"If you leave now," said Jem, "you might survive. You just might."

Another now, drawing closer. He could hear them in the flute grasses, but the four Humans here holding him captive could not. How, with such dull senses, had this race created a space-borne civilization?

"You're threatening us?" Ripple-John asked, viciously amused.

There was no way to control them—the best thing to do would be to get out of the way. Jem tensed up his body, tested the softness of the ground below his feet, scanned about himself for the best route.

"I don't need to be the threat," he replied. "They are." He pointed.

"Vrabbit fobbish," intoned a voice from where he pointed.

It weighed in at about three tonnes and came out of the flute grasses in one great lolloping bound, landing with a heavy thump that shook the ground underneath their feet. As four Human gazes snapped away from him, Jem launched himself sideways, shouldered the ground and rolled underneath the ATV. He glanced back to see the gabbleduck—a young adult yet to attain full massive growth—stand there for a moment like a great bear, then abruptly roll back on its haunches. Kalash chose that moment to open fire on it, which was a mistake.

The shots from his pulse rifle thudded into its chest, burning deep painful wounds. The brainless descendants of a once star-spanning civilization gabbleducks might have been, but they still possessed intelligence enough to know when they were being hurt, and who by.

"Where the fuck did he—" Ripple-John shouted, further words drowned out by th

PRAISE FOR NEAL ASHER

"Asher is a modern master of sci-fi." —*Starburst* magazine

"Neal Asher's books are like an adrenaline shot targeted directly for the brain." —*New York Times* bestselling author John Scalzi

"With mind-blowing complexity, characters, and combat, Asher's work continues to combine the best of advanced cybertech and military SF." —*Publishers Weekly*, starred review

"A wide-screen special-effects extravaganza, a space opera featuring gods and monsters . . . Doc Smith and Olaf Stapledon in a blender, turned up to eleven, with the contents splattering across the ceiling." —Russell Letson, *Locus*

"Asher rocks with XXX adrenaline while delivering a vivid future." —David Brin, *New York Times* bestselling author of *Kiln People*

"Asher has an amazing talent for world-building, for writing larger-than-life characters, for weaving gripping plots and for imagining exotic alien races and wonderful technologies. Huge ships! Big weapons! Space battles! Ground battles! Treason! Revenge! This is New Space Opera at its best." —*Sense of Wonder*

"Asher's coruscating mix of epic space opera, weaponised Darwinism and high-stakes intrigue channels the primal flame of deep-core science fiction." —Paul McAuley, author of *Four Hundred Billion Stars*

"The world of the Polity explored so far . . . is one as complex and as compelling as any created in the genre, and in the breath of biological speculation almost unparalleled." —Lavie Tidhar, *Dusk Site*

"Violence, of course, is what Asher does best—by presenting a stunning, brutal spectacle and taking his readers right into the middle of it. He expertly ratchets up the narrative tension and excitement with high-tech mayhem and technological razzle-dazzle. And it's a genuine pleasure to watch him." —*Kirkus Reviews*

"Asher has lit up the sky of science fiction like a new sun." —Tanith Lee

"Hardboiled, fast-paced space opera . . . Asher's books are similar to the world of Iain M. Banks' Culture universe, but the Polity is arguably a much darker and more vicious environment—and all the better for it." —*The Register*

THE TECHNICIAN

BY NEAL ASHER

AGENT CORMAC
Gridlinked (2001)
The Line of Polity (2003)
Brass Man (2005)
Polity Agent (2006)
Line War (2008)

SPATTERJAY
The Skinner (2002)
The Voyage of the Sable Keech (2006)
Orbus (2009)

NOVELS OF THE POLITY
Shadow of the Scorpion (2008)
Prador Moon (2006)
Hilldiggers (2007)
The Technician (2010)

TRANSFORMATION
Dark Intelligence (2015)
War Factory (2016)
Infinity Engine (2017)

RISE OF THE JAIN
The Soldier (2018)
The Warship (2019)
The Human (2020)

THE OWNER
The Departure (2011)
Zero Point (2012)
Jupiter War (2013)

SHORT-STORY COLLECTIONS
Runcible Tales (1999)
The Engineer (1998)
The Gabble (2008)
Owning the Future (2018)

NOVELLAS
The Parasite (1996)
Mindgames: Fool's Mate (1992)
Cowl (2004)

THE TECHNICIAN

A NOVEL OF THE POLITY

NEAL ASHER

NIGHT SHADE BOOKS
NEW YORK

First Night Shade Books edition 2013. This Night Shade Books edition 2020.

Published in the United Kingdom by Tor, an imprint of Pan Macmillan, a division of Macmillan Publishers Limited.

Visit our website at www.nightshadebooks.com.

10 9 8 7 6 5 4 3 2 1

Library of Congress Cataloging-in-Publication Data is available on file.

ISBN: 978-1-949102-40-6

Cover artwork by Steve Stone
Cover design by Neil Lang/Pan Macmillan

Printed in Canada

For Martin Asher
1955—2010
Too soon, brother. Too damned soon.

ACKNOWLEDGEMENTS

As usual my thanks to the staff at Macmillan, including Julie Crisp, Chloe Healy, Amy Lines, James Long, Catherine Richards, Ali Blackburn, Steve Cox (especially for that "No more gabble") and many others besides. In fact my thanks to all there who help bring this book to shelves in Britain and across the world, so that includes the foreign buyers and translators out there too. I also have to make a special mention here of cover designer Neil Lang and the superb artist Jon Sullivan. Hey, I really like what you're doing with the covers, guys, I like it a lot. Further thanks must go out to all those fans who find me on my blog, on Facebook and elsewhere, to chat, offer support, advice and generally to reply to the stuff I put out there. With you lot a broadband connection away I feel almost as if I've got a social life! And last but not least, all my love to Caroline, without whom I would be a lonely, introvert weirdo, rather than just a weirdo.

PROLOGUE

Three Years before the Rebellion (Solstan 2434)

The sculpture had been mounted on a rock which, though far from the Northern Mountains of the continent, Chanter knew to be the tip of a mountain itself submerged in the underlying tricone-generated soil of the planet Masada. After studying the screen display for a moment longer, he turned to the other displays arrayed before him and did some checking. His mud-marine had risen to the surface pushing up the rhizome mat as a shield above it, so should be all but invisible to the cameras peering down from the Theocracy laser arrays. However, he ensured that the chameleonware shield was functioning too and now extended to the rock, so would cover his departure from his vehicle. It was only by such attention to detail that he had remained undiscovered under the eyes of the Theocracy for so many decades.

He spun his seat round then heaved his bulky amphidapt body from it, traipsing across to the door to one side, his big webbed feet making a wet slapping against the floor. Beside the door he unclipped his root shear from its rack and turned it on. The thing looked like a dental-floss stick, the handle extending to a bow-shaped section across which a monofilament stretched, now vibrating at high frequency.

The door opened with a thump, extruding in towards him then sliding aside into its cleaner compartment. Inevitably, mud and chunks of flute-grass rhizome spilled in towards him. Amidst this mess a nest of green nematodes also tumbled in and began to wetly writhe apart, so Chanter took the time to grab up a sample bag and scoop the worms inside.

Waste not want not—he had not had his body adapted to this environment to no purpose, and here was lunch.

The rhizome mat overhung the exit like a pergola collapsing under an excessive weight of vines, but the work of a moment with the root shear dropped it all back down into the black mud below. Chanter next returned the shear to its rack before stepping out. He paused for a moment to breathe deeply, gill slits opening to increase his air intake and thus winnow out the small amount of oxygen in the air. He held his right webbed hand up before his face, peering at the sculpture through the translucent skin between forefinger and mid-finger, but the infrared image gave him no more data than his mudmarine's sensors had already obtained. The next web across gave him ultraviolet and evidence of some puzzling trace radioactives, but that was all.

Chanter sighed and now trudged through mud then across the flattened layer of flute grass to the rock and gazed up at the sculpture. The structure of carved bones had been joined together with plaited sinew threaded through drilled holes, or small mortise-and-tenon joints carved with a precision normally only available to machines. One of the grazers of this world had been disassembled, its poisonous fats meticulously extracted from its still-living body and discarded, in fact, stacked neatly in a pyramidal Chinese puzzle to one side, glistening in the light of the sun, whilst the rest, excluding sinew and bone, had been consumed. The predator had then taken the hard remains and made this.

As always Chanter felt a species of awe upon seeing such expressions of the artistic temperament, yet though the sculpture had been fashioned with such precision, such symmetry and such definite purpose, he still had no idea what it represented. The thing before him looked like something living, but bore little resemblance to its original form. To his recollection, it also did not look like anything else on this world, nor on any of the other worlds he had visited. The skull had been shortened, the grinding plates removed, cut into spikes along one side then reinserted sideways to give the skull pointy teeth. The thing sat upright, like the statue of some Human god, which was perhaps why Theocracy proctors destroyed these things if they got to them before Chanter.

The rib bones had been closed together vertically and added to at the bottom to form a cone-like structure. The rear legs extended up from behind and had been substantially altered; the long bones sliced thin, lengthways, and splayed out almost like a peacock's feathers. Forelimbs formed a single hoop looping round from the top of the cone to its bottom—a perfect circle.

Chanter whistled, and Mick came trundling out of the mudmarine, long-toed feet extending almost like paddles from the sides of the low, flat louse-like robot to keep its weight supported on the delicate rhizome mat. It headed straight over to the sculpture, stalked eyes hingeing from under its front end to inspect the thing for a moment, then arms folding up from each side of its flat body to reach out with long-fingered hands to probe into the bonework and ensure the thing would remain undamaged when shifted to Mick's flat-ribbed back. Soon afterwards Mick had safely installed the sculpture inside the mudmarine.

Sighing yet again, Chanter realized he was no nearer to understanding the work of this artist. This sculpture would join the rest of his unfathomable collection in his underground base. Of course, he shouldn't be surprised, even after fifty years, at his lack of comprehension. This was no ordinary artist. The Technician, as some had begun to call it, was a very strange and lethal beast indeed.

The Rebellion from Underneath (Solstan 2437)

"Damnation!" Chanter exclaimed.

Hauling himself up by the console from the tilted floor of his mudmarine, he plumped himself back in his chair. Once ensconced, he pulled across safety straps he only used when negotiating particularly moist strata of mud—the stuff that possessed currents and was also navigated by tricones the size of gravcars.

On his screen he called up a seismic map created by the various infrasound emitters he'd planted about Masada, but what it showed just didn't quite make sense. At first he'd thought the shockwave slamming into his conveyance came from a test firing of the Theocracy's new weapon—that massive coilgun they'd named Ragnorak and intended to use to punch missiles right down through the mountains into the rebels' cave systems—but no, they could not have moved it into position so soon and the readings here were just not right for that. The seismic map showed that something big had come down just fifty kilometres away from his present position below the surface, but that it hadn't come down hard enough to be a direct fall from orbit.

He wanted more data—something was going on and he needed to know what it was, and to collect that data he must surface and take a look. He engaged the vehicle's conveyor drive and it began to worm its way forwards, then up as he pulled the control column up. Occasionally there came a bump as the mudmarine shoved tricones aside, but they were of little danger to him, since though their grinding tongues could turn the toughest metal to powder, or sludge, out here he tried not to stay in one spot long enough for them to converge, and when halting did become necessary, he had the means to repel them.

Within an hour he was near the surface, the marine travelling faster in the less dense soil. He slowed almost to a halt below the rhizome mat, taking the precaution of engaging chameleonware before surfacing, then eased the vehicle up. Once it was stable, he first extruded a camera up through the mat to take a look around. No Humans in the vicinity, no technology, and he was a good distance from any Theocracy arachniculture. However, an unseasonal storm was blowing out there, the grasses waving about vigorously and the air filled with broken stems—the aftermath of the same shockwave he had felt below. Also the light seemed odd. It was night out there and, though the nights here were never that dark, it seemed oddly bright. Maybe a distant fire fed by some oxygen supply? Perhaps a spaceship had come down—that certainly matched the seismic profile, but pointing the camera in the direction of the impact revealed no fire. Finally he tilted the camera upwards, and gasped in surprise.

Meteor showers and the extended dull orange blooms that were the after-effect of massive orbital explosions filled the sky. Obviously some major events had occurred above and whatever had come down was probably a result of them. Had the Polity finally intervened here? The AIs had not been showing much sign of doing so over the last few years. As he understood it, intervention here was a bit of a political hot potato that might result in trouble on Line worlds whose Polity affiliation was . . .delicate. He decided the camera wasn't good enough, retracted it and next extruded his main sensor array.

Further surprises. Chanter swore quietly. The Theocracy satellite array was gone or, rather, now formed a cloud of wreckage feeding that meteor storm. However, though the powerful radio telescope in his sensor array showed him much detail of this, and even revealed that the shipyard on the Calypse moonlet Flint had also been destroyed, it did not reveal what had done the damage. He began searching frequencies for Theocracy communications and, slowly weaning fact from rumour and all the religious dross, finally figured out the chronology of events.

The thing they called Behemoth, which he knew as one of the remaining three of four massive alien organisms that originally formed the entity called Dragon, had arrived in rather bad temper. It had destroyed the Flint base then, by pretending to head directly for Hierarch Loman's ship, forced him to call the Fleet away from Masada to protect him. Dragon had then U-jumped to Masada, and the Fleet, with ships that could not engage their underspace drives from a standing start, had been unable to pursue. Here it had destroyed the laser satellites before hurling itself to the surface and crash-landing. Chanter considered what this might mean.

Almost certainly, now, Lellan Stanton and her rebels would take advantage of the situation. They would head for the surface, and he knew there were enough of them, with enough armament, to take it. Loman would then respond, sending forces down from space to retake the surface—those troops presently training in the cylinder world *Hope*. The ballot for Polity intervention, being secretly collected here, might climb above the required 80 per cent but, even if not, there would be such a mess here that Polity intervention seemed inevitable. Chanter was of two minds about that. He rather liked his secretive molelike existence here, enjoyed his singular research and the lack of interference.

He retracted the sensor array and re-engaged his mudmarine's drive. Large events were in the offing and things were due to get a little fraught up there, but he intended to remain underneath it all. Right now, he intended to take a look at a Dragon sphere, from the underside.

Chanter slowly drew his mudmarine to a halt as the seismic image of what lay ahead became clearer and clearer. After checking data stored in his computer system he had ascertained that Dragon spheres were a kilometre across. This one had lost a large portion of its substance and no longer bore the shape of a sphere.

Its impact with the soft ground had thrown up mountains of debris around it on the surface, and within the crater these enclosed, a substantial quantity of alien remains lay visible. The signals from his seismappers revealed incredibly dense bones of a material similar to ceramal but intricately formed and laminated with cellular structures. Other items up there looked like the by-blows of fusion reactors and giant animal organs. Scales strewn about the area reflected as dense as a Polity dreadnought's armour, and other softer items formed an encompassing morass. Anyone stumbling across this would feel sure they had found all that remained of the creature, but it was all for show.

Underneath the ground the story was very different. A half hemisphere of Dragon remained, being pushed deeper into the ground on some thick stalk almost like a mushroom growing the wrong way up. Activity within that hemisphere was intense enough for Chanter to also pick up energy readings through the intervening mud. Seismics showed that internally the hemisphere had divided up into a cellular structure that bore no resemblance to the debris above. Each cell lay about a metre across and was rapidly forming something at its heart. Dragon, it seemed, was not dead and was up to something nefarious, which by the record seemed par for the course for this creature.

Also remembering how dangerous were the Dragon spheres—one had, after all, destroyed a runcible on the cold world of Samarkand, resulting in something like thirty thousand deaths, and this one had just thoroughly shafted the Theocracy -Chanter began to consider just how precarious his position here might be. But no, he was passively picking up data from his seismappers as they transmitted infrasound pulses through the ground. The nearest seismapper lay twenty kilometres away and Dragon should have no awareness of his own presence here, nearby. Chanter sat back with a sigh and tried to dispel his unease, just as the seismap reformed from new data to reveal something snakelike, and two metres thick, punching from the hemisphere directly towards his mudmarine. He swore upon seeing the end of this thing opening like the head of a tubeworm into many strands, just as they closed about his vehicle, jerked it into motion, and began to reel it in.

Nothing Chanter did would shake free Dragon's grip. He tried the device that had been described to him as a "cattle prod for seriously big cows"—the thing he used to drive away persistent tricones when he needed to stop somewhere deep down for maintenance, or sleep—but the Dragon hand of pseudopodia on the end of that massive tentacle shook his mudmarine so hard he thought the hull would crack, so he desisted. Still it reeled him in and now the seismapper images were becoming clearer. There were things growing inside those cells developing within Dragon's remaining body. They looked like nymphs; somewhat similar to the young of mud snakes, though possessing a more alarming *foetal* look. Then his instrumentation went crazy before blinking off and, after a moment, the lights went out.

Chanter awaited extinction, waited for his vehicle to be crushed and for the loose mud here to slide in and engulf him, but then the instruments blinked back on again, and he gazed in perplexity at his screens. Something, it appeared, was going through his files methodically and at high speed. At present he recognized the layout of his journal, though the words were blurring past too fast for him to read. Next came the images of all the sculptures he had collected, along with his speculations about what they might mean. Seemingly in a response to this a hissing issued from his communicator, along with something else that sounded like distant laughter.

"Little toad man," said a voice, spooky, perfectly coherent yet in some manner quite obviously that of no Human, but Dragon itself. "See how in your form I live again?"

"What are you doing . . .Dragon?" he asked.

"I grow ready for sleep."

"I don't understand."

"Yes."

"Why have you seized my craft?" Chanter asked, and when no answer was forthcoming added, "I'm no threat to you."

"No."

Chanter wasn't sure if that was a denial or agreement, but then, judging by some of the documents he'd glanced at under the title "Dragon Dialogues," the ambivalence shouldn't surprise him.

The file search ended and seismic imaging returned. The tentacle had drawn the mudmarine very much closer to the main body now, but had ceased to reel him in. With invisible icy fingers drawing down his back he gazed at those nymphs, those things being created from the very substance of Dragon. They bore something of the shape of Human children, and something very much of the reptile. Was Dragon somehow mocking him? Had Dragon expected him to come? This was madness.

Abruptly, all but one of the pseudopodia released their hold of his craft, the one remaining still engaged with his sensor array, through which Dragon had penetrated his computer system. He considered restarting his craft's conveyor drive, but knew he could not flee fast enough to avoid being snatched up again. He must be given permission to leave if he was to survive this.

"You destroyed the laser arrays," he tried.

"Yes."

"Why?"

"The question you ask."

"Yes, it's the damned question I ask," said Chanter in frustration. "Is your lack of clarity a function of your vast intelligence or vast stupidity?" The words were out of his mouth before he could recall them and he winced. It occurred to him that his long isolation, the years spent speaking to no one but his machines, had rather undermined his conversational judgement. However, Dragon seemed unconcerned about his outburst.

"I go now," the creature said. "I fragment."

And so it was. There on the screen, the remaining hemisphere of this part of Dragon entire was coming apart, dividing into those individual cells which, even as Chanter watched, were inflating and beginning to rise towards the surface.

"Go here, little toad man." Coordinates appeared on one of his screens, precise Masadan coordinates he recognized as somewhere in the mountains—a place he tended to avoid since that meant travelling on the surface. "Or grovel in the mud without answers."

The last pseudopod flicked his mudmarine dismissively and the whole tentacle began retreating into the fragmenting mass, but even as it did so it writhed to an abrupt halt and it too broke apart as the mind directing it went away—ceased to be, as Chanter later learnt, one mind but broken into the minds of many.

Chanter fled the scene just as fast as he could and the chaos above kept him grovelling in the mud long afterwards. Dangerous Jain technology arrived up there in the form of a massive subverted Polity dreadnought and it seemed the whole world was in danger of extinction. Rebel forces battled Theocracy soldiers turned into zombie servants of the one wielding that technology, and those that fought beside the rebels bore some of Chanter's form: dracomen, risen from the ground as from the sowing of the dragon's teeth. Chanter rose once or twice to the surface to view the ruination, as he fruitlessly searched for further sculptures, and he spent long years searching for the Technician, which at some point during the rebellion had managed to shake off his tracking device and gone to ground.

Only later, much later, when it seemed less likely he would end up on the wrong end of a Theocracy or rebel bullet, or be infected by some dangerous technology, long after the Polity finally raised the quarantine, did he take a long hard look at those coordinates. Maybe he was being too damned cautious, maybe his caution was the reason the answers he sought perpetually evaded him.

1

The question to ask is not how the Masadan Theocracy fell, but how such an idiotic regime managed to survive for so long. It allied itself with Polity separatists and arrogantly ignored how much this would annoy the Polity. It allied itself with one of the Dragon spheres, seemingly oblivious to the dangers inherent in adopting Dracocorp augmentations, and to the danger of betraying Dragon. Also deluded enough to think itself destined to win some future war against the Polity, it used a weapon obtained from Dragon to destroy a Polity space station, and grabbed Polity citizens to enslave in its shipyard on Flint. And, as if these actions weren't suicidal enough, below it, on the world it ruled, it had created a slave underclass it treated with joyous sadism, thus ensuring the growth of an underground, truly under the ground, hoarding weapons and supplies and steadily recruiting more and more fighters. The Theocracy had set itself up for a fall, and so it did. Dragon came first and wiped out the laser arrays with which the Theocracy subjugated its people. The rebels took advantage of this and seized the surface of the world, and Polity intervention looked imminent. But, since this shit storm did not seem sufficiently catastrophic, a madman controlling a five-million-year civilization-destroying technology turned up too, in a world-smashing Polity dreadnought, seized control of anyone wearing a Dracocorp aug and incidentally began tossing about apocalyptic weapons like matchsticks. Did I say the Theocracy had set itself up for a fall? Violent obliteration might be a better description of what happened to it.

—From HOW IT IS *by Gordon*

Heretic's Isle (Solstan 2457—Present Day)

The light was different here; the sky a pale violet during the day and only during the night returning to the deep aubergine Jeremiah Tombs recognized. Sanders was here again, her blond hair tied back, and a gauzy wrap, which cycled a slow holographic display of a sun going nova, cinched about her naked body. She gazed at him with familiar pained frustration.

"Good morning, Jem," she said. "How are you today?"

He began mumbling the words of the Third Satagent, and she just turned away, heading over to the steps that led down towards the sea. He touched the ball control on the arm of his chair to roll it to the terrace edge, and leaned forward to peer over the stone balustrade, watched her walk down.

Stunted flute grasses grew in spiky clumps on the rocky slope below, and near where the steps terminated at the pale-grey volcanic sands grew a stand of lizard tails, also stunted, and frazzled and curled like singed hair. Reaching the strand, Sanders strode out, glittering footsteps behind where her feet disturbed luminescent amoebae between the grains. At the shore she discarded her wrap and it fell through the air like flame. He looked away from such shameful nudity, but then his gaze strayed back as she entered the sea and began swimming.

This was all so wrong.

He wanted to shout at her, to tell her that she should not be outside without a breather mask or a scole to oxygenate her blood, for the air here was unbreathable—didn't contain enough oxygen to support Human life. Then he realized that he too was outside, and bewilderment overcame him.

And he retreated inside himself, just as he had the last time, and the time before that. Just as he had been doing for longer than he could bear to remember.

Triada Compound (Solstan 2437—Rebellion Aftermath)

Concentrating on the patterns, on the collections of colourful Euclidean shapes swirling through his mind, helped to keep the agony at bay. This vision seemed to be all Jeremiah Tombs possessed now his sight had faded to a dull snowy blur—that, and a memory of hellish yellow eyes poised above him, surrounded by the clicking whickering of glass scythes sharpening themselves against each other in the darkness.

How had it all gone so horribly wrong?

The chanting of the Septarchy Friars, which kept Behemoth from seizing control of the minds of all members of the Brotherhood, had not been enough to keep the creature from coming to the planet Masada to exact its vengeance. It destroyed the satellite laser arrays then hurled itself to the ground in fiery destruction . . .

No, that's not it.

The agony surged through him and someone groaned, that noise turning into the perpetual chant of the Friars . . .

No, no, they are gone.

After Behemoth destroyed itself, Hierarch Loman had the Friars silenced and grew in stature and power across the channels of the Dracocorp augmentations that all in the Brotherhood wore—their *Gift* from Behemoth. Loman's every order became impossible to disobey.

Liquid over his eye, someone wiping. Vision blurred at first but slowly improving. A jab in his neck, and at once the pain began to recede.

"Look," said a voice nearby, "either take him out back and put a bullet through his head, or let me get on with my work."

"Our people are first," came the gruff reply.

Clearer vision now, and Jem could see a female clad in white overalls as stained with blood as the soldier's clothing. He wore fatigues the colour of old flute grass. He carried a rail-gun strapped across his back, with its lead coiling down to its power supply at his belt. Releasing the woman's arm he stepped back and gazed down at Jem, his expression unreadable.

"I don't take orders from you." Her tone was didactic, precise. "I might have been born here, but now I'm a Polity medtech and my job is first to save lives, then to repair bodies."

She gestured around her at something out of Jem's sight. "None of these are in any danger now." She pointed at Jem. "He needs major reconstructive surgery just to stay alive."

"Yeah, I guess he does," said the soldier, his expression now registering puzzlement and even pity, which was not something Jem would have expected from such as him.

"How the hell is it he's alive?" she asked.

"Damned if I know—no one's ever survived one of those bastards." His voice was gravelly, harsh, that of someone used to bellowing orders.

"You misunderstand me: how is it that he is alive, in this compound? I cut away what was left of his uniform, so I know what he is."

The soldier shook his head, shrugged.

The woman smiled. "So, Commander Grant, you've spent most of your life fighting the Theocracy and, like so many from the Underworld, you're firmly atheist, yet it seems you're not as immune to superstition as you would think."

Jem's vision began to blur again, and whatever she had given him seemed to be running through his body in waves. He felt terribly weary, wanted to sleep. He tried closing his eye, but vision remained.

"Whadda y'mean?"

"It's only because of what he survived that you saved him and brought him here," she lectured. "There isn't a Human resident on this planet who doesn't regard the predators of this world with superstitious awe. Admit it."

"He's got to be questioned," said the soldier, turning away. "We need to know what happened."

"Grant," said the woman as he moved to stride off.

"What?" he shot back, annoyed as he turned.

"Perhaps you should retain that awe."

"Why?"

"Well, oddly enough the hooder saved his life. I've already checked him over and there were signs of burn around the mycelia entering his skull. With perfect timing, it cut off his aug just as that device was being hijacked—cut it off while taking off his face."

The words meant nothing to Jem as the two seemed to draw off down some long dark tunnel, but something about what they had just said impelled new memory to the surface of his mind.

Faith is dead.

After Behemoth's demise and the Hierarch's ascendancy, the Devil had come. It threw Ragnorak, the weapon the Theocracy was going to use to annihilate rebels who were truly underground, into the face of the gas giant Calypse. It burnt *Faith* and it killed the Hierarch—an object lesson in the consequences of hubris. And *Faith*, a cylinder world containing ten thousand souls, eviscerated by the fire of some appalling apocalyptic weapon.

Then through their *Gift*, their Dracocorp augs, the Devil seized control of the Brotherhood—their augs turned ashen against their skulls and their minds dancing to his pipes. Jem remembered trying to fight it, seeing his comrades from Triada Compound turned to zombies all about him, remembered failing as he ran into an encounter during which, in his own personal hell, *something* relieved him of his *Gift*. Then, all at once, Hell came back.

"Isn't that painkiller working?" asked the soldier.

"Yes," replied the woman.

"Then why the noise?"

"I don't know."

The hellish yellow eyes of the demons were back, and they were sharpening their knives again.

A motor whined and the bed vibrated underneath him as the section under his back tilted upwards to slowly bring him to a sitting position. His right eye seemed sealed shut, the vision of his left eye was blurry, but a woman in white stooped close and squirted something in it, and it began to clear. He tried to blink to speed the process but nothing happened. It was as if his eyelid had been glued back.

Like clumsy mist giants, vague memories bumbled through his mind. There had been a fire somewhere, explosions, shooting . . . and clearer than anything else at all, strange Euclidean shapes that somehow made up an overall pattern. A clicking sound sent cold fingers crawling down his spine and he swung his attention to its source: some kind of machine looking like a big chromed insect mounted on a pedestal. They had *Polity technology* here!

He surveyed his surroundings further. His bed stood in a row of ten on one side of the aisle down the centre of what looked like a pond workers' bunkhouse. There were ten beds on the other side of the aisle. Five of the beds were mechanized hospital beds like his own, and all occupied, whilst those remaining were bunk beds separated out singly, a further eight of which were also occupied. The walls of the bunkhouse had recently been painted white, obliterating the words of holy scripture and guidance usually scribed across them, which was puzzling.

Medical machines occupied spaces between the beds; some he recognized as of Theocracy manufacture, others, like that insectile thing, were smaller, neater, *Polity* machines. Directly across the aisle from him, a medic, a man clad in white, was helping the occupant out of one of the mechanized beds. Burns ran down the side of the patient's face, one arm and the side of his body ugly under some kind of transparent coating. There must have been some sort of major accident in which Jem himself had been involved. He shuddered and returned his attention to the woman, who next manipulated something at his throat. A sound issued from there, part sigh, part groan.

"Okay—that's the voice synthesizer keyed in," she said.

Abruptly he remembered waking here before, and trying to speak—trying to demand that she not use anything but Theocracy technology on his body—but his mouth had been frozen and all he could do was issue sounds from the back of his throat. He tried again and, even though his mouth remained frozen, the machine at his throat complemented the sounds issuing from there.

"I do not require some godless Polity machine to enable me to speak."

She stared at him for a long moment, then said, "In ancient times they used to call it being in denial. Surely you've heard enough to know by now?"

Two columns of yellow eyes opened, and from somewhere issued a horrible whickering and clicking. Then all swept away in a swirl of those Euclidean shapes.

"I seem unable to blink," he stated.

"Surely the reason for that's obvious, if you think about it?"

"What have you done to me?"

"Kept you alive. You're the only known survivor of an attack by a hooder, which is why you are alive." She sounded angry now. "Your fellow proctors haven't been so fortunate." She gestured to the other beds. "I've processed three hundred cases through here and you're the only one of your kind I've seen."

Faith is dead.

"That is ridiculous, remove these restraints at once." But even as he spoke he felt terrified by something rising in his consciousness. *Faith* is dead? What did that mean? He tried to make a connection through his aug, his *Gift*, but got nothing.

"Or is it more than denial?" she wondered. "Tell me, Tombs, what do you remember?"

"Some sort of incident . . . an accident." He paused to collect his thoughts. "Obviously it was major or else I would now be in a city hospital rather than in this temporary medical centre." He tried to gesture to his surroundings, but still his arm was restrained.

"The Underground?" she suggested.

Ah, it was obvious now.

"I see—those maggots planted a bomb did they?"

She gazed at him incredulously, then just shook her head and walked away.

Jem inspected his surroundings again and began to wonder if his assessment of the situation was true. There were Polity machines being used here, and the scripture had been painted out on the walls . . . Perhaps, though this place bore some resemblance to a pond workers' bunkhouse, it wasn't that at all. With sudden horror he realized. He was a prisoner of the Underground! They had done something above, at Triada Compound, and snatched him. Those in the other beds were rebels injured during whatever had occurred.

Perhaps he too had been injured but, what seemed certain, soon they would start interrogating him. He tried to fight against his restraints, but moved not at all. Polity technology; they had a nerve blocker on him, which was probably why he couldn't speak properly. He could do nothing.

"I can't do a complete reconstruction."

She was back, placing a chair down beside his bed, something wrapped in white cloth under her arm. This item she placed on the bed beside him as she sat. Then she took another object out of her pocket—a small hand mirror—and put that on the bed too, face down.

"You will get nothing from me," he said. "You may have taken my *Gift* but I am still a member of the Brotherhood."

"At this juncture, shock tactics can sometimes restore memory." She nodded to herself. "But I'm not a mindtech so I can't be sure—in fact there's no one here with that training—I just checked."

"I will reveal nothing, even under electro-stimulation." That he had nothing to reveal was the most frightening thing. They might not believe him and just continue torturing him.

"Yes, you religious police were big on electro-stimulation."

Whickering clicking.

His gaze shot to the insectile machine. Was that what they would use?

"Physical reconstruction from your neck to your knees went well," she said. "Using cellweld techniques, carbon muscle frame and collagen foam I was able to rebuild most of it, though you can no longer produce spermatozoa and it will take about a month for the muscle to grow into the frames."

What in Smythe's name was she on about?

"I've used transparent syntheskin over this, which will gradually acquire skin colour as your skin cells multiply through it—we used up all the precoloured stuff elsewhere." She paused for a moment. "I've used the same skin on your right arm, and your fingernails will regrow, but I was unable to rebuild your left arm. Until such time as the Polity gets here and ships in supplies, you'll have to make do with a prosthetic."

He was beginning to see the shape of it now. This *was* the interrogation, though he had yet to identify the thrust of this woman's technique.

"You have a very convoluted method of making threats," he said, trying to remain calm. But he physically remembered . . . *something* . . . a line of agony ascending from his knees, yellow eyes watching, and something sharp, ever so sharp . . .

"I could do very little about your face."

"Some new rebel interrogation technique," he said, a ball of terror growing in his chest. "We are so much better at it."

She bowed her head. "Yes, the Theocracy was very good at inflicting pain. Some think it a shame it was snuffed out so quickly. Others want some payback on those of you that survived, which is why Grant has an armed guard on this building."

Grant?

Faith is dead, jabbered a voice in his mind.

She raised her gaze to his face and he saw her wince.

"You said earlier you did not need a 'godless Polity machine' to enable you to speak and you also wondered why you cannot blink. Here are the facts: the hooder, one that apparently goes under the title of the Technician, inflicted damage upon you that should have killed you. However, it very meticulously sealed blood vessels as it cut, and it didn't take off your breather mask until it reached your face, where it did the most damage. This might be just the standard way hooders operate. We can't be sure. You're the most we've ever found of one of their Human victims."

"The Technician does not exist. Hierarch Chalden declared it a myth propagated by those whose faith is not strong enough. Anyone caught spreading rumours of its existence must be subject to punishment six."

Faith is dead.

A sound issued from the voice synthesizer. A glitch, obviously, for it sounded like a giggle.

"Punishment Six. Yes, that's when you pin someone out naked over the spring growth of flute grass, so the sprouts steadily punch through their bodies."

Jem suddenly felt flute grass underneath him, dry old grass, papery against his remaining skin. But it wasn't the grass making that sound in the darkness all around him. Stars above? No, even rows of them, yellow . . . He began to recite the First Satagent, as he had *then*.

"Religious babble," she said. "After it took off your mask it took off your face. It took all the soft matter off your skull even as far back as your tonsils. Why it left you one eye is a mystery. Perhaps it's an artist, not a technician. You cannot speak because you have no lips or tongue and you cannot blink because you have no eyelids."

His recitation stuttered to a halt. He was having a nightmare, that was it. This whole situation seemed to possess its own internal logic but, when examined from a distance, the inconsistencies were evident. What was that over there? Something moving at the end of the building, where that big shadow lay . . .

"It went even further than that," she said. "There are numerous holes through your skull, numerous incisions, bleeds, what looks like cautery inside your head and the remains of fibre connections like you get from an aug. All the facial nerves have been removed right back to your spine. The damage is beyond the reconstruction technology I have available. Until we get some real Polity expertise here, all I can do for you is this."

She pulled the cloth from the object on the bed, revealing a hairless human head fashioned of some stark white material. It had one eye, yellow like old glass, the other missing. He stared at that yellow eye then glanced away, but it seemed to leave an after-image in his vision. A clicking sound, he looked back in utter terror, only to see that she had hinged the head open like a clam to reveal gleaming electronics inside.

"It came by special delivery," she said, frowning in perplexity, then went on, "Like the voice synthesizer it detects relevant neural activity and translates it into action. You'll be able to speak, to eat, and your sense of smell will return. It will also route blood to underlying bone to prevent it dying."

She tapped a lump inside the open head, then turned it

over and opened the mouth to reveal a tongue, pure white. He realized the lump she had tapped was a mouth lining seen from the skull side. Turning it back over, she now pointed to the back of the yellow eye, then picked up the wormlike connection extending from it.

"The hooder left your optic nerve in place and, though it did something odd with it, we can still make a connection so you get binocular vision back." She now pointed up at his face. "It left you your eardrums, which is why you can hear me, but with the extra connections in this prosthetic your hearing will improve too."

She closed the head up, and there, again, that yellow eye. He tried to blink to clear the previous after-image of it, could not, and now there were two after-images, then three. The darkness had grown now to fill one entire half of this room, and that medical machine, the insectile one, seemed a lot lot bigger now.

"I don't . . . believe you," he managed.

She sighed, picked up the mirror and held it up to his face. A skull, with one glistening eye in one socket leered back at him. Then he was blind, in darkness, and the medical machine was looming over him. Yellow after-images further multiplied there, became two columns of yellow eyes. The voice synthesizer was screaming; a raw, horrible sound. He began to fall somewhere, Euclidean shapes flashing into being around him and swirling like snowflakes.

"Okay, that didn't go so good," someone said.

But Jem was gone.

"They're here, good," said Sanders. "That's the final nail in the Theocracy's coffin—it's finished."

Jem felt a flash of frustrated anger at her certainty. How could she not understand that the Polity, a political entity run by godless machines, had no future at all? It was a building constructed over a tricone mud vent and the only uncertainty about its fall was the timing. And the Theocracy? Under direct instruction from God, Zelda Smythe had taken the best from the old religions of Earth and written the Book of Satagents: the basis of the true and final religion until The End of Days. So the Theocracy was forever.

"And we've received instructions about you," she added, turning from her new companion to address him. "You're going to a sunny island for some R and R."

He had heard the aerofan outside, the whine of an ATV engine then later the roar of a big transport coming down, and from that surmised that he had to be somewhere on the surface of Masada. For a moment he entertained the hope that Theocracy troops were coming to rescue him but, by the lack of reaction from the other staff here, he suspected not. Then there was a soldier with Sanders—a man he felt sure he recognized.

"So how's he doing?" the soldier asked.

"He'll live," Sanders replied.

The soldier pointed at Jem's face. "So that's the prosthetic? Seems a bit primitive by Polity standards."

"That's the thing," said Sanders, "but if you knew what kind of damage lies underneath it you'd think differently. The only way to complete restoration would be controlled regrowth under AI supervision."

"Which ain't gonna happen while the AIs stay up there." The soldier stabbed a finger up at the ceiling, then gazed intently at Sanders. Jem experienced an odd reaction on seeing that there seemed some *connection* between them. He, Jem, should be the focus of her attention, not this unimportant grunt.

The soldier continued, "I'm told they're gonna install a runcible on Flint but not down here. We just get supply drops and shitty bandwidth com until they've cleared up the mess out there." He gestured towards the ceiling again.

"*Faith, Hope* and *Charity?*" Sanders asked.

"*Faith* is completely burnt out, the other two and the rest of the satellites and stations got three-quarters of their populations brain-burnt."

Faith is dead.

"You cannot break me," said Jem, turning his new white metal head away from them. He would ignore them—that's it. He felt they'd made the wrong move in cutting off his face, for now he possessed no expression that might give him away.

After they put this imprisoning metal shell over his skull it required long introspection for him to figure out precisely what was going on here. This *was* all about faith, but not about the cylinder world of that name being destroyed. In the fiction they had created for him the Theocracy was gone, the Underground victorious and now the Polity poised overhead in all its supposedly gigantic glory.

"My faith cannot be destroyed," Jem muttered, more to himself than them.

That was the crux of all this. The Underground had understood that whilst the faith of the Brotherhood remained strong, neither they nor their damned Polity could be victorious. So now they were trying to find ways to destroy faith. He was one of the subjects of this experiment: they wanted to destroy his belief in God, they wanted him to spit on the teachings of Zelda Smythe. In a way he pitied them, for his eventual martyrdom would mark the end of their self-deception.

"He's nuts," said the soldier.

"He believes none of it," said Sanders. "First time he woke up he remembered most of it, but the trauma of those memories sent his mind into retreat. Second time he woke up he decided he was a prisoner of the Underground undergoing some new interrogation technique. And now he thinks we're trying to destroy his belief in God and His prophet Zelda Smythe. He remembers nothing of what happened between when he was running an inspection tour of sprawn canals two months ago and him being here."

"He don't remember me?" asked the soldier.

"No—the memories will come back of their own accord or he'll need deep mindtech work—probably under AI supervision just like with his physical restoration."

"There's nothing we can do here?"

"In other circumstances I would have said yes," said Sanders. "But the Technician didn't just flense his skull—it did other things inside, physical alterations, and it left things in there too."

There, again, they were blaming his condition on a mythical non-existent creature and as such bringing more pressure down on his faith. If they could somehow prove to him that this mythical hooder had maimed him, he would necessarily then believe in its existence, which would undermine one of the tenets of his beliefs.

Jem turned back and gazed at the soldier. "Why should I remember you?"

But it was Sanders who replied, "You should remember Colonel Grant because he was the one who saw what the Technician did to you, and he was the one who carried you to an ATV ambulance. He's the reason you're still alive."

Jem turned away, ignoring them again.

The main continent of Masada was shaped like a square-rigged sail from some ancient galleon, rumpled in one upper corner, where the Northern Mountains lay. Other large land masses dotted the world, the Subcontinent—a near-circular mass to the east over a thousand kilometres across—and others whose names and locations Jem was quite vague about. However he had heard of the Worry Island chain, for it was to one of those islands, Heretic's Isle, that the Theocracy shipped, for lengthy interrogation and internment, those captives of the Underground that weren't dispatched to the steamers aboard the cylinder world *Faith.*

How did they intend to work this in the fiction they had created for him? Doubtless some drug would be employed, and when he finally became conscious again he would find himself in a different room and be told he was now in the "hospital" on Heretic's Isle, which the rebels now owned having taken it in their apparently victorious war against the Theocracy. As Sanders headed over to him, he awaited with interest her explanation for whatever drug it was she would administer.

"Obviously, you are not entirely healed," she said, gazing down at him, "so you'll experience some discomfort and your body will feel quite strange to you. You should also be aware that muscle regrowth down the front of your torso and upper legs has some way to go, so you will be very weak."

Ah, some kind of painkiller—an anaesthetic to dull his connection with reality.

She reached between the pillow and his neck, where something disengaged with a gristly crunch. Sensation returned; flooded into his body like some fluid filling a man-shaped vessel. His shins and feet felt cold, everything above that, to his neck, felt unreasonably hot yet devoid of any other sensation, whilst his head seemed just a nerveless bulk atop his neck. He tilted this bulk forwards, but not too far forwards because it felt like it might just fall off if tilted too far from the vertical. He lay naked on the bed—no sheet to give him dignity. From his knees up to his chest his body was coated with that same transparent coating he had seen on other patients here, and underneath this he could see the movement of wet muscles, all wrapped in hair-thin gridworks, bloodworm capillaries actually penetrating the skin layer and areas beginning to cloud with new skin-cell growth.

What they had told him about the damage to his body was utterly true, but that did not make it true that some mythical being inflicted it. Perhaps he had been injured during some terrorist outrage when they kidnapped him, or perhaps they had inflicted all this upon him themselves. Now he held up his hands to inspect both them and his arms.

His right arm possessed the same covering as his torso, though it had clouded and he could see small bristles protruding, and small moons of fingernail appearing on his fingers. The detail of his left arm was perfect, down to complete fingernails, the wrinkled knuckles and the skin texture, but the thing was utterly white like the shell covering his head. He reached across with his right hand to touch it, but received very little sensation from his fingertips, yet he felt the touch of those fingertips from the prosthetic, which possessed substantially more sensation than his own limb.

"Feeling will improve as the nerves grow into the dermal layer," said Sanders. "By the time your own skin has displaced the syntheskin, you'll be back to normal . . . well, almost."

He reached up to touch his face and the sensation was quite odd. He could actually feel the touch of his fingertips on his cheek, but in a disconnected way as if he were touching his cheek through a cotton sheet. While he was probing the shell over his skull, Sanders unwrapped a packet containing plain white pyjamas and slippers.

"You should be able to dress yourself," she said. "Or do you want my help?"

"I will attempt to dress myself," he said coldly, feeling it was time to curtail her intimacy with his body.

Leaning forward was difficult. His stomach muscles felt like jelly, their strength seeming only enough to hold in everything behind them, as if the slightest wrong move would result in a hernia. Also his thigh muscles were pulling, and felt as if they weren't securely anchored.

"Where are the other patients?" he asked. "Have they been taken to Heretic's Isle?" He might as well run with their fiction to see where it would take him.

"Most of them are back with their families or friends, or in recovery wards in city hospital," she replied. "Only special patients are being shipped to the Isle—high-level Theocracy patients."

"Prisoners."

With the pyjama jacket finally on he looked with puzzlement at the front of the garment, trying to find buttons. She reached over to pull the edges together and they bonded. As she stepped back he peered down at his genitals. They were transparent: tubes, veins and testes clearly visible. He needed those trousers on, now. He tried to pull his legs up towards him. At first no response, but after a short time he found himself able to bend his knees and bring his feet within reach. He threaded the trousers onto them, up over his knees to his thighs, and then had to stop, because he was gasping.

"I feel too hot."

"You've no sweat glands in your prosthetic, but the rest of your body should compensate," she said. "Just give it a chance—the more you move about the faster the synthetics will adapt and the faster the healing process."

Finally he managed to swing his legs off the bed, down to the slippers there and, supporting himself on his artificial arm, pull up his trousers, though she reached out to do up the stick seams for him.

"Are you ready to try walking?" she asked. "The transport is ready."

He pushed himself from the bed, feeling sick and dizzy, and did not object when she stepped in to support him. Very slowly they made their way to the airlock. Would he conveniently faint now so as not to see what lay outside? When they halted at the airlock she steadied him until he took hold of a rack containing a varied collection of pond-worker tools—nets, goads and telescopic grabs—then she stepped to the other side of the airlock to take up a breather mask from another rack and don it.

"What about me?" he asked, noting she had collected no breather mask for him.

"You've no need—your prosthetic contains a super-dense oxygen supply which it continuously keeps topped up," she told him. "Outside you can last for ten days before it runs out. You're wearing your own mechanical scole."

Doubtless, when they stepped outside there would be some malfunction of his prosthetic, and he would find himself waking up either inside some transport with no external view, or inside the prison hospital on Heretic's Isle.

They entered the airlock together, where he leaned on her heavily, and as it cycled he felt a sudden terror to be in such a situation. Never in his life had he been inside an airlock without a breather mask over his face, and underlying that he felt something of the indignity of this situation. The only people who went through airlocks without breather masks were pond workers, the underclass, who had the big aphid-like scoles attached to their bodies to oxygenate their blood. He tried to deny that terror, because this was all a set-up, all staged . . .

Sanders opened the outer door and they stepped out. The compound was a morass and foamed plastic walkways had been laid across it, one of them spearing over to a Theocracy troop transport. He gazed about himself in utter confusion, trying to make sense of this place. To his right lay the burnt-out ruins of overseers' huts, and just behind them a three-storey proctors' station lay tilted at an angle, its foundations torn up out of the soil. The surrounding fence was down, as were the nearest watchtowers he could see. Beyond this the chequerboard of ponds stretched into the distance, but pocked with crater holes and strewn with the wreckage of armoured vehicles. Distantly, plumes of smoke rose into the sky and on that horizon he saw the tall stilt-legged shape of a heroyne stepping from pond to pond, its long beak occasionally stabbing down to spear something.

"There is a heroyne within the perimeter," he said woodenly, feeling that if he could just stick to that one fact, that one breach of crop-pond security, then in a moment all the rest would begin make sense.

"That's not all," she said. "Take a look over there."

He reluctantly turned to look where indicated. A couple of aerofans were down on one of the pond banks over to the left of the troop transport. Men in uniforms the colour of new growth flute grass were gathered there about a tripod-mounted rail-gun aimed at a massive creature squatting in one of the ponds.

The gabbleduck seemed to be staring directly at Jem, its tiara of green eyes gleaming with unnatural brilliance. It raised its bill from its chest, opened out one of its dimorphic arms and spread one claw. It seemed to be gesturing to the surrounding devastation: here you are, here it is, how can you deny this? Jem snapped his gaze away, those eyes an after-image in his vision and their colour sliding through the spectrum to one he feared. His gaze came to rest on a bullet-riddled sign lying half-submerged in the mud. *Triada Compound.*

Jem's legs gave way and he fell from the walkway into the mud, where he lay clawing at it, dragging himself, trying to get away. But there was nowhere to flee too. Something closed down on every horizon, throwing him into darkness, and out of the sky scythes began to fold down around those two columns of yellow eyes. Something closed on his temples and he could just hear a high whine over his screaming.

2

The Wheelchair

This anachronism can still be seen in museums, but only in the museums of Earth, since it ceased to be an option even before Humans set foot on Mars. In the twentieth and twenty-first centuries many societies began imposing rules and regulations to make buildings more accessible to wheelchair users, but it can be seen that the vast sums involved could better have been spent on something already on the cards. Those working in robotics already had its replacement ready by the turn of the twentieth century with computer-controlled powered exoskeletons but, as was the case with a lot of technologies of the time, viable small power supplies were needed. Later developments of the supercapacitor, ultracapacitor and nanotube batteries quickly swept that problem aside, and within a period of ten years all wheelchair manufacturers went out of business. A Japanese cybernetics company, later absorbed by Cybercorp, was the first to sell its Motorleg and Fullbot exoskeletons for paraplegics and quadriplegics respectively.

—*From* QUINCE GUIDE, *compiled by Humans*

Masadan Wilderness (Solstan 2438—Rebellion Aftermath)

The aerofan motored fast across the flute grasses, raising a multicoloured storm of petals, and Grant realized that flowering would soon be over as the grasses dropped the rest of their petals whilst growing their seed nodules. The fan was a proctor's machine: single big fan underneath the pulpit-like upper section, all gyro-stabilized and fashioned of light bubble metals, a railgun bolted to the safety rail and a single control column, like a lectern, before which the driver stood. But this driver was no proctor, since in the patriarchal Theocracy few females achieved any rank at all. Grant felt something tightening up inside him when he saw her blond hair streaming about her face as she brought the aerofan towards the clearing where he had parked his ATV. Then, when he got a closer look at her vehicle, he felt a brief stab of anger. It seemed Jerval Sanders had made her decision—though she'd come directly from Central Command in Zealos, the aerofan's code number and design showed it came from the southern isles and, since Central had ordered that an effort should be made to keep these vehicles in their designated areas, it was probably due to be returned there.

The vehicle descended, now blowing about itself fragments of the dry old flute grass trampled into the rhizome layer. As it finally settled and its engine began to wind down it also blew out spatters of mud. The rhizome layer here, having taken the traffic of many feet and numerous vehicles, was starting to become unstable. There were even tricones visible on the surface—their three cones connected like Pan Pipes and bearing some resemblance to discarded munitions also scattered nearby. Soon this area would have to be left alone to enable it to recover, and by then there would be no data left to gather.

Sanders opened the gate in the safety rail and stepped down. She wore spring growth fatigues coloured green and purple, heavy boots and a sleeveless insulated top. Her face was clearly visible and he realized she must now be wearing one of those Polity breather devices that contained oxygen about the face under a near-invisible shimmer-shield—one of the most visible benefits from the Polity supply drops—he meant to get hold of one soon.

"Grant," she said, striding over. She looked sad and serious.

He waited until she reached him before speaking. He nodded towards the aerofan. "From Heretic's Isle?"

She dipped her head in grave agreement.

"So you're gonna take that job at the sanatorium?"

"Yes," she replied, then hurried on with, "but that doesn't mean things have to end between us."

Their love affair had been good but brief whilst the rebels finally accepted that they had won, and different for him since his previous relationships had always been with fierce Amazonian rebels—soldiers like himself—but now came the aftermath. Grant did not expect to be in one place for long as their de facto leader Lellan Stanton sent him hither and yon, whilst Sanders would be south of the continent on that remote island. And really, he hadn't expected someone like her to put up with someone like him for so long.

"No I guess not," he lied. Damn, even their meeting here had been wangled as semi-official. She needed to know the full story behind her most important patient at the sanatorium; wanted to hear it from his lips. The fact that he hadn't already told her, and she hadn't asked, maybe indicated that neither of them had taken their relationship seriously. Love in the ruins, need and celebration, that was all. He abruptly felt uncomfortable, groped for something else to say.

"I hear Lellan Stanton wanted you there?"

"Yes," she grimaced, "I was appointed to the position by the military governor of Masada herself. I said I wasn't sure I wanted it. She told me she didn't want her job but we don't get to pick and chose."

"Yeah, I know—heard we're not getting any AI governor here any time soon."

"The quarantine stands," she stated. "We'll continue to get Polity supply drops, but that's all until they consider it safe for them to land."

He nodded, not sure what to say now.

"Let's take a look at the spot, shall we?" she said.

He gestured off to one side of his ATV and led the way, glancing over to an area of charred ground. That was where four corpses had been piled—four proctors he'd railgunned down before chasing after Jeremiah Tombs. They had only been recently collected, and the ground underneath them sterilized. Even after many months they had still been whole—the environment wasn't conducive to human decay. She glanced over that way too.

"They're in cold storage," she said. "All those Skellor touched are being so collected."

"You were over at Central," he said. "Why the quarantine?"

She sighed and shook her head. "It's complicated."

"I've heard some, but not all of it," he said. "They're being a bit close-mouthed."

"You know that our Hierarch's predecessor seemed to believe that the *inevitable*"—the word came out laced with bitter sarcasm—"fall of the Polity was long overdue and decided to accelerate the process. He dealt with an alien emissary called Dragon"—she glanced at him—"who here was known to the Brotherhood as Behemoth."

"The thing that flattened the base on Flint and trashed the laser arrays, yeah, I get that."

"Yes. Dragon gave Amoloran the *Gift* . . .those Dracocorp augs, but it also gave him metal-destroying mycelium it had used once before against a Polity runcible installation. Amo-loran used that mycelium against a Polity Outlink station, and Dragon got blamed. Trying to exact vengeance it attacked a Theocracy ship but was injured by the engine flame, then came here for some payback."

"But why did it crash itself?"

"Suicide and rebirth: it killed itself and, incidentally, turned most of its substance into an alien race here on Masada." She shrugged. "Interesting times."

"That's the reason for the quarantine?"

"Oddly enough, no." Grant saw amusement flash across her expression. "It seems we weren't deep enough into a shit storm at that point—Skellor, the guy in that Polity dreadnought, brought that. Dragon, and some Polity citizens it had brought along for the ride, was being pursued by him—he'd got his hands on something called Jain technology, and used that to hijack the dreadnought. Seems this technology comes from an alien race that's been extinct for a mere five million years. It's very dangerous stuff and, before his departure and eventual demise, Skellor left it scattered all over our world. That's the reason for the quarantine."

It took a quarter-hour to walk to the spot where the hooder had taken Tombs apart but left him alive. All the remaining shreds of the man had been collected and stored in sample bottles, but blood still stained the flattened grass, turned blue-black by the lack of oxygen in the air. The place also swarmed with penny molluscs, the Euclidean shapes and patterns on their shells giving the impression that some piece of ancient electronics had been shattered here. Sanders squatted down and gazed at the blood.

"There ain't much to see," Grant said.

"Where were you standing?"

He pointed into the still standing flute grasses over to one side. These long stalks were bound together in an almost impenetrable mass by their side shoots, which would later break away to leave holes into the hollow stems, holes that later in the year created haunting melodies whenever the wind blew, and were the reason for the name of the plant.

She turned to gaze at him. "So you saw everything?"

"Yes."

"You've no uncertainty about that?"

Grant nodded as he once again described events here. Tombs had run screaming, clawing at his aug, fighting whatever it was that was trying to capture his mind. The other four had gone under in a moment. Grant had hesitated when he got them in his sights, having no idea what was happening. They staggered about like people who had just been nerve-gassed, and two of them fell. Then the two standing grew still, and the two on the ground stood up. Their faces were imbecilic—one seemed to have suffered a stroke, for one side of his face had sagged—but still they all stooped to take up the weapons they had dropped. That's when Grant opened fire, rail-gun bullets smacking through their bodies to jerk them about in a bloody ballet until they dropped. Then he set out after Tombs.

Grant pointed to a peninsula of flute grass they were just walking round.

"I ran round here following Tombs's trail and near fell over the fucker before I got what I was seeing. The Technician, here." He gestured to one side at trampled flute grasses. "I thought that was my lot—I was going to die."

The sight had just slammed him to a halt. The Technician was the size of the largest of hooders, over a hundred metres from head to tail. It had lain coiled across here like the spine of some long-dead giant, only with legs stabbed down from between the vertebrae into the rhizome layer, and this spine terminating in an armoured spoon-shaped head which at that moment had cupped something against the ground, something screaming in raw agony. Then that head had risen, up to ten metres in the air, clear in execution light. In the underside he had seen its close-work eyes—two columns of them gleaming an odd yellow with some strange internal light. And, all about those eyes, the clicking, whickering glassy movement of its feeding scythes and drills. That's when he had jammed the barrel of his own rail-gun underneath his chin and begun backing off.

"You're sure it was the Technician?"

"These are the questions you were instructed to ask?" he grated.

"They are—we have to be sure."

"I'm sure—'less you know of any other albino hooders out here?"

"Okay."

Nobody got that close to a hooder and lived, and that thing that had been writhing on the ground below it, that thing that had once been a Human being, looked as if it would not live for much longer. Grant had felt it would be attended to after the hooder slammed its spoon head down on him, at which point he meant to blow his own brains out—he refused to be subject to its protracted and agonizing feeding process. But the Technician merely watched him for a time that seemed to extend towards infinity, before dipping down and once again covering Tombs. Grant should have run then, but having been a soldier for so long he had accepted his role as a walking dead man -that soldier's trait that enabled him to function in the midst of flesh-tearing metal. His survival instinct was there, but its power over him had waned, and a terrible fascination had held him rooted to the spot.

"We know they're just animals," said Sanders. "Complicated animals with some mysteries about them remaining unsolved, but animals nonetheless."

"So why the . . . intense Polity interest?" he asked. "We've been scraping up samples and making recordings of hooders for them for decades, and then there's that . . . face . . ."

Sanders nodded. "Yes, the prosthetic was unexpected."

It was. Upon hearing about events here, in this clearing, some distant AI had dispatched one of the fastest Polity spaceships here ahead of the intervention fleet. Upon its arrival, that ship had dropped a supplies capsule. Included among them was a new face for Jeremiah Tombs—a thing Sanders herself had fitted.

"You are utterly sure about what you saw?" she asked.

Grant concealed his flare of anger, knowing she must ask the question. Still his deposition was in doubt, especially that part about what he saw after the Technician rose from Tombs for the second time, when he saw Tombs lying there with his breather mask back in place. The hooder had studied Grant with an intensity beyond that of predator watching potential prey, almost as if trying to ascertain if he understood that Tombs must live, then abruptly it swung away.

"Utterly sure," he snapped.

"So what happened afterwards?"

After watching the hooder shifting its massive bulk off and away through the tangled grasses, he had walked over to Tombs, who just lay on his side in his own blood, the portion of his body between knees and throat stripped down to muscle, one arm reduced to bone and that mask grotesquely fixed over his stripped skull. All about him penny molluscs were scattered, though how they had got there so fast, Grant couldn't imagine. He had thought the proctor was dead, but then realized an odd sawing sound was coming from the man, for he was breathing still. It also seemed as if he was studying the molluscs with his one remaining eye.

"So you carried him back to the ambulance?" Sanders asked.

"He was the only other living witness," said Grant, and shrugged.

Sanders fixed him in her gaze for a moment, then turning away said, "Yeah—I understand." After a pause she added, "It seems enough for the Polity that he survived an attack by the Technician."

Yeah, that part of Grant's deposition about the breather mask wasn't on general release—too many of those who heard it believed Grant had made it up after putting the mask back himself.

They began walking back to their vehicles, an uncomfortable silence rising between them. Finally, at the point of departure, she said, "I'll see you soon."

"Yeah, sure," he replied, wondering how many months or years might pass before then.

The Graveyard (Solstan 2448)

"So why is my experience required?" asked the massive iron scorpion. "Though there've been some interesting developments on Masada, there's not been much action there recently. What is there for me?"

"Don't be obtuse, Amistad," replied the head. "You have a special interest and your present project is relevant too."

The polished chrome head apparently floated in the darkness above, but really resided only in Amistad's mind, it being just a representation of the AI the drone was addressing, just as this AI would no doubt be gazing at a big iron scorpion in some temporary virtuality. The head was the standard factory-setting icon used by artificial intelligences yet to choose their own form, yet to choose whether they wanted to live, what body they wanted to live in, and what purpose they might serve, if any. Yet Amistad knew that this intelligence had been around for some time, first as the mind of a Polity dreadnought, and now as the mind running the massive *Jerusalem* spaceship and research station. However,

Jerusalem had not chosen its own pursuits, rather *they* had chosen it.

There were three named ancient and dead alien races: the Csorians, the Jain and the Atheter. The Csorians were the special interest of an AI called Geronamid—a part-time hobby it pursued while holding the position of sector AI, mainly because most Csorian artefacts were to be found in the sector of the Polity it controlled. No single AI had yet to devote itself to things Atheter—to become the leading expert on the subject of that extinct race—but Jerusalem was the leading mind on all things Jain. During the Polity's long-ago war with the vicious arthropod Prador, a war in which Amistad had fought too, Jerusalem had found a small item of Jain technology and used it against the enemy to devastating effect. Only then did the artificial intelligences across the Polity realize just how dangerous this technology might be, and Jerusalem got "volunteered" to look into it. Now, that same technology, having come close to bringing down the Polity, lay outside it, contained in a star's accretion disc. That's where Jerusalem was now, studying Jain technology and, with a strange collection of helpers, ensuring it remained contained.

"What special interest?" Amistad swung his attention to the technological detritus surrounding him, focusing for a moment on a mess of spines and tentacles where it looked as if something huge had stomped on the giant bastard offspring of a black-spined sea urchin and an octopus.

"I know precisely where you are," said Jerusalem.

"Oh yeah?"

The request for direct com had routed to Amistad from some nearby runcible, and the drone had allowed it only after ensuring no tracing routines were attached. Unless Jerusalem was using some programming technique Amistad was unaware of, which wasn't unfeasible, the big AI should not know the drone's location.

"I know the location of the last runcible you used," said Jerusalem, "and, being aware of your interests, I surmise that you are presently in the Graveyard. Next, calculating travel times, it is simplicity itself to nail down that you are presently in the cave where the black artificial intelligence known as Penny Royal met its end. You are probably quite close to that *creature's* remains right now."

"Lucky guess," said Amistad. "So tell me: what do you think my special interest is?"

"When we of the Polity were at war with the Prador, speed of manufacture was the way to win. Independent war drones were made then and, because they were so *hastily* manufactured, some went into battle with minds that weren't quite stable. Some found equilibrium; some went insane and had to be destroyed, if they could be found. Some found their own ending—like that black AI just a short distance from you."

"Get to the point," Amistad said.

"During the war you went insane, Amistad, though it was a useful insanity of greater danger to the enemy than us. After the war, when we were clearing up the mess, you recovered what might loosely be described as sanity. Since then your special interest has been in minds that have been, not to put too fine a point on it, bent out of shape."

"I'll grant you that."

"We want you to study such minds on Masada. There is one Human mind—that of a man who was once a member of the religious police there."

An information package arrived and Amistad opened and studied it. Jeremiah Tombs was certainly an interesting individual, and what had led to his imbalance even more interesting still.

"Such *minds?*"

Another package now.

"Are you sure this Technician has a mind?"

"That will be for you to ascertain."

"And the relevance of my present project?"

"Events concerning Penny Royal's demise have been a closely guarded secret. That black AI died because it tried to install the recorded mind of one of the Atheter into one of its animal descendants, a gabbleduck. Perhaps now you can start working things out for yourself?"

"Yes, I think I'm beginning to see the pattern."

"Then I can leave this to you?"

"You can, though it will take me at least three years to get to Masada."

"The situation is not critical—not yet."

As Amistad pondered that "not yet" he felt some chagrin. He had just been "volunteered" to a task similar to Jerusalem's, only in his case the long-dead race was the Atheter. He had just filled a position that had remained vacant ever since the Atheter were named, and it was just right, for it seemed that entire alien race had succumbed to a kind of mass insanity. It gave him some comfort that the vast intelligence named Jerusalem could get so much so right, for such an intelligence was needed precisely where it was, watching over that lethal technology out there. Then, eyeing the twitching of one tentacle tip, Amistad also felt a degree of satisfaction in knowing that Jerusalem could also get some things entirely wrong.

Masada (Solstan 2451—14 Years after the Rebellion)

Gravmotor rumbling in his guts, the scorpion war drone Amistad descended towards a building surrounded by swampy wilderness. His companion descended on a parallel course—just a ball of black spines three metres across.

From up here the building looked like a black sun surrounded by the white rays of plasticrete walkways spearing out into the surrounding flute grasses. Amistad settled lower, down towards one of the walkways, the black disc revealing itself as a domed roof constructed of photo-electric glass—a material often used in remote Polity buildings. This then, was the place. Having arrived on Masada only a few months previously, it had taken Amistad a little while to orient, and to really understand what was required of him. The Polity needed data, about Jeremiah Tombs, about the Technician, and about the entire Atheter race and what had driven it to self-extinction. This building housed an Atheter AI, though a rather reticent one, and here seemed a good a place to start as any.

Penny Royal landed seconds before him, gently on the rhizome mat and then rolling towards the building, spines shifting like a starfish's feet. As Amistad finally settled on a walkway, he studied his companion pensively. They didn't call them black AIs because of their colour; they called them that because they were the arch bogey men of the Polity around whom no one was safe. After extracting the bitter darkness from Penny Royal's mind and putting the AI back together, Amistad had kept it with him because it might retain knowledge about the thing that had attacked it, and which seemed likely to have some bearing on events here. Having restored Penny Royal to apparent sanity, this entity had become Amistad's responsibility too, and he could not deny a lingering fascination. However, he still wondered if he had made this complex and puzzling entity entirely safe. Keeping Penny Royal around was risky at least.

Amistad returned his attention to their destination, now seeing the supporting ring of pillars below the dome. The whole building looked like an old Greek temple long abandoned here. He stalked towards it, the walkway dipping under his weight, and considered how this thing had arrived on Masada.

The planet from which the artefact housed here originated had been named Shayden's Find after the woman who discovered this thing, and who died there. It would be so easy, Amistad thought, to see what had happened on that world as part of a pattern, for the Jain-infected madman who had obliterated the Masadan Theocracy had gone there earlier, but to do so would be to lapse into the kind of conspiracy theory that Humans, who did not really understand statistics, tended to lapse into. It was coincidence, just that.

A single rocky slab, a small tectonic plate adrift on a sea of magma, had been that planet's only enduring feature. This object could not have survived on such a world but for one circumstance: the magma had accumulated and solidified around a large flat object unaffected by the heat. The woman Shayden went there to study this object, and found that some fragments of its incredibly tough and durable substance had broken away—enough to retrieve and study thoroughly. This substance, something like diamond, also bore certain similarities to memcrystal. Out of curiosity Shayden had attached an optic interface to one piece, and the reams of code feeding back through it astounded her. She had discovered something very important. It was an artefact, later confirmed as being too young to be a product of the Jain, and too old to be something the Csorians made. A product of the Atheter then. But a piece of memcrystal the size of the last joint of a man's thumb could store a Human mind, so what did such a mass of crystal contain? The mind of a god? The stock-market transactions of an entire galactic civilization? Alien porn tapes and family albums? Atheter blogs?

Penny Royal reached the pillars first, folded itself flat and clattered through, expanded into a ball again and rolled on to settle at the centre, shape more oblate now, tentacles squirming out from between the spines. Reaching the pillars, Amistad had to turn himself sideways to squeeze through, finally clanging down on a floor of ceramal gratings. Peering down he saw that a layer of mud had collected below the gratings, perhaps trailed in by the local wildlife, maybe even by gabbleducks. In this mud, over the past twenty years, flute grasses had germinated and spread their rhizome mat. Only the stumps of grass stalks were visible however, the maintenance robot residing in one of the pillars here having cleared the area before Amistad's arrival. The war drone moved over by his companion, reached down with one claw, closed its tips in one grating a couple of metres across, and flipped it aside, used the sharp inner edge of a claw to cut around the space exposed, then scraped up a mat of rhizome and mud and tossed that aside too. Beneath lay a flat surface of incredibly tough green crystal.

"Here," said Amistad.

Penny Royal flipped one eye-stalk from its mass, blinked a hellish red eye and replied didactically, "Anywhere."

Next the black AI extruded a single tentacle. This limb, ten centimetres thick, seemed to be made of liquid glass inside which things shifted and quivered like the internal workings of a diatom. The tentacle terminated in a tubeworm head, which Penny Royal opened out and pressed down against the crystal. The star of fronds the tentacle opened out into melded against the surface, then started to sink into it. Amistad took a wary pace back and as quietly as possible brought his internal weapons systems online.

A science vessel, the *Hourne*, was specially constructed to retrieve this artefact from Shayden's Find, and it was duly retrieved. Next the AI of that vessel had made connections with it, to supply it with energy and look inside. What the artefact contained immediately came to life and seized control of both AI and vessel. Subsequent negotiations had resulted in it being deposited here. It had just wanted to be dumped, hadn't requested anything else, not even power to keep it active. But the Polity AIs had decided otherwise, building this structure and ensuring a power supply, connecting up projectors, sensors and some defences.

Amistad now swung round to study the surrounding pillars with their inset consoles, a deeper sensor probe revealing other equipment inside the pillars. Though all this technology remained active in itself, for two decades it hadn't received any instructions from the entity residing in the crystal below his metal feet.

"Anything?" Amistad enquired.

"You know when I know."

It seemed evident that the Atheter AI here had made a personal choice to cease communicating, that if it wished it could communicate once again. The Polity had respected that choice, even though the likely vast store of data it contained could be very useful. Generally, Polity AIs were prepared to play a waiting game. However, for a war drone, impatience was a programmed-in trait, whilst for something like Penny Royal there were few rules that could be applied.

"Response," Penny Royal noted.

"Good."

If Amistad was to be the prime expert on all things Atheter, he wanted the information that could be obtained here. The planetary governor of Masada, an AI called Ergatis, had warned against doing anything like this and lodged its protest with Earth Central. To no effect, for Amistad had carte blanche.

"Definitely—" began Penny Royal, then fell silent as another huge being joined them.

The massive pyramidal gabbleduck squatted off to one side, seemingly in deep shadow, though that was certainly some effect of the projection. Its forelimbs were folded across its belly and its bill rested down on its chest as if it were dozing. Its eyes were closed and a deep rumbling sound permeated the air. Was it snoring?

"Keep doing whatever you're doing," Amistad instructed, then addressing the gabbleduck, "What should I call you?"

Just a slight twitch from the hologram, nothing more. Amistad waited, then turned to inspect Penny Royal as the black AI made a strange hissing sound, its spines rubbing together like dry reeds.

"Oblivion," said a deep sonorous voice.

The gabbleduck's head was up now, and all its eyes gleaming emerald. A shriek abruptly issued from Penny Royal as it rose from the floor, light glaring from its internal workings. Something snapped then cracked, and a spine shot away, its base a tetrahedral box from which a tentacle trailed—the one attached to the green crystal below. The spine tumbled through the air, stretching the tentacle straight at the limit of its flight, then slammed down against the gratings. The gabbleduck hologram shimmered, winked out, then abruptly clouds of steam began issuing from the gratings.

"Out of here," Amistad instructed.

Penny Royal shot through between the pillars first, rolling across rhizome, spines jabbing deep and sizzling as it used the damp soil to cool itself. Behind, the steam issuing from within the building turned to boiling smoke which, when it occasionally cleared, revealed the AI below glowing a hot orange. But the thing had withstood temperatures much higher than this, so would not be damaged, unless it was deliberately damaging itself.

"What did you get?" Amistad asked when Penny Royal ceased to roll and sizzle.

"Instruction," the black AI replied.
"Like what?"
"Euphemistically, to go away."
"It doesn't want to talk."
"Very definitely."

Heretic's Isle

"His legs didn't stop working back at Triada Compound fourteen years ago," said Sanders. "He came out of it aboard the troop transport as we brought him here, just after I'd cleaned him up and changed his clothing."

"Diagnostics?" enquired the huge scorpion drone.

She glanced at the big machine. She would have to get used to its blunt and sometimes patronizing manner, since it was now apparently her boss. She'd received her orders directly from Earth Central and though she could question them, that was the limit of it. Anyway, it seemed things were changing. At first she'd felt herself rebelling, until she understood that feeling stemmed from a complacency that had grown in her over the last decade and a half. Here she had used her self-proclaimed duty of looking after her charge as a cover so she could hide herself away from the world and pursue lengthy academic studies of Polity medical science, Masadan history and the biology of the Worry Island chain. Now she understood that, she was impatient for change. Hence her recent radical pursuit of change in herself.

"Yes, his medical implants told the tale, as did the readings from his prosthetic," she replied.

As they strolled along the beach Sanders shut down the shimmer-shield of her Polity breather mask and tentatively took a breath. The air smelled just like it would on a beach on Earth but, prior to the nanosurgery she had undergone, after a few breaths she should have been feeling the lack of oxygen. However, the lungs in her chest, the blood in her veins and her muscle matter were substantially different after her three-week sojourn in a somnolence tank, being taken apart and put back together again by the AI surgeon. Alveoli density in her lungs was now three times what it had been, and the extra formed of a semi-organic film much more efficient than the remaining original—a film that actually cracked CO_2. Her haemoglobin levels were double what they were before, complemented by oxygen-gathering nanomachines that operated from the artificial portions of her lungs and that also collected excess carbon for excretion through her kidneys. Her muscles burned oxygen more efficiently than before—much of the dross created by parasitic DNA had been removed.

"And that tale is?" enquired the drone.

Of course this creature had no need of air, just water, which it processed through its internal fusion reactor. And, since this creature was a battle spec drone, it probably also had methods of generating power from every other source available. It probably could breath oxygen, just didn't need to.

"He can walk—all that part of him is functional—he just *won't* walk." Sanders paused to gaze up towards the sanatorium perched at the top of the slope ahead. The Theocracy had used it as an interrogation camp, and though the internees had been moved to City Hospital before she arrived, she shuddered on remembering some of the equipment she had found there when setting the place up as a hospital for badly injured survivors of the Brotherhood. Of course, they were all gone now; cured of their ills and coming under the Polity Intervention Amnesty. Only Jeremiah Tombs remained.

"Won't walk?"

"I've tried everything," she said. "It's why I had him put in a wheelchair rather than an exoskeletal suit—I want his imagined debility to inconvenience him more, in the hope it will drive him to lose it. But that doesn't seem to be working." Understatement of the hour, since Tombs had remained in that chair for fourteen years. She glanced at the drone, but there was no point trying to read an expression there. "The problem lies inside his skull—that area I was specifically ordered to avoid. If I'd been allowed just a little more freedom to act I could have replaced that damned head prosthetic of his—regrown all those burnt-out nerves and filled in all those little holes bored through the bone."

"It is necessary," said the drone. "However, it's interesting that he has retained the use of everything above his waist. Does he do anything with his hands?"

"Like what?"

"Like, perhaps, make sculptures?"

"He draws," she replied.

Once it became apparent just three years ago that Jem wanted to draw, when he started scribing pictures on the floor of his special bathroom with his own excrement, she provided him with the required materials. Fortunately he took to them well and stopped his experiments with the previous medium.

"What does he draw?"

"Molluscs," she replied.

It had taken her some time to figure out what his drawings depicted—all those geometric shapes in intricate and specific patterns that he laboured over for so long, before enclosing them in a circle and then consigning them to the floor. Only one day when she was walking out here and had seen penny molluscs clinging to the shady side of a boulder did she realize what he was drawing. Perhaps the time it had taken her to realize this, despite her studies of island biology, was a good indicator of how far she had disappeared into her own head.

"Interesting," said the drone, but that was all.

"When are we going to put his mind back together?" Sanders asked.

It pleased Jem that the terrace was so wide, but he wished it was wider, so he could get further away from that *thing*. Why it came here to conduct these nonsensical conversations with Sanders he didn't know. He just wished it would go away and never come back. Raising his head again he peered across at it. The machine had been fashioned in the shape of a creature from Earth. From his computer he had learned it bore the shape of an arachnid called a scorpion, though that might not necessarily be the truth, since the information they allowed him was woven with their lies.

"You know the answer to that," the scorpion drone replied, shifting about on tiles the colour of a drowned man's skin.

Jem felt the terrace vibrate underneath his chair. He shuddered and dropped his gaze back to his sketch pad, set his pencil to erase and obliterated the shape there, returned the pencil to draw mode and began again.

"Yes, when you have the answers you require."

Sanders reclined in a comfortable sun chair, a drink on the stone table beside her, its ice glinting rainbows. She now wore a skin-tight bodysuit that terminated just above her breasts and at the top of her thighs. Jem wished she would dress more appropriately. Women should not expose so much of themselves to a man's gaze, much less to the gaze of one of these godless machines.

She continued, "It occurs to me, Amistad, that you've more interest in the state of his mind as it is than in any answers it might provide."

"You are absolutely right," the drone replied, and Sanders sat forward with sudden interest. "But it's only when I obtain those answers will I fully understand what has been done to him and thus satisfy that interest. And we are much closer now."

"Closer?"

"It is," said the drone, "a Human survival trait, this ability to forget pain."

"No one forgets pain."

"You misunderstand me." The drone gestured to Jem with one claw, and he concentrated on his drawing, pretending he wasn't listening. "The AI experience of memory is utterly direct. When an AI recalls, it re-experiences the entire event memorized in every detail, including all sensation. When a Human recalls an event it is a mere tracery in the mind, a dull copy with those sensations that might adversely effect the survival of the organism either erased or filtered. You do *remember* pain, but you never directly experience the memory of it."

Sanders grunted in amusement. "If women of the far past had directly remembered the pain of childbirth the Human race would be extinct."

"That is another mental mechanism," the drone said dismissively. "Human pain is necessarily intense because the lesson of avoidance must be learned by the dull recording medium of the Human brain, but Human memory of pain must not be intense enough to cripple the risk-taking function which is a necessity of species survival."

"Thank you for that." Sanders picked up her drink and sipped. "But the relevance of it escapes me."

"We know about the fibrous structures the Technician left in his brain, and we now know that via them the Technician embedded something very deep and very integral in his mind—we are certain that it actually downloaded something from itself. However, whilst doing so, it was also performing its feeding function—whether out of instinct or as part of the process is unclear—and that memory of pain was deeply embedded too."

"So we're getting somewhere?" said Sanders excitedly.

"Somewhere, yes. But unfortunately, what was downloaded to him is so tightly entangled with his pain, that it remains inaccessible whilst he cannot remember what happened to him."

"So we use nanosurgery to restore his memory . . . '

"No, we considered that, but the embedding process has made his memory of the pain a direct experience, as with us AIs. Recall would be as agonizing to him as what he experienced underneath the Technician's hood. This is why both download and memory are so deeply submerged—he is a Human being and incapable of holding so direct an experience of pain in his conscious mind."

Sanders grimaced and sat back. "So what now?"

The scorpion drone gestured to Jem again. "It leaks through. Very slowly his memory returns to be incorporated in his mind as an indirect experience: a normal Human memory. And with it we get leakage of the download too. It is a process with which we do not want to interfere, at least *directly*, for fear of destroying the data."

"Leaks through?" said Sanders. "Yes, I guess it does, but at least the knockout feed stops him screaming. He just lapses into unconsciousness."

"But remember his drawings."

Yes, the drawing. Jem returned his attention to the clear collection of Euclidean shapes, erased a couple then drew them back in just so.

"Those penny molluscs?" queried Sanders.

Jem looked up to see her standing over him, flinched when he saw that the drone had also moved closer, peridot eyes watching him impassively, then returned his attention to the sketch pad. Yes, he was nearly there with this one. He began muttering the Second Satagent.

"Before the tricones completely churned up the area where the Technician attacked him, Commander Grant had someone make digital two-dimensional photographs there," said the drone. "It's a shame he did not have better recording equipment available to him, but we must make do with these. Penny molluscs had been attracted by the blood and were scattered all about the area. Whether these were all present when he lay there is unknown, but we do know, from closely studying the photographs, that thus far he has precisely drawn the shapes seen on the backs of twelve of those creatures."

"He's remembering them."

"So it would seem."

Sanders turned to the drone now. "By the way, you keep referring to 'we'—who else is here studying Jem? I thought you were working alone. I thought you decided any form of linkage to local AIs would interfere with your thought processes."

"My associate is a little shy of company and wishes to remain incognito for the present."

One last line in place and, satisfied, Jem scribed around the drawing the perfect circle of a penny mollusc shell. The thing itself arose utterly clear in his mind then, there on the bloody flute grass. His skinned hand was closing on that grass, and looking up he saw the scorpion drone—no, it was rising up, two columns of yellow eyes blinking into being down its underside. Then, nothing.

Triada Compound (Solstan 2457—Present Day)

Leif Grant stepped up to the airtight door leading from what had once been a pond workers' bunkhouse, then a hospital, and which had now been returned to its original form and classified by the AI governor of Masada as a planetary relic. Remembering a long-ago conversation at this place, he realized that Sanders had been right about why he had saved Tombs's life, but only partially right. When that massive alien creature Dragon, who he had known as Behemoth back then, came and knocked out the laser arrays before crashing to the ground to enact its peculiar and worrying rebirth, the rebels of Masada took the opportunity to leave their caves and seize the surface. They knew they wouldn't be able to hold it for long, since the rebellion had been all about getting Polity intervention, and inevitably Deacon Aberil Dorth quickly responded by bringing troops down from the cylinder world *Hope* to attack. No quarter was given on either side. The rebels, and those of the underclass freed by them, were especially vicious in their reprisals against the likes of the proctor who had once occupied this very bunkhouse during its brief service as a hospital. The religious police had been the source of all the beatings, the torture and the enforced worship they had endured.

The moment he stepped outside, his Polity tech breather automatically closed a shimmer-shield across his face and began to feed him breathable air, for he still remained wary of undergoing the adaptation to the atmosphere of his own world. He headed out across a meticulously cropped lawn of blue grass. This lawn had not existed when last he was here, and the fence now standing perfectly restored before him had been crushed into the ground by his own side's tanks. It was evening now, and the moon Amok tumbled across the aubergine sky against the backdrop of a nebula like a knotted glass octopus. The light of both of these reflected from the chequerboard of ponds lying beyond the fence, in which the Theocracy underclass had once raised the lethal squerms whose proteins were then the only source of offworld wealth here. There were squerms in the ponds even now, though those that tended to them were armoured swimming robots like metre-long, green-chromed water beetles.

Grant walked over to the gate and pushed it open, then headed out onto the paths lying between the ponds. Remembering that last visit, he glanced over to one pond in which glinted brassy writhing movement. The battle tank had been removed. Back then the burnt-out vehicle had still emitted wisps of smoke, which meant there must have been a leaking oxygen supply inside still supplying the embers. Other wreckage had been scattered here and there, both Human and mechanical. There had been a corpse—a Theocracy soldier, his augmentation grey against the half of his head that remained.

Why hadn't Grant killed that proctor when he found him out there lying on a bed of trampled flute grass? Sanders had been correct about anyone surviving an attack from a hooder likely being held in superstitious awe. In fact, Jeremiah Tombs *was still* held in superstitious awe by many, especially now some portion of the truth about this world had come out. Grant might perhaps have allowed Tombs to live just because of that. But there had been more to it than just superstition, or awe, even though the hooder Grant had seen lift its massive spoon-shaped head from the proctor had been none other than the mythical Technician. There had been that breather mask, that damned breather mask . . .

Grant had been sure that the man had some questions to answer, and the interrogator would probably be a Polity forensic AI tapped directly into his brain to ask them. Yet for over twenty years those questions had remained unasked, and Tombs was a basket case and last internee of what had once been a prison hospital on one of the southern islands. His sanity lay within the compass of Polity technology, yet the AIs did not want to tamper with what had been done to him, and that was probably because they did not yet understand it.

Grant, erstwhile soldier and colonel in the army of the underground, shuddered and peered down at the ground just ahead of him. The particular corpse that had lain here had been surrounded by a few departing dryben, small creatures that seemed related to the sprawns the workers had raised in some ponds, but which were native to Masada and, like maggots on Earth, were the undertakers of this world. Something about the death had called them to the surface, but contact with it was driving them away, for alien meat did not contain the proteins they required. However, Grant remembered how the corpse had been crawling with penny molluscs, their domed shells with their even colourful patterns, just like the same molluscs that had surrounded Tombs . . .

Grant abruptly turned away, heading back towards the bunkhouse and the ATV he had parked behind it, questioning the impulse that had caused him to revisit his past. He understood what drove that impulse. Those discoveries made by Polity researchers here, and the presence of an Atheter AI out there in the wilds, had both weighed heavily on his mind. But now, it seemed, an ancient war drone had arrived, its remit to find some answers. And he felt certain that some of those answers would be to questions he often asked himself, about Jeremiah Tombs.

3

Prosthetics

With the advent of genetic manipulation to enable someone to grow a new limb, or with the technology available for them to just take rejection-proof body parts off the shelf, you'd have thought the prosthetics industry dead in the water. Not so. It being most people's preference to have genetically matched limbs or organs grown in a tank, prosthetics are used while they are growing. Fast replacement prosthetics have also been developed where access to advanced medical technology is limited: plug-in limbs for soldiers on the battlefield, self-embedding syntheskins, pop-in eyes that grow nanofibre connections either to the optic nerve or all the way back even as far as the visual cortex, self-planting teeth and self-connecting chest-pack hearts. The technology is such that now the prosthetics can be more durable, sensitive and stronger than whatever body part they replace, and some prefer them to that part. There are those who, over the years, gradually replace their bodies, ending up in a full Golem chassis, then opting for the ultimate prosthetic replacement by having their minds loaded to crystal.

—*From* HOW IT IS *by Gordon*

Masada (Solstan 2453—16 Years after the Rebellion)

The mud pipe lay between two peninsulas of stone—the foothills of the Northern Mountains—and funnelled in towards his destination. Tricones gathered here in their trillions, intent, in a battle for Lebensraum that would last a billion years, on rendering the whole mountain range down into nice, damp loose mud in which to lay their eggs. Chanter listened to the sound of them thumping against the hull of his mudmarine and noticed, when one hit particularly heavily or loudly, that he was beginning to flinch. It occurred to him that his long years here had perhaps not done his mental condition a great deal of good—he had developed agoraphobia, and the fear of the open spaces he intended to face had begun to grow more and more intense the closer he got to them.

Ten kilometres in and the mud pipe narrowed to just metres across but, having already mapped it, he knew he only had to get through this section, to enter an old volcanic vent, up which he could rise to the surface. Yes, perhaps he did have some fear of open spaces, but it was much compensated for by his utter lack of fear of his claustrophobic environment.

Beyond the narrow section where the pipe debouched into the vent, there were no tricones at all. It was as if the creatures possessed some ancestral memory of narrow escapes from surges of lava, for Chanter could see no other reason for them not to be here. After closing his seat straps across he inclined his mudmarine to the vertical and headed rapidly to the surface, accelerating as soil turned to mud and then finally to water. Here, in the bottom of a caldera lake, he levelled the vehicle again, made his first use in a long while of its buoyancy tanks by releasing a cloud of bubbles, motored in towards the slope to the shore, tractored up this and finally surfaced, chameleon-ware engaged.

Chanter sat for a long moment gazing through the main chainglass cockpit screen as the electrostatics cleared it of filth. The shore here, below a crumbling stone slope leading up to the lip of the crater, was choked with lizard tails of a strange sickly yellow-orange hue. Perhaps some volcanic poison was the cause of this and also the reason for the lack of tricones in the vent. Almost without thinking he tapped instructions into his console, injecting a probe into the mud below to snatch up a sample, then realized he was prevaricating, for this was not why he was here. As the probe retracted, its sample automatically routed to the marine's internal analyser, he used the conveyor drive to drag his vehicle ashore amidst that yellow growth, then unstrapped and stood up. Next, without giving himself time to think about it for too long, he donned tough monofilament overalls, large boots specially made for his webbed feet, took up the backpack he'd made ready, and exited his craft.

Outside Chanter sniffed the air, picking up the distinct whiff of sulphur dioxide underlying the very specific stink here on Masada of putrefaction—something had died nearby, within the last week. Swinging his shear to chop a path he made his way through the vegetable mass, regretting he could not bring his robot, Mick, with him, but it wasn't made for this sort of terrain. The smell grew stronger as he advanced until he broke through into an area where the lizard tails had been crushed flat at the base of a crumbling lava slope leading up to the crater rim. And here he found the source of that stink.

The gabbleduck was down on its belly, as if crouching like some massively obese cat preparing to pounce. Its bill lay flat on the ground and its eyes were now a pepperpot of holes in its bare skull, which prawn-like dryben were using like holes in a wasps' nest. Chanter took a hard sharp breath and quickly scanned his surroundings. This was unusual, very unusual, practically unique. The remains of gabbleducks were a great rarity, for hooders—usually avid predators that avoided carrion—always gathered in numbers when a gabbleduck was dying, or dead. They would then go into a feeding frenzy, crowding each other out in their eagerness to feed upon every last scrap of the creature until absolutely nothing remained. Gabbleducks, it seemed, produced an oddly complex hormone whilst they were in the process of expiring, and this hormone drove hooders crazy. There seemed no evolutionary basis for this, but then evolution wasn't always the answer. It certainly offered no answers for why the Technician produced its grotesque sculptures.

Chanter walked over to the massive corpse, noting further dryben crawling in and out of holes eaten in through its body, and then he glanced up the lava slope. It must have expired up at the top there and rolled down, but still this didn't explain why no hooders had been attracted here to obliterate the remains. Perhaps some connection with the sickly lizard tails and the lack of tricones down in the vent? Chanter grimaced and headed for the slope, further puzzled as he climbed to see penny molluscs clinging in neat spirals to the stone. As he climbed he felt some degree of worry, for a dead gabbleduck would certainly be of interest to the Polity researchers now on this world and the AIs above would know that it was here. His visit might draw their attention, though he was not so stupid as to believe that the AIs weren't already aware of his presence here on Masada.

At the top of the slope he pulled his palmtop out of a side pocket of his backpack and called up the map showing his present location and the path he must tread to reach the coordinates Dragon had given him all those years ago. The arrow directed him to his left along the crater rim, though when he checked, he saw his destination lay twenty kilometres directly ahead. The trekking program had obviously found something there he needed to go round, a cliff or crevasse, maybe a river. He set out, big flat feet clumping down on shale bound together by the mycelial fibres of mountain fungus. Luckily it was early in the season for this growth and it had yet to turn the rocks slippery, though the downside of this was that he would be unlikely to see any of the fungus-sucking herbivores that dwelt up here.

Halfway round the crater rim the arrow directed him down a gentle slope into a canyon formed by black basalt walls standing only a few metres high. He trudged on down to this, but at the base of the slope halted and scanned around. Maybe that gabbleduck back there, and the oddities within the crater, had left him with this creepy feeling, but he got the distinct impression that something was watching him. He glanced up. Perhaps something was, maybe some AI, keeping a sensor directed towards that corpse, now idly tracking his course. He shook himself and stomped on, legs already beginning to ache from this unaccustomed exercise.

After five kilometres, Chanter chose a suitable rock and sat down heavily, telling himself his amphidapt body was as unsuitable for this terrain as Mick's delicate machinery, but he wasn't fooling himself. He would have been just as knackered walking this distance over the rhizome mat of the flute-grass prairie. This wasn't about adaptation, but about him having spent too much time sitting on his fat froggy backside. He unshouldered his pack and took out his lunchbox, opening it to expose a writhing mass of green nematodes, dipped forwards and snatched up a clump with his sticky tongue, chomped them all writhing and salty in his mouth, and swallowed with an eyeball-sucking gulp. Enough. He stowed the lunchbox away, shouldered his pack then, after a long reluctant pause, stood up again.

Fifteen kilometres from his mudmarine Chanter really just wanted to turn round and head back, and it appalled him that every step now took him further from his vehicle, and was one he must take on the way back. However, both determination and self-disgust drove him on—that, and the knowledge that his lunchbox was still full and that his pack contained a nice monofilament tent with integral bed. By the time he reached the long teardrop entrance giving access into the side of a big tubular cave seemingly enfolded in a wave of stone, the sun was setting and Calypse gleamed bright in the sky. Here he paused, scanning through his finger webbing in infrared to check nothing nasty lurked inside before he entered. For a moment he felt panic upon recognizing the shape of a hooder, but soon saw that its individual segments lay some distance apart, perhaps shaken loose by some tremor, like a row of beads on a plate, the carapace of its legs scattered on the dusty floor all about it, and knew it was long dead.

"This what you wanted me to see, Dragon?" he wondered out loud, then shuddered at the echo of his voice issuing somewhere to his left.

Chanter unshouldered his pack and squatted on the dusty floor to open it. His tent was a short cylinder he held in one hand. He pressed the activation button then tossed it a few metres away. The cylinder hinged open along its length, the tent expanding out of it as a small pump forced air into the open foam structure of its walls. Within a minute the domed tent, two metres across, extruded barbs along its lower rim to anchor itself to the ground, then the internal light came on. Chanter ate worms before crawling inside and slumping on the inflated bed, where sleep came down like a hammer.

The remains of the hooder revealed no more than that this particular creature had been a young one, which was surprising—the only hooders to die young on land were those killed by Human weapons, yet Chanter could see no sign of their use here. Only after puzzling over the remains for some while, recording images and taking samples, did he begin to search the rest of the cave. Two hours later he found something quite odd where the ceiling slanted down to join the floor and where the gap was so narrow he had to crawl in on his hands and knees. Here a square of stone had been excised from the floor, laboriously cut out using a diamond saw by the looks of it, but no clues remained as to why. An hour after that he found the narrow cleft concealed behind where one of the hooder's segments lay against the wall, squeezed through the narrow gap and pointed his torch inside.

Rebel cache. On the floor near one wall of the cave were scattered dusty plasmel crates, one of which lay open with its lid propped against the wall beside it. He stomped over and pointed his torch beam inside, noted a single, heavily corroded chemical-propellant rifle, and realized that this must be an old cache indeed—probably placed here when the rebellion was just getting started and before the rebels found their way to the deep underground. He shone the beam around, and felt a sudden surge of incredible excitement when light fell on the object at the back of the cave.

They'd enclosed it—employed what looked like part of the kind of tough, transparent plastic cylinders used in old spaceships to hold deep-frozen members of the crew or passengers. The top of the cylinder was capped off with a steel plate, its lower edge was bolted to the slab of stone it rested upon, and only while studying these bolts and wondering how he might undo them did Chanter realize that the slab was the one that had been excised from the main cave. Incredible. Even while fighting to survive, fighting to get their rebellion under way against the vicious regime here, they had seen the value of this object and sought to preserve it. Here before him stood yet another of the Technician's sculptures.

Moving nearer, Chanter studied the thing more closely. It was definitely old and looked extremely fragile. He could see where sinews once bound it together, those sections now secured with corroded copper wire. The form itself seemed rough, primitive; the product of the young artist in all its gauche brilliance but lack of refinement. The bone itself had faded to a chalky white and in some areas it seemed that pieces were missing; some pieces had also fallen off and were scattered around it. But this was a discovery indeed, and Chanter wondered what truth Dragon had directed him here to find.

He had to get this back to his mudmarine; he really needed to investigate further. How old was this thing? By his reckoning, the Technician, at its present size, would have been too big to enter the main cave out there, let alone to make its sculpture in that narrow place near the cave's end. Even the dead young hooder out there could not have squeezed in. The artist must have made this when still but a worm, still spending most of its time rooting up small mud snakes or ambushing grazer young from below. So maybe, from what he knew of the lifespan of hooders, this was as much as a century old.

Chanter stooped and fingered one of the bolts, but they were corroded in place and he hadn't thought to bring cutting equipment. Next he studied the steel lid and, after a moment, realized only its weight was holding it in place and it possessed no airtight seal as he had suspected. He lifted the edge, and then let it drop back into place—first things first.

Over the next hour he recorded holographic images of every part of this cave, and every detail of the sculpture. He went out into the main cave and packed away all his equipment but for one sample bottle and a pair of tweezers, then returned to the small cave, lifted the lid aside and reached inside to take up some of the scraps of bone scattered about below the sculpture and carefully insert them into the bottle. He could not take the whole sculpture himself—it looked far too delicate—but he couldn't leave this place without taking something, some trophy.

Back out in the main cave he hoisted his pack and exited into bright day. No matter the risks and no matter how tiring the journey, he would return here with Mick to collect his find. It was important, very important, though he'd yet to figure out why. With renewed vigour he stomped the trail back towards his mudmarine, stopping neither to eat nor rest. As he finally approached the crater rim he wondered if his fatigue was why things began to get rather strange.

There seemed a yellowish haze down in the crater, swirling with odd organic shapes like the ghosts of all the creatures the Technician had killed. An odd taste suffused his mouth and he smelt something nutty and sweet in the air, as if he were walking into a cake shop. As he began to make his way down he spotted four figures further round the rim from him, humanoid, but moving with an odd birdlike gait. They made a rush towards him and terror surged up inside. Dracomen—Dragon had lured him here to finish what it couldn't finish under the ground.

Chanter broke into a dogged run, determined to reach his mudmarine before they reached him, but something whirred through the air and wrapped itself about his legs. He sprawled, head down towards the crater, and saw yellow ghosts crawling up towards him, a siluroyne opening diamond jaws and a fungus grazer coming to suck out his brains. Glancing back at his legs he saw a bolas tightly wrapped around them, its string like the linked bodies of snakes and its weights like scaled pomegranates. Writhing, it settled itself comfortably, binding his legs more tightly. It must have also injected some sort of poison, for he was finding it hard to breathe, but still he tried to crawl on down. Then a shadow loomed across him.

One of the dracomen stood over him. Here stood one of those things Chanter had seen forming underground from the very substance of Dragon: humanoid, but with legs hinging the other way at the knees, toadlike head jutting forward on a long neck, scaled green and red skin over most of the body but fading to yellow down the front as on the body of a lizard. This creature clutched a rifle that bore the shape of an ancient muzzle-loader, but also looked like something living.

"Adapted Human," it hissed.

"Hardly edible," commented another dracoman, now stepping into view. "Is it dead?"

"No, not yet."

The first dracoman squatted beside him and tapped the bolas, which abruptly released its hold and wound itself round the creature's arm. Then Chanter's consciousness fled to a hot yellow place filled with the burning sculptures of the Technician.

Chanter opened his eyes and gazed up at night sky, the familiar glare of Calypse somewhere over to his right, a background rustle of flute grasses fading in and out of hearing as he turned his head to the left, to utter horror.

Resting there beside him the thing's lower spines stabbed down into the rhizome mat, the others starred all around. One tentacle with two stalked and lidded red eyes protruding from its tip loomed up above him whilst other tentacles writhed here and there, one stacking single rhizomes, another building cubes out of neatly severed flute-grass stalks, whilst one tentacle snaked into Chanter's chest, which lay open like a butcher's shop display, the smaller tentacles into which this main one divided writhing inside like maggots. He tried to pull away, but knew he was dead: the agony would reach him any moment.

"Keep still, Human," said a voice. "Penny Royal is saving your life—its first-ever experience of putting someone back together rather than taking them apart. Or rather, its first experience of putting someone back together *correctly.*"

"What?" he said, surprised he could speak, seeing as his lungs appeared to be missing.

"The gas vents every five and a half hours," said the voice, closer now. "It was one of those random and very rare occurrences the Atheter did not account for in their very thorough nihilism."

"Gas?"

"Hydrogen cyanide," the voice explained. "It didn't occur in such quantities when the Atheter wiped themselves out, but is now a product of decay of large tricones. They die to eventually form the chalk layer, but whilst dying here their juices enter narrow mud pipes under the mountains where they flow to the old volcano's cap to be cooked up in cyanide-infused sandstone and some metallic remains of the Atheter civilization that were missed. The result is gas, which bubbles up in that volcanic pipe you came here through. It would kill a normal Human within a minute, but on one adapted like you acts as a hallucinogen, and takes longer to kill. It can kill hooders, which is why they avoid the area and why that gabbleduck carcass down below remains intact. In fact it was this same gas that killed that young hooder whose remains you found in the cave—it must have received a small dose and so managed to get some distance off before expiring."

"Atheter?"

"You've been out of the loop for too long, Chanter, and so lack information vital to your own research. Whilst your previous research might also be of value to me."

Something happening in his chest cavity. He watched with an utter detachment from reality as two lungs inflated like little pink balloons and one of the smaller tentacles began negligently flicking ribs back across and zipping up intercostal muscle.

"I've stories to tell you," said the voice.

Chanter turned his head as the speaker loomed into view, and he wondered if the mentioned hallucinogen was still affecting him. But though the massive scorpion drone seemed a fearsome creature, he recognized a Polity entity and felt some reassurance. The other thing sticking him back together also seemed likely to be a Polity entity of some kind . . .

"Where are the dracomen?" he asked.

The scorpion gestured with one claw, and shrugged. "They hunt. They saved your life but did not want to be burdened with you, so they called me."

He felt momentary relief, followed by a touch of confusion, odd images flashing through his mind. "So what stories do you have to tell me?"

The drone advanced a little and he flinched, but then it kneaded the rhizome mat with its numerous legs and settled down. It was almost as if it were making itself comfortable, if comfort could matter at all to such a machine.

"The Atheter, as an intelligent race capable of building civilizations, retreated to their homeworld trashing all their technology behind them, then on their homeworld they committed a form of racial suicide that defies the imagination of an AI," the drone told him. "They reconstructed and reprogrammed organisms they had created for soil building on other worlds, to diligently grind up every trace of Atheter civilization and technology. They sacrificed their own intelligence, utterly abandoned it to revert to the state of animals, but only after they'd reprogrammed and otherwise reformatted some of their organic war machines so that they would obliterate the remains of those animals as each one died. This was an almost irrelevant piece of nihilism, probably stemming from self-detestation. But that's how their minds worked back then, as they sought to destroy what they felt had kept them warring with each other over the millennia."

"Here?" said Chanter, realizing at once that the soil builders mentioned must be the tricones.

"Tricones, hooders and gabbleducks," said the drone. "The gabbleducks are the animalistic descendants of the Atheter, and the hooders were once war machines."

"I don't understand."

"Jain technology," said the drone.

Chanter understood that this Polity machine was now feeding him smaller amounts of information to test the quality of his intelligence, and was probably disappointed by his immediate response of "Uh?" But he recovered and continued, "The stuff that kept this place quarantined for so long."

"A technology created as a weapon, created to destroy civilizations, yet in itself first appearing to be something that offered great power and knowledge. A poisoned chalice the Atheter took up with the result of millennia of war, worlds burnt down to the bedrock, trillions of deaths, and an eventual choice to put away civilization, put away technology and even to shut off their minds. Racial insanity."

"How do you know all this?"

"Polity researchers on this world began to see the shape off it, and a surviving Atheter AI, which now resides here, confirmed the likelihood of some of it, though what happened here happened long after it went out of contact with the kind that built it. There's other proof too. A man called Rho—an adapted Human like you—found an Atheter memchip. Before he could do anything with it, it was stolen from him and taken, along with a gabbleduck, to a black AI called Penny Royal who was willing to do the install." The drone waved a claw towards the sea-urchin thing, which was now stretching Chanter's skin back into place and somehow sealing it invisibly. "The result was messy—Atheter technology hidden in U-space activating and shutting the whole thing down, and nearly killing the black AI concerned."

Again that claw gesture, and Chanter turned to look at the sea-urchin thing with renewed horror. But even as he felt that, Penny Royal gently eased him upright and withdrew its tentacles. Feeling abruptly returned, but just that, no pain. He looked at the AI with suspicion as it nonchalantly continued to stack rhizomes and added greater and greater complexity to its cubic sculpture of flute-grass stalks.

With care, Chanter eased himself to his feet and more closely studied his surroundings, his attention drawn at once to the object standing on the rhizome mat behind the drone. The sculpture was here, still in its glass tube and still mounted on that slab of rock. He gazed at it for a long moment, then swung his attention back towards what Penny Royal was doing, and felt a sudden intimation that he was being told something, but it lay just off the edge of perception, ephemeral, fading when he groped for it.

"I want detail," he said.

"I have transmitted all the relevant files to your mudmarine computer," said the drone. "And I have just summoned your robot, Mick, to collect this Technician's sculpture."

Chanter gazed at the machine steadily. "You've told me stories, but I don't see where your interest lies."

"I study insanity."

Chanter glanced back at Penny Royal. Its presence here made more sense now.

"Did you know that there is a living Human survivor of a hooder attack?" the drone enquired.

"No, but it was sure to happen one day."

"This Human was severely damaged, tampered with—the hooder concerned even did things to his mind, actually downloaded something to his mind."

Chanter felt the skin on his back crawling. "Downloaded?" He looked over to the edge of the clearing to see Mick delicately paddling across the rhizome mat in this direction.

"The hooder concerned was the Technician."

The shivering sensation spread out from his back along his arms and down his legs. He realized that this was a return of further sensation, blocked until now. If he'd experienced all this in a fully conscious state, he'd have been screaming by now.

"We will share information," the drone added, and it wasn't a request. "Go back to your vehicle now and hurry, another gas venting is due in twenty minutes. Study the information I've given you and give me your conclusions—my address is in your communicator."

Chanter set off, but when pausing to watch Mick undoing the bolts around the base of the container and then deftly flip it aside, he came to a decision. Before he moved on towards what appeared to be the crater rim, he turned back.

"You know, Dragon gave me the coordinates of this sculpture," he said.

"Which is why I've chosen to involve you rather than just seize all the information and artefacts you hold."

Chanter nodded and headed on towards the safety of his vehicle, and the depths.

Heretic's Isle (Solstan 2455—18 Years after the Rebellion)

One of Amistad's associates occupied the adjoining control room. Sanders could hear some odd sounds and noted computer displays in the theatre flicking on and running code she did not recognize. Also, the autodocs in the tank were behaving oddly, scuttling around on glass as if anxious to escape something unbearable. Amistad had denied her any kind of access to this entity, even seemed nervous about letting her get close. The whole situation had begun to creep her out until she found out what it was all about. Then she just got angry.

"An essential part of his acceptance of reality," said the big drone, "is him being able to go outside without wearing a breather mask."

"With his prosthetic he doesn't need one."

"Quite."

Sanders tried to contain her anger; to keep to the facts. "So you won't allow any kind of intervention inside his skull, but you're quite prepared, without his permission, to commit him to major surgery elsewhere?"

"You yourself have experienced that same major surgery, you know what freedom it gives you here on Masada. To be able to breathe the air here makes you a true Masadan and not a dispossessed immigrant."

"Bullshit."

The drone continued as if she hadn't spoken. "Once the lung and bloodwork is finished and, incidentally, once we've replaced his mechanical arm with a tank-grown version that's been on the shelf for years, regrowth of his facial nerves and the outer tissues can commence, and he will be returned to your care."

"You're going to let me give him back his face?" Sanders was eager for that, but aware that in some way the scorpion drone had offered her a bribe.

"Yes, we understand now that the damage about his skull, caused during the Technician's downloading process, is irrelevant—repairing it does not in itself have any effect on the download."

"So you've got all you can get from the scanners in his prosthetic. This is still bullshit, Amistad." "Perhaps you would like to explain?"

"Him being able to go outside is not essential to his acceptance of reality," she said, trying to order her thoughts. "In fact, him being able to go outside distances him from his life before—makes his present experiences more unreal to him. If you wanted to rub his nose in reality you'd stick him in a breather mask and dump him out in the flute grasses next to the nearest hooder."

"I see that you understand."

"Damn right I do. You're up to something and I'm not sure it's okay with those above you."

"I have full competence here."

"Why, Amistad? Why?"

"It's complicated."

"I'm used to complexity."

"Integration of elements of the download will reach a crucial nexus, whereupon he will drive himself to face surfacing memory."

"He'll be going on a journey of discovery?"

"Yes."

"He can't even walk."

"As you said: his failure to walk is not a physical problem."

Sanders turned away from the drone to gaze across at Tombs, now floating in the amniote within this newly installed tank, the autodocs scuttling all around him, but not yet beginning their work. He'd rendered himself unconscious again after accessing the Atheter database through his computer. She'd cleaned him up and moved him to his bed and left him there while going to hers, but then strange scrapings and spooky noises in the sanatorium had brought her here, just glimpsing something big and sinister shooting out of sight at the end of a darkened corridor—that "associate"—before finding Amistad and her charge.

"Do you know when this journey will begin?" she asked.

"I have absolutely no idea," the drone replied. "You need to watch him, take note of any changes in his behaviour patterns and notify me the moment such changes occur."

The autodocs all froze for a second, then abruptly launched themselves from the sides of the tank to fall onto Tombs's body, some of them trailing various tubes, optics and other attachments from ports positioned around the inside. They started to cut, and even though this surgery was very precisely controlled, the tank fluid still turned cloudy with blood and other debris.

"Let me know when I can get to work on his face," said Sanders, and walked away.

Chanter's Base (Solstan 2453—16 Years after the Rebellion)

As Chanter brought his mudmarine to the surface, he reached out without thinking to engage the chameleonware, then with irritation snatched his webbed hand away from the controls. Only then did he actually add things up and realize that this was his first time home in almost a hundred Masadan days. Whilst the automatic dock engaged he spun his chair to observe Mick, upright and clamped to the inner hull, the old sculpture cradled delicately against its back. He reached into his pocket and fingered the sample bottle for a moment, then said, "The museum."

Mick detached from the hull, sliding down flat, sculpture still supported on its back. The mudmarine's door slid open into its cleaner compartment as the robot approached. After a contemplative pause, Chanter swung his chair back to his console and without the usual security checks, sent the data here aboard his vessel to the main database in his home. No point in running checks for worms or viruses—if Polity AIs wanted to fuck with him there wasn't much he could do about it. Then he stood and followed Mick out.

The rebels weren't the only ones to discover the numerous cave systems underneath the mountains of Masada. Chanter had mapped many of them from the smuggler's ship that transported his mudmarine and other supplies to this place, and even as he descended to the surface on an antigravity platform, he had already chosen his base. He'd worked in a rush, because he had needed to get to the surface before the Theocracy finished setting up its planetary grid of laser satellites and high-definition cameras, but he remained satisfied with his choice.

The marine sat in a sticky pond twenty metres long by ten wide, nearly occupying it completely. Below this pond a pipe curved for two hundred metres out into the main soil of the planet and within it a specially adapted shimmer-shield kept the tricones out. The pond itself occupied a cavern that was a fifty-metre-diameter cylinder over a hundred metres long, though shortened now by twenty or so metres with the foamstone construction that was both his home and the housing for his collection—a construction he'd have to extend if he was ever to find any more of the Technician's sculptures, which seemed increasingly unlikely now.

He stomped out across his dock, turned right and trailed Mick across the worn basalt. Mick entered a lower door in the foamstone to install the new exhibit, whilst Chanter climbed a stair to the door to his accommodation. He was curious to look at the data Amistad had supplied, and wanted to run tests on the contents of the sample bottle in his pocket. However, so as not to turn into a complete introvert slob, he always followed set rules when back here: first a long soak in his large bath, followed by skin-oil balancing and a medical scan; plenty of food next, which would include those vitamins and minerals the medical scan always told him he was lacking; then a long and contemplative study of his collection.

The bath leached out all sorts of nasty stuff and when, after a brief analysis, his oil machine provided him with the right mix and he sprayed himself, his skin started tightening up and losing its pouchy feel. As well as noting deficiencies of the usual vitamins, the medical scan warned him of a dangerously high deficiency in magnesium, and when he ate fat cherub beetles laced with the required additives, they were nectar, and he soon put away two large platefuls of the fat insects before heading downstairs to his collection.

Mick had already installed the new sculpture in its inert gas case, but had yet to position it in the collection. Using precise isotope-dating techniques Chanter had arrayed the twenty-three sculptures in chronological order, covering a period of nearly a century because, like this latest one, they weren't all sculptures he had seized shortly after the Technician made them. Studying this order he could see steady transitions and occasional abrupt changes as the artist sought perfection, found inspiration, and sometimes abandoned it. This new addition should fit in at the very start, yet it seemed so utterly different in style from the others here. It occurred to him that perhaps some longish time gap—perhaps some artistic block—lay between it and the others.

Further contemplation did not dispel his puzzlement, but then he was used to being puzzled by the work of the Technician. Eventually he made his way through to the small laboratory he maintained next to his collection, and ran his usual battery of tests on the samples from the bottle. Puzzlement returned when only one of the dating techniques seemed to work, but rendered erroneous data. He checked his system then, wondering if Amistad had used something to trash his computers here, but everything seemed to be working. He ran further tests on the mineral content of the bone, and got some odd results there too. Suddenly he grew angry, feeling he had been duped. This wasn't a sculpture by his Technician; it was a carving from some sort of rock!

Chanter nearly abandoned testing at that point, but a microscan of the surface bone revealed the familiar marks, the familiar signature of the Technician, only much much smaller. Widening parameters and trying other dating techniques available to him but never used before, he began to get an intimation of what he had here. This sculpture had been buried in that cave, probably only revealed when early rebels dug out the cave as a hide. Statistical analysis of mineral leaching from bone in this environment—the complex chemical processes of petrification here—finally revealed the truth, and it terrified him.

Since the Technician had made that sculpture squatting in its case out there, quite some time had passed. The artistic gap between it and the other twenty-three was a wide one—about a million years wide.

4

Sealuroynes

Whilst the study of the land forms of Masada progressed quickly, study of the oceans of Masada was put on hold. Further delays ensued when it became evident that the ecology of the land was a constructed one; that hooders were based on war biomechs created by the Atheter which might or might not have been first based on creatures of that world, or might even have no original evolutionary basis at all; that gabbleducks were the (deliberately) devolved descendants of the Atheter; and that the whole tricone basis of that ecology was manufactured. However, a proper taxonomic survey of the sea-life has now begun, with the sealuroynes, and already oddities are being found. These creatures bear some resemblance to the gabbleducks in that their brains are just too large and contain too many complexities for their marine predatory lifestyle. They show the same tendency to play odd games with their prey. For a brief while philologists speculated that the noises sealuroynes make to each other were actually a language, but they were unable to translate it, for it seems that—like the devolved Atheter—they gabble too.

—*From* QUINCE GUIDE, *compiled by Humans*

Present Day

Sanders brought her foot down on a slab of rock covered with domed transparent limpets that were direct relations to the penny molluscs whose shell patterns Jeremiah Tombs drew so intently. Inside the shells she saw writhing movement, peered at it for a moment noting single, spookily

Human-looking eyes gazing up at her from each shell, then waded ashore. She had recorded and studied most biota like this around the island, and these were nothing new to her.

She had been swimming naked again, as had become her custom here, not so much because she was an exhibitionist, but because it drew a reaction from Tombs, and such reactions, she felt sure, slowed his steady retreat from reality. Picking up her towel from the fluorescing sand she dried herself with sensual deliberation, wondering what to do today. Maybe she should check data from undersea probes she had scattered about the islands, or check new research notes transmissions from Earth? Perhaps she could get back to writing her history of the early development of scoles here on Masada? Contemplating these options with a wry smile, realizing that her excitement of two years ago, when Amistad had arrived, was now fading, she coyly looked up towards the terrace.

Surprisingly there was no sign of Tombs. Usually he would be peering over the low wall at her, then abruptly snatching his attention back to his sketch pad when she looked in his direction. She slung the towel over her shoulder, pushed her toes into her sandals and headed for the steps leading up.

Tombs was nowhere on the terrace, and Sanders felt a frisson of excitement at this change in behaviour. She walked over to the stone table he usually parked his chair beside and gazed down at the latest sketches, all held down with a paperweight of jade carved in the shape of a coiled hooder—Amis-tad's idea, that. The sketch on top was complete, and still in the pad, and the erstwhile proctor's electric pencil lay beside it. Usually, when Tombs finished a sketch he abandoned it, then started at once on the next. Never before had he abandoned both sketch pad and pencil, in fact he became hugely agitated if they were taken away from him, then ended up smearing shit on his bathroom floor in just the same way as he had begun his art career—something Sanders did not want to encourage. She gazed at these items for a second, then turned and strode over to pick up her loose dress and shrug it on over her head before returning inside through the shimmer-shield that contained Human-normal air inside the sanatorium.

Just in from the terrace lay what had once, and briefly, been an occupational therapy room. Tombs wasn't here either. Sanders stepped over to a nearby pedestal table, picked up the button of her comunit and stuck it to the material over her collarbone.

"Amistad," she said—the name gave instant access through the unit to the ever-watchful war drone.

"Here," the drone replied perfunctorily.

"We've got a behaviour change."

"Record and detail—I'm busy."

This dismissive attitude from Amistad had been common two years ago after she'd first met him, but less often of late. It had something to do with one of his associates. Sanders got the distinct impression that the individual concerned might be hard to handle on occasions, and dangerous, even to a drone of Amistad's capabilities.

She moved on into the sanatorium, heading directly for Tombs's room. Finally stepping through the door she came to a dumbfounded halt. For a second or two she was confused; trying to figure out what was wrong here. Then she saw it: Tombs's wheelchair stood empty in the middle of the floor. He wasn't in the bed and it seemed unlikely he was in the bathroom unless he had crawled there.

"Jeremiah?" she enquired.

"Right here," he said from behind her, his arm winding round her throat and the point of an oyster knife pressing against her cheek just below her eye.

Sanders made a sudden mental shift: she remembered that Tombs wasn't just a pathetic mental cripple confined to a wheelchair. He had been a proctor, one of the brutal religious police of Masada. He had probably tortured, beaten and killed people, and he had received military training prior to his induction into his latter profession.

"You're out of your chair," she said, trying to keep calm.

"Did you think you could keep me confined here forever?"

he murmured in her ear. "Did you think your pathetic Polity techniques could break my faith?"

"No one has been trying to break your faith," she replied. "We've just been trying to do our best here for you. Your mind and body were severely damaged by the Technician and the process of repair has been . . . difficult."

"Your experiment has failed—now you will show me the way to the surface and I will return to my people."

The surface?

"We're on Heretic's Isle," she replied. "You know where we are—you've been living here for the last twenty years."

Tombs turned her towards the door. "Show me the way out, woman, and understand that I choose martyrdom over imprisonment, but that will only occur after you have died."

"We aren't underground, Jeremiah—just search your memory."

"I have searched my memory and, despite your drugs and your mind-breaking techniques, I know the truth. You have tampered with my mind to create illusions. They are powerful illusions but faith is the tool that unravels them, that and your own foolish vanity."

"Vanity? I don't understand," she said as she walked slowly out into the corridor.

"You cover my face to conceal that I have not aged, yet you fail to cover your own face and you flaunt your youthful body."

So, her looking young had further confirmed his delusion that very little time had passed; his delusion that he *had not* been in this place for twenty years. Ironic, since both her and his youthful looks were a direct result of technology from the Polity now ruling this world—another fact he constantly denied. And the covering of his face was another fiction. She had replaced his head prosthetic two years ago, shortly after Amis-tad's "associate" replaced his mechanical arm and then surgically adapted him to breathe the air of Masada. Though for reasons still opaque to her, Amistad did not want him to know about either his adaptations or the loss of his prosthetic.

Always Tombs claimed that they created fictions for him, yet he lived in his own, adjusting facts to suit his perception of how the world should be. He believed he was still a captive of the Underground, still the subject in an experiment in breaking religious faith, but holes were beginning to show. Her "flaunting" of her youthful body was something that stuck in his mind from his last two years out on the terrace pretending not to see her swimming naked, so he hadn't managed to bury everything from then, and perhaps from the eighteen years before.

She walked on towards the old occupational therapy room and the way out onto that same terrace, but slowly, for she had no idea how he might react when reality in the form of open sky and sea hit him in his *face*. Hopefully Amistad would soon be focusing his attention back here and would intervene.

"You were attacked by a hooder called the Technician," she said. "It did things to you that even the Polity AIs that now control this world fail to understand, and this is why full repair of the damage has not been allowed."

"Just keep walking," he said.

She noted that he wasn't pushing her very hard and had begun leaning much of his weight on her. Though his chair had been running muscle-tone programs through his legs all the time he had been in it, they were still weak and wobbly. Where was that fucking war drone?

In the room beside the terrace he paused, and she was able to peer round at him. She could read little in his expression, but he had grown very still now and his gaze fixed on the view beyond the shimmer-shield.

"Here is the reality," she told him.

"Projection," he said dismissively, and shoved her forward.

As they approached the shimmer-shield he kept hesitating, his gaze straying to the various items scattered about this room.

"I can even see where the projection begins," he said. "This had better be the way out, woman, or I will have to spoil some of the source of your vanity."

He pressed the knife harder below her eye and she felt the sting of a cut. She realized he was seeing the slight glimmer of the shield interface, that effect seen in heat mirages caused by differences in air pressure. He shoved her again and she stepped through, feeling the slight tugging on her body. He followed her out onto the terrace, his gait abruptly turning into a stumble.

"I . . . cannot breathe . . . here," he said.

The knife slid down, cutting her face, but she managed to grab his wrist and push it away, turning and quickly stepping from him, slapping a hand to the wound. He stumbled forward, slicing the knife through the air, once, twice, but he seemed like someone trying to find an opponent in a darkened room. Then something slapped against his shoulder and spun him, and with his mouth moving spastically he reached back to feel that place, then toppled over like a felled tree.

"Interesting," said Amistad.

Sanders snapped her gaze across as the drone suddenly materialized, crouching on the terrace nearby, sting poised above its head glinting clear globules of fluid. It had obviously stung him; knocked him out.

"What did you use?" Sanders asked, heading over to pick up her towel and press it against her bleeding face. The wound was superficial—just a minute's work for an autodoc.

"There's no name for it," said Amistad, "but it blots out memory in the short time it takes to work, which is just as required."

"What do you mean?"

"We let this run." The drone moved forward with silent grace for something so heavy and poised over Tombs, peering closely at him. "Nothing has been achieved by keeping him here. We must let him claw his way to reality by experiencing it, very directly—we let him discover the truth and, in the process, discover the truth about him."

"Hopefully," said Sanders.

The drone turned towards her, then after a moment acknowledged that with a dip of its head.

Jem woke with a start, flat on his back on warm tiles, and tried to collect the disconnected parts of his mind. Abruptly he remembered that at last their security here had become lax: somehow the nerve blocker preventing him from walking had been disconnected, and the guards, grown complacent having to watch over someone confined to a wheelchair, had absented themselves. Only Sanders stood in his way to the surface, the way out . . .

Jem blinked, gazing up at open sky, then sat up and looked around. His thought processes realigned and he realized he had been mistaken about the rebel base. They really had moved him to an island, to another base actually on the surface. This could mean only one thing: there were traitors in the Theocracy who had somehow penetrated the scanning systems of the cameras up on the orbital laser arrays. Somehow those cameras were simply not being directed towards this place. Once he had made good his escape he must be careful who in the Brotherhood he informed about this. Perhaps it would be best to try and get a message directly to the Hierarch. Of course this wasn't Heretic's Isle, but that the Underground had expended so much in resources to create this place, this fiction, showed how important they considered their faith-breaking project.

He stood, gazing down at the bloody knife in his hand, vaguely remembering forcing Sanders to take him to the surface . . . no, out here. His gaze strayed down, then along to the edge of the terrace where she lay slumped in a pool of blood against the low stone wall, a trail of blood leading across the tiles to her. Somehow she had managed to strike him, to knock him unconscious, but in so doing had ensured her own death. He felt a surge of grief, of regret, so much stronger than seemed reasonable considering all they had done to him here. He walked to stand over her. Her blond hair was stuck down in congealing blood which, despite the air here, remained bright red.

"I've been adapted to this world now—Polity technology," her voice muttered in his head. *"I can breathe here."*

He recollected her standing before him, arms spread, wearing only a blue bikini. He shook his head to try and dispel the image, glimpsed the oyster knife still in his hand and with one jerky motion sent it clattering away from him, then stumbled to the steps leading down to the beach. He was gasping, labouring to breathe.

Reaching up he clawed at the covering over his head, seeking to tear it off, but the thing was soft now and transmitted pain. They'd upgraded it, giving it a realistic look and a realistic feel, but he wasn't fooled. It wasn't *his* face. Then, as further memory returned, he abruptly snatched his hands away. Whether the thing was a prosthetic as Sanders had claimed or just there to conceal from him his own face was irrelevant. However, one of her other claims now surfacing in his mind *was* relevant. She had said that, like a scole, it supplied him with breathable air, though unlike a scole it would allow him to breathe for ten days, and here he was *outside* and breathing without a mask.

He raised his wrist, studying the hand of his artificial arm. They'd made that more realistic too, even down to the hairs on the back of his hand. He transferred his gaze to his wristwatch, reached out to set a timer: a countdown of ten days. Unless they were lying about the extent of his oxygen supply, which seemed highly likely, that was how long he had to get back to the Theocracy.

Move, I must move.

He glanced back again at the corpse. Sanders was, to his best knowledge, the first person he had ever killed, and he could not believe that what he felt now was the same thing other killers felt. How could they kill again? As he headed down towards the beach, his legs unsteady at each step, it occurred to him that perhaps they had managed to make inroads into his faith, for surely, his faith being strong, he would not feel such regret on taking the life of an enemy?

Beach sand sank soft under his slippers and, glancing across, he saw her fading footsteps leading up from the sea. How could such fading images be all anyone left to the world?

How could those like Sanders believe that this was all there was? Heaven and Hell respectively awaited the faithful and the faithless.

Sanders would be burning in Hell now.

Jem flinched, a memory of pain so sharp to his perception, a brief image in his mind of her screaming, forever. He found himself on his knees in the sand. God had just allowed him a glimpse of Hell to harden his resolve, yet why did the very idea of what was happening to her now hurt so much?

Move.

He glanced aside, gazed at the object pulled up on the beach. He had no recollection of this boat being here before but perhaps, from his wheelchair, it had been out of his view. He forced himself on to his feet and stumbled over to peer down at the vessel.

It lay five metres long, had a folded-up outboard of a design he did not recognize, twin propellers exposed. How so small, almost infinitesimal an engine could drive such large propellers and propel so large a boat he could not understand. He checked it over, saw that it must be supplied with power from the small cubic unit on the deck below it to which two thin wires ran. He tried the simple controls on the rudder handle and soon had the propellers whirling up to vicious speed, then he stepped back and studied the vessel again. In his weakened condition he doubted he could drag the thing into the water, but he must try. Any time now the guards might return and find Sanders, then they would be after him. With everything he now knew, they would be utterly determined to stop him returning to the Theocracy.

Moving to the bow of the boat he detached a thin line from a post driven into the sand, tossed the line on board then grabbed the ring it attached to on the prow. To his utter surprise the front of the boat lifted with ease—it must be made of bubble metal, like a proctor's aerofan. In a moment he dragged it into the sea, then with a shove propelled it from the shore before rolling aboard and making his way unsteadily to the seat at the rear.

Only when the outboard was tilted back down again and

those twin propellers foaming a wake behind did he think where to go. It seemed likely to him that though the island behind him could not be Heretic's Isle, it did sit in the same crowded island chain. This meant he must head north to reach the mainland. He studied the position of the sun, the position of Amok vaguely visible over to his right, and realized he had no idea which direction was north. Only when his eyes strayed down did he see the small console set below the rudder arm and above the power supply and, inset in that, the compass and map display. The electronic map clearly showed him departing a crescent-shaped island named Heretic's Isle. This had to be a lie, so he ignored it, gazing only at the compass, and set the boat on a course northwards. Still pulling away from the isle he glanced back at the building high above the beach, felt a terrible tightness in his chest and experienced a sudden blurring his vision. Reaching up he touched tears streaming down the covering over his head.

Another lie.

The Underground had not changed its physical appearance much over the last twenty years, but it was emptier now, and the wind sometimes issuing from the cave-borne central river of Cavern Andromeda seemed to be mourning this desertion. Grant, having wended his way down the long stairway from the surface, walked through a shimmer-shield that was not a recent Polity import, but something bought at the cost of lives before the rebellion, from a trader in squerm essence in Zealos. It had always been a dangerous option to approach those who traded with the Theocracy, because the proctors were always on the lookout for such action, such a chance to kill rebels. They succeeded on this occasion too, only one surviving of the party of seven sent to collect the shield projector. Grant sighed. He always felt resentful stepping through that shield, since one of those who had not returned had been his brother.

Trudging wearily down the path to Pillar Town Assos, Grant studied the crop ponds to his right, glancing first at the big blue robotic beetles crouching on the banks, then watching some stilt-legged thing like an iron heroyne stabbing down a beak to remove a deader, a dead squerm, from one pond—a task that Human workers had to do before so as to prevent poisoning of the water. These machines came from the Polity, as did the fusion reactor standing on the banks of the river providing power for the whole cavern, and for the oxygen generator squatting beside it. As always he tried to concentrate on the undisputable benefits now trickling in from that massive realm, and as always could not dismiss his feelings of disapproval.

Entering the pillar town he crossed the lower coin of the building—an area once a weapons workshop but now being converted into a museum. Glass cases contained some of the weapons that had been made here, along with uniformed mannequins and old original-descent boring equipment—the collection gradually growing by the addition of other items of historical significance slowly being unearthed in abandoned stores. There were holographic interactives too, where people could experience a near-facsimile of past events. Grant had tried one once, and abandoned it in a cold sweat, swearing never to try that again. His memories were quite enough. Glancing round he noted that the only people here were parties of schoolchildren come to learn about their past. Beside the teachers other adults were few in number—the memories still raw for them too.

At the end of the museum he climbed into one of a bank of elevators and ascended, finally stepping out into the upper coin and heading out to his apartment on the rim. A hand against the new Polity palm lock gave him access and, as was his habit, he made straight for his fridge, took out and uncapped a bottle of beer, then went out to his chair on the balcony.

Grant perfectly understood his feelings of dispossession and had known for twenty years that he needed to resolve some things in his mind and move on. During that time he had mooched about from job to job, profession to profession—private security, aerofan manufacturing, ATV driver at the Tagreb, the Taxonomic and Genetic Research

Base which was the centre of most Polity research on Masad, even tourist guide, and recently vacuum construction on Flint—but was never able to settle. Now, back here from Flint, it seemed no time had passed at all and memories twenty years old had not lost their immediacy. He needed to find a new direction now, not to sustain his existence, since the intermediate regime had assigned him a pension and this had later been confirmed by the planetary governor, but to give his existence meaning. He had fought the Theocracy for most of his life, and even now the gaping hole it had left remained open—the same rift that all soldiers returning from war found. He sipped his beer, then reached out and picked up a palmtop from the table beside him, which activated to the display he had been looking at prior to his trip to the surface: memory editing.

Apparently, during their war against the alien Prador, soldiers of the Polity had edited their own minds to enable themselves to go on functioning. Upon his return he had discovered that some here on Masada, mentally damaged by the horrors of Theocracy rule and events during the rebellion, had also taken this option. A few surviving members of the Brotherhood had taken it too, as had many other believers trying to rid themselves of the burden of religious indoctrination. Perhaps he should get his head seen to. Perhaps he too should rub out the memories that kept him tied to the past, so he could at last step into the future he had been fighting for?

No.

He put the palmtop aside. That option just seemed too much like cowardice to him. He was the sum of his past. He was Commander Grant and so he would remain for the rest of his life, no matter if he never fought as a soldier again.

"The editing techniques are much more refined now," said a voice. "You can actually retain memories, but have them scrubbed of emotional content. You can be reprogrammed to acceptance, have old habits excised and the pleasure and pain wiring rerouted."

Grant sipped his beer again, then glanced over to his left

at a wide stretch of apparently empty balcony. "I'd say why don't you use the door just like anyone else, but I'd have to have it widened."

Amistad appeared like a scorpion-shaped bottle filling with iron colour. The drone reached out one long claw towards him, then down, delicately closing claw tips on the palmtop and picking it up for inspection. "I knew someone whose mind was edited when he was a child—his mother trying to save him from pain. Only when he reintegrated those memories and that pain did he become whole." The drone put the palmtop down again. "I too edited my own mind to return it to sanity, and only after I'd gradually put back those cuts, absorbing the pain as I did so, did I find the way to my future self."

"Trite philosophy—I expect better of you, Amistad."

"Editing out pain edits out its lessons too."

Grant shrugged, sipped his beer. "What do you want with me?"

"Jeremiah Tombs is on the move," the drone told him. "After drawing some final penny mollusc shell, he regained his ability to stand up and then he escaped the sanatorium."

"Escaped?"

"The only fiction we have created for him. He believes that he killed Sanders and escaped, and is on his way back to his Theocracy."

"He's in for some shocks, then."

"Precisely."

"You think the shocks'll unlock his skull?"

"I do, but we need him to stay alive long enough for them to work."

"Should be simple enough for you."

"Yes, even though Tidy Squad assassins have been dispatched after him."

Grant glanced up at the drone. "I ain't in disagreement with 'em."

"Neither is the runcible AI, which is why they've been allowed to operate for so long—some Humans are irredeemable."

"Yeah, okay, but you still ain't explained why you're here."

"I want you to guide and protect Tombs, and I want him to remember you," said the drone. "Your presence will help him find the gateway to sanity. He'll reintegrate his pain and become whole, and at last we'll find out what it was the Technician put in his mind."

"You seem confident."

"The mathematics of insanity," said the drone obscurely.

"And you'll tear his mind apart again."

"Do you accept the commission?"

Grant glanced at his palmtop, finished his beer and put the bottle aside. "Of course I do—I need the work."

Shree Enkara gazed through her binoculars at the apartment building, noting the foamstone construction of the walls, flicking her gaze down to the cams positioned above the main entrance glassed in above the covered street, then to the logo on the box they fed into. Old security there: armour glass, static cameras, palm locks, the armed guard she'd earlier seen enter the building for his morning shift, and perhaps some extras Mulen had placed in and around his apartment and in the offices of Glaffren Shipping.

Lowering her binoculars, Shree scanned across the rest of Zealos City. Lots of new buildings going up, lots of renovation, and many here were taking advantage of Polity technology becoming available. But of course Mulen, who now called himself Andrew Glaffren, had refused to have any of that godless stuff near him; refused the security drones and AI oversight. He'd foolishly assumed that his new identity and new face would be enough, and not reckoned with the fact that the Zealos police, now with its large complement of ex-Underground rebels, was full of Tidy Squad supporters who had been feeding her and her comrades the information they required to . . . tidy up. Of course, Shree was fully aware that their freedom to act here would soon be curtailed as the Polity tightened its grip. She was also aware that the Polity AIs did not seem overly anxious to close down Tidy Squad activities—perhaps they did not entirely agree with their own policies.

She closed up her binoculars and shoved them into her pack, hoisted that up to her shoulder then strolled over to the head of the stairwell leading down from the glassed-over roof. Mulen's biggest mistake, the one that had made information on him easier to come by, was that he had not been prepared to give up the family business. Though he himself had gone on to special training for his position in the Theocracy, his family had owned numerous squerm ponds. They had lost half of those ponds—confiscated by Lellan's intermediate regime—but retained the remainder which, now kept in business by Polity robotics Mulen did not seem adverse to, were bringing in a good income.

The stairwell wound steadily down to the apartment building's foyer, where Shree deposited her pack in a rental locker. The items it contained had been very useful on other occasions, but here she needed none of them, just her skin with its sprayed-on layer to prevent the shedding of skin cells and other DNA evidence, and her hands. Inside the public toilet here she checked her make-up in the mirror, brushed her ash-blond hair, making sure it covered the small crescent-shaped aug behind her ear, ran her hands down the clingy dress she wore, ensuring that the neckline was sufficiently low and that the slight tranlucency of the material made it quite evident that she wore nothing underneath.

Heading out of the foyer she stepped into the covered street. This area of the city had been one of the wealthier suburbs, generally occupied by those in the higher echelons of the Theocracy. It wasn't a place where you had to pay to breathe the air in a walkway, or where oxygen debt could lead to enslavement, scole implantation, and eventual demise labouring in squerm ponds. Now, however, things had changed. There were none of those white uniforms with text of the Satagents running from underarm to ankle, and the only bearded fool in long robes was the corner preacher, who hadn't been in the Brotherhood at all but was a city resident who delighted in lampooning religion and getting into arguments with the believers here, who still formed the larger part of the population.

Within a few minutes she had wended her way to the steel stairs leading up to Mulen's apartment building, climbed these and walked out into the glassed-over area before the doors and there halted. She gazed about herself with interest for a moment, then reached out to thumb the comscreen beside the door. A dour-looking security guard peered out at her.

"I have a delivery from Soola's for Mr.. Glaffren," she said.

"I don't know you."

"I'm new, but not without training."

"Let me see it, then," the guard replied.

Resting one hand on her tilted hip she replied, "You are seeing it."

The guard's face receded a little way as he obviously sat back in his seat. "I think you can do better than that."

Having watched this place for some time, Shree knew precisely what the man required. She ran a finger down the stick seam of her dress and opened it for him, cupping her breasts for a moment and squeezing her nipples, then sliding a hand to her pubis to gently play with herself.

"Come see me afterwards," he said huskily, and the doors unlocked.

Closing up her dress she entered the foyer and headed for the stairs. The whores who regularly came here from Soola's conducted their main business with Mulen, but then had a little number on the side with the security guard. Apparently the man did not like to go where Mulen had already been, and was conscientious—he kept on watching his camera screens all throughout the ensuing blowjob.

Three flights up, Shree reached the door into Glaffren Shipping and tapped the com screen beside it.

"Delivery for Mr. Glaffren."

His new face peered out at her for a long moment, then the door unlocked. "Remove your clothing in the lower office then come up," he said.

The office contained two desks with old computer terminals mounted on them, a collection of squerm essence cylinders in one corner and a scattering of empty wine bottles on one desk. Litter lay scattered across a floor that looked none too clean. Mulen had been letting himself go, just as she intended to let him go. She shed her dress and draped it across the cleanest surface she could see, then climbed the spiral stair to his apartment.

"Mr. Glaffren?" she said, scanning the kitchen diner she found herself in.

"Through here."

He awaited her in his bedroom, flopped back naked on his bed, the half-empty bottle of wine he had been swigging from clutched in his left hand, his penis in his right. Shree wrinkled her nose at the smell of sour sweat and alcohol, then stepped over to the window overlooking Zealos and the covered street two hundred metres below. As she had surmised, the window was one that simply locked down on a seal, and generally outside atmosphere was kept out by a pressure differential. She reached up and began undoing the catches.

"What in Smythe's name do you think you're doing?"

He was up off the bed and coming unsteadily towards her by the time she undid the last catch. She turned, smiling cheekily as he drew close. He hesitated, and in that pause the heel of her hand came up hard into his nose, crushing it and depositing him on his backside on the floor.

"Whah!" he managed nasally.

"I'm here to bring you to account for the fifteen pond workers you personally executed, Proctor Mulen," she said. "I am a member of the Tidy Squad and it is not our policy to accept the Polity Intervention amnesty."

"D' fuck!" He reached round and smashed the wine bottle he still held on the corner of a cupboard, then surged to his feet, fast. Shree was glad about that; he was fat, heavy, smelly—she hadn't wanted to pick him up. He came at her with confidence inspired by her naked, petite and vulnerable-looking female body. Intercepting his arm as he thrust at her with the bottle, she snapped his elbow, turned him and slammed his head against the window, once, twice. As he staggered back she heaved the window off its seals and propelled it aside on its hinge. When he came at her again the throw was simple and neat, and all she'd need to wash was her hands and the hip she rolled him over. He didn't even touch the window frame, though he did touch the roof of the covered street, and hard.

Ten minutes later, Shree had retrieved her pack, having given the guard the kind of blow he had neither expected nor wanted, before going on to trash the image files of the surveillance system. She was a number of streets away when an icon appeared to the far right of her visual field informing her of a call through her aug. With a slight mental effort she'd always found difficult to describe to those who had never tried these devices, she accepted the call, and halted to lean against a nearby wall.

"It's done?" enquired the man whose face seemed to appear in midair before her.

"Certainly." Shree studied him.

Thracer was a tough TS unit commander, the maple-leaf scar on his shaven head indication of his route to the Squad from the Overlanders. Perhaps it was time to tell him about how things were changing, to let him in?

How did the Tidy Squad survive whilst being hunted down by AIs and dangerous ECS agents? It did seem that the AIs secretly agreed with the Squad's work, but she reckoned they were reluctant to close down units like Thracer's until through the likes of him they'd found and caught the Squad Leader—that person whose identity few knew.

"Then get your wilderness gear together—you'll be needing it."

"Found another one out there?"

"No, but it seems target Alpha has left Heretic's Isle and they're letting him run."

"Dangerous—we know there's AI interest."

"Even so, I have a standing instruction to pass this on to you."

"Send me the details," she said.

Jeremiah Tombs possessed an iconic status here on Masada, and the Tidy Squad wanted him swept away most of all. But as Shree well knew there was so much more to it than one ex-proctor. The AI interest in Tombs related to the entire status of the planet Masada and getting close to him might lead to a chance to remove even bigger threats to this world. Certainly this would be a very risky kill, very likely a suicidal one, but it was one Shree had always wanted and, as Squad Leader, it had been easy enough to secure it for herself.

As the shore continued to recede, Jem tried to shake from his mind the image of Sanders lying in a pool of blood, and concentrate on the present. He began to examine the controls available to him through the console set just below the rudder arm. Eventually he noted that wrapped around the rudder pivot were small hydraulic motors, connected by an optic into the same console, and surmising that the boat possessed some kind of autopilot, soon found and engaged it, keeping his course due north.

While the boat sailed on, he sat back, flinched at that same bloody image, and again tried to turn his thoughts to other things, but memory seemed a perilous place. His inspection tour of sprawn canals lay clear in his mind, but he struggled, his eyes watering again and an unknowable dread coming to sit on his chest, when he tried to get beyond the point when he landed his aerofan inside Triada Compound. Something unusual had been happening, because he recollected his fellow proctors being stirred up like a mid-pond filled with meat flakes. Something about the rebels? He reached up and touched his head where his *Gift* had once been attached. It was as if, with its removal, a large portion of memory connected to it had been excised too. There had been fear over the aug channels, he was sure of that, terror even.

Behemoth . . .

The name, and some attached meaning, seemed to sit in his skull like a weight bristling with barbed hooks. Behemoth had given them the *Gift*, but knowledge of that creature's nature remained confined to the upper echelons. He tried to shake the memory free and realized he was sweating, and yet cold at the same time. Then he saw an image, a brief flash with visual file bar coding running down the side of it, someone in the shipyard of Flint glimpsing some immense shape on a screen, just before a wall of fire fell down on him. Next came screaming, channels snuffing out, a whole portion of the aug network disappearing . . .

Jem found himself coiled in the bottom of the boat in darkness, but painful recall remained with him. Flint had been snuffed out, hadn't it? That much he retained: one small fragment dragged out of a darkness guarded by something terrifying. And now he just did not have the will to venture there again. He kept himself in the present, found with extreme disgust that he had shit himself.

Forcing himself into motion, Jem removed his pyjama trousers, cleaned them and himself with seawater, then tossed them to the far end of the boat. By the time he was done he realized the dawn was coming—he'd been out of it for over ten hours. He just sat listening to the thrum of the motor and the steady lapping of the sea against the hull, his mind shut down, nothing to see . . .

The sun, eating a diamond chunk out of the horizon, set him in motion again. He searched lockers set along the sides of the boat, finding a pair of overalls to go over his pyjama jacket, cinched with the belt of a large sheath knife, and a life jacket that he immediately donned. He also found a complex medical kit with inset autodoc like a hibernating metal spider—certainly Polity technology—some fishing gear, then food and drink. A gun would have been useful, but the short, vicious-looking harpoon gun he uncovered would have to do. Thus kitted out, he uncapped and sipped from a bottle containing cold coffee with a vaguely salty taste, ate preserved sausage and dried fruit, and gazed into the distance.

By his estimation it would take him a further three days to reach the mainland, but his hope was that before then one of the cameras up on the laser arrays would spot him and a proctor be sent out by aerofan to investigate. But if this did not occur, what to do?

Peering down at the console screen, he used a small ball control to bring up a map of the main continent. Generally there wasn't much civilization along the south coast, since the climate, though good, wasn't right for crop ponds. However, on the other side of the eastern peninsula lay the port of Godhead, where ships docked to unload a kind of alien guano, mined on some island out that way. Abruptly he came to a decision. He had to presume that some of what the computer here was telling him was true, as proven by the position of the sunrise, and so made a course correction to take him round the south-eastern peninsula. Further investigation gave him an exact figure for the journey time of five and a half Masadan days. Time to explore his memories, if he dared.

It took Jem four days to finally drag enough memories clear of the darkness inside his skull to form a small but coherent collection; four days of probing a wound and often finding the pain too much for consciousness. After the second occasion of having to wash his clothing in the sea, he learnt that it was best to strip off his trousers when he tried this, because each time he lost all self-control. Sanders must have cleaned him up each time before . . .

Sanders? Before?

Yes, the rebel doctor he killed while escaping. He saw her clear in his mind naked on a beach, but that memory had to be false because she wore no breather mask.

Surgical alterations. Polity technology.

He shook his head trying to clear that. He would have to sort out the truths and fictions there later, for he did clearly remember her walking outside with him before . . .before he cut her throat. He swallowed, the artificial lining of his mouth dry, concentrated on memories retrieved, sitting there in his skull like a precise interlocking collection of geometric shapes, and studied them closely . . .

Behemoth was an intelligent entity, a massive sphere of alien flesh able to propel itself through vacuum like a spaceship, and wielding weapons from within its body more potent than those of a Theocracy dreadnought. It had destroyed such a warship, but had itself been injured in the process and, wounded and angry, it had come to the Braemar system to exact vengeance. It had arrived screeching for

Hierarch Amoloran, who had betrayed its trust, using against the Polity a weapon it had provided so that blame would fall squarely on the creature itself. Upon its arrival it became clear why the Septarchy Friars occupied so many of the aug channels with their chanting: Behemoth had provided the *Gift* so it could seize control of the Brotherhood and only their racket kept it out. Not finding Amoloran, for he had been replaced by Hierarch Loman, it had turned its weapons on the shipyards of Flint, obliterating them, then it had . . .

Nothing. He couldn't get beyond that point and now he was weary, needed to sleep rather than render himself unconscious again. Deliberately maintaining a void inside his skull, Jem lay down in the bottom of the boat, allowing the thrum of the motor to lull him. Sleep came and went like a black juggernaut, dragging daylight in behind it as the only indicator that he *had* slept. He sat up and stretched, then peered out across the sea.

At first he thought he was seeing a bare rock sticking up from the waves, but when he detected movement he realized that yes, a rock was sticking up over there, but it was covered with sealuroynes. Knocking off the autopilot, which obviously wasn't taking into account the local fauna, he swung his boat away from the colony hoping to bypass it before being seen. However, having only just woken he hadn't seen the danger soon enough, and the heaving movement there culminated in a wave of the creatures diving into the sea with a concerted splash.

"Zelda Smythe, guard me now," he muttered, and grabbed up the harpoon from by his feet.

He didn't know for sure whether sealuroynes were dangerous. But they possessed a similar name to the predatory silu-royne, and now they appeared to be in pursuit of him he didn't want to wait to find out. He turned the motor throttle right round to its stop and the outboard roared, throwing spume out behind and lifting the bow clear of the water. But even this did not seem likely to be fast enough, for the creatures behind were accelerating, playfully hurling themselves up out of the water as they came.

For long minutes he stayed ahead of them, then they were into his wake, their bodies churning the sea like oiled rubber, then leaping out beside his boat, then ahead of it. Seeing one of them leap airborne close to the boat, he shuddered. The things looked like shroud-wrapped corpses, bones more than a mere hint through translucent obsidian skin, underlying arms enwrapping torsos but terminating in odd fan-shaped fins which at the tail opened and closed like the petals of a rose, long stretched bird heads and teardrop eyes containing turning wheels of linked familiar shapes.

Jem found himself choking on terror. He couldn't look at those eyes. They gazed straight into the darkness in his mind and seemed to be the key to unravelling it. In the rush and splash of their movement all about him, he heard the underlying sharpening of scythes, and it was as if the surrounding creatures were all merging into one menacing whole, rearing up out of the sea into a nightmare hood. Another sound now, and Jem realized it was issuing from him, a chesty keening that seemed to be using up all his air. He dragged his gaze away, the confusing image of the thing they were making spreading before the boat, sharp edges and grey-scaled hide.

Then the boat slammed into it, hurling him forwards. Jem smacked his head on one of the lockers, but though his head covering transmitted pain, no blessed unconsciousness arrived. He curled in the bottom of the boat, crying. When he finally surfaced it was to observe a sea filled with nothing more threatening than waves, and to see his map screen indicating that he had hit the western side of the peninsula he had been trying to navigate around.

5

Heroyne (an introduction)

As indicated by its name, this creature does bear some resemblance to the heron of Earth, this emphasized by a similarity of environments—of mud flats covered with the reedlike "flute grasses." However, there are no flying creatures on that world that have not been introduced by Humans, and to call an alien organism a bird is to descend into fundamental error. Heroynes look like birds, hatch from eggs and make nests, but there the resemblance ends. The eggs are not hatched in the nests, but carried about on the back of the prime male (image one) of the species, whose body resembles a thick bucket seat, its long curved neck extending from what would have been the backrest. Below this neck, to the creature's fore, are two sets of arms terminating in spadelike scoops, whose sum purpose is to load the eggs onto its back. The prime male also possesses a long beak just like the secondary male and the female (images two and three respectively), but it is serrated, and no one knows why. The female builds a night nest—a thick pad of interwoven flute-grass stems. After being fertilized by the primary and secondary males it lays eggs in this nest after three months' gestation, then abandons them, whereupon the primary male collects them up and carries them around until they hatch. Heroyne chicks must then get away from the male as fast as they can whilst the male goes into a brief fugue, after which it will eat them. One thing is known for certain about these creatures: more study is required, because much of their behaviour doesn't seem to have a logical evolutionary basis. However . . .

—*From* THE MASADAN PLANETARY ALMANAC

The Atheter had constructed the mechanism with meticulous precision, and deeply graven their purpose into its structure. It must erase the active higher thought processes, the sentience and intelligence of the Atheter themselves—a wipeout process affecting not only the content of those minds, but their physical structure too. Upon first initiating, it had spread its pattern disruptors all around the Homeworld to carry out its function on a massive scale, and sometimes, when it was done, too little survived of the animal mind to keep the target alive. However, many did survive the process and, as had been planned, the Atheter returned to the level of animals: gabbleducks. This done, the mechanism followed through with its secondary function: matter disruption to shatter remaining Atheter technology, to render it down small enough for the tricones and the depredations of time.

Upon completion, the mechanism packed away its disruptors and next sent out all its probes as it turned hunter, tracking down those minds that had avoided the initial holocaust at its location on the Atheter Homeworld. It also began to move itself away so as to be able to more easily bring its power to bear. Whenever a probe found a living, thinking Atheter, the mechanism took a disruptor out of storage and dispatched it to that location, to erase the mind found there, and shatter the technology the Atheter had surrounded itself with. These Atheter had either fled or not been part of the return home, and most of them, existing in situations that required technical expertise to sustain, did not survive losing both their minds and their artificial environments.

This hunt took it a realtime period of fifty thousand years, towards the end of which span it seemed the mechanism's task was nearing completion and the moment approaching for it to destroy itself, breaking the last link between the gabbleducks and the Atheter civilization. However, those long years and its numerous battles had taken their toll. Necessarily it had needed to repair itself, many times, and its programming had degraded throughout the process. When the time came for it to die it found the parameters of completion of its mission too vague to act upon. Instead it settled itself in U-space adjacent to its realspace position at the limits of the Atheter realm, its touch light on its probes, which now encompassed thousands of light years, and watched.

Proof that its task remained incomplete came to its attention a million years into its vigil when a rogue war machine of its masters tried to load a static recorded Atheter mind to one of the animals. The war machine was a formidable physical being. It possessed defences against the kind of direct attack the mechanism had been intending to launch, and wielded weapons at the peak of Atheter technology.

The mechanism considered the necessity of relocating to the actual scene to bring the full force of all its pattern disruptors to bear, considered how dangerous that would be to itself. It frantically sought some way of fulfilling its programming without a direct confrontation and, because that programming had degraded, found it.

Through its probe, it found a situation it could manipulate to a satisfactory conclusion. The war machine was vulnerable at that moment, rather like some predator in the process of giving birth. The attack was brief, specific, involved no apocalyptic weapons. The result was a war machine with a scrambled mind, and the failure of its attempt to resurrect one of its masters. A better result would have been the complete obliteration of the war machine, but the mechanism just settled back like a senile cat watching an injured snake.

The next situation that impelled the mechanism to fulfil its function occurred a million years later, the circumstances surrounding the event, and its location, utterly unexpected. It found one of the animals located away from its Homeworld and in the process of having an Atheter mind-recording loaded to it. Data from the probe that found this was murky, and the mechanism mistook the occurrence for some automated process, some Atheter machine, missed by the hunters, at last firing up. It first tried to halt this process by working through the probe only, deeming only minimal interference necessary. Something rebuffed this attempt, violently, the mechanism assailed by killer programs suddenly loading to it from the probe. The mechanism fought to destroy them, meanwhile waking and dispatching one of its pattern disruptors. Through the disruptor its power ramped up, as did its ability to see through the murk. It found a powerful alien intelligence there; an artificial intelligence calling itself Penny Royal. They fought, their battleground the disruptor itself, and their own mental strongholds. It managed to fulfil its programming and prevent the loading of an Atheter mind to a gabbleduck. But the fight had taken a further toll and it did not completely destroy its enemy, and retreated, its physical structure damaged and its programming further disrupted, to again settle back, watching, and not quite understanding why.

It couldn't be a coincidence that they had contacted her now. Jeremiah Tombs was on the move—apparently he'd stolen a boat and was currently en route to the mainland—and the Polity AIs were watching him closely. As she drove her mud buggy hard through the wilderness north of Greenport, Shree felt an excitement twisting her stomach she hadn't experienced since . . . since the rebellion. She felt sure her offworld Separatist contact had seen an angle here, some way of striking a blow for freedom.

Her buggy collapsed the flute grasses before it, occasionally disturbing creatures from hiding: mud snakes shoved the tips of their horse-skull snouts out of the ground, and sprawns that had escaped during the rebellion, and now thrived out here, would go flitting up to fill the air with the mica-like glitter of their dragonfly wings. At one point a heroyne rose up from its woven nest of grass and stalked away stilt-legged. She shuddered at the sight of the big birdlike monstrosity. Certainly there were more dangerous creatures on this world, but none that gave her the creeps like a heroyne. She had seen one of these creatures gobble down whole one of her comrades, then stride away with the man still struggling as he slid down its long throat. What a death—drowning in stomach acid. However, there was nothing in the vicinity that could be a danger to her whilst she remained inside the bubble cabin of her vehicle. No hooders or big gabbleducks—she got that direct from one of the Polity satellites.

When she finally motored her buggy out into a muddy channel, she brought it to a halt and checked her map screen. Yes, this was the place she had been aiming for—just a kilometre along this channel and she would be at the coordinates. As she turned her vehicle she wondered if her contact, Halloran, would be here. It would be nice to at last put a face to the voice—communications had been necessarily limited in bandwidth to prevent Polity interception, so no image data had been used.

Finally the coordinates' tracker zeroed. She brought the buggy to a halt again and gazed ahead. The channel had reached its terminus here, the flute grasses once again closing in, and beside the wall of stalks stood a twin-disc aerofan. She shut down the engine, unstrapped herself, picked up her stubby Zatak melee gun—it fired a load of fibre-linked glass beads on different choke settings and was capable of taking down three or four people if they stood close enough together—opened her bubble-cab door and stepped down.

"Shree Enkara." The voice was instantly recognizable—flat, emotionless, almost as if the one speaking had some difficulty with spoken language: Halloran.

He stepped out from behind the twin-disc, a squat bulky man who bore some resemblance to Unit Leader Thracer. He wore a long heavy coat, baggy trousers and inadequate shoes now stained with mud, and seeing that the two companions walking out behind him were similarly attired, Shree wondered if they adhered to some sort of Separatist dress code. The other two, a man and a woman who might have been twins, what with their pale hair and narrow aesthetic faces, both wore breather masks. Halloran, however, wore none. Was he adapted to the Masadan atmosphere like herself, Shree wondered, or was he adapted to all sorts of different environments? She just didn't know.

"Halloran," she said. "Good to meet you at last."

"Yes, good," he said, without any emphasis.

The next thing she noticed was that all three wore scaly

organic augs clinging to the sides of their heads like adolescent scoles. She didn't like that. Though she had been aware that Separatists used Dracocorp augs, they were too much of a reminder of others who had worn the same: those in the Theocracy Brotherhood, her enemy.

"So what's the urgency?" she asked. "I take it you know that I've got an important hit coming up?"

"Yes, Jeremiah Tombs."

"That's what this is about, isn't it?"

"Yes."

Shree felt a surge of frustration. She felt like stepping over to slap him across the face to elicit some sort of Human reaction.

"Perhaps you can elaborate?"

"The AOP," he replied.

"Yes, I'm aware of the Alien Occupancy Policy."

"Then you are aware that this place could end up being classified as an alien Homeworld, with the result that you would have little or no say about your future here."

"Yes, I get that."

"More Polity control, more restrictions." Still that flat tone, yet he was talking about something Separatists had been fighting for for years. He continued, "The greatest dangers to you are the Atheter AI and what might be inside Tombs's head."

"Which is why he needs to die."

"You need to think bigger."

"Go on."

"We calculate that the AIs presently watching over Tombs will guide him to certain locations. They will confront him with the realities he has avoided through his madness. It seems likely that one of these confrontations will involve the Atheter AI."

"And?"

"You need to get close to him; you need to be with him when he reaches the AI. The Atheter AI is perhaps the larger danger and needs to be eliminated."

"No one can get close," Shree replied. "The barrier

around it is loaded with force-fields and sensors. You need permission from the planetary governor, the AI Ergatis, to get there, and I'm damned if I want that thing inspecting me so closely. Anyway, as I understand it, no one has been granted that permission for years."

"We calculate that Tombs will be permitted to approach it."

"Right, so all I have to do is get close to Tombs, stay with him when he goes to the AI, meanwhile smuggling a bomb in under my blouse?"

"Circumstances are now in your favour. You can use your cover as an Earthnet reporter to get close to Tombs."

"Yeah, they'll choose me over all the other reporters who'll want to be in on this."

"Circumstances are now in your favour." The repetition gave Shree more of the creeps than the sight of that heroyne. Was it the Dracocorp augs that had seemingly dehumanized these people? She glanced at Halloran's two attendants. They hadn't moved since she and he had started talking, and their expressions were blank.

"What circumstances?"

"We understand that a Human will be recruited to shepherd Tombs. That Human is the erstwhile rebel commander, Leif Grant. You know him, he knows you. This is your entry point."

Shree grimaced. Halloran said "Human" like he wasn't a member of that species.

"Possible," she agreed, wondering if Halloran knew her history with Grant. "But that still leaves the problem of how I 'eliminate' a fifty-metre disc of memory crystal with a building sitting on top of it." She paused for a moment. "You can guarantee that getting any form of chemical explosive past the barrier will be impossible and a CTD containment flask would be detected at once."

Halloran held up his hand and clicked his fingers. The attendant on his left, the man, stepped forward and just stood there dumb for a moment. Halloran clicked his fingers again, in irritation, and the blond-haired man abruptly opened his coat and then his shirt to expose a bare pale chest and saggy stomach. He then turned over his right hand and stared at it for a moment, before twisting his fingers in some odd fashion. A knife shot out of his sleeve, delivering the handle straight into his hand. He flipped it up, turned it, then stabbed it back in just below his breastbone.

"My God!" Shree exclaimed, then was suddenly annoyed with herself for using those words.

The man slit down, almost with the indifference of someone unzipping a carryall. Blood gouted and spattered down his trousers. He reached inside himself, grabbed something and pulled it out with a horrible sucking sound, then held it up. The slit in his stomach bulged intestines.

Halloran turned and gazed at him, perhaps conveying some silent communication through his Dracocorp aug. The man removed a thick pad of cloth from his pocket and cleaned off the squat glassy cylinder he was holding, before handing it over. Halloran nodded. The man turned, pushing his intestines back inside, walked with a slight stagger over to the twin-disc then abruptly sat down next it and leant his back against it. He was going to die, Shree realized. He was just going to die.

"Was that entirely necessary?"

"It was the safest way of smuggling this"—Halloran held up the cylinder—"to this world. It possesses electronic camouflage to screen it from scanning, but not to conceal it from a physical search of our luggage."

"CTD?" Shree enquired. "I thought it almost impossible to hide an antimatter containment flask."

"So the Polity would have us believe, but no, it is not a CTD."

The blond man had bowed over now. His trousers were soaked with blood, as was the ground all around him.

"Then what is it?"

"The one thing that will utterly ensure the destruction of the Atheter AI." Halloran held the cylinder out to her and, with some reluctance, she took it. "There is a simple DNA fingerprint console on the end, you will notice." Shree observed a small glassy circle, almost like an old-style camera lens. "You press your finger against it once and it records your fingerprint and DNA. Do so now." Shree did as she was told, heard a little chime issue from the cylinder.

"Now what?" she asked.

"Only you can open it now," Halloran continued. "The next time you touch the reader and press, hard, the cylinder opens."

"And then what happens?"

"You unleash Hell." It was the nearest he had come to saying something emotive.

"Then I don't want to be in the vicinity when that happens."

"You can throw the cylinder and run but, having used this weapon, you will be hunted by the Polity."

"Nothing new to me."

"You misunderstand. The most powerful Polity minds will be seeking you and, should they catch you, their forensic AIs will take apart your mind. A better choice for you would be to stay with the cylinder when you open it."

"What does it contain?" she asked, feeling that excitement again, that response to a challenge.

"Active Jain technology."

That dumbfounded Shree for a moment, then she managed, "It will destroy the Atheter AI?"

"No."

"What do you mean 'no'?"

"It will do what it always does. It will begin to hijack technology or even any life it comes into contact with."

"With what result?"

"The Polity satellite network will detect it within minutes and the AIs will react within seconds. They consider the Atheter AI a potential danger, but an Atheter AI being infested with Jain tech they will consider a system-wide lethal threat. The AI and probably a great deal else within the barrier will be vaporized. You will have to run very fast."

Shree weighed the cylinder in her hand, nodded an acknowledgement and turned away. Would she run? She didn't know, but she did know that she would deliver this item to the designated place.

Jem stepped out of the boat and took a couple of paces away before turning to study it. Though damaged, it still appeared serviceable and, with some effort, he should be able to drag it back down off the shingle strand and relaunch it. But he didn't want to go back into the sea. He didn't want to risk the sealuroynes again. Didn't want to see the patterns in their eyes. Yet even here on the land, he didn't feel in the slightest bit safe. There were dangerous animals here, he knew, and now, almost as if it had woken the moment he contacted solid land, something, somewhere, was muttering like a giant stirring in uneasy slumber. He concentrated on it, realizing it was distant from him, somewhere far inland. Then abruptly it seemed to retreat, and he felt fear, though whether his own or from that other source he could not tell. Once it faded it seemed that it had been the only thing holding him in place, and he impelled himself into motion, and stepped back to the boat.

After searching through the lockers he unloaded a collection of supplies then packed them into a bag that he emptied of some sort of inflatable. Checking the map screen again he saw that if he crossed the peninsula to Godhead the journey would only be twenty kilometres, but that meant crossing flute-grass prairie occupied by the kind of horrors he had always tried to see only from his aerofan, nervous even when fifty metres up in the sky. Also, the mapping computer of the boat could not be detached and there were no portable direction finders amidst the rest of the equipment. He could very well end up lost, then dead.

Better, he felt, to stick to the shore and take the sixty- or seventy-kilometre route round to the port town. He didn't know what dangers might lurk in that margin between flute grasses and sea, but at least across the open stretches of shingle or compacted mud he would be able to see them coming. They wouldn't surface like a mud snake through the rhizome mat and chomp him down, nor creep up on him concealed by chameleon skin and only at the last moment reveal an improbable mouthful of teeth, nor come down on him like . . .

Jem abruptly found himself sitting with his back to the boat, shivering, his gaze fixed on the flowering flute grasses a few hundred metres inland from him, cold horror wrapped around his guts.

"With perfect timing it cut his aug off just as it was being taken over—cut it off while taking off his face."

He could not put the words into context, could not remember where or when they had been spoken. Certainly he recognized Sanders's voice but could not see much beyond that, just some shadowy figure she had been addressing. And even though he knew it had been something that was staged for him, to reinforce their fiction about this mythical hooder the Technician, the terror he felt was undeniable.

How long he sat there he did not know. It was only when the slow counting down of the timer on his wristwatch impinged upon him that he managed to force himself back to his feet. Four days left of his prosthetic's oxygen supply—somewhere along the line he had lost a day, but he couldn't figure out if that had been while at sea or while here on the shore. He took up his bag, managed to slip its handles over his shoulders to make it a backpack, and set out, small nodules of stone hard through the soles of his sanatorium slippers. At first walking was difficult, his legs feeling weak and rubbery and his breathing harsh. He started to get hot too, but after a few hundred metres found himself settling into a steady rolling gait. After a little while he glanced back, noting that the boat was now out of sight, then he began to study his surroundings more closely.

The shore here, like all the shores of the continent but for the one against the northern mountains, consisted of stretches of compacted mud or shingle. The shores were in a perpetual state of flux, having no rock to anchor them. Tricone-generated soil was perpetually washed away or redeposited, and often the steady scouring processes of the sea washed out all but the largest items the tricones left after their constant grinding processes, that being this shingle with no stone larger than a ridiculously precise three millimetres across, each drift topped with lighter pebbles of foamstone scraped from the undersides of numerous structural rafts inland. Also, flute grasses fought to reclaim land, whilst the sea fought to take it back. A frequent sight at sea, Jem knew, were floating islands of dying flute grass, which had been snatched away by late summer storms.

Other things now began to impinge upon him, almost as if he was waking up from nightmare to bright day. He saw a drift of snow-white tricone shells like the back of some beast preparing to dive into the mud below, each shell no larger than three fingers. These were those killed in the mud here by the high concentration of salts their kind had generated by grinding up the land and which were subsequently washed into the sea. Remembering some Theocracy-approved biology, he knew that some time in the past there had been tricones in the ocean, but they could no longer survive there. He saw red nematodes writhing through a bank of hard mud like slow veins, a crowd of mudslappers skittering towards the waves at his approach, then he ducked down upon seeing a small heroyne striding across the mudflat now extending to his right. Only when he passed what looked like an oddly sculpted boulder of lava until he realized it was a segment of a dead hooder did some of the brightness go out of his day. And the other sound from the flute grasses to his left took the rest of it.

"Yissock blaggerslog," said a voice quite distinctly, whilst some huge shape shifted there.

With utter cold dread he realized that a gabbleduck was keeping pace with him.

The muttering was back, that thing stirring, somewhere. At first it seemed it might be coming from the gabbleduck, but somehow, deep inside, he knew it wasn't the original source. The creature was a relay, its presence somehow amplifying that . . . sense of something else.

There seemed no point in running, because the only predators here that a Human on foot could outpace were the ambush ones like mud snakes. A gabbleduck, with its odd loping and rippling gait, would be able to bring him down within a few tens of metres, so if it wanted him dead, he was dead. But even there, he suddenly found room for optimism.

A heroyne big enough to consider him viable prey would have been on him in an instant, gulped him down whole to suffocate and burn in its acidic stomach. A siluroyne would have shown no hesitation either and would have grabbed him and eaten him alive, even though his flesh would have later sickened it enough to throw up his remains. But gabbleducks were odd contrary creatures whose actions often defied the conventional behaviour of predator with prey.

Gabbleducks sometimes pursued their prey with outrageous stubbornness—Jem distinctly recollected a story of a proctor, high up in his aerofan, being followed by one all the way back to Agatha Compound. The thing managed to get through all the compound's defences, though badly wounded, then ignored the man and trashed his vehicle, before expiring on its way out. Both compound and surrounding crop ponds then had to be abandoned when the scent of dead gabbleduck brought in a swarm of hooders, and the mess they left took months to clear up.

Gabbleducks sometimes caught Human prey and just chewed them up, spitting out the remains. They did other odd things too, like drowning their victim in mud, then carrying the corpse back to some settlement. But they also sometimes chased those on the ground but then did nothing, and on other occasions just ignored Humans completely. And there were even stories of people being lost out in the flute grasses and then guided back home by the creatures.

Jem hoped that his case would be one of the last.

As he walked, he caught glimpses of the creature's hide through the grasses: greyish-green with odd purplish swirls. The grasses stood three metres high and he also caught the odd glimpse of its back, which meant it had to be a huge example of its kind. Diverting his course outwards, he walked as near to the sea and as far from the flute grasses as he could get without sinking into sticky mud. However, sweat chilled on his back when ahead he saw an area where the mud had been churned and torn up, and his only way through was a firm strip only three or four metres wide between that and the grasses.

As he drew closer to the churned-up area it seemed to him that the creature was moving about with more eagerness, as if something prevented it coming out into the open, but that it knew he would soon draw close enough to grab. He studied the ground ahead more intently in the hope of seeing a way through, and it was only then that he saw the area was not the result of some storm or land slippage, but seemingly of battle.

What he had at first taken to be a chunk of torn-up rhizome mat came abruptly into focus and made clear everything beyond it. A tank lay there, its rear end sunk in the mud, its turret half torn off and the blackened barrel of some kind of gun pointing up towards the sky. Other wreckage lay scattered in the area, all spattered with the mud that initially disguised it from him. He saw Satagent script etched into a chunk of armour and only after studying other debris around it did he realize he was seeing the remains of a Theocracy lander.

"The Hierarch's brother, Aberil Dorth, brought the troops down from Hope to attack us," said Sanders. *"He might even have succeeded in flattening us, if it weren't for the fact that our rebellion was just a side show in a bigger and more lethal drama."*

Jem looked round to see Sanders wading ashore, naked again. He averted his eyes for a moment, but then could not help glancing at her once more, but she was gone. Her spectre had been sent to taunt him, straight from Hell.

"The Devil came," he muttered to himself, not sure where the words came from, but an image clear in his mind of Proctor Shaunus turning towards him, expression dull, one eye reddened with blood, his augmentation, their *Gift* from Behemoth, turned into something scraped from an ash pit. Terror accompanied the vision, old remembered terror of something trying to take control of him, and his need to flee. He felt his legs starting to give away, a blankness spreading in his mind, but he fought it, straightened up and struggled to breathe evenly air that should have killed him.

"Lies," he said.

He was like one of the prophets out in the wilderness being taunted by demons, haunted by visions, going through a trial to arrive at the eventual truth. However, when he again raised his gaze to the wreckage strewn before him, he could not deny it. This was no vision, no illusion, nor could it be something that had been staged just for him. A real battle had occurred here and he must accept and integrate the fact of it. Now, abruptly, he did sink to his knees, but to begin reciting the Satagents, to try and drown out that constant background mutter and more importantly to find some inspiration in their truth, some guidance. But the Satagents gave him no comfort and even as he started on the second Satagent, the words felt empty. He stood up, paced forward. He would find the truth in Godhead. Revelation would come, it had to.

Keeping out near the shore, a feeling of unreality, emphasized by that odd muttering, distancing him from the frightening reality of the gabbleduck over to his left. He walked closer. There was definitely a hole in his mind. He did not remember how the rebels got hold of him so perhaps just a small amount of truth lay in the things Sanders had told him because, in the end, all the best lies were laced with truth. Now closer, he noted something else. The wreckage looked old; there were growths of moss on some of it, and webs of fungal mycelia.

Twenty years . . .

He shook his head, trying to see all this clearer, and then he saw the machine.

It was working out in the middle of the devastation, foamed-metal treads supporting it on the soft mud, its cylinder body covered in dirt, mantis arms excavating the ground before it and churned mud mounded up behind. Then he saw the next machine—ovoid body on spider legs, the thing probing the ground with a proboscis almost like the beak of a heroyne. Then another—this one scooping soil with one flat arm into some kind of sieve and shaking it through, advancing its metal body with a caterpillar humping motion. These, he realized, were what had made this area impassable, not the battle that had been fought here.

He had never seen anything like them, could not integrate them into his reality. Abruptly he headed inwards, towards that narrow strand between the area they occupied and the flute grasses, his fear of the gabbleduck lost in the sheer incomprehensibility of this scene.

Upon reaching the narrow pass, Jem broke into a slow jog, determined to put this behind him, to get somewhere he could straighten out his mind, but as he rounded a jut of flute grass it seemed as if someone, or something, was determined to stick things in his way. Ahead, across his path, a wide silvery sheet lay pegged to the ground, glassy objects neatly arrayed across it. Coming to the edge of this he peered at one of the objects, and realized he was seeing a coffin. Inside lay the corpse of a Theocracy soldier, black-stained by mud, wrinkled and partially preserved in an environment that did not provide the means for Human decay. Every coffin here, and there were hundreds, contained a similar black atomy.

"Sapple clogger," said the gabbleduck knowingly.

Jem turned to stare at the mountainous pyramidal creature squatting less than ten metres away from him. It seemed like some rotund jolly Buddha relaxing prior to some enormous feast, the food laid out before it in glass coffins.

Jem ran, hurdling coffins, a sound issuing from deep in his chest that might have been a scream, and might have been laughter.

6

Squerm Essence

The biggest export from Masada was and still is squerm essence. Squerms, which are a genetic splicing of tubeworm, sea louse and lobster, are capable of surviving in low-oxygen-content water. They take five years to grow from egg to the aggressive and hard to handle adult form. The whole process is fraught with problems, since just one dead squerm decaying in a rearing pond will poison the water and kill all its fellows. Upon reaching adulthood they are caught and placed in presses, the essence crushed out of them and immediately bottled. Whilst sealed in the bottle it undergoes an odd and highly complex fermentation and maturing process resulting in long-chain protein molecules. Only very small amounts of squerm essence are used in cooking and work as a flavour enhancer for sea foods and some other dishes. The flavour is one that Epicureans claim cannot be reproduced chemically and, despite numerous comparison trials in which said Epicureans could not tell the difference, the more expensive essence shipped from worlds like Masada remains a favourite. But then, this inability to accept that the cheaper version of a food or drink is absolutely no different from the expensive version, has a long and well documented history.

—*From* QUINCE GUIDE, *compiled by Humans*

The mechanism stirred uneasily in a state that would have been called slumber had it been a wholly conscious being. Its probes, strewn along the interface between realspace and its own domain in underspace, were registering input with a direct relationship to its function, but because of its confused state of mind, this input only served to raise it to a higher level of inner alertness and did not impel it to act.

Time passed in realspace, marked by those probes, which in turn confirmed the veracity of the new input. The mechanism became aware that certain patterns were in evidence and they possessed a spacial relationship with the two problems it had encountered before: the war machine and the black artificial intelligence, both of which had tried to resurrect the Atheter by loading ancient mind recordings of those creatures into the brains of their animal descendants. The mechanism woke, increasing its capacity as it did so, but still it could not act, for it had yet to detect clearly active Atheter thought processes.

However, preconditions for its main function evident, and something quite odd and difficult to nail down about them, enabled it to bring online back-up programming previously unused, and new processes woke in the mechanism's disrupted consciousness. It began to model reality in ways it had never done before, began to extrapolate, began to use a mental function now available that in another being might be called imagination. New data also became available, and the mechanism understood, beyond automatic function, the "why" of its existence.

Jain technology destroyed civilizations and, having taken up its poisoned chalice, the Atheter had proceeded to the precursor to that destruction of internecine war that had lasted for tens of thousands of years. In the end they decided to free themselves of this technology by removing its target. That target being civilization, it became necessary to remove the uttermost basic building blocks of that: the minds that build it.

That the Atheter had done Jain technology's job by returning themselves to the level of animals to avoid it, the mechanism did not question. Nor did its new imagination have the sheer extent to contemplate the level of despair and self-hate that led to such self-immolation. Nor did it see that as a product of the Atheter their fear and madness were integral to its own systems. Deeply ingrained in its programming lay its self-destruct. If it became infected by Jain code it must destroy itself. No other option had been provided.

This extra programming capacity, however, did not resolve the puzzle it was sensing on the Atheter Homeworld. An Atheter mental pattern existed there, yet it seemed to exist in a grey area between function and non-function.

There was only one way to deal with this. Remaining in underspace so far from the action, or potential action, was no longer an option. Within the mechanism, components of matter, pseudomatter and patterned energy, which hadn't been used for nearly two millions years, powered up. They unzipped the fold that had concealed the mechanism for that time, everted it into realspace where relativity snatched it up, and the rules of existence hardened into immutability.

Janice Golden, the interfaced captain of the Polity dreadnought *Cheops*, swore loudly and vehemently, scared for the first time in eighty years. In that time she had always resided deep inside her ship, which bore the shape of an Egyptian pyramid sitting over U-space nacelles like two conjoined iron cathedrals. Here she commanded weapons which, though not nearly as effective as those of newer Polity warships, could still trash a planet. She had patrolled the Line, the Polity border, as it expanded towards the inner galaxy where, thus far, nothing as nasty as the Prador had been found nor had any lethal alien technologies crawled out from under a stone to spoil her godlike insouciance. But that looked like it might have changed.

Something had disrupted U-space in the Wizender system, and had done so with enough force to slap *Cheops* back out into the real just seconds after it had U-jumped. Janice at first thought a USER had been deployed here, but the readings she was getting were nothing like the disruption caused by an Underspace Interference Emitter. In fact the readings weren't like anything either she or the *Cheops* AI she was interfaced with had ever seen. Something had certainly disrupted U-space, but why the massive ensuing energy flash?

Anything? she asked, mind to mind, the question not even really a word.

Patterned, Cheops said, the reply ghosting over a feed of a five-dimensional shape far too regular to be anything but artificial. *Cyclic point disruption into the real, here . . .*

Image feed from *Cheops*'s long-range receiver array gave her the location close to a green gas giant, a Jovian planet yet to acquire anything but a number. Only now it wasn't the plain green orb it had been. A bruise much the size and shape of Jupiter's eye storm had appeared, striations spreading out from it of storm-feeding atmosphere flows that Earth could float in. However, unlike the storm on Jupiter, this phenomenon wasn't confined to the surface of the giant. From its centre a tail of gas extended hundreds of thousands of kilometres out into space, there terminating at . . . something.

Not clear, she said.

Too much interference, Cheops replied, *but I will try*.

Close imaging gave her something dark and blurred at the tip of that tail of gas. Janice tracked the clear-up programme in her mind as EM emissions directly attributable to the spiral were subtracted from the data and all that remained gradually built into a clear image. The mass came through first—about that of Mars, which made it perfectly understandable that its exit from U-space had caused so much disruption. Then its shape came clear.

Janice felt her spine crawling. The thing there looked woven, a horn of matter made from evenly woven strips of a material whose density put it just a spit away from being neutronium. It was sucking inside itself the gas from the giant below, using an irised gravity field like a million-mile-long syringe. Within the horn itself, where the gas arrived as plasma, conglomerations of dodecahedrons were swirling and reordering in bewildering complexity, and fast, so very fast.

Janice had hoped to find explanations to dispel her fear; all she found was something more frightening. However, she would not let fear govern her. Though Human, she was the interfaced captain of a Polity dreadnought, and her years in this position had refined her intellect, ground away the animalistic responses, hardened her mind into something strictly governed by logic. Yes, this alien object would seem powerful and frightening to a lesser being, but all she needed was more data, more input, so as to come up with a suitable response to it. She would not let herself down, she would not let Cheops down.

What do you think? she drily enquired of her partnered artificial intelligence.

I think we should run like hell, Cheops replied.

As ordered, Halloran had delivered the cylinder and accompanying instructions. He continued to watch until Shree Enkara's mud buggy was out of sight then abruptly turned. Gleet had served his purpose and was nearly dead from blood loss, his aug link erratic and questions arising in him that Halloran had managed to suppress in the small network he and the twins formed. Melet, though he had thought she would still be useful when they got back offworld, was straining against his control—her dying brother tearing at those parts of her original mind that remained.

Perhaps he could suppress Melet's nascent rebellion after Gleet finally died, but that was too great a risk to take. He couldn't afford to have her escape enslavement as they entered Polity-controlled areas. She might give him away, and if the Polity got hold of her and managed to unearth what was concealed in her mind, the whole operation was dead. He reached inside his coat and drew his thin-gun, hesitated for a second, then abruptly thrust it back into its holster. No, better to wait until after they met his other contact here—the one who named herself Agent Azure. Apparently it was through her that the Jain technology had been obtained, and smuggled off Masada just after the quarantine ended.

Halloran walked over to Gleet, prodded him with the toe of his muddy shoe. All aug contact with him blanked at that moment as if that final prod dispelled the last of his life. He noticed that without instruction Melet had turned to watch him, so hardened his control of her.

"Bury him," he instructed out loud to reinforce his nonverbal instruction.

She just stood there shuddering for a moment, until he really pressed her, then she lurched into motion and walked over to the twin-disc and unlatched a toolbox positioned between the two fans. She took out a monofilament cutter, then turned. Hal-loran walked away from Gleet's corpse, now aware that Melet might be a physical danger to him. She walked over, activated the vibro on the monofilament, then cut into the ground, soon heaving out a chunk of heavy sod and tossing it aside.

"It is not the Dracocorp network that dehumanizes," said a voice. "It is the choice of those who rise to ascendancy within it."

"Who is that?" Halloran asked, looking round.

"The female, Melet, is slipping from your control."

A hissing sound ensued and something sped from the flute grasses. Halloran thought for a moment it was one of those flying prawnlike things here, but realized it wasn't when it thumped straight into Melet's chest. A glassy tube protruded, with two testicular sacs on the end of it. These things started pumping, eagerly, obscenely. Melet started choking, grabbed hold of the thing and fought to pull it out. She fell, at last pulling the thing free, and hit the ground on her back. The thing landed at Halloran's feet, still pumping a bile-like fluid from the hollow point ahead of barbs in which chunks of flesh were caught. Halloran's link with her turned grey, shot through with screaming shadows shimmering like heat-haze, then abruptly blinked out.

"Gleet," she said on her final exhale.

"The Humans would call it a mercy killing," said the voice. "We don't tend to believe in mercy."

A figure hurtled from the flute grasses, humanoid, but something wrong about it, about the way it ran. It seemed to be clad in chameleoncloth, for it was difficult to see. It slammed into Halloran before he even managed to reach inside his coat. Next thing he knew he was up on his toes with a rough scaly hand closed around his face.

"This is necessary," said the draconic visage gazing at him.

Then it closed its other arm around his body and turned

his head like someone undoing a jam jar. Halloran felt it snap, felt everything wrenched, then gagged into blackness.

Before the rebellion the population of Godhead had numbered over ten thousand, consisting of a large contingent of the upper echelons of the Theocracy and a substantial force of proctors to protect them and watch over the thousands of enslaved workers. There hadn't been many mid-level citizens here, which was part of the reason why the population was now less than two thousand. Grant, climbing out of his ATV where he had parked it on a hard standing by the harbour, gazed across at other reasons why there were so few people here.

The long and heavily laden cargo ship coming into dock was controlled by a submind of the planetary AI, Ergatis. That sub-mind also controlled the conveyor buckets that steadily unloaded its cargo either into parked lorries or the massive complex of storage bays, whilst a second harbour submind controlled most of the other machinery ashore: the big loaders, the autohandlers and the maintenance robots. People did work here, but out of choice not necessity. Some were aboard the cargo ships, some drove harbour machinery or the trucks transporting the guano up the continental highway to the northern crop ponds and fields. Others just lived here, enjoying the sea air now they could breathe it.

Grant remembered how it used to be here. The ships were commanded by members of the Brotherhood, had crews of over a hundred, consisting of enslaved workers, some citizen personnel and proctor disciplinary units. They also transported a steady stream of workers out to the islands, to replace those dying in the guano pits from horrible skin and lung diseases usually contracted after just three or four years of work.

The trucks that ran the guano up north were worker transporters on the way back, bringing in needed replacements for those expiring both on the islands and here, where much the same routine had prevailed. Inefficient machinery was used in the loading and unloading of the guano and there were frequent spillages that the workers had to clear up with shovels and barrows and brooms, thus exposing themselves to the highly alkaline stuff. Very primitive.

In Godhead it had been very easy to distinguish the workers from those overseeing them, for all the proctors, Theocracy bigwigs and citizens wore protective clothing as well as breather masks. This ease of identification was probably why so few of them survived the rebellion.

After Dragon destroyed the laser arrays, those working under cover here received notification of that, and an instruction to delay their rebellion until ground units from the Underground were in place. Guano-based homemade explosives and hidden weapons were distributed, and preparations began, but so bitter were the workers they didn't want to wait. Using loading machinery as armour they attacked both the ecclesiastical central town and the proctors' station. Fighting was fierce, and though better armed, Theocracy soldiers found themselves up against people who had little to lose. Just over three thousand workers died to inflict casualties of about five hundred on the Theocracy. The surviving hundred or so of proctors and upper echelon ecclesiasts were stripped naked, though allowed to retain their breathing gear, thrown into a guano storage bay then buried alive in the stuff. Whether they died when their air ran out, or were killed by the stuff eating into their skins, was a moot point.

Pacing out the edge of the harbour, Grant watched the ship slow to a halt beside the long unloading jetty, then be drawn in by magnetic docking gear to lock in place with a resounding clang. Immediately its conveyor arms extended like opening limbs and dipped down to open-top trucks. The stuff that spewed from the throats of the conveyor tubes was like talc. Despite special cowlings and an array of filtration devices mounted along the jetty, a haze arose from it, and after only a couple of minutes Grant felt a slight tingling on the skin of his exposed hands. He quickly turned around and headed up towards the main town.

When Underground forces arrived here the main battle

was over and, but for the worker huts, most of this place had been turned into a smoking ruin, the workers having run riot destroying the place that had been killing them. After the vengeance killings, both workers and the rebel forces took the road north, abandoning Godhead. A year and a half later, whilst Masada remained under quarantine, northern crops began to suffer from lack of guano, and military governor Lellan Stanton ordered the port reopened. A large group, consisting of surviving workers and technicians from Zealos, came south and, assisted by Polity drops of equipment, put this place back together again. The largest share of the inhabitants now consisted of those who had once been enslaved here, and many of them were Tidy Squad supporters, so it definitely was not a safe place for a lunatic proctor who thought the Theocracy still existed.

The ecclesiastical section, with the proctors' station looming at the edge, had been built on a fat foamstone coin with a life, estimated when it was laid, of two hundred years. The new town had been built on the ruins of all that. Like all such towns or compound rafts on the tricone-infested soil of Masada, a steady hum almost below perception filled the air as the tricones below steadily ground away at the stone. Stepping onto a slabbed street, Grant paused to listen for a moment, before heading over to a covered walkway, recollecting that they no longer called this place Godhead. Officially it had been renamed Greenport, and the residents stuck to that. Those still embittered and vowing never to return here unofficially named it Shit Harbour.

Pausing at the walkway door, Grant unholstered his sidearm and checked its action. The proctors' disc gun possessed an electrical trigger and a magazine containing seven discs, each with five rounds. Grant extracted the cylindrical magazine and inspected it for a moment before slotting it back into place. The weapon could fire single shots, five-shot bursts, or empty the entire magazine in five seconds. There were many better weapons available, but Grant had become attached to this one. It was the one that nearly killed him when he himself ran out of ammo, before he managed a throw that put the ceramic stiletto now holstered in his boot through the owner's eye. He holstered the weapon and pushed through the door into the walkway, a slight breeze slipping past him because of the pressure differential. And as the shimmer-shield of his Polity breather mask automatically shut down, he turned right to head directly to his destination.

Time to deliver a warning.

Amistad found Chanter amusing: one of those borderline cases whose low-order autism balanced out his sociopathy, so that rather than being antisocial he was asocial. The man had chosen not to have his head rewired, rather had gone in for heavy physical adaptation to enable his monastic, highly introvert pursuits. On one world he'd been a piscine, limbless, sensorium boosted so he could study the colony patterns of some odd oceanic life-form like a slime mould on speed. On another world he'd returned to full Human to study the paintings of an artist in vogue at the time, until he became something of a nuisance and needed to be warned off. Then, upon learning about the Technician here on Masada, and knowing there would be no danger of him being classified as a stalker, he went in for heavy amphidaption, converted all his funds into that mudmarine and some other equipment, and had come here to study the creature.

Six years ago, upon being informed of Chanter's presence here and the nature of his interest, Amistad had thought him an unnecessary complication and considered having him removed. However, since the rebellion the man had done no more than follow the Technician about like some eager puppy, only abandoning that pursuit to return to his underground base or to chase rumours of sculptures or sculpture fragments found on the surface. He seemed harmless, and another element to Amistad's calculations prevented him from sending the man away: deleting complications to try and find simplistic patterns, simplistic solutions to puzzles, was a Human approach. It was why they'd ended up with religions like the one here, and why throughout their history they'd been hampered in their advancement by superstition, crippled value judgements and a tendency to accept facile explanations. Amistad's own research had shown him that retained complications often helped permanently resolve a puzzle, or could provide outfield components to that puzzle. And four years ago Chanter had done so in spades.

His discovery of that ancient sculpture had revealed that the Technician was a living artefact, a creature that definitely dated halfway back to the time when the Atheter rubbed out their own minds and ground their civilization to grit. But it went further than that, further than Chanter had seen. Hooders, though long-lived, did not have the physical and genetic ruggedness to survive for such an appalling length of time. That a mutation capable of doing so had arisen a million years ago was about as likely as a flipped coin turning up heads a thousand times in succession. Amistad precisely recollected his brief exchange with Penny Royal at the time:

"Give me your thoughts," he had asked.

"Two million years," Penny Royal had replied.

The sea urchin AI, once classified as black but now, to Amistad's mind, just a slightly darker shade of grey than himself, clacked a tentacle against the platform rail, then returned that tentacle to a process that seemed alarmingly like it was sharpening its black spines, but which Amistad knew to be an odd way of making dataport connections between its seven states of consciousness. Perhaps it too was remembering that exchange.

Amistad's claw gripped the same platform rail, as if the drone was steadying himself against the slight sway up here at the top of this stalk as its lower section, a hundred metres below, cleaved through the rhizome mat. The observation tower was still on the move—an underlying conveyor drive much like the one in Chanter's mudmarine driving it along. But soon it would be stationary again, for their target now lay in sight.

They had been inspecting that cave shortly after Chanter had relayed his news about the ancient sculpture, and now Amistad replayed the rest of their brief exchange in his mind, relaying it to Penny Royal so the AI would know what he was thinking about:

"Elaborate," he had said.

"It was made, and no makers here for two million years."

"Agreed."

"Surprising that this wasn't discovered before," Penny Royal had opined. "Unless knowledge is being kept from you to prevent mental crippling."

It was often an AI technique: provide all the information to an investigator and that individual would probably come to the same conclusions as you. Be sparing with information and that same investigator might discover something you missed.

"Not something we should concern ourselves with."

Penny Royal had writhed, doubtless something surfacing from one of its states of consciousness about its own past when it disagreed with AI research policy, before going on to conduct research in its own violent and sadistic manner.

"Mind ungoverned by evolution," Penny Royal had stated. "And yet to be sized to ultimate technological purpose."

Amistad had dipped his head in acknowledgement, and dipped it now, as the observation tower drew to a halt and spread its nacelle anchors below, concentrated on the creature lying just a couple of kilometres away.

The Technician had brought down a big grazer, a thing resembling a six-legged water buffalo with a tined lower jaw to fork up rhizomes, extended head to accommodate the numerous grinding plates used to mash them up, and big flat feet to stop it sinking into mud it exposed while feeding. The animal was so large that the big hooder could not accommodate all of it, and so was working its way along the creature section by section. The back half of the grazer had been skinned, muscle and white fat removed with surgical precision and ingested, whole unbroken guts, veins and layers of black fats flapping about grey-blue bones in a loose shreddy mess. The thing was making a sound like a flock of rooks being sucked into a combine harvester, as it continued to fight for freedom.

"A prototype," said Amistad, repeating verbatim the observation he had made four years ago, "made before the Atheter extinguished themselves."

The Technician was a leviathan albino centipede whose head had been squashed flat then dished underneath; perhaps, as many had remarked, it was similar to a giant Human spinal column. Though of course, those who made such comparisons were usually at as safe a distance as Amistad and Penny Royal. Using his own sensors and those within the platform, Amistad studied the creature, the machine, on numerous levels, and made comparisons. It became evident, almost at once, that it had changed further.

Since the rebellion all the data the Theocracy had gathered on the Technician had been collected and collated. This and all Chanter's data had been added to that gathered by the Polity researchers and stored in the Tagreb. Prior to the rebellion, scans of the Technician did reveal all sorts of anomalies, but within the recognizable structure of a hooder. The scanning methods used had not been sophisticated enough to reveal what those anomalies were. After the rebellion, Chanter's intermittent scans of the creature yielded a steady decrease in information, for it seemed evident it had started undergoing major internal changes, which it was somehow shielding. Later scans by Tagreb researchers revealed complex nano-structured materials, high-density energy storage and that internal shielding. Now, even using state-of-the-art scanning routines, data had become increasingly difficult to obtain, and large portions of its body were completely opaque. Notable, Amistad felt, that this transformation had accelerated after the Technician did what it did to Tombs.

"Perhaps *the* prototype," Penny Royal opined, flipping up its two superfluous eye-stalks so as to gaze at Amistad with eyes like glowing rubies.

"Explain," since they were moving to new territory now.

"Final hooder form given limited lifespan and ability to breed," Penny Royal stated. "They were made to fit an environmental niche even if the environment is, in essence, artificial."

"You still haven't explained why you think it might be *the* prototype."

"At this technological level only one would be required," Penny Royal explained. "All the necessary data to make the current hooder form would be downloaded from it."

"So is that what we'll find in Jeremiah Tombs's head: hooder schematics?"

"No."

"Why are you so sure?"

"Why, when they made the final form of the hooder, didn't the Atheter destroy the prototype?"

Amistad had already wondered about that. "Maybe, just maybe, not all of the Atheter agreed with racial suicide."

Penny Royal sharpened some more spines, neither agreeing nor disagreeing.

Despite first using Theocracy medical technology to save their lives, then Polity technology to heal up lung damage and the worst of their progressive skin complaint, the Overlanders retained their scars. Or rather, Grant noted as he entered the covered market, they retained those scars that weren't horribly disfiguring, usually on their arms and the backs of their hands, with maybe the odd example on cheek or forehead. They said they wore their scars with pride as a reminder of all they had gone through and as a memoriam to all those who had not survived. Grant knew that their scars helped them cling to their bitterness and hate, but how could he judge them when still, as to a familiar lover, he clung to his own?

The stalls sold locally manufactured goods, local produce and Polity goods shipped down from the north or obtained from the occasional trader spaceships that landed on the foam-stone rafts, once supporting worker huts outside the town. Amidst these the Overlanders were easy to spot. As well as their scars, they favoured black clothing often like a photo negative of a proctor's uniform, though the script running from armpit to ankle consisted of the kind of Euclidean patterns found on the backs of penny molluscs. After the slaughter the creatures had appeared in great numbers here, like poppies on some ancient Earth battlefield.

All the Overlanders had accepted other Polity medical

technology and had their bodies adapted so they could breathe the air outside. They didn't need a breather mask like Grant, and didn't need the parasitic scoles. However, many of them carried scoles—gutted out, preserved and lined and turned into shoulder bags. Grant approached the first Overlander he saw, a woman inspecting the contents of an upright glass cylinder standing before an enclosed surgical saucer that had to have come in through the main market doors. The cylinder contained various styles and makes of augmentation, excepting Dracocorp augs, which were now banned from sale here on Masada. She turned towards him as he approached and nodded cautiously—she recognized him.

"I need to find Edward Thracer," he said.

"You're Commander Leif Grant."

He felt only a brief inclination to say that he *was* Commander Leif Grant; that such titles were for the past. But it was not something he really felt, and grabbing at the future was not something he yet had any enthusiasm for.

"Yeah, that's me," he replied.

"I'll take you to him." She pointed across the market, and then led the way.

As he walked, Grant noted a stall selling parboiled squerms and sprawns, a form of protein it had been an offence for anyone outside of the Hierarchy to eat, and now being sold in paper funnels for just one New Carth shilling or equivalent. Other food and drink being vended here consisted of the big grapes harvested from grape trees in the north, wine from the same source, preserved sausages of all kinds, sliced and served up in pepper sauce between slices of pillow bread, and other more exotic concoctions from offworld. His mouth started to water until the woman spoke again, killing his appetite.

"It's an honour to have you here," she said. "Have you come to join us?"

"Nah, not now," he said, wincing a little.

She led him round a market corner where stallholders were selling Theocracy relics: proctor uniforms, various forms of ecclesiastical clothing, badges, medals, jewellery, daggers and other hand weapons—the various guns in a locked chainglass case—numerous ornate paper books and standard electronic Satagenials. It surprised him to see such stuff on sale.

He gestured towards the stall. "Don't it bother you?"

She had been about to question him further, but now glanced at the goods on display. "No, it doesn't bother me, nor does it bother any other Overlander or any with allegiance to the Tidy Squad. We like it that all the Theocracy valued so highly is being sold off as trinkets, collectors' items or decorations. It puts the Theocracy firmly in the past, where it should be."

Grant glanced at her. That really didn't sound like the opinion of someone who wore the negative of a proctor's uniform and kept her money and make-up in a hollowed-out scole. It occurred to him that they had been forewarned of his arrival here, and that she had been waiting for him.

Beyond the trinket stalls lay a carousel vending machine about which a collection of tables and chairs had been set out. Such alfresco drinking and dining, albeit undercover and sealed from the air of the world, was something that had never been seen on the surface of Masada until after the rebellion. It was a novelty Grant had noticed spreading, especially amongst those who could *really* eat and drink alfresco. He'd sat in such a place actually outside and watched the diners and drinkers enjoying a freedom they hadn't imagined before; he still having to wear a breather mask.

Edward Thracer, along with two other Overlanders and another individual in plainer dress, sat at a table drinking white wine and sampling mezes from a varied collection of bowls. The four seemed to be having a good time at their feast, and Grant felt like the arriving skeleton.

"Commander Grant," the woman announced as they approached the table.

Grant felt himself cringing as other people all around looked towards him, some giving a rebel salute, others grinning and nodding. Chairs were shuffled aside to leave a space and a new chair pulled over. Grant sat down, ignored the glass of wine poured for him and gazed across at Edward

Thracer. The man was a rock, solid muscle, and a shaven head revealing a purple scar almost the shape of an oak leaf.

"So what can we do for you, Commander?" Thracer asked.

Grant decided to play it gently at first, not to get too heavy-handed. Here he could not be as terse and abrupt as was his wont, nor could he bark orders and expect them to be obeyed. "You know where my sympathies lie, Edward, and I know where yours are," he said carefully. "What I'm about to tell you, you're probably already getting set up for."

Thracer just folded his arms and sat back, waiting.

"During the rebellion I saved a proctor's life—took him to our med unit in Triada Compound." Grant flicked his gaze around all the other faces at the table. "Y'know the story; he survived an attack from the Technician, survived it because the Technician replaced his breather mask."

"So *you* say," said Thracer.

Grant felt a flash of annoyance at that. The fact that Tombs's mask had been replaced by the Technician after its attack on him had been in the public domain for over a decade, but still there were those, like Thracer, who questioned Grant's word. But instead of arguing the point he nodded acceptance and continued. "We've always thought there was something odd about the gabbleducks, the hooders, the siluroynes, heroynes and tricones. Now, with that stuff from the Polity Tagreb and that Atheter AI, we know it: gabbleducks are the descendants of the Atheter, hooders and tricones are artificial, and hooders were war machines, either that or they were made from them."

"You're not exactly telling us anything new," said the woman who had guided him here, now seated astride a chair behind Thracer.

"Well I didn't know that bit about hooders once being war machines," said the man clad in plain clothes.

"That's because you weren't paying attention, David," she shot back.

Thracer held up a hand. "Let him continue—he at least deserves a hearing."

"Okay," Grant grated, "let me tell you something y'don't know about Proctor Jeremiah Tombs."

"We know he's heading in this direction," said Thracer. "And that it's quite likely that Greenport is going to be his final destination."

Grant shook his head. "No it ain't, and here's why." He took a deep breath, gazed at them steadily. "All you know about Tombs is that he's a proctor loon who can't accept his Theocracy is dead. He's become an icon—represents all proctors to some. He's the prime target for the Tidy Squad, but until now stayed safe on Heretic's Isle. But he's more than that, a lot more."

"How can a proctor be any more than a coffin dodger?" asked one of the other men at the table, his words succinct, vicious.

Grant dipped his head. He wanted to slap some sense into these people, but he also perfectly understood them. His stomach tight, he raised his head and focused on the speaker.

"When the Technician took Tombs apart, it plugged into his brain and downloaded something," he said succinctly.

"Bullshit," said the man.

Grant shrugged, which was not the response he wanted to make, and continued, his tone even but hoarse. "I guess you never wondered why Tombs is still a madman, why Polity mindtechs haven't straightened out his kinks. The AIs don't want to damage that download because of its source."

"So why'd they let him get away?" asked Thracer.

"Because the realities now, here on Masada, should shock him back to sanity and allow the AIs to get to that information." Grant said it straight, succinct, hiding his own doubts.

"Oh, we can acquaint him with realities," said the vicious man.

Thracer glanced at the man, expression blank, then said, "You're asking us to accept that a hooder is capable of inserting information into the mind of a man. They may be the descendants of organisms fashioned for war, but I know nothing about such a capability. Hooder biology is mostly known and understood."

"The Technician used to make those weird sculptures—we all know that. Do other hooders do that?" Grant asked.

"So it's a bit different," said one of the others, shrugging.

"A lot different," said Grant. "Even during the rebellion some Polity gink was here tracking the Technician and snatching its sculptures before the proctors could find and destroy them. He found one in the mountains four years back. It's a million years old. Hooders don't live that long, so it seems the Technician was made practically immortal, and there ain't been anyone capable of doing that on this world for two million years."

"And your final point?" asked Thracer.

"Don't try to kill Tombs, don't try to have him killed, and warn off any Tidy Squad members preparing to kill him." Grant glanced at the vicious man, then returned his attention to Thracer.

"Are you threatening us?" Thracer asked.

"Just delivering a warning," said Grant, now standing up. "I'm going to be watching over him, and others will be watching too."

"What others?"

"One's a Polity drone that fought in the Prador war. It's a machine you seriously don't want to fuck with. But concern yourself with me first. Anyone tries to take Tombs and I will stop them."

Mr. Vicious looked up. "How does it feel, Grant, trying to keep alive a piece of shit like that?"

"It makes me feel filthy," said Grant. "But the Theocracy is gone and the AIs are here—we can't be selective about what parts of their rule we'll accept."

"Yeah, whatever," said Mr. Vicious.

"You've delivered your warning, Commander," said Thracer. "We'll consider it."

It was a dismissal. Grant nodded and moved away. He hoped that Thracer would realize that Tombs alive was more important to Masada and its people than petty vengeance—hoped the man could rein in the hotheads in his organization. Really, he didn't fear for Tombs's life, he feared for theirs. Amistad had recently made it quite plain to him. The drone itself wasn't watching Tombs, that job had fallen to one of the drone's "associates," and it would not limit its response to any threat to the man's life. Something had worried Grant about the way Amistad referred to that "associate." It was almost as if that individual might be more lethal than the drone itself, and since Amistad was a veteran of the Prador war, carrying enough munitions to take out a city and enough bile to enjoy the process, that didn't bode well for any assassination attempts.

Some time in the past a storm had detached a clump of flute grasses from the main inland growth and one of the complex retreating tides had dumped it. Here the continent was reclaiming some of its land as the grasses now spread their rhizomes across waves of shingle. Jem had felt certain such a small stand of grasses would not contain anything nasty, for within it there would be nothing to hunt, so there he fell into a sleep of exhaustion.

He woke once in the night, the glare of Amok turning the grasses around him to silver, and noted penny molluscs scattered on the damp ground all around him. Staring at the patterns on their shells he tried to make some sense of it all, but found only an unbearable sadness rising in him. He tried to find comfort in the First Satagent, but the world around him just drank up the words and replied with a distant and mocking "Sudburf hogglemiff," and he fell silent, both sadness and fear mingling in his chest.

Everything seemed to be testing his faith. Reality seemed to be testing his faith. And with that disconcerting thought playing in his mind, he tried to find sleep again, but that background mutter haunted a mind stirred by flashes of scripture, memories of childhood and the endless theological classes, and easy sleep now evaded him. At some point he slid into dream and found himself gazing at the words of his Satagenial and simply not comprehending them, terrified because the teacher would be along soon with his flute-grass cane that hooted and whistled when the man delivered the inevitable thrashing.

Jem jerked awake, Calypse high and misty above, and sunlight casting cage shadows across him from the surrounding grasses. He sat up, not sure what proportion of the night he had spent in real sleep. After a moment he opened his pack and took out his remaining flask of cold coffee, drank deeply, then eyed the sealed packs of food he had brought along. He knew he should eat, but did not relish the prospect. Already doubts were coming back to haunt him; a continuous nagging pain at the core of his being. What Sanders had told him seemed the only rational explanation for the things he had seen: twenty years ago there had been a successful rebellion here, after which the Polity brought in its satanic machines.

He ate because he needed the strength, but without relish, then repacked his supplies and lurched to his feet. Heading out onto the shingle he first noted that Calypse had drawn the sea in close, the waves lapping at the rhizome mat here, then he saw two trails running across shingle and the mudflat, drawing two lines between where he stood and the inland grasses. Something big had come out here in the night and then returned. He shuddered, took a diagonal course back towards the mudflat where walking would be easier, then finally reaching the compacted mass, which was much interwoven dead grasses, he picked up his pace, realizing that by now he had rounded the peninsula. Checking the time display on his watch he saw that over a day of his air supply remained, so he must cover a distance he estimated at about thirty kilometres within that time. He should have no problem, just so long as this world did not throw new barriers in his path.

Still linked via her aug to Thracer's comunit, Shree turned to gaze through the panoramic window of Thracer's apartment as Grant stood up from the table in the market square below and departed. He'd been recruited to act as close protection for Tombs, a guide, a mentor. Obviously Grant's past history with the proctor was why he had been asked, but though for her own plans it was what she wanted, it surprised her that he had accepted. His dislike of the Theocracy had been as fanatical as her own, and he had often been considered for recruitment to the Squad. Something had changed, obviously, but as Halloran had said, circumstances were now in her favour.

She listened in on further discussion at the table. Miloh and David Tinsch were having none of it. Fuck the Atheter. What value was information about a race that trashed its own civilization and lobotomized its descendants? They lived in the untidy now and it was time to make Masada just a little bit cleaner. Protection? Right. Let's see how Tombs would be protected from an HV bullet at a thousand metres, though, of course, they'd much prefer to bury the bastard up to his neck in guano and see just how long he managed to keep screaming.

"I disagree, I'm afraid," said Thracer. "We've only glimpsed what these Polity drones are capable of. Remember, just two of them here took out most of the Theocracy air force and they, apparently, were nothing like the things made during the Prador war."

"So we let the fucker live?" said Miloh incredulously.

"When the AIs have got to whatever it is inside his head, they'll lose interest in him." Thracer smiled. "Then we take him down."

Miloh pushed his chair back and stood. Tinsch, who wore rather ordinary clothes to disguise a gut full of hate, stood also.

"Bullshit," said Miloh. "You damned well know that this might be our only chance at him." He stepped away from the table and departed.

"I never thought you'd go soft on us, Edward," said Tinsch, just a hint of disappointment in his voice, and he headed off after Miloh.

The party began to break up then, its earlier conviviality now dead. After the last of them departed, Thracer stood and took his leave, wending his way across the market, out along the covered walkway, then up to his apartment. Shree shut down her aug link, then gazed at the door as he entered. He paused to stare at her, his look unreadable, then tiredly walked over and took the seat opposite her.

"So?" he asked.

"He told you no lies."

"Then Tombs can't be killed—you know how things are now. We need as much information as possible about the Atheter, about the history of this world. We need to be able to fight our case."

Shree gave a slow nod, then said, "Did you think Tidy Squad's interest was only in turning him into a corpse?"

"What else?"

"Politics."

Thracer suddenly looked even more tired. "Tell me."

Shree stood up and walked over to the window to peer down at the market. "Under the Theocracy the idea of AI rule seemed like utopia, until we really understood what the Intervention Amnesty meant. Now we start to see other symptoms of autocracy and begin to realize what Polity Separatists are all about."

"Separatists, yeah—like those fuckers the Theocracy was supplying."

She turned back towards him, feeling a slight twinge of regret. "AI rule is absolute—there's no room for disagreement -and now we learn that under that rule this world is a spit away from being classified under the AOP."

"AOP?" Thracer was puzzled.

"Alien Occupancy Policy." Shree grimaced to herself—she'd further explored what that meant after her meeting with Hal-loran. "Masada could cease to be classified as a Human colony but be classified as an alien Homeworld occupied by illegal Human squatters. A whole new set of AI rules start to apply then and we end up thoroughly shafted. We end up having little or no say about our future—population strictly controlled, travel through alien areas limited, all further construction put on hold."

"The gabbleducks?"

"Precisely—they appear to be unintelligent animals, but still there're doubts about that. Their brains are too large and in some areas defy analysis. And of course the Atheter AI might be considered an original indigene too."

"So how does this relate to Tombs?"

"Tombs received a download from the Technician—and as we know, the hooder species was originally made by the Atheter before they threw everything away. It's quite possible that whatever it put into his skull could have some bearing on AOP classification. We need to destroy it."

"Then why not a straight assassination, here in Greenport?"

"If he's being watched over by a war drone then that's near impossible." She strolled back to her chair and sat down. "We're talking about nanosecond response times." She paused for a moment. "If Miloh tries with a high-velocity rifle a war drone could shoot the bullet out of the air and be on him shoving the rifle up his ass before he gets off a second shot."

"So what's your plan?"

"Tombs is on a journey of discovery, and it is Squad Command's bet that he will be led to certain locations to try and free up whatever lies inside his skull. He can, in fact, give us access to certain locations presently closed to us." She reached into her pocket, took out the squat glassy cylinder Halloran had given her, and placed it on the table between them.

"What's that?"

"A little something snatched from under the noses of the Polity clear-up teams, taken offworld after the full quarantine ended and cooked up in a Separatist lab on Cheyne III."

"Jain tech," he said, then gazed across at her with obvious disgust. "You're dealing with Separatists?"

Shree felt her regret increase. Despite his cruel past Thracer was a good man. His problem seemed to be an unrealistic romanticism that made him unable to understand the necessary political expediencies of their continued fight for freedom. He thought that fight ended with the fall of the Theocracy. He was a fool.

"You find that distasteful?" she enquired.

"I find that practically treasonous."

He was a useful unit leader here in Greenport but, really,

she did not need him, the Overlanders or the Tidy Squad unit here.

"You do understand how things have changed, don't you?" she asked. "In the past the Theocracy supported Separatists and vice versa, but that does not automatically make Separatists enemies of the people of Masada."

"They're not our friends," said Thracer. "Remember, the Theocracy supplied them with wealth and resources in exchange for stolen Polity technologies and expertise. Without them the Theocracy would not have been able to complete the laser network so quickly, nor build Ragnorak."

"That may be so, but things have changed now."

"They're the enemies of the Polity—that's good enough for me. Every world that's been pushed by Separatists to secede from the Polity has ended up a disaster zone."

Shree frowned, aware that she shouldn't have taken their conversation this far, and that now Thracer possessed too much information to be safe.

"Polity intervention has brought great advances, but that does not automatically make the AIs our friends, Edward. They have their own agendas and, in reality, if we get in the way, we'll be stepped on. The Polity is as totalitarian as the Theocracy."

Thracer shook his head and gazed at her. After a moment he said, "Polity intervention has taken a population out of slavery and raised the living standard of every individual to something beyond that of a bishop. Their medical technology has given everyone on this world a chance at real immortality, not the crap promised by religion. All enjoy even justice without favour." He paused for a moment. "And though that last comes after the Intervention Amnesty and allows those who should be dead a second chance, it's good for the population as a whole. I think, Shree, that you've lost sight of what we were fighting for."

"I haven't, it's freedom."

"An airy concept often used by people who are really saying: I'm fighting for the freedom to tell you what to do."

"All we have done here is swap our chains for another kind," Shree said woodenly.

"I think you'll find some disagreement from those who once wore scoles and spent their every waking moment labouring, those whose lives were at most forty years long, and those who can now walk free on the surface, have the chance of living for ever and are supported by the labour of machines. Don't you?"

"Chains are chains," Shree insisted. "After suffering the Theocracy we shouldn't accept the next manacles because they are fur-lined."

"So you think that without the Polity AIs running this place, by following the Separatist route, people will end up with greater freedom? You think *that*, despite the entirety of Human history refuting it? To paraphrase some ancient historical figure: Polity rule is not the best form of government, but it's better than every other kind that has been tried."

Shree felt the anger surging up from the pit of her stomach, but cold and controlled and flowing into her limbs like a stimulant. The same controlled rage had kept her alive during some of the worst fighting of the rebellion, and powered her through the numerous assassinations she'd conducted afterwards. And the same controlled rage had enabled her to meticulously build the Tidy Squad network whilst keeping her own position at the top hidden. Thracer, despite being an Over-lander and despite being a member of the Tidy Squad here in Greenport, had demonstrated that he was a liability. Her pulse-action handgun was in her hand before she even thought about it.

Thracer gazed at the weapon for a long moment, then said, "I guess you just won't see that you've proven my point."

Shree shot him through the face.

7

Black artificial intelligences have been with us right from the start. They were there during the corporate exploration of the solar system, occasionally slipping the leash of their Human masters and causing atmosphere ventings and machine-driven slaughters aboard space stations; they were there during the Diaspora of that time, some seizing full control of cryoships and playing interesting games with hibernating Humans, in one case the game being target practice, that is, firing two thousand frozen people at an asteroid; they were there during the Quiet War advocating the extermination of the Human race, or at least a radical involuntary redesign of the same; and they are with us still. Names resound, but are spoken in whispers: Glee-of-Murder, Mancer-ator, Scuttler, Penny Royal and Jack O'Gravestones. They are the serial killers of the AI world, but cannot be compared to real Human killers, rather more to fictional ones like Hannibal Lecter, Elm Street's Freddy Krueger and Jason Vorhees. Nightmares in metal, these beings are not defined by hate of Humanity, rather more by an amoral delight in everything dark in the Human mind, and in their own. And they are dangerous because they bring terrifyingly powerful intelligence to the pursuit of what we deem evil, and because they are not damaged rejects of the Polity but creatures that have advanced beyond it, though not to a place many would want to go. To call them insane is not meaningful; they are far beyond such trite classification.

—From HOW IT IS *by Gordon*

From a distance Godhead had looked no different from how he remembered it, but as he drew closer he began to see changes he just could not account for. Where was the monolithic proctors' station? Where were the workers' huts? How was it that the entire central town seemed to have changed its shape? A few kilometres out he reached a railed foamstone platform with steps leading up. He climbed up and gazed out to his left to get a clearer view of what had once been the worker compound, then tried to make sense of the scene before him.

The compound fence was gone, as were all the neatly ranked huts, but the foamstone rafts remained and on four of them had been erected a very modern-looking complex of buildings, from whose centre arose the stalk of a tower topped with some kind of observation structure in the shape of an onion. Why would the Theocracy demolish perfectly adequate worker huts and build such a thing, he wondered. Why, even if the huts had been destroyed, maybe by a particularly violent summer storm, had the huts not been re-erected on those perfectly adequate foamstone rafts?

Because, replied the treacherous part of his mind, Sanders told you the truth: there are no more enslaved workers and there is no Theocracy. Jem closed his eyes tightly and slammed the palm of his hand against his forehead. It hurt, the false covering over his own face transmitting all the pain to him and seemingly causing that distant muttering to grow in volume. When he opened his eyes nothing had changed. He felt a sudden hardening of resolve. No more doubts. He would find the truth and be done with it. Almost angrily he stomped down off the platform and made his way along a path consisting of slabs of epoxy-bound flute-grass stems—the slabs attached to each other with metal hinges, so the path was an unbroken chain on ground that moved like a slow sea.

The path took him in towards a floating breakwater beyond which lay the entrance to the harbour. Though he could see the central town lying a little way inland and still not looking quite right to him, the harbour, but for the tops of a few cranes, lay out of sight behind flute grasses sprouting from thick mud and layered rhizome. Within a few minutes he had reached the steps leading up to the shore-attached end of the breakwater and climbed. As he did so he checked the time remaining to him—how long he had before he needed to get into properly breathable air. Still plenty of time, but his satisfaction with that turned to horror when he mounted the breakwater and gazed towards the harbour.

The breakwater itself curved back inland, connected to the foamstone supporting the machinery, storage bays and harbour buildings. For a second he stared at all this, at the ship now departing and the one presently in dock, and saw no more nor less than he had expected. Then it began to impinge upon him: he could see no people, and there were new gleaming machines there that moved with a terrifying animal grace.

The Polity.

How could he deny it any longer? Sanders had told him the truth. He rubbed his hands over his face. Polity technology was here on this world, it was here as the prosthetic over his skull, here in Sanders's body so she could breathe the outside air, here in those machines digging up Theocracy dead, here in that small motor on the boat he had used, and here, right before him.

His gait wooden, he trudged in towards the harbour, now seeing the machines even more clearly and more undeniably of offworld manufacture. He felt sick. How could this be? How could the rebels have won? Maybe they didn't, maybe the Polity simply attacked? But how could the Theocracy have fallen against godless machines?

Endlessly he questioned himself as he drew closer, finding answers supplied to him by Sanders, but answers he just could not accept. Next, she was walking beside him, clinging wrap about her body, endlessly cycling a slow nova.

"You can keep on denying the facts," she said, *"but how far will you go?"*

"To the ends of the Earth," he replied.

As if she hadn't heard him she continued, *"How much in the way of resources do you think the rebellion has? Enough to create this and keep it hidden from those satellite eyes above?"*

She was referring to the sanatorium perched above the sea on that ersatz Heretic's Isle, whilst he sat in his wheelchair, trying to make the patterns work, trying to get them *right.* He turned towards her and she winked out like the star her wrap depicted.

A wide expanse of foamstone lay before him now, and to his right a docked ship, silvery *things* on its deck. Without them it would have been fine—it would have looked right. It was almost as if the Polity machines were some kind of evil overlay on his world.

"Hey, how many times do I have to tell you people?"

"Tell us what?" Jem asked, wondering what Sanders was on about now. Then abruptly he realized it wasn't Sanders's voice he had heard. He glanced to one side and saw a woman clambering down from the cab of an old and familiar loader. A transparent oversuit covered her clothes and she wore a breather mask.

"Just because you can breathe the air doesn't mean the g-dust isn't going to hurt you," she said as she stomped towards Jem. "We've got it cut down, but you breathe enough of it and it'll eventually fuck you up."

"Be careful how you address me, citizen," said Jem.

She gazed at him with some surprise through her transparent visor. He realized that she was wearing a proctors' breather gear, not the breather of a citizen. Perhaps he was mistaken about her being just a citizen? No, she wasn't in uniform and she had been driving a loader.

"Who the fuck do you think you are? Hierarch Loman?"

"I am Proctor Jeremiah Tombs," Jem stated portentously. "And I want you to take me to the proctor station here." He gazed across at central town. "Apparently it has been relocated."

She stared at him for a long moment, then said wonderingly, "Right . . . you're the spaghetti-head we were warned about." She abruptly grinned. "I'm so sorry, proctor, please forgive me. What I suggest you do is head into town, try to find the market square and ask there. I'm sure you'll find plenty of people there willing to help you rejoin your

Theocracy." She abruptly turned away, heading back towards her loader.

"Wait! Did I give you leave to depart?"

Without turning she gave him the finger, and continued towards her loader. Jem unshouldered his harpoon and pointed the weapon at her back. "I will only give you this one warning." She had to obey, she must obey, else the world just wasn't right.

She glanced back, saw the harpoon and came to a halt.

"Oh, a dangerous lunatic," she said. "Well, be sure you're on target Tombs, because if you miss I'm going to be rubbing your face in—'

She stuttered to a halt, looking at something off to one side, just as a shadow loomed over him. His harpoon gun fired. He must have pulled the trigger but hadn't intended to. The weapon made an odd thwacking sound and shuddered in his hand. A panel had opened up in its side and a large spring was hanging out, and as he lowered the weapon the harpoon itself fell out and clattered on the ground. He dropped the weapon, obviously useless to him, his gaze still locked on the woman.

"Sweet mother of God," she whispered, backing up, her eyes wide with fear.

Jem did not want to turn to see what was standing beside him. He could see hints of something out of the corner of his eye, but to turn would reveal what loomed there, and he was terrified that it would be a gabbleduck. The woman turned and ran, clambering up into her loader and slamming the cab door behind her. Engaging the drive she spun the vehicle a hundred and eighty degrees, its tyres smoking, and took it hurtling away just as fast as she could. Jem wanted to order her to come back, to beg her to come back, and then, finally, he found the courage to turn.

Nothing there. He was just gazing across flat foamstone towards the docked ship. He felt laughter bubbling up in his chest, then it abruptly died. He could see nothing, but some invisible presence loomed close by. He could feel an imminence, some kind of heavy force pressing against reality and, terrifyingly, a twisted black eagerness. In an instant he knew that if he took a few paces in that direction, he would be stepping into Hell. Satan was here, the Devil himself had come here during Jem's time of revelation.

"You won't have me," he whispered, then turned and ran towards the central town, sure in the knowledge that Hell hounds were on his trail.

Chanter surfaced his mudmarine and, as was his habit, reached out to engage the chameleonware. He hesitated for just a second, then did engage it. For a while, after the fall of the Theocracy and the arrival of the Polity here, he'd stopped hiding his vessel. What was the point now there were no proctors to spot him and those who now ruled here were thoroughly aware of his presence? However, as he discovered only a year after the rebellion and a year into the two-year quarantine period, the thorough changes this planet was undergoing had not changed one thing: the wildlife.

He had surfaced, as was his habit, at a location the Technician had occupied for a full day-night cycle, which meant it had probably fed. The transponder signal from the beast, still somewhat intermittent, told him it was now fifty kilometres away, so he was safe from it. The second hooder, half the size of the Technician but still a formidable beast, had slammed into his mudmarine and spun it over once. It then came down on it again and started to try and take it apart. Chanter was able to engage the drive and take the vessel back under, the hooder only releasing its hold when he reached a depth of thirty metres.

Later on during the quarantine period, he learnt that the erstwhile rebels had started a program to affix beacons to every living hooder, so as to give warning to any out on the surface of their approach, and by searching frequencies he found that of the beacons. Later still, after the quarantine ended for most of the world—still some areas were prohibited even now—every hooder had received a beacon, and a satellite surveillance program watched for young hooders surfacing and ensured they were tagged soon afterwards. He'd felt safe then, and again ceased using the chameleonware when no hooders were nearby. An enormous gabbleduck, turning his mudmarine on its side and seemingly trying to play it like a drum with its huge black claws, had cured him of the inclination. It was only after this particular attack that he realized just how lucky he had been to have survived on Masada for so long.

Now, here was definitely a place for chameleonware while he exited his craft, and other precautions afterwards. His own transponder and the Polity beacon placed the Technician only five kilometres away from him and, whilst that was far enough for him to safely exit his vessel and head to his destination and yet close enough for most other wildlife to have fled the area, there was always the chance that a gabbleduck sat out there, for hooders ignored them until they were dying.

Whilst still inside his vessel Chanter used his sensors to check the area, then linked to satellite surveillance to check further. The Technician was precisely where it should be, lying coiled in a perfect spiral as if taking a snooze, whilst the upper disc of the mobile observation tower lay almost over his own present location. Nothing else hostile was visible in any section of the electromagnetic spectrum he used to scan, but he now checked a seismic map of the area.

Two hundred metres away from him, just under the surface, lurked a three-metre-long mud snake, its presence there seeming to justify his new paranoia. What if, during all those times he had walked out to check out some new sculpture, a mud snake had been sitting directly below him? Thus, very messily, would his studies have ended.

The mud snake lay too far away to get to him before he reached the tower and, as was often the case when a big hooder was about, had burrowed down deep and curled into a wood-louse ball. Chanter unstrapped himself, picked up his pack and exited his craft and, when a few metres away from it across the rhizome mat, instituted another of his new precautions. A signal from a remote control he held sent the mudmarine down under the surface. Really, sophisticated chameleonware would be no use at all if a big hooder blundered into the craft by chance—it would be like the thing being hit by a monorail. He then turned to look up at the tower and platform silhouetted against the sun.

Bases down on the surface had to be defended, with fences, autoguns and all sorts of devices to discourage the voracious wildlife. Going overland out into the wilds was plain dangerous—it might be that you could know the location of hooders in the area, but what if they moved while you were out there so you ended up surrounded, and what about the other wildlife? Polity AIs tended to want citizens to adhere to the laws, but made no laws to stop people suffering the consequences of their own stupidity. Hundreds of would-be researchers and solvers of the puzzles here had ended up having to be airlifted to safety, whilst hundreds more with less luck had ended up inside the things they had been studying. Observation of the wildlife from the air wasn't energy-efficient, whilst satellite observation, though presenting clear images, was too divorced from the ground.

The engine that drove the observation tower lay well below ground and was made of ceramics tough enough to withstand the depredations of the tricones. The platform stood too high for any of the wildlife to reach, whilst the stem, also tough ceramic, was as ignored by the wildlife as a rock. It was a workable solution to the problems inherent in studying the Masada fauna, but to Chanter seemed too intrusive, too massive, too much of a statement of Polity arrogance.

As he set out towards it, Chanter recollected that this tower had been designed by one Jonas Clyde, working from a Polity Tagreb—the Taxonomic and Genetic Research Base. He had made a comprehensive study of the biology of the hooders and, along with another researcher called Shardelle Garadon, who had been studying the non-language of the gabbleducks, the "gabble," was credited with putting together everything about the Atheter racial suicide here. However, Chanter very much doubted they were the first to know about it, just the first to bring it into the public arena. An Atheter AI had been down on this world since just after the rebellion, and it seemed likely Polity AIs had been in communication with it and knew everything there was to know about that race.

When Chanter reached the base of the tower, a ring-shaped elevator girdling the stem descended towards him, fast. It slammed to a halt just above the ground, a ramp door folding down to touch the rhizome. Chanter climbed it, his feet slapping wetly on the diamond pattern metal, seated himself in one of the ring of chairs. The moment his bottom touched the seat the elevator ascended, not so fast this time, but fast enough to press him down into the seat, then lift him half out of it as it slowed to a halt below the platform. A door opened into the stem, and he found his way up to the top, and walked out onto the platform where Amistad lurked.

"My application?" he asked as he approached the scorpion drone.

"Ignored," the drone replied, turning to face him with metal feet clattering against the floor that sounded like an old diesel engine starting. "But you're not unique. Only on the world Shayden's Find where it was discovered, during its transportation here and for three years after it was installed here on the surface, did the Atheter AI communicate with anyone. After that it ceased to react in any way."

"Is it dead?" Chanter asked.

"It's still drawing power and other monitoring shows it's still . . . thinking, but that's all. The speculation is that having ascertained for certain that the Atheter are effectively extinct, it has chosen mental ascension."

"Why don't the AIs do something?" Chanter asked in frustration.

Only after finding the Technician's ancient sculpture had he realized that during all his years here on Masada he'd fallen into a kind of fugue. Now, when he studied his journals, he saw a man who had dropped so deeply into esoteric explorations of *art* that he'd utterly lost his way. Now, with the revelations about the Atheter, he had begun to see his way to the surface again. Some resolution to the whole picture seemed just about within his reach, yet, frustratingly, even intelligences like Amistad were still in limbo. So what chance did he stand?

"That's problematic," said Amistad. "When the AI was powered up aboard the ship used to transport it here, it took over the ship AI. It is powerful indeed, perhaps beyond even the power of a sector AI or something like Jerusalem. Intervention could be very dangerous. And there's also a moral issue."

"Moral issue?"

"The Atheter AI is an alien intelligence, so cannot be judged by Polity standards of mental health, of sanity. We cannot really know whether intervention is required, nor do we have any right to intervene."

"Seems specious to me—and you're not so wary of intervention when it comes to a Human mind."

"Definitions of sanity and mental health are clearer there," Amistad replied.

"So we're just nowhere, it seems," Chanter grumped.

He walked out to the rail, for which there was no need, since a very sophisticated shimmer-shield surrounded the platform—the rail was just a psychological prop for the Humans who came here, and a place to mount sophisticated scanning controls. He gazed across at the distant Technician, still coiled in a perfect spiral, then activated a field lensing control. Immediately a section of the shimmer-shield before him framed out, and he expanded the view until it seemed he stood as close to the Technician as he had only once before, when he got close enough to it to fire his transponder into its body.

"Not very active today," he noted.

"According to your journals it's been going somnolent like this ever since the rebellion, or rather ever since you found it again after the rebellion—perhaps this is some sort of response to the threat of Jain technology here."

Chanter glanced round, but the drone remained unreadable as ever. "What makes you say that?"

"It was that same technology the Atheter suicided to avoid, so their biomechs are probably aware of it too. Also the Technician has been undergoing some major internal changes during its periods of sleep."

"It stopped producing its sculptures during the rebellion too," Chanter said.

"How can you be sure? Throughout your time here you discovered one sculpture every couple of years on average, and not necessarily new ones. It could have stopped years before or years afterwards."

"Perhaps it'll begin again . . ."

"You are no further in your understanding of those sculptures?" Amistad enquired.

"I'm thinking that maybe it tries to recreate the creatures it destroys—some primitive form of prey worship as seen in cave paintings done by prehistoric Humans."

"You try to understand art, Chanter, but only with your own mind because to you it has to be something more than the mathematical, the scientific. It has to be something mystical, mysterious, almost beyond the grasp of logic. It's almost as if you are searching for a substitute to worship."

"Fuck you," said Chanter, but without heat, doubt lodging in his skull.

"It's a shame that beyond the scientific tools you use to study the physical structures of those sculptures, you use nothing else. Copious analytical tools are easily at your disposal, and using them you might discover something . . . interesting."

"Art is not science," said Chanter stubbornly, now turning and heading for the exit from the platform.

"That everything can be analysed, catalogued and understood does not destroy its value. Mysticism is the function of a mind looking for alternatives to reality."

Chanter fled the platform, went back down into the mud.

During the rebellion many buildings had been destroyed here in Zealos, but now they had been replaced and Polity technology and building materials were evident everywhere. However, to Sanders it felt very strange to so freely wander these streets. Even now, after coming here intermittently over the last twenty years, she still expected the hand of a proctor on her shoulder and a demand for identification. This had happened just prior to the rebellion, when she and some other rebels had come here to steal medical supplies from a Theocracy store. Luckily they escaped with their lives, though the proctor concerned ended up in a city sewer.

Church Street lay ahead, and two of the four churches that lined it were still frequented by the many believers living here, though they came furtively and often disguised, aware that Tidy Squad spotters were in the vicinity, and that if they were recognized they might find themselves subject to public ridicule. The two other churches, however, had been put to different use. Episcopal See, which had been a burnt-out ruin just after the rebellion, had been rebuilt as a meeting hall for rebel soldiers. The big Church of Zelda Smythe, its dome collapsed and two of the four steeples extending above its bell towers toppled, had been lovingly restored, its steeples plated with silver and its dome with gold. But no one went there to recite the Satagents and sing the praises of the prophetess, though it was true that communicants came to speak with something akin to a god.

A covered walkway terminated at a side door to the church, but the main doors were now exposed to the open street. Sanders climbed red marble steps to the big, arched grapewood door, turned the single black iron ring at its centre and pushed the door inwards against the internal pressure differential. She stepped inside, the door swinging silently closed behind her, and studied the interior.

Pews still stood on either side at the back of the central aisle, and ahead of these lay the rough stone prayer floor where the deeply religious could bloody their knees and graze their foreheads as they worked up a lather reciting the Satagents. At the four corners of the church, doors opened into the residences of the Bishop, his vicars and staff, along with apartments for those attending for an intensive course in faith reinforcement. Of course none of these people were here now. All those in the Brotherhood, within Zealos, who had been turned into zombies, were shot by the rebels and buried in a massive pit outside the city, until Polity machines came to retrieve the dangerous corpses. Many of those in the Theocracy yet to receive their *Gift* were hunted down and slaughtered too, others fled and some survived—Sanders had tended a few of them on Heretic's Isle.

Walking down the aisle towards the altar and the twin lecterns, Sanders looked up at the paintings decorating the inside of the dome. Depicted was a mishmash of religious art: the cupids as winged Buddhas, classical Christian demons, along with the goddess Kali and other more obscure monsters, supposedly tormenting the unrighteous, whilst the righteous wore glowing crowns, flowing robes and Dracocorp augmentations. Sanders had only come in here twice before, both occasions after this place was restored. However, she felt sure that then the righteous had not worn such expressions of sickening piety, nor had the damned seemed to be having such fun, or the demons been so amused.

The lecterns stood just ahead and off to either side of the altar. From the big lectern on the right the Bishop would have delivered his sermon, whilst from the left-hand lectern one of his vicars would have controlled the pictures appearing on the screen wall behind the altar, presently concealed behind heavy gold-braided curtains, whilst also keeping a close eye on the congregation. The altar itself was a Bridge console from an ancient First Diaspora U-space colony ship—the one Zelda Smythe supposedly brought her people here in. Upon it stood a framed picture of the woman herself—a religious icon—around which rested a bizarre collection of religious artefacts: a Christian cross with Christ nailed in place, a wooden carving of Ganesh, a small stone Buddha, amber worry beads and a scroll reputed to be one of those from beside the Dead Sea. All these, the religious believed, belonged to Zelda Smythe and helped her towards revelation and her amalgamation of religions, as did the library behind the left-hand lectern, numbering such works as the Koran and the Bible, actually on paper, and numerous other religious texts.

"I see you've been playing with the artwork, Ergatis," she said, finally coming to stand before the altar.

"I like to keep myself amused," replied a deep godlike voice. "It's a specially formatted family of nanites in the paint itself. They also have a random evolutionary component so I won't know what they'll do next."

Sanders very much doubted that. The being she was now addressing could probably calculate every possibility and encompass every one in its mind, all within a microsecond. It just chose not to. Ergatis had, unusually, not named itself after the world it governed, but then this AI was in a slightly unusual position for one of its kind. It did not control the planetary runcible, since the still extant danger of Jain technology here made it necessary to place the runcible on one of the Braemar moons—Flint, where the Theocracy shipyards had once been. Also, a question hung over its governorship, what with Masada maybe ending up being classified as an alien world inhabited by illegal Human colonists.

"So," Ergatis continued, "you've come to register your protest and try to obtain some sort of explanation. Am I right?"

"Of course you're right," Sanders replied impatiently. "You were probably running a copy of me as a subprogram before I walked in the door."

"You may be memchipped and backed up, Sanders, but your mind is your own property. Anyway, I don't need to run a copy of you to make that prediction. So, state your objections and ask your questions."

"Two years ago Amistad, without Tombs's permission, had him adapted to the environment of this world. I let that go because my pay-off was to be able to replace his head prosthetic, to regrow his face, and because I felt sure the drone knew what it was doing—it had after all been given carte blanche in Tombs's case." Sanders paused in frustration. How to logically put her case which, really, was just based on a gut instinct?

"Do go on."

"Amistad did nothing to stop Tombs believing he still wears a prosthetic and actively intervened when I tried to convince him that his face is now his own. I would have been dismissed from my position at the sanatorium if I'd brought up the subject again."

"Yes, unfortunate, that."

"Amistad is partnered with an ostensibly 'cured' black AI called Penny Royal. I did some research on that creature, and there's still an outstanding 'do not attempt to apprehend but destroy at a distance' order on it, yet it's here supposedly working for the Polity."

"The order you discovered in an outdated databank has since been deleted."

"There's never any amnesty for Humans who commit murder," Sanders stated, feeling the injustice.

"The situation there is more complicated. Penny Royal is not a singular distinct being. Of its previous eight states of consciousness just one of those states was the murderer. That conscious state has now been . . . removed."

Sanders nodded. She'd just have to accept that. "Tombs reached some critical mental nexus when he finished drawing his shell patterns, assaulted me and attempted to escape—not that he was really a captive anyway. Amistad intervened, then went on to allow him to escape, incidentally rendering me unconscious and setting the scene so it looked to Tombs like he had killed me. The man is now out on the surface of Masada—a danger to himself and to others."

"That's so, but what precisely is your problem?"

"I am not entirely convinced that Amistad's aims concur with those of the Polity. I think the drone's interest in madness outweighs any interest in curing it."

"Oh I agree."

Sanders took a step back, stunned, gazed up at the ceiling where a steel angel wore a smile she was sure it hadn't had before. "You agree?"

"Oh yes."

"Then isn't it time you intervened? Isn't it time this was taken out of Amistad's . . . claws and handed over to someone more capable, more responsible?"

"One would think so, yes," replied Ergatis, then, after a

surprisingly long pause, "Six years ago I had the power to negate Amistad's carte blanche, but not now. You have to understand that war drones were the grunts of the Prador war, the slightly dim fighting machines we used and, traditionally, that is how those that remain are still thought of. However, many of these drones are like the soldiers who came back from the front with a great deal of anger and drive which they threw into educating themselves."

"It's still a war drone, not a planetary governor AI."

"Not so. Amistad, it seems, long ago surpassed the memory, experience and intelligence of an artificial intelligence like me. And it seems that after reintegration of his consciousness, Amistad will acquire huge processing power and become the prime authority on all things Atheter. The drone will climb to the status of AIs like Geronamid and Jerusalem."

"What?"

"I can no more give Amistad orders than can you. Only Earth Central itself is higher, and that AI just told me to butt out."

Sanders turned in a daze and left the church, the eyes of fat lecherous cupids tracking her departure.

Miloh kept his eye utterly fixed on his rifle sight and swore. Whilst Tombs had been talking to Deela—a dockworker Miloh recognized—he'd got target acquisition, the crosshairs locking over the proctor's head and the rifle's gyros shifting the weapon about in his hands to make minor adjustments whilst he kept it in the targeting field. But now the man was running, the rifle just wouldn't acquire. This was ridiculous—he'd checked the damned thing over for hours before coming here to wait, he'd even run a full diagnostic of its internal workings, including structural scan of its moving parts. The rifle was as near to perfect as possible, yet now it was malfunctioning.

Without acquisition Miloh tried one shot, but saw no sign of the bullet hitting anywhere near the fleeing proctor. He next tried a five-shot burst, but again saw no sign of impacts. Swearing, he took his eye away from the sight and just aimed down the barrel, firing another five-shot burst. It was then, his eye away from the sight, that he saw them: ten slugs hanging in the air just a few metres away from him, all edge-on and arranged in a slowly turning circle. Then abruptly all of them turned back towards him.

"You have got to be kidding," he said.

Suddenly the bullets were in motion, accelerating towards him one after another as if the circle they had been arranged in was some sort of invisible ammo can rotating to present each bullet in turn to an invisible breach. The first slammed into the crane's metalwork beside his head before he had time to even duck or flinch. Then the rest were impacting all around him, splinters of metal and broken rifle slugs exploding apart and filling the air like a swarm of sprawns. He managed to cover his eyes, tried to draw back to cover, but with the certainty one of those bullets would soon slam home. However, the tenth bullet hit and it was all over. He checked himself for damage and saw none at all, which seemed an impossibility considering the amount of metal that had been flying about.

"Protected," he said, his heart thundering in his chest.

He swallowed drily, then reached with a shaking hand to his water bottle and uncapped it, took a sip. Suddenly he was just grateful to be alive, the feeling of relief swamping the constant anger he felt, at least for the moment. He considered what he had seen. Somewhere about here there was a Polity war machine concealed by chameleonware. Perhaps that accounted for the reaction first of Deela, then of Tombs himself. Tombs had been about to put his harpoon into her, but the weapon malfunctioned. She must have seen the thing, which was why she ran rather than take the opportunity to beat the crap out of Tombs for threatening her, as Miloh knew she was quite capable of doing. Tombs must have seen it too, which was why he ran. It seemed there was something damned scary about whatever—

Miloh froze, and felt a shiver running through his body. The crane stood on a loading jetty not currently in use, so would be powered down. It was also heavily built and well anchored into the jetty, which itself was reinforced enough to take the loading stresses imparted by the magnetic docking system dragging in half a million tonnes of cargo ship. There was no wind today and the sea was calm. So only one thing could account for the vibration Miloh could feel from the box-section he was sitting upon and the I-beam he rested his back against: something heavy was climbing up the crane towards him, and very soon he was going to die.

What could he do against something invisible, and capable of stopping his shots in midair, playing with the bullets like marbles, then firing them back at him? He peered down the length of the crane to the ground and for a moment could see nothing. Then came displacement, occasional prismatic distortions, a glimpse of something black and sharp at one moment, then the writhe of a metallic tentacle. The thing could do total invisibility, Miloh knew that—it just wasn't bothering to conceal itself from him. He considered emptying his rifle down towards it, but feared it would only send the bullets back.

"I'm not a threat," he said. "I'll not try again."

"Yess," a voice hissed up at him.

"Shouldn't you be sticking with Tombs? The central town won't be safe for him."

The thing relentlessly continued its slow ascent. He pointed his rifle down towards it, then hesitated. What rules did this thing exist by? If he deliberately fired upon it would that give it the excuse to kill him? Was that why it had revealed its location to him? Abruptly he raised the rifle, clicked across the safety, then ejected the magazine and pocketed it.

"I'm done," he said, peering down at the thing again.

"Yess," it hissed, and came up at him like an express elevator from Hell.

Black spines and metal writhing like squerms, cutting, nerves winking on and off like party lights, a single red eye inspecting him dispassionately. For just seconds, or maybe eternity, Miloh lived in some nightmare place and understood he was being given some hint, some small taste of a realm Jeremiah Tombs had once visited. It didn't end abruptly, just seemed to fade away, and he found himself with his face pressed against the I-beam, arms embracing it, legs coiled on the box section below, a tight cramp in his side. He tried to push away from the beam, but realized the thing that had assaulted him had either cuffed or tied his wrists on the other side, probably very tightly too, for he couldn't feel his hands and his forearms felt . . . odd.

Shuffling himself more upright, he tried to bring his wrists into view to see if there was some way he could free himself. When he finally did get a look at his bonds he at first felt a slightly irked puzzlement, which gradually grew into horror. His hands were gone, and his wrists terminated at his rifle, one at the stock and one at the butt. They were melded into the rifle, skin and metal blended into some whorled woody substance. He could feel the rifle between, actually *feel* it as a linking extension of his arms.

It took three hours before dockworkers responded to his shouts for help, and they wondered why the harbour submind had ignored him. He soon learnt that his *feeling* of the rifle was no illusion when those workers tried to cut through it to free him, and he screamed in pain and the weapon bled. Eventually they sliced a section out of the I-beam and lowered him to the ground. Later, in Zealos hospital, Polity medical technology swiftly restored his hands, but that technology could not free him of the sudden stabbing agony in his palms any time he touched a rifle, nor could it return to him his hate, which had withered and shrivelled away like a tumour starved of blood.

8

Being Human

Terms change as times change and language is necessarily protean in order to keep up. When we were still confined to Earth, a Human being was easily defined by body shape, mind and genetics. The first of these to go was body shape, as cosmetic surgery and deep body surgery improved then claimed new territory. This started with cat's eyes and elfin ears, then went radical as it became fashionable to take on other animal characteristics. Thereafter it ventured off into both the weird and the grotesque as some considered the utility of, say, an extra arm, a fish tail rather than legs, wings or the head of a crocodile. Mechanical augmentation played its part as people also turned themselves into cyborgs, with maybe an extra mechanical arm, or some steel tentacles or a motorized shell. And body shape became an irrelevance when it became possible to record and download a Human mind to any vessel. The shape of the Human mind disappeared with cerebral augmentation, much of it necessary to control different body shapes or those mechanical augmentations, much of it to expand mental watts, memory, or to turn the mind into a specialized processor. Human DNA, already being adjusted for medical reasons, came in for major adjustment as Humans began to adapt themselves to new environments. Initially surgical alterations and technological augmentations played their part, but their limited scope was not enough for a people who wanted to colonize a whole world—they wanted alterations the body could repair, and that they could pass on to their children. So, in the end, what is it to be Human now?

—*From* QUINCE GUIDE, *compiled by Humans*

Jem staggered out of the still standing harbour gates, his sprint through the guano storage bays to get away from the Devil seeming to have drained the last of his strength. He went down on his knees in an area that appeared more familiar to him, a row of open-top trucks parked to his right and a small proctors' guard post to his left, neglected and its windows smashed.

He fought to regain breath, return some strength to his limbs, wondered if his air supply was running out early and, so thinking, lurched to his feet and headed for the short road leading up to the central town.

Worker huts had once stood on either side of the road, but now new structures were being erected on the foamstone rafts—long low buildings which, when he saw one yet to acquire a roof, seemed packed with complex and already moving machinery. Other machines worked between these huts, perfectly designed for laying foamstone blocks, or cutting and welding into place bubble-metal beams and plastic-laminate roof panels. Then amidst them, amidst that madness, Jem saw something to utterly confirm that Hell had arrived here at Godhead.

Skeletons walked amidst these new structures: the skeletons of men and women but coated with gleaming chrome. They were labouring to build the engines of damnation here on Masada. Only now, seeing this, did he truly comprehend that phrase "godless machines." It wasn't that the Polity denied the reality of God, rather, the Polity had accepted and welcomed to its steel heart the legions of Hell. When one of these skeletons turned to gaze at Jem with utterly Human eyes in its silver skull, that seemed more horrifying than either empty sockets or some satanic red gleam. He moved on as fast as he could manage, gasping, eyes blurred with tears.

How could this all be true? How could it possibly be true?

The road ramped up onto the thicker foamstone raft of the central town and, though Jem recognized covered walkways for what they were, and saw hints of old structures, most of the buildings here were new. He recognized so very little of this. What had happened here?

Avoiding one of the larger covered walkways, he turned into a narrower street, hoping to reach a walkway perhaps less used, and then find access to breathable air. Maybe inside somewhere he could find a breather mask and an oxygen supply, then perhaps he could head back here and steal one of those trucks. He didn't want to stay inside Godhead and find it turned into some Sodom and Gomorrah.

Twenty metres into this street he saw a man and a woman jogging towards him from ahead. He turned towards the entrance into an alley; someone there too, then another approaching from behind. He continued walking, moving over to the side of the street to avoid the two ahead, but they came straight towards him—it was him they were coming for.

"I'm guessing you've noticed some changes here, Proctor Tombs," said the man, halting before him.

"Who are . . .you?" Jem managed, studying him, noting the lack of a breather mask and the metal aug affixed to the side of his skull.

"My name's David Tinsch," the man replied. "But you don't know me. Me and my son were sent to work the ponds after someone just like you accused me of heretical speech, had me beaten and took away everything I owned. My son died of septicaemia when the scole attachment went wrong."

Jem wanted to say sorry, then cursed himself for the inclination.

Tinsch looked over to one side where the woman now squatted on the paving, some sort of control panel before her on fold-down legs.

"Where is it?" he asked.

"Coming this way, and fast," she replied.

Jem stared at her. She was wearing the negative of a proctors' uniform, demon script running from armpit to leg. He recognized the writing at once. How was it he recognized that, yet even at that moment could not visualize the writing of the Satagents? Was he being absorbed into Hell?

"How long?" asked Tinsch.

A resounding crash echoed from somewhere distant, seemingly back along the route Jem had traversed. He glanced round to see a pillar of lightning stabbing up into the sky above the buildings. A curved hardfield flashed into being up there, something black and nebulous briefly visible behind it, then both the shape and the field flashed out of existence, sending a wavefront of fire speeding overhead. He watched this pass out of sight, then lowered his gaze to the two men now approaching him from behind. Both wore the same negative uniforms as the woman.

"At this rate, five minutes at best," said the woman. Jem returned his attention to her, dizzy, a sickness in his stomach, but noting her fear as she continued, "It just took out the first hardfield."

"Best we get this done now," said one of those behind Jem.

Hands closed on both his arms. The two dragged him forward and threw him down on the ground, nose smacking agonizingly against the paving and lights flashing across his vision. Before he could recover they were on him, turning him over on his back and pinning him there. Tinsch, whose clothing was of a plainer cut than the others, strode forward and squatted over him, holding out between his finger and thumb an aug just like the one he wore. It was a metallic version of the *Gift*, Polity tech, and Jem realized they were about to take him into a brotherhood of a very different kind. In this final act they would recruit him to their legions.

"That necessary, David?" asked one of the black-clad men whilst drawing a big evil-looking dagger from the sheath at his hip. "This doesn't have to be complicated."

"When that thing gets through it might kill us all," said Tinsch.

"We know that," replied the other. He scraped the tip of his knife against a package affixed to the front of his belt—a series of antipersonnel mines. They all wore these, Jem realized. They each wore enough explosive to gut this entire street.

"But if we ream out his brain we've got a bargaining chip." Tinsch tapped a finger against the metal aug. "The AIs will want this, and it's directly linked to my aug—if I die then the small explosive inside it detonates."

"Small comfort to the rest of us," the knife wielder quipped.

Another crash, and another line of fire flaring across the sky.

"Second hardfield gone," the woman called. "For Christ's sake get it done!"

"Turn his head."

Jem fought just as hard as he could, but the arms holding him were like steel. Out of the corner of his eye he could see Tinsch lowering the aug to the side of his head. He could see the standard anchor ring there—designed to attach the aug to the bone behind the recipient's ear—but the thin needles already beginning to extrude from within that ring weren't standard at all.

A low thunk issued from one side, and Jem recognized it as the sound of a stun-stick connecting. The pressure came off him and the aug retracted slightly. Managing to turn his head a little he saw the woman sprawled across her console.

"Put it away," said a gravelly voice.

That big knife swept in towards his throat. Another impact of a different kind and the knife wielder yelled and spun aside, the handle of another knife protruding from his shoulder whilst his own blade clattered to the paving. Something cracked—a disc gun firing—and the other one pinning him sprawled away too. Jem grabbed up the fallen knife and scrabbled across the paving past the figure striding in. He should have felt some relief, some gratitude, but felt only a tugging, gnawing fear deep inside his head. He recognized the newcomer's voice, and that recognition lay deeply embedded in the darkness within his skull—threatened to tear it open.

"You fucking traitor!" Tinsch still clutched the aug in one hand, his other hand straying to the explosives on his belt.

"That's debatable," said the newcomer.

Reaching a wall, Jem heaved himself up and, gasping for breath, rested his shoulder against it. He held the knife out to fend off any new attack, but it seemed he had slid into irrelevance. The newcomer stood with his back to Jem. Short grey hair topped a wide-shouldered rangy physique clad in flute-grass fatigues. The disc gun the man held pointed unwaveringly at Tinsch's forehead. One of the other men lay on the ground, hands pressed to his stomach and blood leaking between his fingers. Jem's other attacker stood with one hand at the handle protruding from his shoulder, his other hand sliding down towards the explosive on his belt. Jem closed his eyes. They were all going to die now, but that was alright, just so long as the one with the gun did not turn, did not reveal his face.

After a pause the newcomer continued, "Did you really think you could do this? Did you hear your last two hardfields crash? Did you get another dramatic fireworks display?"

Jem opened his eyes. Tinsch and the two negative proctors all had hands at the explosives on their belts, the one with the stomach wound repeatedly, desperately, stabbing a bloody finger at some control. And all three explosives were simply failing to detonate.

"I get that you thought Miloh would delay it long enough for you to put up hardfields between." The grey-haired man shook his head sadly. "Good plan, but you have no idea what you're up against. It divided out there, sent one half of itself off to deal with Miloh, while the other half continued to shadow Tombs here. And it didn't even have to do that—Miloh was no real danger, nor are you."

"It's here?" said Tinsch, his hand finally dropping away from his suicide bomb.

"Been playing with you all along." The grey-haired man gestured to the woman sprawled beside her console. "It was turning off your hardfields from the inside, while its other half provided the fireworks display. But I've stopped the game, and just hope that's enough—that it'll let you walk away from here."

The gut-shot one was dying, Jem realized, his face deathly pale and blue under the eyes, his black clothing soaked with blood, the demon script stained red and a pool spreading all about him. An artery torn open. Where had Jem seen such a wound? Why did he know?

Grey-hair tilted his head for a moment. "Seems you get to live."

The knife wielder suddenly accelerated backwards and slammed into the far wall of the street. He shrieked, the knife in his shoulder sinking deeper, the handle disappearing inside him. Oddly no blood leaked from the wound, and then he was just hanging there, pinned by the shoulder, his feet kicking half a metre above the paving.

Tinsch next, his arm coming up against his own volition—he seemed to be fighting it, his hand moving round in a smooth arc whilst his body writhed and kicked. His hand slapped against the side of his skull, then dropped away. Now having acquired a second aug on the opposite side of his skull to the first, he abruptly went down on his knees.

"No . . . please," he said, then after a moment started crying.

The demons haunt their own, Jem realized. Hell offered no relief, no better treatment for its allies. He swung his gaze to the woman. She was sitting up, her console in her lap, eyes closed as if in meditation. Jem could not see her hands, for her wrists ended against the sides of the console, seemed to be connected to it.

The wounded man now. He stood upright in that pool of blood, and the pool seemed to be growing smaller, whilst colour returned to a face locked in a rictus of terror. As the last of the blood disappeared something seemed to happen down by his feet and he abruptly dropped, sinking up to his ankles in a paving slab. He looked down, terror transforming to a knowing horror, tried to move and went over on his back, his knees in the air.

"Nooo!" Tinsch wailed. "Please, I'm sorry . . ."

"You get to live," said Grey-hair. "To live."

He turned to look at Jem, features utterly clear now behind a practically invisible visor: a hard face, dull green eyes, a scar across the back of his cheek leading to where part of his earlobe had been severed. Utter and complete recognition now. Here stood *the soldier.* Jem got to his feet and ran without a further thought. The constant background mutter turned to a growling, like some engine starting up. Horrific painful memories clamoured in the vaults of his mind and he abruptly realized the truth.

It was all lies.

Everything he had seen had been twisted out of shape, for wasn't the one trying to destroy his faith the Prince of Lies? From the moment Sanders affixed this demonic prosthesis over his skull, it had been feeding him its bile, its fiction, its madness routed straight out of Hell. It had overlaid his world with false visions of the aftermath of a successful rebellion and Polity intervention here.

He had to remove it.

The Tagreb sat amidst the flute grasses like an iron lily opened on the surface of a weed-choked pond. Here it served as a base from which its AI and its staff could make a taxonomic and genetic assay of the fauna and flora of Masada, create a database, then from that make the planetary almanac. After this was done, the base was supposed to remain as a permanent fixture for the use of the planetary residents, as specialized researchers completed their work and moved on to the next world, the next Tagreb landing. However, the specialists here were becoming a bit of a permanent fixture, the life of Masada having the fascination of a monorail crash.

Chanter approached the place from underneath, studying with interest the seismic images presented on his screen. He could see the various pipes terminating in extraction heads the Tagreb had injected into the ground to suck up water for internal supply, for the fusion reactor and to crack for oxygen. These, Chanter understood, were often pulled back up when too many tricones gathered, only to be injected elsewhere. There were also sensor heads down there, and the flat, scan-proof interfaces of hardfields, between which extended cattle prods to keep tricones at bay.

Some time after the Tagreb established itself on the surface, its AI decided that mobility might be a good idea here, so constructed bubble-metal treads for it to run on. Beneath the defensive perimeter fence lay a four-metre-wide foamstone raft, below which tricones gathered like barnacles. Four huge spokes attached the whole engirdling raft to the Tagreb itself and so propelled it along with the base. The research Tagreb seemed a living organism, perpetually shifting its underparts to prevent them being bitten, slowly shifting itself across the surface. A starfish maybe, or a sea urchin—that last being something Chanter did not want to think about too much as this particular creature's mind finally got in contact.

"I wondered when you would be paying us a visit here." The Tagreb AI, Rodol, spoke from his communicator. "Leonardo Da Vinci invented machines, explored the structure of the Human body and other structures besides, and he painted and drew with great skill. But he was from a time when the false division between art and science had yet to be firmly established."

AIs talked to each other, Chanter knew. They talked to each other a lot.

"Why do you claim the division is false?" he asked, at a loss for any other words.

"Art is just another way to describe and classify reality—its mystical aspects merely a function of ignorance."

"Yeah, whatever," said Chanter, already finding himself disliking this particular intelligence. "I'm here to see Jonas Clyde and Shardelle Garadon."

"Shardelle is unavailable, since she is presently working with the haiman Kroval Liepsig on Earth studying the deliberate disconnection from coherence and derision factor of the gabble. Jonas Clyde, however, is here but presently deliberately disconnected from coherence himself. I'll check if he is prepared to see you."

"Where do I go?" Chanter asked.

"Surface your mudmarine beside ATV Ramp Three—it is behind my direction of travel so your vessel should remain within the perimeter fence for four days," Rodol replied, a schematic of the Tagreb appearing on Chanter's screen with Ramp Three indicated. "If your stay is going to be longer, then link your system to me and I'll keep your vessel beside the ramp continuously." Now a linking icon appeared.

Chanter did not want to link up because he did not expect to be here for long, and to do so would also breach his security; however, if Rodol wanted to take control of his mudmarine, there wasn't really much he could do about it. He reached out and touched the icon, giving his permission, then motored directly to the ramp he had been directed to.

Once again stepping out onto the surface of this world, Chanter studied his surroundings. The ramp extended from an all-terrain vehicle garage, but one ATV stood out here too, its big fat wheels turning with incremental slowness as it kept pace with the Tagreb. The base itself sprawled across the ceramal petals it had folded down when it landed, after having first been ejected from the research spaceship the *Beagle Infinity*. Now cluttered with numerous additional buildings—storehouses for organic samples, additional laboratories and accommodation areas—it looked less like the single complete and sparse structure it had been. Here lay a small circular town, perpetually on the move. He climbed the ramp, walked in past two ATVs, one of which gleamed like new, the other being washed free of mud by a hose-trailing robot like an upright iron cricket on wheels. A third ATV lay beyond these two. It looked like someone had fed it between the rollers of a massive mangle.

"The ostensible reason for her departure," said the voice of Rodol, issuing from nearby.

"What? Who?"

"Shardelle Garadon felt there was still more to learn about the gabble by direct study. She wanted to find another old gabbleduck who was close to death, since she believed that in that state part of its real underlying mind might show through," Rodol explained. "She found her creature and kept track of it, whereupon it abruptly changed course and headed at great speed up into the Northern Mountains, to a place called the Plate—a circular plateau—where it turned back to her ATV and sat on it. You see the result."

"So nearly dying destroyed her spirit of scientific inquiry?" Chanter asked, unable to keep the sarcastic tone out of his voice.

"No, she thought the gabbleduck's actions, in leading her to where its attack on her ATV would have more effect than just pushing it down into the mud—an indication of hidden intelligence revealing itself," said Rodol. "The real reason for her departure was so she could work closely with Kroval—she gave her near-death experience as an excuse to disconnect completely from communication and so avoid the massive amounts of incoming data from the sudden proliferation of would-be gabble experts springing up all over the Polity."

Chanter snorted as he stepped through the door at the back of the garage, pressure differential impinging, the oxygenated air almost aseptic. He now stood in a room racked with various survival suits and lined with glass-fronted cases containing discrete Polity breather gear. One of the suits, until then utterly still, stirred into motion and he realized it was occupied. The individual inside glanced at him with reptilian eyes, a glint of frost slowly clearing from the visor below them. An adapt like himself, wearing a suit to keep her cool on a world too hot for her. She headed through the door into the garage. He turned and eyed the two doors exiting from this place.

"Where do I go?" he asked.

"Jonas has taken some aldetox, and when he has also finished his triple espresso he will see you in the museum," Rodol replied. "Take the door to your right and follow the directions now entered in your palmtop."

Through the door, palmtop out and direction arrow clear, Chanter stomped down corridors clean and white, feeling a childish satisfaction that he was still leaving muddy footprints behind him. By the time he reached the museum his webbed feet were dry and his skin felt decidedly papery, but the sight that met him when he stepped through double sliding doors dismissed the discomfort from his mind.

The dead hooder extended along the length of a hundred-metre wall—the spinal column of a giant. Of course he had seen all this before, but it was the spoonlike hood, turned so its underside faced out, that drew his attention. He'd seen hooder remains, and he'd seen anatomical schematics, flatscreen and holographic, but to actually stand beside something like this and gaze at what was the last thing some people had seen before the darkness closed over them and the agony began, held a horrifying fascination.

Down either side of a ridge that ran on the underside of the hood were rows of eyes like glassy beads. At both ends of the ridge jointed limbs were folded, these terminating in curved spatulas, small spikes extending from their bases along their inner faces. To either side of the ridge lay rows of glassy tubes, some flat, some turned in and some folded out, these last showing telescopic sections, all toothed. Next out were rows of glassy scythes, some shedding their inner faces to expose sharper material, much in the way a cat sheds its claws. Outside these lay tangled organics like the insides of some animal, looking soft at first then hardening down into the rim of the hood. Here and there protruded black tentacles, some terminating in pincers, others in things that looked oddly like paint brushes.

Chanter stepped closer, eyed a column-mounted scan scope—a device that could scan any of the EM spectrum, and at any focus from nanoscopic upwards—then abruptly stepped back when the eyes lit with a red inner glow and all that surgical cutlery began to move like the workings of an ancient mechanical printer running a diagnostic.

"The red glow isn't the real thing," said a voice behind him.

He turned to see Jonas Clyde standing there. The man wore slippers, knee-length trousers and sleeveless shirt, and he clutched a coffee beaker in his right hand. His blond hair was cropped, eyes electric green and skin bearing a tan that didn't come from Masada. Though he looked athletic, there was a distinct unsteadiness to him now—the aldetox had yet to purge from his body the effects of whatever he had been drinking.

"I'm hoping none of this is real." Chanter gestured to movement within the hood.

"All synthetic muscle and electro-nerves," Clyde explained. "This exhibit was sprawn-infested and long into decay when it was discovered."

"So what causes the glow?" asked Chanter. "What makes their eyes glow when they're alive?"

"The same luminescent amoebae you find on some of this world's beaches. It's not mutualistic, symbiotic or parasitic really—just a foible of the designers."

"The gabbleducks," said Chanter. "The Atheter."

Clyde nodded like someone whose head might not be firmly attached. "Glad you're here, Chanter—I've been wanting to talk to you for some time."

"And I you."

"Though not for so long."

"No."

They stood staring at each other, and to Chanter it felt almost as if he had finally come face to face with some old enemy. He could find no real reason for the feeling, it just existed.

"So what's brought you here?"

"I've read your studies, your reports and your précis for the almanac, but I'm here to find out what else you've learnt. You've said nothing about the Technician, yet one would think that creature would hold as much fascination for you as it does for me."

Clyde winced, walked over to lean against the scan scope. After a moment he tossed his cup down on the floor and just watched as a beetlebot scuttled out of its alcove and snatched the cup up, polished away the spill of coffee then shot out of sight again.

"The thing you learn, being a Tagreb researcher, is that half the time you're looking into things that have already been studied by minds far in advance of your own." He turned to look at Chanter. "We're not researchers, Chanter, but research tools. They withhold stuff, they sometimes give us false information or information with a particular emphasis or slant. All this is to direct their tools, us, to a particular point, to elucidate it, to expose some new angle. It's quite depressing."

"But the Technician?"

"All I knew was that it was an interesting legend among the people here," said Clyde. "Not really my territory but that of the social anthropologists. I was preparing to leave this world, having mapped both the hooder genome and its physiology, having ascertained that it's really an organic machine, an artificial creation."

"But learning that the Technician is a reality kept you here?"

"No, not really—I learnt about it a little while after I was going to leave." Clyde now gestured to the other side of the long room. Here stood a row of exhibit cases, but they were all empty. "So, Chanter, don't you think it's about time you allowed others to study your collection of sculptures?"

That threw Chanter. They were his sculptures—how dare this man make such a demand? Then he felt a moment of chagrin. The art of the Technician should be on display for all. How could he allow his own selfish greed to keep this work from the world?

"I suppose," he said reluctantly.

"Fair exchange," said Clyde. "You bring your collection here where, frankly, it would be much safer, and you get to use the specialist pattern- and shape-analysing programs Rodol designed, which, as we both know, is your real reason for being here."

AIs talked to other people a lot too.

"Very well," said Chanter then, after a pause, "but tell me what kept you here, if you didn't know about the Technician."

Clyde shrugged. "It was a toss-up between me and Shardelle. We were given a non-negotiable instruction that one of us had to remain here. Shardelle won the coin toss."

"Who instructed you?"

"An arachnid associate of yours."

"Amistad?"

Clyde nodded.

"Why?"

"Apparently one Jeremiah Tombs needs to speak to us, when he's ready." Clyde pushed himself away from the scan scope, the aldetox obviously having fully kicked in now. "Seems he'll be ready sometime soon."

Information, once out of safe storage, was like something Pandora might recognize. Usually, when a supposed secret escaped out into the public domain, it was because the AIs were using the time-honoured technique of aptly timing leaks. However, it seemed to Shree that the news of Jeremiah Tombs's escape had leaked too early. What purpose could be served by alerting Overlanders, the Tidy Squad and Theocracy haters everywhere that the erstwhile proctor had become a viable target? Unless, of course, this was all about entrapment.

Tidy Squad members had been apprehended whilst attempting to kill Tombs, but then the likes of Miloh were all too obvious in their hate, and had probably been closely watched by the Polity anyway. No, the entrapment had been aimed at ex-rebels who apparently bought into the regime, were generous in their forgiveness and did not openly reveal their hate, like Tinsch, who it seemed might have been captured, and like her.

Perhaps the AIs had unearthed something about the alliances she had been making with offworld Separatists and understood Tombs's importance in that respect. Perhaps they understood that Tombs was precisely the one they needed to draw out the Squad Leader. It seemed likely he was bait in a trap but, unfortunately, he was bait she could not ignore.

"Uffstetten here," said the face appearing in her visual field—fed directly to her optic nerves from her aug.

Uffstetten, a pale, thin-faced and bald man, possessed double-pupil eyes, twinned augs and internal visual interlinks. His ears had been replaced with squat cylindrical multidrums and he was also processing direct mental feeds. She knew that his screen image must be partially adjusted, for he appeared to be talking to her only, whilst in reality he was conducting numerous conversations, reading numerous texts and studying numerous images. He was a haiman, his augmentations perfectly designed for his job as Earthnet News Editor.

Shree allowed her own face to appear to him, doubtless as one icon of many on some mental screen, just a little explanatory text appearing when he focused his attention on it. "Ah, Shree Enkara—our local Masada correspondent," he said after a thirty-second delay. "What do you have for me?"

"Jeremiah Tombs," she stated.

A beat, then, "I have four correspondents as close as I can get them—there's an AI intervention on this. So what's your angle?"

"Tombs is being protected by Leif Grant, Commander Leif Grant, who was my commander during the rebellion, in fact my lover during the rebellion. I think, because of that, I can get close enough for direct recording and interaction."

"Human interest?"

"Not just Human interest," said Shree. "We're all aware that there's something odd about the situation. Why has Tombs been allowed to remain insane for twenty years? It all relates to how he received his injuries during the rebellion—the hooder called the Technician. This also has planetary status implications in that it very likely relates to the Atheter."

"You make the approach and I'll back you from here." Uffstetten also did something else, for a new icon appeared in her visual field. Checking it she found a funding link through her aug to her bank account here on Masada. Not that she needed the money, but it all added to her veracity. "If you're blocked, then the usual fee structure applies for something on the whole situation with your personal connection. Agreed?"

"If I'm not blocked?"

"Full coverage of your expenses plus eighty New Carth shillings an hour, doubled if the hour is aired."

"Make that one hundred shillings and we have a deal."

After a short pause Uffstetten said, "We have a deal," and his image blinked out.

Shree sighed out a long breath. Those kinds of pay rates might be enough to tempt someone away from the fight for freedom, but not her. She would take their money and send it where it would be of use. And she would complete her mission, which meant she might not be able to spend it herself anyway.

Shree reached out and picked up her glass, sipped contemplatively whilst attempting to aug back in to the various cams she had positioned about Greenport. She had watched Miloh and Tinsch make their preparations, then seen Miloh fail before her cams at both locations went offline. Still nothing. Something had got to them fast, punching through Tinsch's quite plausible approach of blocking Tombs's minders by using hardfields. Certainly Commander Grant was the visible protection of Tombs, but he had powerful invisible protection in the vicinity too.

Shree now tried a direct communication, mentally dialling up the address of Tinsch's aug. For a moment nothing, then connection.

"I'm *sorry, I'm sorry, I'm sorry,*" Tinsch whispered to her, before his communication drifted into a distant sobbing. She cut the link quickly, and just sat there with cold fingers tracing her spine.

Then, suddenly, a cam view called to her attention by a recognition program: Tombs stumbling out towards the site of the old worker huts, the place now used as a spaceport. Coincidentally, she also received a general notification of an imminent landing at the spaceport—something big was coming down. Shree stood up and headed for the door.

Grant gazed in morbid fascination at what had been done to the four here. Conscious again, the woman stared in horror at the console that had now become an extension of her wrists. The Overlander man who had been bleeding his life out only minutes ago was tugging at his ankles. Someone would have to lever out the slab and carry him like a living statue on a plinth to the hospital. The knifeman would be going to the same place with a chunk of wall attached to his back. And Christ knows what that *thing* had done to David Tinsch: the man was still crying and begging for forgiveness. And it had been so terrifyingly fast.

When Amistad had told Grant that this Penny Royal, an apparently reformed black AI, would be watching over Tombs, he had done a little research. Penny Royal had haunted the Graveyard, that wasteland of worlds lying along the border between the Polity and the Prador Kingdom. It had done things there for which there should never be forgiveness, using its capability of separating a Human into whatever size of living component it chose, and then putting that human back together in whatever order it chose, to horrifying effect—the result often being something that simply could not be described as Human.

"Why?" he asked the air, but no reply was forthcoming.

He sensed now that it had gone, shadowing that yelling madman now rounding the end of the street and heading off towards the side exit from Greenport central town.

Grant sprinted off after Tombs. His own role in all this had been carefully directed, supposedly, yet it all seemed like the kind of horrible game Penny Royal had played during its time in the Graveyard. What possible purpose could be served by what it had done to those four back there?

Tombs came back into sight, now heading through the exit, straight out towards what had once been the main worker compound, its rafts now serving as a landing field. Grant slowed to a jog, trying to catch sight of Penny Royal, but seeing nothing. He had only caught glimpses of it before, so had no real idea about its actual form, those glimpses hinting to him that he might not want to know. It had communicated, but the brevity of those communications rendered them almost nonsensical and he'd had to contact Amistad for translation. Amistad laid out the whole drama to be acted out here, but failed to explain what Penny Royal meant by "cerebral pressure juncture," "Gleason limit" and "green-stick point upon acting out." Tombs was being pushed towards sanity and full recovery of his memory, pressure being loaded upon him, but to Grant it seemed that the man was just getting crazier.

As Grant exited Central Town, a shadow slid across the ground towards him, covered him for a moment then slid away again. He glanced up in time to see a spaceship in a U-shape formation, ports dotting its surface like mica crystals in rock, numerous sensor arrays, signal drums and other instruments protruding from its surface like components on an ancient circuit board. The thing was massive: it would encompass the entire landing field, and as far as Grant knew, nothing so large had ever landed here before. The field had been used by occasional private traders, most of the big Polity stuff coming down on the rebuilt landing field up by Zealos. The timing of this vessel's arrival was almost certainly no coincidence.

Continuing out, Grant noted that Tombs had halted in the middle of the landing field to gaze up at the descending ship. The man fell to his knees—something of a habit of his. Grant picked up his pace, realizing that he needed to get out near Tombs if he didn't want to find himself underneath a few million tonnes of curving hull. Strange forces seemed to be tugging at his body, and dry flute-grass stems swirled through the air to create a wailing symphony. The ship's antigravity also seemed to be interfering with Penny Royal's chameleonware and something formed of sharp honed shadows poised like a wave ready to fall on Tombs.

"Lies!" the proctor bellowed. "All lies!"

He now held up the dagger he had grabbed, as if hoping to stab the descending spaceship out of the sky. But still it descended.

When twenty metres away from the erstwhile proctor, Grant slowed his pace, aware now that he was within the compass of the ship, and that beside himself, Tombs and the black AI, someone else had come out here. He drew his disc gun and held it down at his side as the woman approached, something recognizable about her flowing walk.

"Lies!" Tombs shrieked, as finally the ship's lower hull made contact with the ground. The thing touched light as a feather, but when its gravmotors shut down the interlinked foamstone rafts all sank abruptly, half a metre of rhizome-tangled mud thumping up between them like the walls of a maze.

Numerous ramps now folded down, first spilling holocams like silver bubbles into the Masadan air. Next came the people, and what people they were. It seemed the full, weird mind-numbing diversity of the Polity had arrived at this one spot. There were adapts: catadapts, amphidapts, ophidapts, saurodapts, avidapts—human chimera in forms limited only by imagination. Golem walked here too, some in the shape of adapts, some like normal Humans, some skinless chrome skeletons and some metalskins in brass aping a legendary figure. Other robots of all kinds strode amidst this crowd, pets and auto-luggage yapped around ankles, tails, claws and elephantine feet. Coldworlders and hotworlders wore strange esoteric suits. Many wore masks, many did not, still others occupied aquaria striding along on iron spider legs.

"Lies," Tombs whispered.

Grant, now standing just a couple of paces away from the man, could hear him, despite the nearby uproar.

"Reality is a heavy load to bear sometimes," said a voice.

He glanced round. "Shree Enkara," he said, puzzled to see her here now.

She wasn't looking at him but gazing at Tombs, her eyes widening in surprise, then her expression twisting with horrified fascination. Grant whirled back and just for a moment could not believe the scene before him. Tombs had pinched out a handful of his own cheek, had cut down behind his ear to his jaw bone and, making a horrible keening sound, began sawing the blade forwards.

Grant hurled himself towards the man but it was as if he had thrown himself at a jagged rock face. As he bounced he momentarily glimpsed black spines and a single stalked red eye, before he hit the ground heavily on his back. Tombs continued to cut, that keening becoming a shrieking which turned wet and bubbly as he exposed his back teeth to the air. Things then went slightly hazy for a moment and Grant found his head resting in a warm lap.

"They can't see or hear us," said Shree.

It was true, the crowd departing the spaceship were just moving past as if he, Shree, Penny Royal and the screaming bloody thing that was Tombs occupied some blister in reality. Grant wished for that haziness again—some small escape into unconsciousness—but it never came, and he saw the whole horrifying thing to its conclusion: Tombs returned almost to the state in which Grant had first found him, but kneeling with knife in one hand and his sacrifice to his god in the other.

9

When resurrection and actual corporeal immortality are real facts of life, the threats and promises of old-style organized religions become laughable. When education is taken out of the hands of the doctrinaires, religion is castrated at source. With knowledge and experience able to bypass the senses and be loaded directly to the Human mind, the standard level of Human intelligence rises, and religion wilts under its inspection, for religion thrives on ignorance. But when religion crawls away from the light of reasoned inspection it sheds its damaged skin and returns with something thicker and more durable. When science explains the universe, and gets everything right, century after century, one would think that religion should turn into the quaint pursuit of the intentionally deluded, or be a matter for historians. However, the virus that is religion is a difficult one to kill. Over the years it has mutated and adapted to changes in its environment. It turns holy writ into allegory, turns true stories into parables, styles angels as metaphors, admits to embarrassment at demons. It tries to downplay its gods and concentrate on the good it perceives in itself, like the comfort it offers to the faithful, for surely comfort can be found in the knowledge that if you infringe on arbitrary rules written down thousands of years ago you will burn in hell for ever.

—*From* HOW IT IS *by Gordon*

"Since its arrival here its mass has increased by about half," said Janice Golden. "But still there's no clear indication of what its purpose is, where it comes from, or who built it."

The bridge of *Cheops* had the decor of an Egyptian tomb, and Janice had departed her sarcophagus to sit herself in a perfect historical reproduction of the throne of Rameses II, or rather what some deeply anal historian had decided it might look like. However, her connection to the ship AI remained firm, optics trailing from her bodysuit like a mummy's unravelled bandages to the sarcophagus.

Her visitor surveyed his surroundings then strolled over to the scroll-edged stool positioned before the throne and sat down. She studied him like an aged parent inspecting a grandchild. In a way he was her descendant, or perhaps a better definition was that he was the next stage, the next evolution of what she had done to herself.

Janice was interfaced with the AI of this ship—as close a connection to an artificial intelligence as had been feasible a century ago. Optic links transferred data between her and Cheops, but only at a speed her augmented mind could handle, because anything more would cause a feedback effect, a brief synergistic loop which for a few seconds would create a supernal melding of AI and Human, but afterwards would leave her a burnt-out husk and Cheops a crystal-minded lunatic.

This man before her was a haiman. The crystal disc with its steel scallop-shell hub on the left-hand side of his skull contained the artificial intelligence he interfaced with. Such AIs were usually at the lower limits of the Turing band—argued by some to be outside present definitions of AI—whilst his own heavily augmented brain, with its cooling grids, its massive amount of implants spilling from the right-hand side of his skull into a half-face augmentation, its bio-electronics, and the whole array of physical supports from his also heavily augmented body, stood at the upper limits of Human function—argued by some to be outside any realistic definition of Humanity. Here, in this being, the gap between AI and Human had been narrowed but, as yet, not closed.

"I would question your choice of the words 'since its arrival here'," said the haiman Drode. "Having studied your original data recordings before you ran, I see it quite likely this object was concealed in an adjacent U-space fold within the Wizender system."

"Position is a rather debatable feast when talking about U-space," said Janice, not liking his hectoring tone.

"As you are aware," Drode said, "the least energy an object in U-space uses to surface into the real brings it out in its *adjacent* position there." He waved a dismissive hand. "This is all semantics."

Janice blinked, glanced over to her viewing wall, now showing Egyptian tomb paintings, dismissed them and replaced them with a view from her probe nearest the object. Now they looked upon a spectacular view of this thing, still poised over the gas giant but no longer sucking up gas. Below it the surface of that Jovian world still roiled with the storms the thing had caused. They were beautiful, the world striated with all the finely aged colours of the paintings previously occupying the viewing wall. She grimaced to herself and decided not to point out that it wasn't his criticism of her wording about position in U-space that had annoyed her, but his offhand comment about her running.

It seems that to attain a higher form of Humanity it was necessary to sacrifice tact, Cheops commented, directly into her mind.

No, she replied, *I think all aspects of Humanity were upraised here, so if he was an arsehole before they started screwing metal into his head, that means he's an even bigger arsehole now.*

"So why are you here?" she asked.

He'd requested a face-to-face talk, docked and boarded when she agreed, and first asked about the current state of the mechanism out there. She couldn't understand why. Since she'd been instructed to come back here and watch over the thing she'd sent regular reports, and the instrumentation aboard his own vessel should have been quite sufficient to give him an answer to that question.

"I'm here to make an assessment of all available data and report back," the haiman replied.

Ah, commented Cheops, *a specialist . . .*

"I still don't understand why we don't have more of a presence here," said Janice. "Surely this thing warrants at least a couple of the newer dreadnoughts and a science vessel?"

"Calculated risks. The object showed no reaction to *Cheops*, which was why you got sent back. Bringing in anything bigger or making more aggressive studies of it might result in precisely the kind of reaction we want to avoid."

It's big, it might be dangerous, keep watch on it but leave it alone, Cheops interpreted.

From her throne Janice peered through a hull-mounted camera at the haiman's docked vessel. It was one of the new attack ships, a lethal-looking squid of a vessel which she knew possessed the kind of firepower that ought to worry even Cheops. Beneath notice? She thought not.

"So tell me," Drode continued, "in your own words, precisely what you have discovered."

All her data were available, but she understood he wanted more than that. He wanted the opinion of the watcher on site, wanted to make his special assessment, to process data in ways that might yield unforeseen results. Usual AI technique—you throw diverse minds at the weird ones. She sighed, thought for a moment about all that data, then said, "The tip of the iceberg." She paused. No, that wasn't right. "No, the body, the head of an octopus sticking its head above water, its tentacles all splayed out with their tips peeking out of the same surface some distance from it."

"Yes," he said, "it retains U-com to other transceivers scattered across a realspace region estimated at over a thousand light years across." He paused. "I am, however, interested to know more about your octopus analogy. You see whatever lies at those other locations as the tips of octopus tentacles—as something less than the object here."

"Perhaps a bad analogy." Janice tried to see her way through it. "My feeling is that this thing is the centre, and that those other transceivers are part of it, part of a network of sensors or perhaps other devices spread out from it."

"It does, however, lie on the edge of the region it covers, not at the centre."

"Metaphorical centre."

"The other objects could be exactly the same as it," he suggested.

"No way—that region you mention extends into Polity space and a large collection of things of the same mass as the thing here, no matter how widely dispersed, would have been picked up." She hesitated for a second. "Have they been detected? Did the big-fuck AIs know all about this thing before it appeared?"

"No, they did not." He smiled, a twist of the mouth only, nothing reaching eyes containing a scaly metallic glitter. "Their assessment of it is much the same as your own: this object sits at the centre of a sensor net, those sensors occupying U-space interfaces." He stopped there. Janice was sure he had been about to add more. "What do you think its purpose is?" he finally asked.

"Some kind of alien defence system, maybe left over by one of the dead races?" she suggested.

"Employing what manner of weaponry?"

She shrugged, sending a ripple down her optics to her sarcophagus. "Could be anything. It can suck up and remodel matter in just about any form as far as I can see, and it can—" She stopped dead, making a sudden intuitive leap. "You've found one of the sensors haven't you?"

He bowed his head in acknowledgement. "It is being studied, passively, as we speak."

"What can you tell me about it?"

"It scans, across the EM band, all material objects within its vicinity. However, passive analysis of its scanning format reveals that it is tuned to recognize precise bio-electrical patterns."

"Searching for some long-dead aggressor?"

"Perhaps—it certainly shows no great interest in Polity activity within its scanning area."

"What else?"

"It draws energy from the realspace U-space interface."

"Then it's also an anchor."

He blinked, paused for internal calculations.

"Yes, it seems so."

She gestured to the screen wall. "Probably an efficient way of drawing this thing to its location should it find that old aggressor, or perhaps so it can more easily send something. With an anchor the thing out there could penetrate some levels of U-space disruption."

Again that slight bow of the head.

"So we have some possible answers," she said, "but not the main one we want."

"Which is?"

"Why the hell has it surfaced here, and now?"

"Which is precisely the question I was going to ask you."

"It found something—it's preparing to act." She studied him intently but could read little from his expression. "Where is this sensor you found?"

"In the Graveyard."

"So maybe the Prador?"

"No—they've been in the region for centuries."

"Then what?"

"We don't know."

Why do I get the feeling, interjected Cheops, *that shit and fan are moving into conjunction, and that we might be in the way?*

Probably because they are and we are, she replied.

"I have to question why the Polity isn't taking this thing a little more seriously," she said to the haiman. "Is that a question you can answer?"

I think our answer is just arriving, said Cheops.

Janice felt the disruption through her connection with the ship AI, like something dragging at her skin, or a wrongness, a distortion seen through some extra eye she had not possessed until then. The dreadnought that surfaced into the real was instantly recognizable: a thing like a giant bracket fungus made of steel, snapped from some titanic world-tree. They called it *scold*—an understated light-hearted label for something very dangerous. It seemed the Polity had decided to take that thing out there very seriously indeed.

Jem opened his eyes to a bright comfortable place, and a feeling of utter disjointed confusion. He remembered the agony, and so much more: the demon falling upon him like a wave of writhing sharp-edged blackness, snatching away his knife then sliding the bloody mess from his other hand, inserting wormish tentacles into the ruin where his face had been. The demon took away the agony in gradual stages, knitting ruination back together in a way that exactly mirrored what had been done to him two decades ago, that mirror opening his mind to clear slaughterhouse memories of the Technician, that time preceding it and much that came after. He remembered seeming to float in the demon's swirl of darkness, up the Polity ship's ramp, through internal spaces more like city parks than any ship he had known, finally to this place, this garden.

But though memories now lay clear in his mind, he felt utterly disconnected from a reality seemingly wholly distorted. Gazing at the two nearby he recognized them from outside the ship, yet some deeper part of him could not quite integrate them. They were such an odd shape: small, simply jointed limbs, flat-faced and just two eyes—almost like something put together by a child.

"Earthnet," said one of them. "You're working for Earthnet?"

The words possessed a strange clarity and in a second he realized why. The muttering was gone, that constant sound, as of a discussion being conducted one room away, had disappeared. The man's voice also brought him into focus for Jem: Leif Grant, commander of the eastern forces of the rebellion, the first Human face he had seen this side of the Technician's punishment and that flow of Euclidean shapes. He hadn't remembered the man at the time, but now recollected that Grant had been on the Theocracy hit list for some time. The woman he didn't recognize. Perhaps she was one of the crew of this Polity spaceship—certainly she looked far too *Human* to be one of the passengers.

"I'd perfectly understand if you told me to go away right now, Leif," she said. "But since I was allowed to send a recording of what happened out there, the story just became huge and, really, someone has to report it. If I provide that story, Earthnet will be able to farm out portions of it to some of the other Net News services, and that way you won't be bothered by other reporters."

Grant gazed at her steadily. "Reporters ain't no bother unless they're allowed to be. I just don't get why it let you through."

He gestured off to one side at something black and sharp-edged in this colourful paradise. Jem concentrated his attention on this thing, but wasn't quite sure what to make of the form the demon had taken now. It had reduced itself to a flattened ovoid, hard angles, glinting protrusions, gutlike metallic and glassy folds—almost like a metal brain with crystals of obsidian in the process of breaking out from inside it. Yet, this strange thing seemed almost more *logical* than the two Humans. Movement off to the side of it swung his attention that way.

Jem gazed in puzzlement at the sight that met his eyes, simply failing to understand it, feeling a niggling terror of the thing. Then, abruptly, he realized what he was seeing. Datura, a datura tree—he'd seen them in his Bishop's garden. But it wasn't movement of the long trumpet-like pink blossoms that attracted his attention, but the zipping flight of the electric-blue humming bird feeding on their nectar. Utterly fascinated he watched it proceed from bloom to bloom, as if seeing something for the first time he knew he had seen before.

"Hasn't it told you?"

The two were at one of a scattering of tables in the enclosed garden, close to Jem and sitting higher, a bottle and two glasses on the tabletop between them. He lay on some sort of lounger. This place in fact rather resembled a Bishop's garden with its collection of exotic plants and comfortable furniture, though he couldn't see any walls and the ceiling looked like a blue sky with a yellowish sun burning in it—a sky some deep part of him recognized, though he had never gazed upon one like it.

"As you can see, Penny Royal's shut down," said Grant. "It don't like to be aboard this ship—don't want the mind here takin' a close look."

The woman now turned towards Jem, who quickly closed his eyes and pretended to still be asleep, which was an easy pretence when lying in such ridiculously luxurious comfort.

"So what the hell happened back there?" she asked.

Hell indeed, thought Jem. He had tried to cut off his own face. Yes, his own face—the prosthetic had been removed long ago and, using Polity technology, Sanders had regrown his own flesh.

Jem's stomach tightened with deep gnawing guilt, and suddenly he no longer felt comfortable, no longer felt either disconnected or confused. He clearly saw Sanders lying in a pool of her own blood. He had cut the throat of the woman who had looked after him for so long, and her being on the side of the enemy did nothing to assuage his guilt. Even his madness seemed no excuse and the suffering he had self-inflicted no recompense. So intense was the feeling he felt the heaviness of tears behind his face, his repaired face. But to cry seemed like self-indulgence, self-pity and childish denial of his responsibility. He tried to step back from it; to be more analytical and rediscover that earlier disconnect, but it just wouldn't come.

"Call it . . . catharsis," said Grant.

"You've got to be kidding."

"What do you know about him?"

"He was a proctor who survived an attack by the Technician, which was why you saved his life. What happened to him drove him off the other side of weird and he's spent the last twenty years believing the Theocracy still exists. It also seems likely that Polity mindtechs have been let nowhere near him because, just maybe, the Technician did something to his mind."

"You've got it about right," said Grant.

"Do I have your permission to send this to Earthnet?"

"You're recording now?"

"I'm always recording—got a link straight to my visual cortex perpetually downloading into terabyte storage."

"You need permission?"

"Not really—everything is vetted by the news service AIs."

"In what way?"

"For distortion of the truth by reporting methods, reporter narrative and subsequent cutting and pasting. I'm just asking you personally."

"Then you can send, but only if it's vetted by Amistad first."

"Amistad?"

"Ask Ergatis."

Jem opened one eye slightly to see her tilting her head, her expression slightly unfocused. He realized she must be communicating through her aug, just as that communication ceased and she returned her attention to the soldier.

"I'm informed that Amistad is unconcerned about what I send to Earthnet, but that whether I can accompany you and continue reporting is up to you," she said.

He tapped a finger against a comunit in his ear. "That's what I've been told too."

"And your answer?"

"How important is this to you, Shree?"

She slid one of the glasses across the surface of the table as if moving a piece in some board game. "You know how it is—you dedicate your life to the rebellion, to fighting the Theocracy, and when the fight is won that leaves a great hole inside you. Some of us can never recover from that—the likes of the Overlanders and the Tidy Squad are an extreme example in the way they cling to the past." She moved her glass again, checkmate. "As a sometime Earthnet correspondent over the last twenty years I've found a way to fill that hole, but there have been so many strictures on what I can report and so much I've looked into that Earthnet simply dumped that it's been difficult." She looked up at him. "This, really, is my big break."

"Okay, I understand," he replied. "But I want a say in what you report. It can't be realtime—you'll send at the end of each day when I get the power of veto on what you send."

"That's standard when reporting like this. Your power of veto begins with you being able to just walk away from me," she said, then smiled, reached out to take hold of his chin and planted a kiss on his lips.

The two were revisiting some previous relationship, Jem realized. Remembering Sanders's attempts to manipulate him—her sometimes crude efforts to get a reaction out of him—Jem felt he knew the reality here. The man was a Human male being twisted by the wiles of a female, deliberately ignoring her equivocation because his own instinctive imperatives had some other goal in mind. For a moment Jem complimented himself: obviously his Theocracy training, and his faith, made him more able to see through such subterfuge. Then doubt trammelled that away, because he had no memory of ever thinking so analytically before. Abruptly uncomfortable with the workings of his own mind, he sat upright and let the outside world back in.

"So you're back with us," said Grant.

Jem stared at the two of them for a long moment and quailed inside. They had no welcome in their expressions, they weren't glad he had recovered his mind for his own sake, but because it served a purpose of their own. That made him sad and, though he tried to ignore the feeling, he wanted their acceptance of him.

"I am back and I am remembering," he replied, his voice catching.

And he was. He remembered being on an inspection of sprawn canals when Behemoth arrived to destroy Flint, then the satellite lasers, before crashing to the ground. He and his fellows broke out the heavy weapons because at that point the possibility of the rebels attacking overland became a certainty. After that the Septarchy Friars were silenced and the Hierarch became impossible to disobey. However, no matter how forceful his orders to crush the rebellion, Jem and his fellows had been unable to resist the force that attacked Triada Compound—Commander Grant's force—and beat a steady retreat through the flute grasses. Then came that other thing in a subverted Polity dreadnought, the destruction of Ragnorak, the concerted scream over the aug network as thousands died when the newcomer gutted cylinder world *Faith* with fire, and next the worm in his skull, trying to flee it and running straight into an albino hooder, darkness and agony descending . . .

"But how much do you remember?" asked Grant.

Jem swung his legs off the couch and inspected himself. He was clad in clothing with a cut the same as a proctor's uniform, even down to the boots. However, the material wasn't white, but a pale pearly grey, and the text running from armpit to ankle was not the usual from the Satagents, but something else from Zelda Smythe:

"You are the vessel of divinity and perfect copy of some fragment of the mind of God" ran down one side, whilst up the other side ran, *"But your internal vision is imperfect."* It ended there, the text that side terminating at his waist, the bit about the strength of faith enabling clarity of vision being missing. Jem looked up.

"I remember all that happened to me during your damned—" He caught himself, recognizing deliberate provocation arising in him from set patterns of thought and an anger that he groped for but couldn't find. For a moment the two before him slid in and out of his mental compass, one moment looking utterly alien, the next becoming utterly recognizable. And, though they were recognizable as the enemy, their familiarity felt like a refuge, a haven. He began again, "I remember everything that happened to me during the rebellion, and some of what occurred after is returning to me." Jem inspected the memories of his perpetually adjusted self-delusion; how he had considered himself the subject of some faith-breaking experiment and had twisted new data to fit that delusion—the delusion that had resulted in him killing Sanders.

"But, I'm told, 'with insufficient emotional investment'," Grant replied, obviously uncomfortable with the words. "Apparently, to become sufficiently invested, you need to see the Monument."

"Monument?" Jem wondered just what they considered "emotional investment," for guilt hung inside him like an axe head.

"We're no longer on Masada, Tombs," the soldier said. "This ship's taking a little journey just for you."

In retrospect, Amistad felt that leaking the news that

Tombs had left Heretic's Isle had been a mistake. It had resulted in Tidy Squad killers being apprehended, as intended, but the direct mind interrogations being conducted even now had revealed nothing new about "Squad Command" or the "Squad Leader." And now news services were onto the story and pushing for more, especially after Shree Enkara's recent broadcast. Amistad didn't like it, but the offer Uffstetten of Earthnet had made, after making deals with other news services to farm out the story to them, seemed the best one going. Having just Shree Enkara watching and recording would be better than having Masada swamped with reporters. But still, Amistad should not have allowed the news to be leaked in the first place. This whole issue with Tombs was so much more important than netting a few Squad killers. Perhaps, after the coming upgrade, such errors of judgement would be less likely?

Poised upon the viewing platform, Amistad rattled his feet against the metal as he watched the upgrade unit descending. The octahedron lay five metres across, its eight polished plane faces revealing nothing of the incredible complexity packed inside it. It came down on internal gravmotors, tumbling silently.

Now that events were rapidly heading towards their resolution, Amistad felt an unaccustomed impatience. Perhaps this was the result of thorough mental dyspepsia and the subsequent lack of mental integration. So much information, so many facts to put together, and still no shape emerging as to what that resolution would be. Perhaps the upgrade would help, perhaps not—Amistad felt that it was the information from Tombs that would impart clarity, yet that information would not be forthcoming until after the man had been scrubbed of all his illusions. At this point the temptation to instruct Penny Royal to key directly into the man's mind and tear from it said steadily surfacing information had become almost irresistible. However, Amistad calculated that an over 10 per cent chance remained that such contact would distort the information. Too much of a risk to take, despite the fact that within the calculated period of that percentage dropping below 2 per cent, there remained a large risk of Tombs now being assassinated.

The unit slowed to a hover over the platform, turning slowly as if inspecting its surroundings, which was highly likely because the thing possessed intelligence, though of a rather odd kind. Then it finally descended the last few metres to crunch down on the diamond-pattern metal.

There were no other observers up here today. Those presently aboard this strange pillar of a vessel had been instructed to remain below, whilst today there would be no more specialists heading out this way from the Tagreb. Amistad had decided he did not want anyone watching this particularly personal time.

With one face flat against the deck, the octahedron clunked, separating along the edges of each of its faces. These then folded out and down, gleaming technology revealed within also unfolding, unpacking and expanding, almost like some incredibly complex chrome fruit being turned inside out. Jointed arms stretched, coils of optics and segmented pipes unravelled, short telescopic towers rose and opened brassy tubeworm heads, and a squat tic-like robot unpacked itself and inflated, testing limbs terminating in multi-purpose tool-heads. Next, sliding plane faces across the deck, the whole thing opened out further to leave a space—a space just large enough for a scorpion war drone to walk into.

Amistad hesitated. For over a century he had borne this outer shape and only a slightly adjusted interior. Acquiring more *mind* had required some swapping about of internal components but little else, since additional processors and memcrystal had taken up very little space. However, over that last century Amistad had reached both physical and mental limits to expansion. His mind was like a much repaired and strengthened wall which now, to be stronger, needed to be torn down and rebuilt. But did Amistad want to go there?

He had been perfectly happy with his investigations of madness and perfectly equipped for the limited tasks he set himself. However, if he was to become the prime authority on all things Atheter, which currently extended far beyond

Masada itself and also incorporated the Atheter AI, then he needed to transcend, needed to integrate at a higher level.

"I am ready," the tic-like upgrade robot informed him.

Amistad hesitated for a second longer, then realized it wasn't fear of the upgrade itself that held him back but, quite simply, fear of the responsibility. Really the time had come for Amistad to stop pissing about out on the periphery of the Polity, to stop playing, to come home and at last grow up. He advanced amidst the complex machines and settled down on his belly plates, extending his limbs and placing his claws tip-down against the deck. A nervous shudder ran through him, then he forced himself into stillness and waited.

"Close down autodefences," the tic instructed.

Amistad began shutting down a weapons system that had nearly acquired a distinct intelligence of its own. Beam weapons, railguns and munitions carousel powered down, whilst his immune system, which would automatically react to computer, microbot and nanite attack, reluctantly went offline.

"Autorepair too," the tic added.

It comforted Amistad to detect a note of nervousness in the upgrade robot's communications. But, of course, working on something made for total war against an alien race was a risky procedure at best. Amistad offlined all the internal microwelders, recasters, nanoscopic reconstructors and other internal repair bots, shut down the rerouting systems and instructed the nanite armourers all over his outer shell to go on hold. Suddenly, at that point, he felt something he had felt only once before, at his inception aboard the factory station where he had been built: vulnerability.

"I commence," said the tic.

Telescopic tool heads and crane-like mechanisms bowed to the task, closing on Amistad like the spikes in an iron maiden. Cutting lasers began firing up, but merely to soften metal for the hypersonic neutronium cutting discs that followed. Amistad observed armoured shell coming away in sections to expose internal ceramocarbide bones, powerful stepper motors, optics and s-con cables. He *felt* this happening until shutting down millions of microscopic sensors underlying the departing shell. When his claws went he writhed with the feeling of inconsolable loss, even though he knew these would be returned. And soon he looked nothing like a scorpion, had become almost indistinguishable from the machinery that surrounded him.

Now the tic robot itself moved in close to work on the main internal components of Amistad's body. A fusion reactor just half a metre across connected up whilst Amistad's own reactor disconnected and slid away. Upload connections established, one after the other, to each of the previous upgrades to his mind, and data began to slide away in a destructive process that nearly autostarted his immune system until he clamped down on it. Very shortly Amistad forgot things and began to feel less intelligent, only the sensed presence of the quantum protomind offered any reassurance, that being where Amistad was going.

Next the download connection established to Amistad's main processor, even as the large lozenge of crystal began to disconnect. Consciousness began to fade and he asked the question of himself that many a Human asked when loading to crystal, to a new vessel: "Will I die?"

Utter blankness, timeless.

Amistad woke abruptly, now in a place so huge his mind almost diffused away in the first second of consciousness. Also, in that second, he re-engaged his immune system, autorepair and weapons even before his senses. His particle cannon and close antipersonnel lasers briefly flared in response to a perceived attack before he could shut them down, then his senses connected fully in time for him to see the wreckage all around him: tools slagged or chopped into pieces, glowing pools of molten metal, occasional secondary explosions and chunks of hot metal raining down.

"Damn," he said, then, "Er . . . sorry about that."

"Not unexpected," said the tic robot, now climbing back up onto the platform from where it had previously concealed itself. "You have sufficient control for me to finish the job now?"

The thing had dragged up with it a cable net bag containing Amistad's armour, which had yet to be replaced. Amistad grasped at once that in preparation for this moment the upgrade unit had moved its entire mind into the tic robot, which had been provided with the tools to complete its task. Something else occurred to Amistad too: he still had no idea about the purpose of another tool that went under the name of Jeremiah Tombs.

After his first trial runs with the specialist programs, Chanter realized that all physical objects possessed congruent patterns if you broke them down sufficiently for, in the end, they were all made of matter, which at its basis was all the same and in the end broke down into nothingness. The programs here stretched into the territory of various unification and chaos theories, whilst also straying into the perpetual revisions of those theories and incorporating AI solipsism. He found it far too easy to end up losing himself in speculations about the meaning of it all. Perhaps this was because he was distracted. He felt naked and without an escape route now his mudmarine and Mick, under the control of Rodol, had returned to his base to collect his collection of sculptures.

"Any joy?" asked Clyde.

Chanter looked up. The man was thoroughly sober now he had found something to interest him. He had explained to Chanter that after his and Shardelle's depressing discoveries about the gabbleducks and hooders, and his orders to remain here on Masada, he had allowed his addictive personality free rein. But now there was some research he could get his teeth into he had allowed Rodol to suppress that part of him, and the autodocs here to shave the fat from his liver and purge the toxic build-up in his body.

"I've gained some understanding of why some choose the easy escape route called God, but fail to understand how they can't look beyond that construct."

Chanter returned his attention to the screens before him. Icons represented each of the sculptures in his collection, whilst bar graphs detailed the performance of the program he was using, each bar representing adjusted data inputs. Thus far he knew that all the sculptures were made of animal bone, that parts of them had been fashioned in shapes similar to structures in creatures on this world and others, but no congruent pattern or order to that. Construction methods were congruent: mortise-and-tenon joints, bone pegs and micro dovetails. One of the searches related to Human woodworking and Human artisans of the past—Gibbons, Boulle and Chippendale—but he doubted that would make anything clearer, for the Technician's use of such joints just represented the best physical methods of accurately joining cut materials without glue or welding.

Clyde pulled up a chair before the next console along and sat down, elbows on the chair arms and fingers interlaced before his mouth. He then reached out and waved a hand over the console and the screen before him came on to show the kind of data maps Chanter just couldn't read.

"You're only searching for physical patterns or matches," Clyde said. "Perhaps you should extend your search outside such limitations?"

"To where?"

"Perhaps your concentration on the artistic endeavours of Humans might be a dead end and you should take a look at the Atheter databases and the fauna and flora of this world."

Chanter repressed the urge to snap at the man. Maybe he was right about what would be the original sources of inspiration, and from them Chanter could run new comparisons with Human art and then find the Technician's core.

"Perhaps this." Clyde leaned forward and reached out to the screen, directly manipulating the data maps with his fingertips. A new search bar appeared on Chanter's screen.

"What's that?" he asked.

"I'm running a comparison program between the structures of your sculptures and the gabble database."

"But the gabble is gabble," said Chanter. "It's nonsense—your own Shardelle has been unable to make any sense of it."

"Let's just see what happens shall we?"

Chanter was about to protest this foolish use of processing power, for the gabble database was huge, when one of the icons before him flashed and his console chimed. He concentrated fully on the screen and saw a sketch outline of that sculpture descend towards a three-dimensional shape that had appeared on a subscreen. The two shapes melded, turning and twisting, then flashed red and another subscreen appeared. On this a shape slowly sketched out. Chanter could make nothing of it.

"What have we got?" he asked.

Clyde stared hard at his data maps. "Could be a complete coincidence—the match is not in the main gabble database but in a mindtech research—'

The console made that sound again, another sculpture selected out for comparison with another three-dimensional shape. Again a match was made.

"Then again, perhaps not," said Clyde.

"Are you going to make yourself clear?"

Clyde pointed at his data maps. "The program is finding structures in your sculptures that match the neural structures of a gabbleduck's mind."

The console rang again.

"Really weird," Clyde added.

"In its art," said Chanter, feeling a moment of victory, "the Technician has been trying to express the minds of its masters."

Clyde just continued staring at his screen, his expression blank.

"I rather think," he said, "that with the limited tools at its disposal, and limited and wholly distorted understanding, it has been trying to rebuild them."

Jem struggled with the unfamiliar fastenings of the spacesuit, then stopped and looked over his shoulder for expected help, and yet again realized Sanders wasn't standing there. The feeling of loss, and guilt, surged up again and he just stood, unable to continue. Grant gazed at him for a moment, then abruptly stepped over and helped him. Jem felt a sudden huge gratitude, his throat tightening and tears pricking in his eyes as the soldier demonstrated the simplicity of stick seams and the automatic seals. The suit clung over his clothing, film-thin and terribly insubstantial, a bowl helmet covered his head and just a few discrete packages decorated his belt. How could such a light garment be sufficient to protect him from vacuum? The answer was always the same here: Polity technology.

"Okay, you're done," said Grant.

Jem felt this warranted some sort of reply, but for a moment didn't trust himself to speak.

"You're ready?" Grant enquired.

Jem cleared his throat, turned to look at the airlock door so the soldier could not see his face. "So . . . what is this monument I must see?" he asked, not for the first time.

"You'll see soon enough," said Grant.

Jem glanced at Shree, then away again. "Will you tell me?"

"It might spoil the effect, and effect is what I'm all about," she said. "But I'd have thought you would have guessed by now."

Grant turned towards the airlock door—an arched contraption with segments that opened like an iris, disappearing into the surrounding walls. After they stepped inside, the iris closing behind them, Jem saw vaguely familiar text appearing in the glass of his helmet and guessed it indicated pressure and atmospheric readings within the airlock as it drained. About him the suit gained a degree of rigidity, but still did not constrict movement.

"We've arrived on quite a day," said Grant. "They've finished repressurizing and are starting to spin it up again."

Shree glanced at him sharply. "Interesting timing."

"Ain't it just," said the soldier. "Makes you realize how important the AIs consider what's rattling round in his skull—they were ready to repressurize over ten years ago."

"All for my benefit?" said Jem, puzzling over why Polity AIs might have such interest in him. Hadn't Shree mentioned that the Technician had done something to his mind? Hadn't Sanders once said something . . .

Jem winced, the heavy boot of guilt coming down hard on his chest again. It was unbearable, but he couldn't see what recompense he could make—beyond acceding to their demands right now. But no one died—they all went to Heaven or Hell, didn't they? No comfort there either, for his own beliefs damned Sanders to Hell.

The outer door of the lock drew open to reveal a long framework tunnel extending to something looming in the dark of space.

"Perfect timing right now too," said Grant, his voice as clear over suit radio as in the air. "Sunrise in about three minutes."

"Sunrise?" asked Shree.

"When it comes out from behind Calypse."

Grant stepped into the tunnel first and Jem followed, feeling as if he had stepped from a cliff the moment he moved out of the airlock. *Gravplates*, he realized, nausea rising in him. The Hierarch Amoloran had spent the entire planetary budget on getting such things smuggled to Masada for his tower and his own ship, yet aboard the Polity ship they were even inside the airlock. A prick in the side of his neck made him jump and his nausea at once began to fade. The suit had *doctored* him, he understood, dispelled his nausea, looked after him, and that seemed to make the undercurrent of guilt even harder to bear.

Down the length of the tunnel handles were provided with which to propel themselves along. Though clumsy at first, Jem soon got the hang of it, recalling his brief stays offworld during his proctor training. Ahead, the massive object hanging in vacuum was visible only as a blackness blotting out a large portion of the starscape. Jem began to feel an odd familiarity about this thing, then a growing fear of that familiarity.

"Starting to feel reluctant?" Shree asked spitefully.

Realizing he had been moving ever and ever slower, Jem picked up his pace, Grant having moved some distance ahead of him. He caught up with the man in time to hear him say, "Here it comes."

Sunlight lit the scene from behind, casting the Polity ship's shadow directly ahead and blotting out much of what lay there, but off to the right, truncated by perspective, the light revealed a curved surface of bare metal, char, and occasional areas of unburnt vacuum paint. Slowly this shadow slid leftwards, exposing more of that surface and uncovering Theocracy script. When it revealed a few letters Jem finally realized where they had brought him.

"*Faith,*" he said, his voice catching.

"The laser blast," Grant explained, "hit the Up Mirror and reflected up inside the cylinder world. The mirror lasted about two seconds before evaporating, but long enough to cause the firestorm that gutted this place." The soldier pointed to where the shadow was now sliding aside to reveal the ring-shaped, heat-distorted Down Mirror sitting above an oddly misplaced gothic tower at this hub end of the cylinder, a concentric window around it through which reflected sunlight shone into *Faith* itself. "Amoloran's Tower has been restored. They found most of it drifting into a decaying orbit around Calypse and towed it back. Some other stuff inside has also been restored." Grant fixed Jem in his gaze. "The dead, or rather what's left of them, have not been removed."

"Why have the dead remained unburied?" Jem enquired, his voice at last steadying, a fading and resentful part of himself wondering if the dead had been left visible so the victors could gloat.

"Effectively they have been—this has been classified as a war grave." Grant continued on down the docking tunnel.

"The Polity is above gloating," said Shree, almost as if she could see into Jem's mind.

He glanced at her, then noted the look Grant flashed back at her. With a sudden cold certainty Jem realized it would take the soldier a while, but eventually he would see through her. Then, as he followed, Jem felt grief nibbling at the edges of his own consciousness, but weak, more like sadness. It seemed for a moment he had managed to step away from it into some other part of himself. He wondered how actually seeing *Faith* twenty years after the firestorm could be any stronger than feeling the tens of thousands die here over his aug. It hurt him that they thought that whatever horrors awaited beyond that distant airlock would give him "sufficient emotional investment." But that hurt stemmed from the soldier's opinion of him. Did Grant think Jem so shallow?

Soon they reached the end of the docking tube, passed through the large outer door into Amoloran's Tower and propelled themselves inside an airlock large enough to hold a Hierarch and his retinue. Jem eyed Satagent script running around the wall, the snouts of two stun blasters peeking from their high alcoves, and lower down the recesses from which tangle wire could be ejected. High security here, this being direct access to the Hierarch's abode, but it wasn't lethal security—Amoloran, and then his successor Loman, would certainly have wanted to question any assassins who got this far, prior to sending them to the steamers. Jem winced at the thought of the agony anyone caught here would have endured, then immediately upon that felt surprised at his own empathy.

"Tower gravplates are active on the other side," Grant informed them. "And there's air."

The inner door admitted them to a fire-charred corridor, the drag of gravplates dropping them hard onto the remains of lush carpets. Ornate sconces protruded from the walls and burned with pink-tinged artificial flame. Each of these seemed to be made from a decorative lacework of precious metals and stones. The walls themselves were decorated with icons, many blackened by fire, whilst alcoves held alabaster sculptures of previous Hierarchs—a display of wealth suitable for this place, surely?

Grant removed his helmet and hung it on a hook at his belt. Shree copied him and Jem did the same only when something clicked in his neck ring and, coming loose, it threatened to topple away. The smell hit him immediately. It was as if he had just stepped inside a furnace that had been dead for years.

"Mind where you walk," said Grant.

Jem's gaze strayed down to the charred corpse stuck to the carpet just ahead, and his throat tightened. Some of its proctor uniform remained, but this individual's occiput, back and the backs of the legs had been seared down to ropes of now desiccated muscle. Next, his colder mind studied precisely what had been burned here, how the burn damage seemed directional, and he realized the fire must have travelled up this corridor from the end they were heading towards.

"A lot entirely evaporated," Grant explained. "In other areas fires burned until the air got sucked out."

"The Hierarch?" Jem enquired.

"Lot of windows and other openings in his upper tower, so most of it was flash-burnt inside. Not much to see up there, but we'll go take a look anyway."

At the end of the corridor they reached a spiral stairway, every step gravplated on the way up. Having earlier considered the cost of smuggling these plates into the Theocracy, Jem couldn't help but feel some disapproval at such profligacy, yet even as he felt that, he understood why. Ever since being a child he had been aware of a schism between planet-bound and cylinder-world theocrats. Those down on the surface of Masada, like himself, had always been more puritan, more stoic in their faith. But both possessed such faith, which made the gap between the two minuscule compared to the gulf between them both and the Polity.

"Oops, here's another one," said Shree.

There wasn't much left of the corpse on the stairs, just a foetal atomy sculpted in charcoal—impossible to tell its rank, sex, or even if it was an adult or a child. The wall sconces here hung melted, and further up were gone entirely, replaced by softly glowing globes strategically stuck to the walls to highlight this item or that: a gun seemingly etched into a gravplate step that wasn't functioning and caused Jem's stomach to lurch as he stepped over it, a steel sculpture slumped over, seemingly bowing in obeisance.

Finally they came to warped double doors which creaked open ahead of Grant, driven by Polity-tech hydraulic arms attached on this side. The huge apartment lying beyond had obviously been a high-echelon abode, but little remained of its furnishings. Jem identified the glass top of a low table melted against the floor, an ashen mess along one wall all that remained of a mass of computer hardware, the remains of a motorized massage chair standing like a weirdly distorted Human skeleton.

"Loman's place," said Shree. "But only for a short time after he tried to have Amoloran tortured to death. I think he only occupied it a couple of times." She shot a look at Grant for confirmation.

Grant had moved over to a window slanting out from the edge, runs of molten glass all around it showing that the original had melted and that this glass was a replacement to hold the air in. "That's right, and from here he watched *Faith* die."

Wavering between simple intellectual curiosity and sadness, Jem walked over to stand beside Grant, and peered down through the cylinder-cap window into the eye of *Faith* to see a fire-scorched tube, crammed buildings seared down to cubic skeletons, metal ripples visible on the central spindle.

"How do you know Hierarch Loman was here?" he asked.

"Because he's still here," Grant replied.

"Where?" asked Jem, that being the only response he could think of.

Grant turned and gazed at him. "Look up."

Jem didn't turn, felt something prickling the back of his neck. All the ruination here had been a sideshow to the main event, which was now. They'd brought him here to see whatever lay above him. He fought for resolve, found only confusion, then turned and looked up, straight into the face of his Hierarch.

"Within a microsecond the coherent light turned his body into ionized matter and plasma," said Grant, "carrying it straight up in line with the laser blast."

The grey ceiling held an image of Hierarch Loman from the waist up, distorted towards the sides by the ceiling's curve so it seemed he was in the process of sinking into a grey pool. He held his arms out and up—his last position as he tried to fend off the fire that consumed him. Other flaws in the ceiling -spatters of metal—looked like stars. Seeing them suddenly switched patterns in Jem's mind. For a moment the Hierarch did not look like he was sinking away but rather as if he was rising out of starry void, his arms held up in blessing.

"Makes me think of the Turin Shroud," said Shree.

Yes . . .

A sudden feeling of inconsolable loss bubbled up inside Jem, an inner self, a core that seemed in the process of forming. Orbiting this core were two other perspectives.

One considered the huge error they had made in bringing him here to try and twist him to their purpose: they sought to weaken him by showing him the devastation, the evidence of the Theocracy's death, the charred shadow of Hierarch Loman here on the ceiling. Being so utterly sucked into their machine world of cold facts and logic they were blind to evidence available here to anyone with any religious sensibility at all. Hierarch Loman was not dead. Hierarch Loman had been martyred and achieved sainthood, and here, traced by the very hand of God for Jem's eyes alone, was the evidence.

The other perspective saw a simple mind in which imagination had been wholly slaved to the task of reinforcing long-term indoctrination. A terrifying, intelligent perspective devoid of contempt, full of understanding, yet distant from such *Human* concerns.

Jem turned away, not sure if he was doing so to avert his gaze from the power of the image above him, or to hide from the other two the tears glistening in his eyes.

"We identified him from DNA scraped from the floor," said Grant. "There was none on the ceiling because the blast burnt the top half of his body down to its elements."

No, cried the older of Jem's orbiting minds, *Loman's base matter was transformed into something supernal, even the essence of God.* The other orbital mind looked on with utterly alien understanding, translating, reassessing, and coming to its own nihilistic conclusion, *It is just a shape; only extinction is real,* whilst Jem's inner core cried in the darkness, and believed neither of them.

10

Super-dense materials

The invention of force-field and gravity technologies capable of producing pressures previously impossible for our industries ushered in the era of super-dense materials and the compacting of matter for numerous uses. Whole new sets of names needed to be devised to describe new materials, so we ended up with, for example, ND12 Iron, for iron doped with neutronium on the newly invented 1 to 24 proportional scale; fibre-diamond (commonly called monofilament); chainglass; cutting application shearfilm; hyperlead and hypergold. Gases could be highly compressed to give us super-dense air supplies and a whole new range of high-explosive devices, and new stable solids were found, like metallic hydrogen, oxybloc and nitrox geodes. Whole new branches of materials technologies opened up, and for these we must be grateful. This technology also ushered out the gemstone market, but that's a subject for another time . . .

—*From* QUINCE GUIDE, *compiled by Humans*

In the first few seconds after it materialized in the real, the mechanism concentrated on its own condition. Having sat in underspace for nearly two million years, it found that its maintenance schedule was lagging. Its U-space engine, having been battered by currents within that continuum for so long, wasn't up to spec. A great deal of rebalancing needed doing for it to function, but beyond that the mechanism did not know whatelse to pursue: it seemed to have lost the ability to actually repair the engine. When it also discovered that viruses and worms surviving its battle with Penny Royal had taken control of some units within its structure, it reacted with Jain-tech-inspired paranoia.

Internally it manufactured scraps of antimatter and fired them towards these units, at the last enclosing them in full-sphere hardfields. A series of violent but contained explosions ensued, rendering the units down into concentrated energy too violent for the mechanism to utilize, so it ejected this through hardfield tubes.

Destroying those units used up energy which it replaced in the usual manner by drawing power from its network of probes spread out across the old Atheter realm. However, it discovered that traces of Penny Royal's attack had spread through them. It began sending self-destruct orders to those affected. In the ensuing five seconds eight hundred probes everted into the real in the chromospheres of suns. This left a further five hundred probes and a dearth of energy supply. Also, the mechanism had lost material mass, had reduced itself from the optimum in the initial orgy of destruction. A second later it turned its attention to the nearest available resource: the gas giant by whose gravity well it had made the underspace fold in which it had hidden itself until now.

It took whole minutes for the mechanism to make a gravity lens, to effectively punch a million-kilometre tube down to the surface of the gas giant. Pressure at the surface, now no longer restrained by the massive gravity of the giant, forced matter up within the tube like hydraulic oil squirting out of a ruptured hose. Sucking this in, the mechanism drained off and utilized thermal, chemical and isotope energy, routed appropriate materials to the variety of fusion reactors it contained. It also began to crystallize, forge, form, twist and manipulate materials within internal structures that fell somewhere between the cells of an organism and auto-factories.

A pyramidal alien spaceship appeared whilst the mechanism worked and it scanned the vessel for the patterns it was set to recognize. No sign of gabbleducks, no Atheter minds, but it upped its alertness when it recognized that this object contained an artificial intelligence similar to Penny Royal.

The mechanism felt something that in another being might be labelled frustration, for its ability to respond to something like this remained limited, even though it recognized that if one of these AIs had tried to resurrect the Atheter, then others might too, so they were all a danger. That frustration only increased as the ship folded itself away into U-space and departed. But even frustration was new to the mechanism—lay outside its original programmed parameters. The years of battles, rebuilds and the attrition of time had changed it.

The mechanism continued to rebuild what it had destroyed within itself, began making new clean probes to send out to occupy the positions of the eight hundred it had burned, and whilst it did this the alien vessel returned.

Obviously the new alien civilization here was now aware of the mechanism. This presented dangers previously not programmed for. A civilization in itself was a danger, for any such was effectively the prey of Jain technology, the greatest danger of all. The mechanism used its frustration to push against the limits of its programming, and found their previous rigidity had faded.

Another smaller vessel arrived, docked with the first. The mechanism observed these for a moment, then turned to further self-analysis and repair, and further straining against its chains. A bigger alien vessel next joined the other two here. All the mechanism's problems were interlinked, that seemed clear, but the developing situation on the Homeworld was its first priority.

Focusing its attention through those probes in position about the Homeworld, the mechanism studied the situation there with greater intensity than before. Traces of Atheter mental thought patterns were plain, but barely active. They seemed to have an organic basis, and though there was something quite odd about that, it was enough to enable the mechanism to force further leeway in its already loose programming.

Time for action.

Being located so far from this activity, with only a few probes through which to operate, the mechanism could not be fully effective both in data gathering and in responding to that data, for there was no unequivocal proof of Atheter resurrection. It was also plain that it had failed in its previous two attempts to suppress such a resurrection. Why else were Penny Royal and the Atheter biomechanism so close to what it was detecting now? It must relocate itself to the scene. There it would be able to more easily assess the developing preconditions for its main function. There, should the situation warrant it, it would also be able to bring online and distribute around the world the full array of its pattern disruptors, those machines now stored and somnolent inside it that it had used to first erase the minds of the largest portion of the Atheter race and then to tear apart the remains of its civilization.

"*Emotional reintegration in process,*" Penny Royal informed Amistad.

The scorpion drone integrated that and slotted it into the complex formulae in his expanded mind before returning to his contemplation of the distant coiled shape of the Technician, and internally to a growing angst. In retrospect there was something to be said for the lesser intellect he had possessed before. Though aware the universe could be a dangerous place he had reneged on responsibility because, of course, there were other higher intellects taking care of things and because, in that lesser state, he had remained utterly ignorant of the sheer extent of that danger. Take, for example, Jain technology.

Amistad had been aware that this dangerous technology had been created as a weapon by one divergent part of the Jain race to destroy another part, an almost separate race. Analysis showed that after taking care of its intended target that technology must have turned on its makers, since they weren't around any more. Reappearing recently it had caused some serious problems in the vicinity that had wholly occupied the attention of some of those higher minds. Now included in that select group of AIs, they vouchsafed Amistad further information. Jain technology had come a spit away from annihilating the Polity, and it still hadn't been nailed back in its box. Yes, Amistad knew that right at that moment a vast bloom of it occupied an accretion disc some hundreds of light years away where a vast engineering project was being made to contain it. But that select group of AIs estimated the chances of success there at something like fifty-fifty.

Now this.

"Clyde tells me it was trying to make Atheter minds," Chanter had said. "Structures within its sculptures match up with gabbleduck neural structures."

Clyde?

Amistad just got to Rodol in time to tell that AI not to permit Jonas Clyde's request to be allowed to switch back to alcoholic mode. Clyde had been rather unhappy about this.

"Look," he had said, "you don't fucking need me. When have you quartz-heads ever needed organic input?"

"Tell me," Amistad instructed.

"Some massive twist in the Technician's perception of reality," Clyde explained. "It was got at."

And there lay the problem. The data indicated that the Technician was over two million years old and to say it was a rugged biomechanism would be to venture into farcical understatement. The most powerful force on this world, ever since the Atheter opted out of civilized existence, had been the Theocracy. All the data on the Theocracy's hunt for that creature was now easily available to Amistad. Even with satellite weapons the Theocrats had failed miserably. The disaster that occurred the one time they managed to track it down and close in had remained a secret throughout the remainder of the Theocracy's existence—not that there were many survivors of the hunting party to tell tales.

They'd hit the creature with their satellite lasers, bombed it from the air with conventional explosives, then nuked the area where it went to ground. Their big mistake had been to land and search for remains. The search party had consisted of eight hundred troops, fifty-eight ground transports, forty aerofans and twenty-six tanks, of which just enough remains were found to fill a small squerm pond. An interesting footnote to this was that though Ragnorak's first targets were to be the rebel caves, its next target was the Technician. The thing scared the Theocrats in ways that outreached its sheer destructive might.

"Perhaps damaged during that attack?" Penny Royal opined from its present position inside the Monument.

"I think you know better," Amistad replied. "A self-repairing biomechanism might have lost data but its own genetics dictate that it would have rebuilt itself to some earlier form. The likelihood of its perception of reality being so distorted, even by nuclear mutation, that it conflates physical structures with mental ones, is remote. Clyde was right: it's been got at—most likely by what got at you."

That ancient Atheter device that had reached out of under-space to prevent Penny Royal from loading an Atheter mind to a gabbleduck, and had all but destroyed the black AI in the process, had been active before. It seemed certain now that what the Technician had been trying and failing to do for about a million years with its sculptures, it had tried before, but that time with a sufficient probability of success for the mechanism to reach out and interfere with the biomech internally. It had not only reprogrammed the Technician but physically altered the structure of its mind.

"So what initiates it?" Penny Royal enquired.

"You have no idea?"

"All a blank to me."

There was the rub. Penny Royal had fought some savage informational battle with that device and, just like with Jeremiah Tombs and the things Amistad needed to know from him, knowledge of that battle was locked up in some dark part of its consciousness. However, unlike with Tombs, that dark region no longer resided within the mind that gave it birth but in the state of consciousness Amistad had removed to turn Penny Royal into a more acceptable being—the eighth state had been where all Penny Royal's murderous impulses had resided.

"Assumptions can be made," said Amistad.

"Dangerous."

"The Atheter destroyed their civilization and their own

intelligence. The thing reacted to you, reacted to you trying to resurrect one of that kind, so quite simply it was built to prevent that—to keep the Atheter extinct, to prevent the gabbleducks from being more than animal."

"Obvious," Penny Royal stated.

Yes, certainly, but they needed more than that. The device resided in underspace and could reach out to the physical world to flatten an AI, to tamper with a powerful biomech, and it seemed likely that what was happening with Tombs might activate it again. They needed to know how to stop it.

From his position aboard the platform overlooking the scenery of Masada, Amistad first firmly cut all connection with Penny Royal then mentally reached out. The heavily encrypted signal he sent, via a U-space transceiver inside his own body, activated another such transceiver inside an armoured sphere anchored to a plate of ancient coral deep in the southern ocean. Inside this shell rested a chunk of AI crystal, powered up but connected to no sensorium. Trapped in a virtual environment entirely of its own making, Penny Royal's eighth state of consciousness perpetually tried to escape, searched for the door that Amistad now entered through.

That Eight, as Amistad had designated this thing, had created a virtual world based on a model of existence as viewed through the Human senses only confirmed reality: AIs weren't something separate from Humanity, but its descendants. That Eight had chosen to make its home in such a place indicated something else, though what, Amistad had no idea.

Amistad manifested on the floor of some huge cathedral cavern whose walls seemed to be in perpetual motion. With Human senses this would be all the drone could see, however, magnifying things revealed the walls were made of millions of Human beings writhing together in black slime, slowly tearing each other apart and also slowly reassembling. Amistad had not yet ascertained how deep was the reality of these . . . things. Quite possibly they represented the recordings of Human minds Penny Royal had tormented and now continued to torment. Certainly, just this one eighth of the AI possessed the capacity to contain them. Herein lay the reason why Amistad had not simply obliterated this thing, or at least so he told himself.

In places these bodies formed the entrances to further caves and, observing these, Amistad awaited the perceptual representation of the attack the thing here always made as it tried to find a way back through the door into here. Odd, that on this occasion those caves did not immediately spew their complement of flying, hopping and crawling horrors.

"Eight," said Amistad.

Nothing for a moment, then in one cave a red light surging forwards. Eight manifested as a great black squid with glowing red eyes. It shot out, spewing an ink consisting of highly destructive nanomachines in this virtual environment, but as com line chewers in reality. The cloud of machines washed over Amistad, darkening his carapace, tried to find a way in but, as always, blunted molecular teeth on sheer armour and were torn apart by the drone's own complement of nanomachines. The comline chewers hit the same wall for, quite simply, Amistad was the door and remained stronger than the thing beating against it.

"The Atheter device," Amistad stated.

No verbal response from Eight, but a flash of some broken computer architecture underlying this virtuality. The ink cloud dispersed and now the squid sat right over the drone, trying to find some purchase on Amistad's shell, its tentacles screeching across adamantine armour. In a flash of irritation Amistad reached up with one claw and snipped a tentacle away. Eight fell writhing through the air, breaking into small spiny black stars. It shrieked, drew back, then attacked again.

"We need to understand the Atheter device," the drone insisted.

Eight offered some construct. Here in the virtuality the tormented began bursting like sporulating puff balls, spewing internal organs that flitted through the air like grotesque birds to coagulate in a glistening squirming sphere above. Hints of knowledge of the Atheter device's abilities to reform matter and suck energy from somewhere. Hints also that it was damaged, no longer functioning as it should, and that it possessed vulnerabilities. Amistad was left in no doubt that deep knowledge of the Atheter device existed here, and that by seizing the sphere above he could possess it. The only problem was that by doing so Amistad would open himself to Eight, open the door, and the thing would escape, probably damaging Amistad as it opened up a channel back to its original home inside Penny Royal.

Amistad had once managed to extract and imprison this eighth state of consciousness from the erstwhile black AI, but that was when Penny Royal had been poised on the edge of extinction. Now, even though Amistad was much much more powerful, he doubted that he could extract Eight from a fully functional Penny Royal and put it back in the box.

Amistad demurred, retreated, slammed the door shut on his way out.

The shadows on the walls here were low-echelon vicars, bishops and others in the priesthood, mere proctors like him, women, and even menial staff of the cylinder world. He gazed at them and felt only sadness, regret, but that seeming to arise out of a growing strength in his inner self, which recognized that these images denied Hierarch Loman's sainthood.

"Same effect as with the Hierarch," said Grant. "These images are all across the Polity now in picture-wall memories, though it ain't the kind of decoration I'd choose."

"I don't know," said Shree. "They have their appeal."

Jem gazed at the ruin of the Friar Hold. The stone wall before him now possessed a glaze into which the ghost of the garden, now blackened soil underfoot, had been etched. He could see roses, shadow stems, a soldier hunched over something, his honour guard rifle a metallic splash distorted into a curve over his shoulder.

"I'm sure you can see some of the bodies," said Shree.

Bodies?

"So I'm told," said the soldier. "Though I can't."

"Bodies?" Jem asked out loud. He looked over his shoulder seeking an answer, but again Sanders wasn't there, would never be there.

"When Loman had the Septarchy Friars murdered he had the bodies left here in the garden," Grant explained. "Some say they can see the shapes of those bodies in that charred mess at the foot of the wall."

Jem shook his head, tried to dispel ghosts, then bowed low and peered hard at the drift of fused and scaly ash. Yes, maybe a hint of a limb there, and could that be a face? No, what looked like eyes were rivet holes in some half-molten lump of metal. He abruptly stood upright again, realizing that even those without faith distorted their perception of reality for the purpose of confirming their own beliefs.

"Your . . . Penny Royal gave me back my mind," he said. "Was that so you could have something whole in which to break my faith?"

"Whether or not you believe you got an invisible friend in the sky is irrelevant to us," the soldier growled, turning to him. "The Theocracy is dead, and the number of believers dropping daily as they come out of the darkness and choose sanity. Polity AIs don't much care about people's beliefs, just so long as they obey the law."

"The Theocracy may have fallen," Jem said, the ghost of a shrug shifting his frame for a moment as he allowed his obvious indoctrination to take over, "but you cannot destroy the teachings of Zelda Smythe."

Grant glanced across at Shree, some amusement in his expression, before returning his attention to Jem. "The biggest lesson she taught was that Human gullibility should never be underestimated, including her own. Seems Smythe's problem was too much belief—she bought into any mystical crap thrown her way, including all the major religions back then. In trying to sort out all the contradictions she wrote it all down and began work on her teachings—what you call the Satagents. However, her own excess of belief didn't blind her to the benefits when those searching for belief started knocking on her door."

"What do you mean?" A rote question; a game played out to its end.

Shree interjected, "What he means is she used her

patchwork religion to become extremely wealthy, and she used that wealth to later explore some new interests in memcording, exotic drugs and what she described as "transcendence through sexual ecstasy" with her highly paid staff of young men."

Jem nodded, continuing the game. "Yet, with her wealth she brought her followers here and established the Theocracy. Whether you believe or disbelieve her teachings, her own faith in such an act cannot be doubted."

"She funded it," said Grant, "but shaved enough corners it's a wonder the cryoship got here." He stared at Jem with puzzlement, perhaps sensing a lack of sincerity. "Nearly a quarter of the passengers died during thaw-up. The death rate then was pretty high for those taking the landers down to the surface to establish a foothold there. Not so many died up here where the upper Theocrats started asteroid mining and building their cylinder worlds."

"There seems to be a hole in your logic," said Jem. "Why would she risk herself by "shaving corners" as you put it?"

"Probably," said Shree, "because she didn't come here."

"Zelda Smythe walked amidst the flute grasses and heard the music of angels mingled with the raucous cries of demons," Jem quoted, tired of the game now.

"Zelda Smythe," said Shree, "died aged a hundred and eighty-six in her Antiguan palace. The combinations of drugs she was using to control the AIDs VII she suffered did not sit well with the other drugs she used for recreational purposes."

"Lies," said Jem, the robot.

"Why?" asked Shree.

"You are just trying to break—'

The back of Grant's hand slammed into his mouth before he could finish. Jem fell and skidded along the ashen ground, lights flashing behind his eyes. In a moment Grant had him by the throat and dragged him up, slammed him back against the charred wall.

"Listen, you little shit," he said. "If we wanted to 'break your faith' by feeding you lies we could have rigged you up to an aug just like that one I stopped Tinsch from sticking into your skull. We could tear your mind apart and stick it back together in any shape we chose. We could make you believe Zelda Smythe is a transsexual orangutan living on bananas on Mars. We could make you believe anything. But why should we? Do you really think you're that fucking important, that your belief is that fucking important we want to waste resources on it?"

"Evidently . . . you do," Jem choked.

Grant stared at him, then abruptly released his hold. "You're not important, your damned religion isn't important. What's important is what a biomechanism may have shoved inside your skull."

Jem rubbed at his throat. These two would never like him, never understand the long journey he had made and was still making, never see him as anything more than Proctor Jeremiah Tombs. Continuing that journey he would make what recompense he could, for Sanders, not for them. But he would damned well have their respect.

"Only extinction is real," he said, Euclidean shapes clamouring to escape the wells of his consciousness, a cry of loss turning to sound that could not have issued from a Human mouth. "But belief in a negative is incomplete, when the penny has two sides."

"What're you talking about?"

"I am ready to hear the truth, soldier," Jem replied. "And maybe that will uncover the truth of what the Technician branded into my mind."

Its last inmate now no longer here, the sanatorium had taken on a ghostly, almost doleful air. Sanders gazed up at it from the small landing field cut into the mountain slope on the landward side, reluctant to return there, because she was also reluctant to bring this part of her life to a conclusion. Then, angrily, she stepped out of her rented gravan, walked to the side loading door and thumped the lock plate.

Inside rested two large plasmel trunks. Taking a remote from her pocket she selected "follow" on the screen menu then turned and headed for the crushed-stone path that led straight up, rather than taking the curving supply road—best get this over with quickly. After a short while her anger waned, and she glanced back at the two hover trunks dogging her footsteps, gratified to see that the rough path seemed no problem to them despite their usual environment being runcible terminals or space ports.

Soon she reached the grapewood door into the rear courtyard. In Theocracy times this door had been closely fitted and sealed and she would first have had to pass through the outer door of an airlock to reach it. Now, what with the airlock having been removed along with the roof of the courtyard within, the weather had got to the old wood and it had shrunk, and its seals peeled away. Yanking down the central handle she pushed it open and entered.

The courtyard had once contained all sorts of exotica grown here by the Bishop of Heretic's Isle. The image of that man quietly tending his plants before heading off to oversee the bloody games they had played here sat uncomfortably in her mind. She noted that though native growths were sprouting from the pots and raised beds within, some of that man's plants had survived. It seemed significant—some things could never be wholly erased. She crossed flagstones, the trunks emitting a low whine as they followed, entered through the next grape-wood door, the seals round this new and working, felt the puff of pressure differential as she entered and noted the abrupt slowing of her breathing as her adapted lungs themselves adapted to the extra oxygen here.

In from the courtyard lay a long room containing all an enthusiastic botanist would want, then beyond this the kitchens. Treading a familiar route, Sanders passed old confinement cells, torture rooms stark and empty but for the occasional fixture that once supported frames, manacles, gallows. Finally she entered the modernized section of the sanatorium—redecoration here, no sign of the past use of this place—then eventually came to the door into her quarters.

Gazing around at the place she had slept in for two decades, she felt a surge of nostalgia and old regret. She focused on a chair over the back of which her nova wrap still cycled its hot display of a dying star, walked over and picked that up, then took the remote control from her belt and pressed "packing."

The two hover trunks obliged by settling down on the whitegrass carpet and hinging open their divided lids. Sanders tossed in the wrap first, then her clothing, a small collection of items she'd found washed up on the shore, including the much-eroded upper beak of a gabbleduck, then other items she considered personal possessions. By the time she had finished she'd only filled one trunk. Of course, before the arrival of the Polity she would have also packed a large collection of books, memory crystals and other singular data-storage items, but now all that just sat in her personal store somewhere in cyberspace, and she could recall it wherever she settled. She eyed the laptop on her desk here. Even that wasn't really hers—just disposable and easily replaceable tech. She walked over to it. Keyed into the offworld excursion site to check on her booking, for with things not quite as functional here as in the rest of the Polity, there could be problems.

Cancelled.

Sanders stared at this a long moment, then keyed in a query. The laptop blanked, then two words appeared on the screen: Disposal Confirm?

What the Hell?

Sanders reached down to cancel the order, but now "Confirmed" flashed up. The screen blanked again, then rainbow faults spread and it began to crack. The keys started to shrivel and the whole case of the thing distorted.

Her hand instinctively strayed to the button of her comlink now on the lapel of her jacket, then she hesitated. This could have just been some sort of glitch, or it could be that the computer hardware here had been set to wipe itself anyway, but she doubted it. She pressed her right forefinger to her comlink, which read the whorls and activated.

"What the fuck is going on?" she said out loud.

"Sorry about that," a familiar voice replied from her link. "But I wanted to get your attention."

"Well you have it now, Amistad. Why've you cancelled my booking?"

"Jeremiah Tombs still believes he murdered you," the drone replied. "It will be necessary, quite probably in the near future, to apprise him of the reality."

"I thought you wanted him to carry on believing that," she said bitterly. "I thought his guilt over supposedly killing me was one of the driving factors to enable you to get to what lies inside his mind?"

"Not so much for that, but rather to impel his cooperation over a limited time span. However, since one of the main drivers in religious indoctrination is guilt for which there can be no recompense, examples being original sin, guilt about wholly natural sexual impulses, and the general guilt at being unable to live up to deliberately unattainable ideals, those with that mindset tend to revel in it, and for our purposes it could now become a hindrance, even destructive."

"Just show him recordings of what you did—of me getting up afterwards and cleaning off that artificial blood."

"Too little drama," Amistad stated. "Humans always require drama when changing underlying belief structures else they fall back into the old patterns. They need an excess of pain, joy, strong emotion or new experience, to impress the change upon the dull recording medium between their ears."

"Y'know, Amistad, you can be really irritating sometimes." Sanders took out her remote control again, hitting "follow." The two trunks closed up, rose a few centimetres off the floor, then trailed her as she headed out of the room. "So what do you want of me?"

"I require you to remain available—preferably in the vicinity of Dragon Down, which I calculate is where Tombs will be when he reaches his next mental nexus."

"They've got Human accommodation there, haven't they?"

"Of a sort—dracowoman Blue has prepared for your arrival."

"You seem pretty sure I'm going to do what you ask," said Sanders. "My opinion of your methods and your aims has not changed. If you finally get to what the Technician downloaded into Tombs, if there's anything of value in his head at all, that will also result in a sane individual and someone of no interest to you whatsoever."

"Tombs has returned to what you Humans classify as sanity," Amistad told her. "He has even become, by your definition, more sane—his whole belief system collapsing and reconfiguring."

"What?" Sanders halted outside the door leading into the Bishop's garden.

"It's amusing really," the drone continued. "He maintained his own fiction by believing your aim was to break his faith by feeding him false information. That false information is the truth, yet the reality is that even the truth cannot break faith—it is by its nature not dependent on truth."

"So what returned him to sanity?" Sanders opened the door and stepped into the garden, her breathing now deeper and faster.

"His return to sanity was an acceptance of the truth, impelled by him trying to cut off his own face, which he believed to be a Polity prosthetic."

"What!" Sanders's throat tightened with horror. What horrible grotesque games was this drone playing with Tombs's mind?

"The damage has been repaired," Amistad added.

"He cut off his face and lost his faith?"

"No."

"You just said—'

"I just said that truth does not destroy faith—exterior input does not change that kind of indoctrination."

"So how is he losing his faith?"

"Something internal—something that wasn't there before."

"The download."

"That seems the most likely explanation."

Once she stood on the path outside the sanatorium, she turned and looked back. "What's going to happen to this place?"

"There was a proposal to turn it into a museum, but there are enough museums covering the Theocracy's distasteful rule here," the drone replied. "I believe another proposal is being considered—turning the place into a holiday resort."

For a second Sanders felt that wrong and wanted to protest, then she reconsidered. What a perfect denial of the island's hideous past. How much better to move on rather than revel in that past.

Finally reaching her gravan she stowed the two hover trunks inside before climbing into the driver's seat.

"So you will be heading for Dragon Down?"

"When will he be there?"

"I would like you there, and ready, within the next two days," the drone replied. "Will you go?"

"I think you know the answer to that."

Sanders set the van's gravmotors running, grabbed the joystick and lifted the vehicle from the ground. She still didn't like what Amistad was doing, but for twenty years she had conducted some utterly one-sided conversations with Tombs. Now, it seemed, he had become a functional Human being. Neither Amistad's requirements nor the drone's power to order her obedience informed her decision to go to the place beside where the dragon sphere had come down and given birth to a new race from its substance. She just wanted to talk to Tombs and have him talk back to her.

As the ship ascended Grant watched Tombs taking a deep breath of Masadan air he should not be able to breathe, then return his attention to his two companions. Something had changed about the proctor, the man seemed somehow more assured, yet sad. Even his speech patterns seemed to have changed, and not once during the rest of their tour of *Faith*, then the cylinder world *Charity*, had he mentioned his own faith or resorted to mindless recitation of something by Zelda Smythe.

In *Charity* they'd walked The Aisles; the walls formed of giant honeycomb structures, each one of their tens of thousands of cells containing the brain-burnt body of a Theocrat, awaiting some future time when Polity AIs had finished their investigations and deemed those bodies safe enough to serve as vessels for the mind recordings of dead Polity citizens. There Tombs had said nothing about decent burial, had not prayed, though his reaction to the news that the Polity Soul Bank contained millions of mind recordings had not been unexpected.

"Do all Polity citizens . . .back themselves up?" he had asked.

"Not all," Grant had replied.

"How do you know who?"

"You don't, unless they tell you—it's personal."

Tombs turned to Shree. "Like me you breathe the air here. Have you taken advantage of this mind-recording technology?"

"No, not yet."

Turning back to Grant, "And you have not either?"

"No," Grant replied. "This stuff is new to us—we weren't born in the Polity."

"Was Sanders?"

"Born in the Polity?" said Grant. "No, born in Zealos, though got herself smuggled out of Masada and trained as a medtech in the Polity."

"She wasn't backed up?"

"Not as far as I know," Grant lied.

Tombs shook his head, his expression miserable. Grant had expected more of a reaction from the man, expected him to talk of souls or some other religious claptrap. Was he now sufficiently emotionally invested? Grant didn't know. Penny Royal, once again awake, close, and looming like an invisible wall of knives, was silent—nothing coming over Grant's comlink.

"So what now and where now?" asked Tombs, still gazing up at the ascending ship.

Grant did not want to admit that he didn't know. Tombs had returned to sanity, perhaps a sanity he hadn't possessed before, but revelations were not forthcoming and they still had no idea what the Technician had done to him.

"What do you think?" he asked—easy response of question to question.

Tombs reached up and touched his face, switched his gaze to the nearby town and stared at it with a bitter intensity. "I am an outcast, a pariah, and an anachronism who only has value by dint of what is hidden in my mind. But I am curious about the things I have heard that relate to that." His attention now snapped to Grant. "Unless you want it otherwise I want to hear direct from those involved about what has been discovered here on this world, so I can assess the truth."

"What sort of truth would that be?" Shree asked.

"There is only one sort of truth," Tombs shot at her.

"No, there's our sort of truth and there's your sort of religious truth."

Tombs just stared at her bitterly for a long moment then swung back to Grant. "I heard you talking about this Tagreb, about the researchers who revealed the *truth,*" he emphazised the word, "about what the Atheter did to themselves. I want to go there and speak to these people."

"That can be arranged," said Grant. Now Penny Royal was being uncommunicative he needed to put some distance between himself and the other two so he could talk to Amistad—to find out what should be done next, maybe arrange transport to the Tagreb if that was what the drone wanted.

"Slowly."

The word ghosted over his comlink from Penny Royal. Grant was beginning to understand the brevity of the AI's instructions. He glanced over towards Greenport and came to an instant decision. "Come on then."

He led the way in towards the port town, towards the gate, but turned right before reaching it, following a foamstone path circumventing the town, finally connecting to the road leading down to the port itself. Shree walked close at his side while Tombs walked a pace or two to the right, keeping a small but significant distance between them. The man also surveyed their surroundings with singular focus, often halting to gaze at those structures that had appeared here over the last two decades.

"I saw Hell," he said when they drew athwart the factories being built on the foamstone rafts to one side of the port road. "What do you see?"

Grant found no reply for a moment, stumped by Tombs's use of the past tense. "I see pond workers' huts swept away and replaced by Polity technology, Polity wealth and a better life for us here."

Tombs nodded then abruptly headed over to the edge of the road, squatting down beside where a bank had mounded up, perhaps by the action of tricones underneath, and where purple-orange spikes of lizard tails were sprouting.

"Where the hell are we going, Grant?" Shree asked.

"To my ATV."

"Surely this is important enough to warrant some fast transport?"

"Apparently not." Grant gazed at her, not wanting to reveal his interpretation of Penny Royal's *Slowly*.

She stared at Tombs, showed a flash of irritation, quickly concealed. "Why does he dawdle so?"

Though at first Grant had liked the idea of her coming along, he had begun to find her company grating. On the face of it, it seemed action was all she wanted, that providing drama for her news service was all-important to her, yet he sensed an underlying viciousness that made light of her claim to be seeking a new life. He felt it in himself too. Why had he struck Tombs? Why react with such anger to the kind of nonsense the man had been spouting for two decades? Trying to step back from his contempt for the man, Grant could see that maybe that had been his last chance, that his anger arose from the feeling that Tombs was changing, and that in the future such anger might no longer be justified.

"We're in no hurry to get anywhere but inside that man's head," he replied.

"So we just let him saunter along doing what he wants," said Shree. "He should be pushed. He should be forced."

"How, precisely?"

"Confront him with the realities here. Rub his nose in

them. Show him the dracoman town, maybe Zealos, maybe even the Atheter AI—that should wake him up."

Perhaps she didn't know that the Atheter AI was now even less communicative than Penny Royal—it wasn't common knowledge.

"What's he doing?" she added.

Grant shrugged and walked over to the erstwhile proctor. Tombs was now down on one knee, looked like he might be praying, and Grant felt a momentary justification for his violence up in *Charity*. But no, with gritty mud-smeared hands the man was raking his fingers through the soil, picking out mollusc shells and making a small stack of them beside him. The soldier felt something cold touch his spine when he saw the shells bore Euclidean patterns; they were the shells of penny molluscs.

"Who designed my clothing?" Tombs asked.

"It's what they provided aboard the ship, but I reckon Penny Royal or Amistad had something to do with it."

Tombs nodded, scooped up the shells and deposited them in his pocket. "Yes, I remember Amistad—a machine made in the shape of some arthropod. It terrified me." He looked up at Grant. "I have to wonder why they make themselves into such shapes."

"Amistad was a war machine, once," Grant replied. "Its shape was both functional—evolution still comes up with the best designs—and intended to terrify the Prador, an alien enemy the Polity once fought." Even as he said it, Grant felt unsure. Many Polity machines bore shapes that were a cause for unease, and they weren't all made for war.

"The Prador, yes, I know about them." Tombs stood and peered back the way they had come as if looking for someone, but Shree wasn't over there, no one stood over there. The man then closed his eyes for a moment, dipped his head then raised it, eyes open now and glistening. He continued, "Evolution . . . but how much of it is there here?"

"You mean since the Creation," said Shree from just behind Grant, saying precisely what he had been about to say.

"No, since the uncreation of the Atheter race."

Grant now felt contempt for himself—how easy those old patterns of thought.

Tombs still held one shell which he cleaned against his clothing, smearing mud over the text in the cloth with almost blasphemous unconcern. He gazed at the pattern on the shell, then nodded towards Greenport.

"Those who tried to kill me used shapes like these to replace Satagent text on clothing that was a negative of that worn by proctors." He paused, forehead furrowed. "I saw it as the writing of demons."

"You *saw* it? So how do you see it now?"

"Patterns."

Grant tried to make sense of that but found only confusion. "Shall we get on?"

Tombs followed him as he moved off. Grant noticed how the erstwhile proctor now walked at his side whilst Shree kept her distance, perhaps better to record them for her news service.

Soon they were down on the hard-standing where Grant had parked his ATV. Gazing across at the port he saw that no ships were docked, though one was visible out on the sea, either heading away or heading in, he couldn't tell.

"We'll take the North Road up towards Zealos, turn off at Bradacken, then it's wilderness driving all the way to the Tagreb." Grant hauled open the ATV side door and climbed inside, ducking forward to head for the driver's compartment. Here were seats for driver and co-driver, with two further seats behind. He glanced back as first Tombs then Shree entered. The proctor halted in the rear compartment and studied his surroundings with the same peculiar intensity with which he had been gazing at Greenport. Did he recognize this vehicle? Did he recognize the since much modified and updated vehicle that had served as an ambulance—the one in which Grant had taken him back to Triada Compound after the Technician tore him apart?

After a significant pause, Tombs moved forward and took one of the rear two seats, whilst Shree moved up and took the seat beside him. Grant had expected at least one of them to come up and sit beside him. Why Shree hadn't done so became evident shortly after Grant started up the ATV's engine and headed towards the port road.

"So, Jeremiah Tombs, perhaps you would like to give me your opinion on the Theocracy, on the Polity occupation of Masada—your impressions of everything you've seen and experienced since your . . . recovery?"

A personal interview, then. Was Tombs aware of Shree's position as a reporter for Earthnet, and what that entailed?

"Shree Enkara is your name," said Tombs.

"Yes."

"Once a rebel whose main enemies were those in the same position as I used to occupy," said Tombs. "If one of our number disappeared we would hold a wake precisely ten days afterwards, the presumption being that if they were lost and out of communication in the wilderness they would be dead within that time, or that if they had been captured by you they were dead anyway. How impartial is this interview going to be, Shree Enkara?"

It seemed Tombs knew the situation precisely.

"If partiality on my part doesn't result in this being pulled, it's usually detailed by secondary narrative, either from an Earthnet presenter or, if not, by AI. You'll get a fair hearing, though whether or not you deserve one I leave to others to decide. Tell me, Tombs, how many beatings did you deliver, how many people have you killed?"

It seemed Shree had decided on partiality.

"I delivered one beating, with a stick, whilst in proctor training. This was overseen by the Bishop of Triada and considered an essential part of my induction."

"Did you enjoy it?"

"I vomited publicly afterwards and the Bishop had me beaten by one of the other trainees as punishment."

"I'm sure the Bishop wanted to ensure his proctors received *proper* training."

Shree's voice had an edge to it now. This wasn't going anything like she wanted.

"I am sure he had time to regret that when rebels sewed him up in a sack and threw him into a squerm pond," Tombs shot back. "I wonder if the squerms tore him apart before he drowned."

"We're getting away from the subject now, which is you. How many people have you killed?"

"I may have hit someone during the fire fight in Triada Compound. I cannot be sure—we were too busy running and dying at that point."

"Surely you were involved in executions? Surely you were present when someone was pinned down over new flute-grass growth?"

"No, I never saw nor was I involved in that. I saw my commander shoot a pond worker through the head once, but that's all."

"How did that make you feel?"

"I threw up—safely out of sight that time."

"So you've never killed anyone."

"As a proctor, no."

"So you have killed someone?" said Shree, sniffing blood.

After a long pause Tombs spoke slowly and distinctly, but with a catch in his voice, as if he were on the edge of tears. "I killed a medtech I only know as Sanders as I escaped Heretic's Isle."

Why had he given Shree that, Grant wondered. "Her full name is Jerval Sanders," he said and, only after saying it, realized why Tombs had spoken about this. He was making his confession.

"Jerval," Tombs repeated.

"Did you vomit after you killed her?" Shree asked nastily.

Grant concentrated on his driving. If this interview went out, Tombs would not look so bad and Shree was damning herself, especially when it became known that Jerval Sanders wasn't dead and Tombs had been fooled into believing he killed her. Grant grimaced. Only a short time ago he had felt that the burden of guilt Amistad had loaded on the man was a just punishment. Now he wasn't so sure. He knew it was one of the mental drivers that had pushed Tombs to mutilate himself and thus, by some weird form of sacrifice, restitution, recover his sanity, but was there any need for it now?

"This interview is over," said Tombs.

"Why, I haven't even got to the good stuff yet. I want your thoughts on the Theocracy and the occupation, on the Polity . . ."

"No, Shree Enkara, you want to hold me up as an example of why you think you are right. You want to affirm your own bitterness, your own faith."

"Faith is a good subject too."

Tombs didn't reply and, when Grant glanced back, the man was leaning against the side of the vehicle, gazing out of the side window, his expression grim, bitter.

"Perhaps you can explain your belief in God, and why you think Zelda Smythe is His ultimate prophetess," Shree persisted. "Perhaps you can explain why your god is any more true than the thousands of gods primitives have worshipped or why, as a godly man, you're quite happy about people burning in Hell." Grant noted Tombs wince at that. "Maybe you'd like to detail why the great and wonderful Theocracy needed torture, multiple executions, satellite lasers and an orbital coil-gun to keep order on its world, and why it fell to the godless machines."

Tombs simply wasn't biting and Shree had begun to sound like some expression of her name.

"Shree," said Grant, "leave the man alone and come sit by me."

After a brief silence, she stood and moved forwards, plonking herself down in the seat beside Grant.

"Waste of time," she said. "That'll never be broadcast."

If Earthnet and the vetting AIs were searching for impartiality, Grant guessed it would not. He pointed off to the side of the North Road—which was essentially a layer of compacted flute grass five metres wide leading all the way to Zealos—towards a small hill with a single garage door in the side of it. "Bunker One."

"No hooder warning," said Shree, nodding towards a light positioned atop a pole, like many other lights spaced at half-kilometre intervals along the road.

The lights don't signify anything now," said Grant. "If there're hooders nearby I get a warning straight through this console." He gestured to the console lying ahead of the control column. "Along with the warning I get details on the best bunker to run for."

The system was more efficient now. In the time of the Theocracy hooders were picked out by motion sensors out in the flute grasses, backed up by satcam when available. The moment a hooder was spotted within ten kilometres of the road all the lights on that section would begin flashing and the cargo trucks would run for the nearest bunker. However, depending on the positioning of the hooder, the nearest bunker might not be the safest one to run to. Their loss rate in trucks, and drivers, had been about 10 per cent. Now the only driver deaths out here were of those who did not heed the direct warnings they received, and there were a few.

As they motored past the bunker Grant settled himself for the five-hour drive ahead. Wondering where Penny Royal had positioned itself, he reached past the steering column and keyed in a query on the console. Some figures came up on the small computer screen there. The loading of the ATV was precisely what it should have been with three people inside, so it seemed unlikely Penny Royal was squatting on the roof. Out there somewhere then, keeping pace with them.

"Under Polity law," said Tombs abruptly, "I am guilty of murder."

Yes, his apparent killing of Sanders still occupied his mind and now he was starting to ask the questions Penny Royal had told Grant to expect, and to which Grant had been given replies.

"No, apparently not."

"I killed her. I cut her throat."

"Whilst the balance of your mind was disturbed."

"That's nonsense," said Shree, turning to peer at Grant. "Under Polity law mental disturbance is no excuse. Murder is murder and cannot be recalled, and a mind sufficiently disturbed to commit it is a mind not worth saving."

"On the face of it, yes, but Sanders agreed to waivers before she began looking after Tombs here, probably because she thought him no danger to her while stuck in a wheelchair.

With it also being likely he'd been subjected to an involuntary mental download, legal matters get a bit murky." He glanced at her. "A cynic might say that because of his value the AIs brushed aside the law." He shrugged.

"Fucking Polity," said Shree, turning to look out of the side window.

Revealing, thought Grant, then he glanced round at Tombs, who seemed disappointed and sad. *And no restitution for you, he* added.

11

Flute Grass

The flute grasses of Masada are thoroughly tedious plants closely resembling numerous rhizome-based plants on Earth, like reeds, irises, papyrus, ginger, turmeric—the list is a long one—but there is something odd about them. They sprout from their rhizomes in the spring, the shoots sharply pointed and tough enough to punch through even seasoned wood. Throughout the year they grow to heights of up to four metres, the hollow stems being up to ten centimetres wide and numerous side shoots binding the whole mass together. In late summer the grasses produce flowers, the over fifty identified separate species of grass producing just about every colour in the spectrum. And here we have the oddity, for there are no naturally occurring flying pollinators on Masada. These flowers eventually fade, drop away, to leave pods which eject "pollen" with three distinct sexes, and pollination is carried out by the wind, as with the trees of Earth. After pod pollination the grasses drop seeds, very few of which get a chance to germinate in the rhizome-packed ground. In the Masadan winter all the side shoots drop away to leave holes in the hollow stems, which play like flutes in the Masadan winter winds, hence the name. But we have to go back to it: why the flowers? Pure chance or, with what we know about that world now, design?

—From HOW IT IS *by Gordon*

"Katarin, about time!" said Ripple-John.

The woman peered at him from his laptop screen, some indecision in her expression.

"Hey Ripple-John," she said.

"So, tell me what happened," said John, lifting the laptop up and crossing his legs below it. "Damn com was jammed for a day and, ever since, Tinsch has been out of contact. I saw on Earthnet that Tombs is on his way up the North Road. Am I taking a wild guess to say the hit was unsuccessful?"

"It was unsuccessful."

"So what happened?"

"It did something to them." Katarin looked scared, her attention straying away to one side. John had never seen her like this, even during the rebellion. She had been as avid for revenge as him, and included herself in those who had dragged off the Bishop of Triada for his swim in a squerm pond. Did her fears relate to the Polity and what might happen if they were caught, or was she having second thoughts about plan B, Ripple-John mused. He had always been aware that many in the Tidy Squad entertained some moral uncertainties.

"You're going to have to be a little clearer than that, Katarin," he said. "Tell me *exactly* what happened."

She returned her attention to him. "Miloh tried to take his shot and, as planned, Tombs's protection went after him, giving David and the rest their opportunity. They activated the shields between Tombs and that protection and grabbed him. Now all but one of them are in Greenport hospital." She shook her head, looked bewildered.

"So this protection, some intelligent hardware of some kind, got through to them," Ripple-John stated. "But it didn't kill them. Are they badly injured?"

"Difficult to describe."

"Do your best my love."

"Miloh lost his hands, but it's worse than that. His wrists were fused into his rifle, which itself became a semi-organic extension of his body."

"What?"

"Whatever attacked him left him looped round an I-beam, his rifle acting like a set of cuffs. Port Maintenance tried to cut through it." She paused, trying to find the words. "They had to take him to the hospital with a wound dressing on his fucking rifle!"

Ripple-John sat back in his director's chair, and absorbed that. Tinsch had wanted a nice neat hit with zero other casualties and John had known that approach was wrong from the start. Because of Tombs's importance to the Polity he had heavy protection, and the only way to get to him was by using something a bit more substantial—a bomb, nerve gas, the kind of weapon he couldn't be protected from by a bodyguard of any kind, something like the contents of the canister standing beside the balcony rail just a couple of metres from Ripple-John.

"What about the others?"

"Franklin, Amira and Joden are in a similar condition to Miloh. Franklin is melded to a street paving slab at the ankles, Amira's console is now an extension of her wrists and Joden's got a chunk of wall attached to his back."

"So, whatever's protecting Tombs likes to play the comedian. But we'll be seeing how it deals with the reception I have for it here."

"You're at the way station?" Katarin asked.

"I certainly am."

"He's got other protection too," she said. "You must have seen that on Earthnet."

"I certainly did. Leif Grant—I never had him pegged as a traitor. So tell me, what about our David Tinsch?"

"The aug he intended to use on Tombs ended up on his own head."

"I said that was a bad idea from the start—we're Tidy Squad and we don't try for deals with the Polity." Ripple-John paused, feeling a sudden surge of doubt. When, after his close comrades in the Squad went out of contact, he had used the secure comline he was only supposed to use in circumstances of extremity, whoever he spoke to there had told him to stand down. In light of that it seemed likely the Polity had penetrated the upper command of the Squad, and that he could only trust those he had always trusted. "So his brains got scrambled or something like that?"

"Something like that."

"Explain."

"When I saw him in the hospital they'd finished interrogating him. He just sat and cried and said he was sorry. Yesterday they transported him to Zealos hospital, where I'm told Polity mind-techs are going to take a look at him."

"So now it's down to me only."

Katarin just stared at him for a long moment before replying, "Maybe we should just drop this. Is the death of one crazy proctor worth the casualties?"

So, she was softening, she'd lost sight of the ideal. Masada could not move on until every damned Theocrat was dead. It could not move on until every trace of the Theocracy had been erased. It could not move on until every believer chose either atheism or death. The Tidy Squad's task, John knew, might be centuries long and, in face of that, they could not pay heed to a handful of casualties now.

"I think you know my answer to that."

"Yes, I do."

"Tombs got taken to the Monument, didn't he, Katarin?"

"He did."

"And to *Charity*."

"Yes."

John nodded to himself. They would have to go. He'd been pushing for some plan to obtain either nuclear or antimatter explosives to take out those cylinder worlds, to erase those visible *monuments* to the Theocracy. Many other members of the Squad had always argued against that, saying the function of the Squad was retribution against individuals, not against a belief system and not against inanimate objects. They failed to understand the persistent strength of the enemy. Ripple-John understood.

"Then back to Greenport, and now they're still on the North Road?"

"Yes, they're still heading your way."

"Good. Be good enough to let me know if there's any change in the itinerary." He reached forward to cut the communication but Katarin's expression made him hesitate. "Something else on your mind, Katarin?"

"What did Thracer do wrong, John?"

Puzzled, John replied, "Thracer? He's doing a bundle of things wrong all the time—he lacks balls. He dismissed the idea of a hit in Greenport and he pooh-poohed my idea of poetic justice. And he won't even look at us destroying the cylinder worlds."

"Is that reason enough to kill him?"

"Not yet . . . what is it you're saying?"

"His body was found about five hours ago, in his apartment—someone shot him through the face."

Not before time, thought John, but said, "Not me, nor any of my boys."

She stared at him speculatively, then said, "I'm out of this now, John. I've had enough."

Ripple-John felt completely unsurprised. Though Katarin had been Tidy Squad right from the beginning, she was not the first hardliner to renege on promises made during difficult times. She had just joined a long procession of those Ripple-John thought he could trust but who had abandoned the Squad. Those that hadn't understood their comrade Ripple-John and remained on Masada, now resided here permanently, under the Masadan mud.

"You'll be understanding, Katarin, that if you're loose at the mouth I'll be having to hunt you down," he said.

"I understand," said Katarin. "I've booked passage offworld."

Yes, perhaps she understood that whether she opened her mouth or not, he would try to hunt her down anyway. Only by leaving Masada could she ensure her own survival.

"Well, I wish you luck."

"Sure you do," said Katarin, shutting down the communication.

Ripple-John closed his laptop and peered contemplatively up at the glass dome over Bradacken. With no large agricultural areas to put off the local wildlife—the creatures of this world tended to prefer the flute grasses and stayed where their natural food remained available—the way station bore similar construction to that of the bunkers.

First a thick foamstone raft had been laid, then buildings erected on it in a ring at the centre, all their openings facing inwards. From above the roof-line of this ring of buildings, reinforced concrete sloped down to the edge of the raft. A dome of armour glass four centimetres thick covered the circular parking and maintenance area the buildings enclosed, and entry to this place was via a long tunnel through the concrete, armoured blast doors forming a vehicle airlock. Gabbleducks, siluroynes, heroynes and mud snakes just had no way of penetrating.

Hooders were the greatest danger out here; few structures could survive a determined attack from one of them. However, they took no heed of this place, skating over it as if it were just some mound—in fact there was a recording that could be viewed here of a hooder doing just that, seen from the underside as it went over the dome. Had that same creature been able to see inside, been attracted by the lights and movement, it could very likely have broken through the glass and caused mayhem. But the designers had thought of that and the glass was one-way, its flat hemisphere appearing just a dull rocky grey from the outside.

Ripple-John stood, putting his laptop aside, then stepped over to the corner of the short balcony provided for his apartment. Here stood a tall plant pot, its contents, a plug of soil bound with roots, standing messily to one side with stunted multicoloured lizard tails sprouting from it. John resumed the chore he had been at just as the call arrived from Katarin. Using his hands only he scooped more remaining soil from the pot and deposited it in a bag, then he pulled closer the canister from beside the balcony rail and keyed instructions into the control pad on the end of it, then after second thoughts, added further instructions.

There was always the possibility that the same sort of jamming as had been used around Greenport might be used here and block his signal, even though he was using seismics to a transponder actually within this place. He therefore set a timer for seven hours hence. Either at that time, or when he sent a signal upon knowing for sure that a certain ATV had arrived here, the canister would open and discharge its contents into the atmosphere. The canister did not contain nerve gas or any other sort of lethal gas, though it did contain a biological substance. However, even that was harmless when breathed by a Human. The stuff would spread throughout the way station and, since this place maintained its breathable atmosphere more by pressure differential than by atmospheric security, it would leak out through the many holes in this place.

Then the killing would start.

Jem tilted his head, listening. The muttering was closer now, seemed clearer somehow as if, with some effort of will, he could divine meaning from it. It also seemed to be more under his control. He could tune it out, concentrate on the ATV's engine and let that other sound wane, recede somewhere to the back of his mind.

As the big armoured door swung open ahead of the ATV, Jem returned his attention to the shells arrayed on the seat beside him. Puzzles with a religious motif being one of the few entertainments allowed Theocracy children, he remembered doing jigsaws when a child, and gazing at these shells he felt the same as he felt when doing them. It was almost as if each shell was a circular segment cut from some larger picture he had yet to see. Certain lines and shapes seemed concurrent; seemed like they ought to link together in some way. Moving the shells about, trying to match one line to another on a different shell, he felt both frustrated and fascinated. He felt that jigsaw feeling of engagement to complete something, yet a joy in the process that he did not want to end. It also distracted him from what felt like an unhealing wound inside his head.

"Didn't they give you any toys when you were a child?" asked Shree.

Her statement seemed to mirror some of his thoughts, but her words were only bile, bitterness. He knew, that given the opportunity to do so without bad result for herself, she would hurt him in any way she could. No, that's not right. He looked up into her face, which at that moment appeared utterly alien to him yet simple and open to easy inspection. Double bluff, he realized. Her reporter persona was allowing her hate free rein for she could justify her provocation as an attempt to obtain newsworthy responses. She could claim to be pretending a plausible hate she did not really feel. But she really did hate him, and he knew in that moment that she intended to kill him.

"Softly spake the gabbleduck in words of meaning lost," he said.

"They gave you a book of rhymes, then."

The cab of the ATV darkened as Grant drove it into the tunnel, grew darker still as the big door closed behind, then an eerie blue glow infused the tunnel as lights flickered into life. Jem blinked, Euclidean after-images in his eyes, overlaying her face like fractures.

"I booked us three small apartments," said Grant. "Lucky really, since now there's not much room—a road crew is staying here."

"The ones working on that damage we saw?" asked Shree.

"Probably." Grant shrugged.

It had delayed them for a couple of hours, during which time they set up a brief camp and broke out supplies. Shree hadn't let up then, continually pressing Jem about his beliefs, about his opinion of the Theocracy, the Polity. To escape this Jem had taken a walk up to look at the damage. A great scar had been ripped across the road—the rhizome mat completely torn apart to reveal black tricone-infected mud beneath. Apparently this was a common occurrence, the tricones attacking the road as if it were a real structure rather than just a path hammered through the flute grasses. Over the other side of this had stood a large truck with a loading arm, the back of it filled with sheets of plastimesh to make repairs, but no workmen had been in sight.

Other supplies quickly packed away, Grant had taken the ATV off the road, barging through flute grasses beside the tear, labouring over raised mud banks, the beaked monstrous head of a mud snake, like a giant horse skull, briefly surfacing to one side as if they had run over its body. Going off-road being so easy, Jem had wondered why they bothered with a road at all, but that detour made him realize why. Though capable of going off-road the trucks that generally used this route were not as agile as the ATV, and with the road open ahead of them could travel much faster. After that, two hours' travel had brought them to the way station, which remained invisible to Jem until its main door opened, for flute-grass rhizomes were spreading over its upper surface to disguise it.

The inner door opened, flooding the tunnel with a brighter artificial light from within, and Grant drove the ATV into the central area. Here vehicles were parked directly on the foam—stone raft, whilst around these, raised beds contained gnarled grape trees shading grey grassy masses starred with flower flashes of red, yellow and white with exotic combinations in between. Jem wondered what bishop had made this place his gardening project, and whether his remains resided in his flower beds or outside. Grant drew the ATV to a halt beside a large dozer and shut it down.

Both Grant and Shree picked up packs to carry out of the vehicle with them and, seeing this, Jem felt a sudden surge of loss. His only possessions now were the clothes he stood up in, and even they might not be considered truly his. He didn't even have a bag containing a few personal items, toiletries, a palmtop or even a watch. Directly upon this feeling he felt a sudden nostalgia for his room in the sanatorium. Only as he stepped out of the ATV after the other two did he wonder at his lack of yearning for his proctor residence at Triada Compound. It seemed so utterly distant from him and, though he had spent the intervening years since in something like delirium, their impact remained. Even further in the past lay the family home in Zealos, parents struggling with oxygen debt and his father dying from the strain, a debt Jem paid off with his first year of proctor wages, only for his mother to die just as the account cleared.

That past now lay utterly disconnected from him. It belonged to a person Jem no longer recognized; one with simple beliefs and few questions, one who accepted the world as he found it and his position there. The Jeremiah Tombs of right now recognized that the world was a lot more complicated than he had supposed and that the questions storming in his head only began with the ones Humans asked themselves day to day. Shree had helped bring this into focus; her hate had brought it into focus.

Above the gardens enclosing the parking area, the ring of apartments and other concerns rose to four storeys; short balconies ran in a ring around each level. Jem could see some people up there, and more in the restaurant they passed on the way to one of the four reception entrances. Inside, a tall woman with scars on her face and a shirt open to her navel to expose a scole scar took Grant's details, handed over room cards and gave him directions. With wary doubt she stared at Jem for a moment, at his clothing, at the script running down it. Perhaps she'd seen something about him on Earthnet. He wanted to tell her that a lot more resided inside these clothes than she was seeing.

"You can buy new clothing direct from your rooms, if you like," she said, her gaze on Jem. "In fact there's a lot you can buy here now." She flashed a sympathetic smile at him, her gaze again straying down. Confused, he looked down too, saw that his clothing was stained with mud and there were rips in both knees of his trousers. When had that happened? He turned and followed as Grant led off, realizing the woman had seen only a person, not an erstwhile proctor, and that to her his clothing might only have been some odd fashion, like the open top she wore. Glancing back as they mounted the stairs he saw her watching him with just a hint of a smile, her look something he had no recollection of any woman directing at him before. But he had to turn away, angry that his sudden gratitude tightened his throat and squeezed tears into his eyes.

Corridors decorated in bright colours and soft thick carpets led to their rooms.

"I do need a change of clothing," said Jem, as Grant directed him to one door and handed over his room card.

"There'll be a console inside," said Grant. "You can order what you want through that."

"Got some proctor back pay?" Shree enquired.

Grant took a wallet out of his pocket, opened it and extracted a thin memory stick. "Use this—your credit rating should cover anything you want."

"So now he gets Polity credit?"

Grant glanced at her. "He's on a retainer—he's working for the Polity now." The soldier turned away and headed for his room.

"You'll find it difficult to buy yourself a Satagenial here," said Shree, turning to Jem. "Though there are plenty available for sale in places more often frequented by tourists. It seems Theocracy artefacts sell well to Polity citizens, who always like to snatch up the remnants of a dead past."

"I will let go of my religion the moment you let go of your hate," Jem replied.

She snorted derisively and moved away.

Entering his room Jem gazed around at the luxury cluttering the shell of land-bound Theocratic minimalism. It didn't take much imagination to mentally remove from this small space the soft bed, cupboards, combined high-tech shower and toilet unit and auto vendor, and replace them with institutional paint, sleeping mat, prayer stool, slop bucket and the scourging tools resting in an icon alcove now containing a holographic projector.

He nodded to himself, not sure what this confirmed to him, then deliberately allowed that distant muttering to impinge on his consciousness again. It definitely had a source, he felt, outside his skull, distant but definitely directional. Something was stirring, over there, he could face where it came from. And its unease came from him. What it was he didn't know, but felt sure he would know. He shrugged it away, walked over to sit before the room's console.

It was of the kind he had been familiarized with at the sanatorium and it automatically came on, sensing his presence, to show him the wonderful shopping opportunities here at Bradacken way station. He sat staring at it for a long moment, resisting the urge to check over his shoulder, utterly aware that no one was there, that he was alone. If only he hadn't killed, if only she could be here . . .

Abruptly angry with himself, he jabbed into its slot the memory stick Grant had given him. His credit rating blinked up on the screen, and he proceeded to spend it. Half an hour after that he took a shower, then sat on his bed wrapped in a towel until the door buzzer snapped him out of reverie. He opened the door to find a low, flat oval platform piled with his purchases, and wondered if maybe the woman from reception had brought it. Puzzled that no one was here, he picked up the various packages and took them inside. When he took up the last one, the trolley said, "Have a good night, Jeremiah Tombs," rose up on six fat insectile legs and scuttled off down the corridor.

Jem slammed and locked the door, stared at his bed and contemplated the certainty of nightmares.

A notification went to every aug, comunit and console inside the observation tower, and many in the monitoring rooms below the main platform returned to their instruments to begin recording and analysing their subject with a depth and precision never used before, yet with so much more concealed from them now. Accepting all data feeds from the tower's sensors, and using many of his own sensors, Amistad watched the Technician wake.

After its last kill the biomechanism had lain coiled on the flute-grass rhizome mat for eighteen days, as if digesting that meal, yet this had been a common occurrence only over the last twenty years, so this certainly wasn't an after-lunch nap. At the centre of the coil its spike of a tail twitched, then the creature rippled, that ripple spiralling outwards from the tail until it reached the spoon-shaped head, which rose a little. From where that head had been cupping the ground, a mist of vapour dispersed, and Amistad saw that the Technician's body temperature had risen, in some areas beyond anything seen in it before, and now even higher within its cowl. Other readings, where they could be obtained, revealed high chemical activity, the kind of electrical readings to be expected from a busy computer, running as a background to disperse neuro-chemical firings. This had been seen before, but never at this density.

Amistad opened a channel to the Tagreb where the AI there, Rodol, replied.

"Something you require?" it asked.

"What is Chanter doing now?" Amistad asked.

"Right now he is enjoying a meal of orange-back nematodes, which he seems to prefer to the more common green variety. Having adapted his body to this world it seems his taste is for more cyanide in his food, though he has convinced himself that he prefers orange-backs because they tend to wriggle more in his mouth."

"And his work with Jonas Clyde?"

"They're avoiding each other now," Rodol replied. "After Clyde's assertion that the Technician, through its sculptures, was trying to rebuild an Atheter mind, Chanter has ventured into more esoteric studies of how artists try, through their art, to erase the same traumas of their early lives that, so he believes, resulted in their artistic impulses. He is theorizing that it is impossible for them to erase those traumas and so they will always remain artists, though, should such erasure be possible, they would kill the impulse."

"In other words he's disappearing up his own backside again."

"That about covers it."

"Then it's time to give him something more constructive to do. I'll consider how best he can be used."

"Haven't things moved beyond his rather distorted and simple view of reality?"

"Perhaps . . . what about Clyde?"

"At first resentful that I won't allow him to lapse back into alcoholism, but right now back in his laboratory studying data now being transmitted from your location. I believe he wants to talk to you."

"Okay."

Contact followed immediately.

"Amistad," said Jonas Clyde.

The man peered from a virtual screen in the drone's mind, him seeing an image of the drone from one of the cams on the platform.

"Evidently," Amistad replied.

"I've been making some comparisons." Obviously excited about something, Clyde ignored the sarcasm. "Biochemical activity is about on a par with any other hooder's, but that doesn't account for the amount of bio-electrical activity being picked up."

"Theorize," Amistad instructed.

"Okay, the Technician is probably over two million years old. Its musculature is about four times stronger than a normal hooder's, the complexity of its cowl manipulators up there with that of an autodoc or even an AI mindtech. Its armour is not only resistant to energy weapons but to massive shock and possesses molecular dense layers that would give it resistance to nano-attack."

"This is all known."

"Yes, and from the excess of redundancy you theorized that it might well be a prototype—the redundancy removed to result in the other hooders."

"That was a hypothesis, not a theory, and a questionable hypothesis too."

"Okay, I'll give you that."

"You yourself hypothesized, because of the resistance of their armour to energy weapons, that the hooders of this world were an adapted strain of war machine—that the Atheter took their war machines and simplified them for the chore of obliterating gabbleduck remains. Presupposing this was the case, then the possibility that a high-redundancy prototype *hooder* was made seems unlikely."

"Yeah, you got it."

Clyde sounded disappointed, defused. In that moment Amistad realized that though he himself now possessed as much brainpower as other high-functioning AIs across the Polity, he had yet to acquire another of their traits: diplomacy. The likes of Jerusalem and Geronamid tended to let those researchers under them enjoy their discoveries—perpetually being second-guessed by an AI could be depressing, and would reduce the efficacy of those same researchers.

"Do go on," said the drone.

"Right, I guess the Technician could still be loosely defined as a prototype . . ." Clyde paused for a moment to get his thoughts in order and, though already way ahead of the man, Amistad let him work his way through it. "Look, the Technician may or may not be the machine on which the Atheter based the common hooder, that's irrelevant, but there's other things we need to consider. You know what I thought when I measured that electrical activity?"

"Please continue," said Amistad, not quite able to express surprise and say, *"I've absolutely no idea!"*

"The readings looked just like those you'd get if you pointed sensors at a haiman: biochem, bioelectrics, then a big ramp of electrical activity from their computer additions."

Amistad did suddenly feel some surprise, not at what he knew Clyde was coming to, but at where that reference to a haiman—a Human being partially blended with an AI—might lead.

"But I guess that's to be expected—a biomech can't alter its physical structure quite so fast as can you, Amistad. There's all the problems engendered by the organic blueprint in the genome."

"Where are you going with this?" Amistad asked, his tone one of perfect puzzlement after he removed the prior tone of get-on-with-it exasperation.

"I think the Technician is one of the original war machines."

How very surprising.

"I agree, this seems likely."

Clyde's enthusiasm returned. "This means we're dealing with an alien version of you, and all that entails. It means adaptability and maybe the ability to create new weapons, which probably accounts for the changes it's been undergoing for the last twenty years. I need to get closer and run some tests. I bet it's got nanite defences in its armour, just like you."

"I wonder about that comparison you made between sensor readings from the Technician and those you might get from a haiman . . ." Lead him there, but ignore that bit about him wanting to come to the observation tower. Clyde had to remain where he was in readiness to tell his story to future visitors.

"The proportions can vary, depending on the amount of hardware a haiman has installed, though for a Human there is an upper limit."

Gently, gently.

"But no upper limit for the Technician, it being a manufactured life form?"

"I guess."

"Well, it's a certainty that it is manufactured—its genome is far too precise, lacks numerous alleles and junk genome."

Clyde was dismissive. "Humans have been dumping junk DNA and altering their alleles for centuries."

Amistad waited in hope that the penny would drop. It did.

"Hey, you know, there's nothing to say that hooders are completely artificial. They might be adapted from an original evolved form."

"Horses, dogs, cats," said Amistad.

Originally the product of evolution, then of selective breeding, which then extended into genetic manipulation. There were dogs now with opposable thumbs and maths degrees, and pursuing myth, the first Pegasus took flight on a low-gravity world even before the Prador war.

"They might even be native to here," said Clyde. "Though physiologically they're very different from other native forms."

"A new line of inquiry perhaps?" Amistad suggested.

"What?" Clyde was distracted, already manipulating his data maps.

"I suggest that you return your attention to all the hooder data you gathered before and now view it in a different light. Perhaps, rather than concentrating on all those elements of hooder biology that classify them as biomechanisms, as artificial creations, you should now look at everything else, perhaps try to ascertain if an original evolved creature is their basis."

"Already way ahead of you," said Clyde, waving a dismissive hand.

Of course you are, Amistad thought, even as the communication channel closed.

But would Clyde be able to take an overview of all this: organisms turned into war machines by a race descending into self-destructive insanity; speculations about where the main intelligence of a haiman might lie; organisms capable of manipulating their environment in complex ways; rampant Jain technology and thousands of years of civil war.

Some very, very unsettling possibilities were now coming to light.

Amistad returned his attention to the Technician, now fully uncoiled and writhing through the flute grasses. For a moment its choice of direction gave him even more reason to feel unsettled, but then, through an anosmic sensor on the observation tower, he got his explanation. Somewhere out there a gabbleduck had died. The Technician, like many other hooders over a large area, was heading off to obliterate the remains. It was following instinct, or programming. Same difference.

Fuck, they've used a bomb, was Grant's first thought as he rolled out of bed and pulled on his undertrousers. He reached his door, which was still shuddering from the assumed blast, and stepped out expecting to find the corridor full of smoke and wreckage. He found only Shree rapidly exiting her room, thoroughly sexy in only a pair of knickers, and it was evident to him now that she'd had her body cosmetically enhanced.

"What the hell was that?"

She'd felt it too—it wasn't some mental replay of his past, some nightmare making the transition into waking.

"I thought it was a bomb." He glanced at the weapon she held—a thin-gun, and not the kind of thing you would expect an Earthnet reporter to be carrying—then swung his attention to the door to Tombs's apartment, which remained closed. After a second he returned to his own room to grab up his comunit and turn it on.

"Penny Royal?" he asked, whilst inserting the receiver into his ear.

"Get out," the AI replied, just as some other unknown impact shuddered the floor. *"Leave ATV—too large a target."*

"What's happening?"

"Hooders."

"Surely it's safer here?"

"Gabbleduck death hormone," the AI replied. *"Am searching for source. You remain, you die."*

"Hooders," Grant said to Shree, who was hovering in his doorway. "Someone's released gabbleduck death hormone in here and if we stay we're dead."

"If we go outside we'll probably die too," she said, oddly fatalistic.

"Get your stuff," he instructed, himself pulling on the rest of his clothing.

She stared at him for a moment longer, then turned away. He dressed fast and efficiently, ensuring his Polity-tech breather gear was in place at his neck before then checking the action of his disc gun and holstering it. The weapon would be no use against hooders, but if one of them got to him at least it would provide a get-out clause. Next he slung his pack over one shoulder and left his room. Tombs's door was still closed and he hammered on it. "Tombs! We go now!"

The door slid open and Tombs stood there clad in heavy walking boots, black trousers tucked into the tops of them, a green denim jacket open to reveal the silvery padding of a temperature-controlled undersuit. He also had a backpack slung from one shoulder, and had even made use of other facilities in his room, his jet-black hair now cropped down to his skull.

"They've come," he said.

How did he know?

"Who's come?" Grant asked.

"The morticians," Tombs replied.

The man wasn't even looking at Grant, but staring slightly off to one side, almost as if gazing through the very walls of the way station. His hand strayed up to his chest and fingered a penny mollusc shell now depending from a string about his neck.

"Hooders," said Grant.

Tombs abruptly focused on him.

"Oblivion," he replied, just as Shree stepped out of her room and strode over.

"Not if Penny Royal or I have anything to say about it," Grant replied. "We run. We'll use one of the emergency exits—'

"West side," Penny Royal whispered in his ear.

"—on the west side of the station, get as far from here as we can."

"Canister located, shut down," said Penny Royal, *"but hormone level at twenty gabbleduck deaths—many hooders."*

Grant glanced at Shree and continued, "Hooders go crazy when they're looking for a dead gabbleduck. They'll attack this way station and probably ignore us."

Probably.

"Come on." Grant reached out to grab Tombs's shoulder and found his hand closing on iron, then his wrist closed in a similar grip. The erstwhile proctor pulled him close, then put a hand against his chest and shoved. Grant slammed into the other side of the corridor, the wind knocked out of him. As he slumped down the wall he saw Tombs, his expression blank, turn and take a pace towards Shree. She stepped back, sudden fear there, drew her thin-gun and pointed it at the man.

"Oblivion," said Tombs, taking another pace and backing Shree up against the wall, the barrel of her weapon only a metre from his face.

"No," Grant managed.

Tombs abruptly looked puzzled. He gazed at the gun then took a pace back, before turning to look at Grant.

"I am sorry," he said. "I am frightened."

Grant struggled upright. "Put it away Shree—we go now."

Shree hesitated, a brief yearning fleeing across her features, then holstered her weapon. Grant stepped forwards and caught Tombs's shoulder again, felt only Human resistance before Tombs turned and set off in the direction Grant propelled him.

"Let's pick it up." Grant broke into a jog, towards the end of the corridor, Tombs and Shree keeping pace.

You're frightened, thought Grant. *Not half so much as me.*

The west-side emergency exit lay on the side of the station directly opposite their rooms. The quickest way to it was down, outside, across the parking area then through the apartment block over there. A crowd milled in reception, and through its glass doors he could see vehicles pulling out of the parking area and queuing up at the main exit from this place. The people here must have been warned about the danger of staying put, but obviously hadn't been warned about the danger of taking large noticeable vehicles outside. Had Penny Royal delivered a warning, or had someone else? Had it been decided by some horribly cold mind that those departing vehicles would act as decoys whilst the one they considered important, Jeremiah Tombs, made his escape?

They made their way to the glass doors, following others out, just as something like thunder rumbled above. Grant looked up to see an image similar to one recorded in the past here—a hooder up there on the glass dome—only it wasn't on its way across, it had paused, its legs trying to scrape purchase and a blur under its hood where it was scratching the glass to opacity. It rose up, a jointed tower, gleaming red navigation lights at its top, then it came down like a giant fist.

With the impact, the floor of the way station seemed to drop half a metre. Grant staggered, saw others falling over, noted Tombs squatting and retaining his balance, head tilted upwards and eyes closed as if he was enjoying some sun. The whole dome bowed inwards and with a sound like mountains clashing, shattered and rained down, the hooder flowing down with it like black oil. It hit the parking area hood first and the rest of it thundered down in a rain of armoured glass like quartz boulders. Its hood came up again, crowned with wreckage, and it shook itself. A mangled ATV, perhaps Grant's vehicle, smashed into the buildings to their right, just as Grant grabbed Tombs's shoulder and pulled him on.

"We go round!" Grant shouted into the din of demolition and screaming. Shree moved ahead of him even as he spoke. They ran round along the aisle between buildings and gardens, partially shielded from falling wreckage by the spread of grape-tree branches. They passed the fallen ATV and Grant saw that it actually was his vehicle. Some people were here, staring stunned at the scene, others with more purpose were running, and one group of three were down on their knees, praying.

Even as they reached the other side of the way station, a second hooder flowed in from above. The first now speared into the apartment block and swung across, cutting through the buildings like a finger drawn through soft cake. The second hooder, a smaller version, slammed its hood down on something, then up again, spewing abattoir wreckage across the foamstone. It looked like more than one person. Seemed the hooders here weren't slow-feeding, just obliterating.

Grant kicked open a door ahead, followed emergency exit signs to where people clad in armoured work clothes were already cramming through a door into a narrow tunnel through the surrounding reinforced concrete. It seemed the work crew here had a better idea of how they might survive this.

"Why would anyone do that?" The woman ahead had been injured—blood all down her leg, leaning for support on a coworker Grant at first thought was an adapted Human, until he recognized the birdlike legs and knew it to be a dracoman.

The dracoman did not reply, but one of the others did. "Probably some Smythian."

How wrong you are, thought Grant. This had Tidy Squad written all over it. After attempting a straight hit the Squad had upscaled to something more careless of casualties to get to Tombs. And how appropriate those murderers must have thought it to set hooders on one who had once survived an attack by such a creature—a tidy resolution to the existence of Jeremiah Tombs that took no account of other consequences.

A door stood open ahead through which the road crew were spilling out into Masadan night, pastel-lit by the cabochon face of Calypse on the horizon. Grant pushed out, slid down a concrete slope turned slick by crushed rhizome, regained his balance on compacted flute grass and looked round for Tombs and Shree. Over to his left, crouching, Shree with her thin-gun in her right hand and a handful of Tombs's jacket in her left.

"Penny Royal?" Grant asked.

There were creatures out here, three of them. Grazers? Something like that but lower to the ground with odd protrusions from their backs. Then Grant realized he was seeing mounts of some kind, single dracoman mahouts astride thick scaled necks, the road crew scrambling up the flanks of the mounts to cling onto cargo frames. Even as he saw this, one of the mounts turned and disappeared into vegetation, its departure strangely musical as it disturbed old flute-grass stems. Another sound then—the music of demons as a high-speed train arrived at Hell's way station. The hooder just appeared out of darkness like such a train spearing from a tunnel, flicking one of the dracoman mounts onto its back and going over it like a blunt saw over liver, then rising up into the night.

The thing reared up and up, in silhouette against Calypse, some monstrous cobra, but one fashioned of slick, hard black components moving with oiled smoothness against each other. But as it surged forwards and down, the hollow machine movement in its cowl became visible, then its columns of red eyes, as if some power breaker had been switched on inside it at that moment. Almost certainly its targets were the other dracoman mounts nearby, but it would come down across where Grant, Shree, Tombs and other refugees crouched.

I'm dead, was all Grant could think, frozen to the spot.

Then the hooder slammed to a halt against some invisible wall, which became visible at that moment: Penny Royal, ten metres up, a curved face with inward-pointing spikes, tentacles wound into a trunk rooting down into the ground and bowing under the impact. The hooder itself arched with the strain, a terrible hissing shrieking cutting the night, then came a sound as of a tank going over a glass greenhouse. Lightning flashed, a single static electricity gunshot discharge. Debris began to rain down as the two opponents swayed back and forth, and Grant was horrified to see a single black spine spear down into the soft ground beside him. Then an explosion between the two, blinding bright, and more debris, flute grass flattened as if under some giant aerofan, dracoman mounts and their Human cargo fleeing under it. The ground came out from underneath Grant and when another explosion ensued, then another, he put his hands over his head and fought the urge to pray.

"*Keep moving west,*" whispered Penny Royal.

Grant peered out, saw the hooder, headless, writhing as it fell, Penny Royal bowed over—some carnivorous plant suffering terminal indigestion.

"*Wesst,*" hissed the AI, a strange reverberating echo behind its instruction.

Up on his feet, Grant ran to the other two, pulled up Shree, Tombs following. He couldn't hear what they said, ears ringing, and perhaps they couldn't hear his instructions. But they followed him out into the wilderness, fleeing a writhing destruction as hooders tore the station apart.

12

After the Quiet War, when art was no longer supported by state funds or by those more interested in iconoclasm, the grotesqueries of the previous centuries died a deserved death. People were no longer satisfied or impressed by political messages in an age when politicians and ideologues had become objects of ridicule. Higher general intelligence and broader knowledge of the world, of the solar system, also enabled them to at last see through the obfuscations and justifications of lazy but glib pretenders to art. Something of a renaissance occurred when art returned at last to its natural state of being beautiful objects or elegant design that people are prepared to pay for. Thousands of artists, who previously would not have considered producing objects of beauty, now started producing. Legions of art critics whose greatest skill was analysis of non-existent meaning discovered an urgent need to retrain. And the time had returned at last when a gorgeous painting taking weeks of skill to produce might garner more praise than a frozen pig's penis in a glass of vodka.

—From a speech by Jobsworth

Chanter slammed shut the door of the room provided for him, pack slung over one shoulder containing both his special food and a copy of his research notes—the latter because he didn't trust Rodol to consider them as important as he did, and so keep them safe. He felt a confused amalgam of excitement and anger, and he didn't know if he was angry at himself for doubting beliefs that in the past had been firm, or angry at believing such stuff in the first place.

The Technician is on the move.

It had been so easy to wrap himself up in his esoteric pursuits and deep analysis of the wealth of data that had become available. He had convinced himself he was forging a lot closer to understanding the Technician's art, but now it was on the move again and new data was flooding in from the observation tower, new hypotheses were arising that threw his speculations into further doubt.

It's a war machine.

When Clyde told him that, Chanter had felt a deep offence, his instinctive reaction being that nothing made for the specific purpose of delivering destruction and death could have artistic sensibilities. He had argued with the man, even then realizing how infantile his reaction was but unable to stop himself. Wartime produced some of the greatest art, and only the exigencies of survival, and a lack of excess wealth and spare time for those involved, limited its quantity. Even so, when Clyde went on to inform him that the Technician might also be an evolved creature adapted, genetically altered and augmented for the purpose of battle, he had grasped at that as a man sinking into some quagmire would grasp at overhanging flute grasses.

"Then there is the trauma from which the art arises," Chanter had said. "A natural creature twisted to kill, destructive technologies sewn through its body, all that it was repressed, crippled, broken."

"You're assuming it wasn't a killer before. You're assuming prior sentience and enough of a mind to suffer." Clyde had gazed up at him from where he sat before his screen, data maps cycling spookily like bone sculptures. "The organism from which the Technician arose might have had no more mind than some Terran arthropod—might have been no more than something programmed by evolution to kill, eat and breed."

"The sculptures tell me otherwise," said Chanter. "How appropriate that a creature distorted for war should choose so bloody a medium for its art."

"What analytical mind the Technician had, and might still have, could all be additional, could all be the kind of add-ons you see in a haiman. Its mind could be the most artificial thing about it."

"Artificial intelligences produce art," Chanter responded, then realized he had just contradicted something that had been a contention of his for most of his life, from which his earlier offence had arisen. He *believed* that machines did not produce art. He had always felt that only evolved creatures could produce it, that AIs only copied, they did not have the *soul.* Then, out of that thought and all that dodgy word—soul—implied, he felt a deep confusion. Clyde just looked at Chanter pityingly, probably understanding, even from their brief association, that he had just shot himself in the foot.

"You just don't understand," said the amphidapt, hot anger purple-blushing his warty skin.

"On the contrary," said Clyde. "I understand that your house of cards is collapsing, Chanter, and that despite everything, you have the intelligence to see it."

Chanter just turned and left, feeling stupid and very annoyed with himself.

His mudmarine was just where he had left it, still keeping pace with the slow molluscan crawl of the Tagreb. He pointed his remote control at it as he stomped wetly across ground churned up by the movement of the base, and its door opened for him offering welcome retreat inside. Ensconced in his chair he pulled across and fastened his safety straps. Grabbing the control column he tilted it forward and down, the machinery responding with a comforting roar, soon muffled as the marine speared down into the mud. Next checking the location of the Technician's beacon on his screen and the intervening seismic maps, he changed course ten metres below the surface and headed for a nearby undercurrent of slushy mud flowing between ancient layers of decayed rhizome.

If the Technician didn't change its present course he would intercept it in about two hours. Thereafter he would be able to keep pace with the creature until its next kill. He felt certain that the creature must be aware, in some way, of recent events. It had to be aware that its living artwork, Jeremiah Tombs, was on the move too and was in some way responding to this. And, maybe, even after twenty years of no product, no art, its next kill might be turned into something new, something different, something from which Chanter would be able to extract explanations, find some sort of resolution . . .

Twilight brought no rest, just better visibility in which to observe the devastation. The way station looked like a titan had segmented it with some immense cleaver, then torn out its guts and strewn them about the surrounding landscape. The big tricone shell, almost the length of Grant's ATV, offered welcome cover for the three of them. Others had hidden in some of the debris—Jem had seen people peeking out from the large chunk of apartment building lying canted where it had landed in the mud a hundred metres away. Still others had not been so lucky. Just a few metres away from where they crouched behind the shell lay a woman's head, whilst a little way beyond it lay what might have been her enviroboot, the foot still inside.

Debris both Human and machine strewed the surrounding landscape. Judging by the wreckage lying smeared across from where the way station main entrance had been, not one of the departing vehicles had escaped. As he studied the whorls in the curve of shell before him, Jem wondered if anyone at all had managed to get clear of the area, including those the dracomen had come for.

"I think it fairly fucking evident that they're missing nothing," said Shree.

"They're still looking for dying gabbleducks," said Grant. "And anything that moves they'll come down on."

"So when do they stop looking?"

"After that last hit Penny Royal told me the hormone had spread over an area of twenty square kilometres and mentioned something called catastrophic cascade."

"Oh yeah?"

Grant seemed perfectly calm, thought Jem, perfectly at rest in this madness, and so, it seemed, did Jem himself. *Where is my guilt?* he wondered. *Where is my pain?* The answer to those questions seemed astounding in its simplicity: the organism he was could not afford them whilst fighting for its own survival. Guilt and other emotional sufferings were an indulgence, a luxury only afforded to those with the resources to waste on them.

"The death hormone from one gabbleduck is, depending on wind direction and air quality, enough to summon hooders from the surrounding fifty square kilometres of flute grasses," the soldier explained. "Unless we get a north wind to blow this out over the south coast, there could be enough hormone in the air to send hooders crazy from east to west across the entire continent down here."

"Let's hope they follow the wind into the sea," said Shree.

Grant gazed at her steadily. "I'm told that's a possibility, which is why every vehicle in Greenport is being used to transport the population there to the east, including the cargo ships, and which is why no vehicles are available from there to help us here."

"I thought he was important." She stabbed a finger at Jem.

"He is, but we're safe now."

"Penny Royal tell you this?" She nodded towards where a tower of shadow knives was sliding to put itself between them and the line of a hooder crossing below the horizon like a black monorail train. Convenient that the huge number of hooders in the area had crushed down most of the flute grasses, for now they could see them coming.

"No, I got that from Amistad," said Grant. "Penny Royal ain't saying much now."

"It's been damaged, hasn't it?"

A slight whine in her voice caught Jem's attention and he looked at her curiously. Ostensibly she seemed to be showing fear of her own demise, yet it came with an underlying frustration. Gazing at her flat Human features, the tense pose of her body and the way her hand never strayed far from the butt of her thin-gun, he understood that fear of death was not her greatest concern, but fear of *inappropriate* death. Returning his attention to the shell whorls he traced one with his finger, further hints of meaning now apparent under a Braillelike sensation. "Of course Penny Royal has been damaged," he said.

They both turned to look at him, but when he offered no further explanation, returned to their conversation.

"Amistad is getting us out of here," said Grant. "Transport should arrive for us in about an hour."

"Shit, where's it coming from? Zealos?"

Jem removed his finger from the shell, looked over towards where the corpse of the hooder Penny Royal had killed lay just visible between them and the remains of the way station. It had been that first creature that damaged the AI, immediately demoting it from the legions of Hell to reality; a reality excised of the supernatural, but nonetheless strange and frightening. Penny Royal had underestimated that first attacker, taken the full brunt of its attack like a hand raised to stop a falling blade. Jem had seen parts of the AI smashed away before it resorted to more conventional weaponry to blow off the creature's head. With the other two hooders that came close the AI used different techniques, presenting a hard surface to divert their course, actinic light, other radiations and an output of complex hormones to blind and confuse. Of course, the soldier and the killer, Shree, only averted their gaze from the light; they did not have the other radiations screaming in their heads nor taste and smell the contradictory messages of those hormones in the air, as did Jem. So blind and dull these Humans.

"Most vehicles to the north of us are being used to evacuate areas up there," Grant explained. "But these are here for the survivors."

He pointed towards the horizon where three black shapes became visible, catching sunlight on their sides from the rising sun. Watching these things approach Jem recognized old Theocracy troop transporters.

"They'll get torn apart," said Shree.

"I think not," said Grant.

Shree gazed at him, her expression all suspicion. "I see . . . so we should board them." She turned as something crashed in the way station and the cowl of another hooder rose out of it. "Seems pretty fucking dangerous round here."

"We're safe," Grant repeated. "And we've got other transport."

Jem watched the transporters drawing closer, three fifty-metre-long bricks of bubble metal kept in the sky by aerofan, thruster nacelles protruding at the back should their usual lumbering pace not be enough to get them out of trouble. No gravmotors, no sleek, fast and efficient Polity technology—they had probably been requisitioned from a museum. No way, on their own, could they survive both landing and take-off in an area swarming with hooders like this. Jem transferred his gaze to the sky directly above. Though Calypse still occupied the eastern sky and though the sun lay close to rising, some stars were still visible, one of them steady and metallic, and which hadn't been up there twenty years ago.

"Dragon destroyed the laser arrays," said Shree, a hint of bitterness in her voice. "It destroyed the Theocracy's main power for oppression. How free are we now, Grant?"

The soldier shrugged. "A gun ain't evil—only the fuck pulling the trigger is that."

"Far too trite and easy," she replied.

Grant shrugged again, gave her an estimating look as she turned away from him to watch the transporters start a circling descent. Jem watched for a moment too, then abruptly switched his attention to Penny Royal, now rolling across the landscape like a lost cloud full of steel crows as it moved to position itself between them and the hooder departing the way station. He felt that sensation again—the one he had felt arising when the AI had turned away the third attacking hooder—that feeling of denial and an upswell in his mind that deposited penny mollusc shell patterns across internal vision, encoded for external inspection.

The first old troop transporter came down near the wreckage the hooders had made of the departing ground vehicles, and a surprising number of people fled their hideaways, some running, some limping, others being carried. The hooder from the way station turned towards this scene and accelerated. A roar of aerofans above and a second transporter descended nearby, coming down by the chunk of apartment building. Refugees fled that like parasites departing an old mattress doused with insecticide, soon reaching a rapidly lowered ramp and clambering inside. Jem watched these for a moment. Distantly another hooder had been drawn in, but it wouldn't get there in time. The way station hooder was a different matter so, with a feeling of regret, Jem returned his attention to it.

The strike ruptured air molecules all the way down, a violet fire seeming the refined essence of the aubergine sky, concentrated and hurled down. It lasted for only an eyeblink, but left a black after-image like a column of shadow. A sphere of fire expanded ten metres back from the hooder's cowl, bright red at first then swiftly guttering with little oxygen to maintain it. The blast peeled up rhizome and black mud, whilst the fore-section of the hooder tumbled away like a discarded spoon. The rest of its body bucked up and peeled back, came down again writhing—a beheaded snake.

"How different are Polity satellite weapons from the Theocracy's?" Shree asked.

"A damned sight more powerful, for one thing," the soldier replied, then he tilted his head for a moment, listening. "Amistad tells me we need to head west—the hooders were starting to move off but this is pulling "em back."

"This doesn't make any sense," said Shree angrily. She pointed towards the transporter down by the ruined chunk of building. "A couple of minutes and we can be away from here."

"No one's stopping you," said Grant. He turned to Jem. "You coming?"

Jem considered the question very carefully. If their remaining in this area was to result in further strikes, he would have objected—why destroy more of those fine creatures just so three Humans could get to a particular designated transport? So wasteful. He concentrated on Penny Royal. The AI had begun to close in on them, meanwhile becoming less and less visible. It had been repairing itself, its latest repairs evidently to its chameleonware shield, so it seemed likely it would be able to hide them, and that no further satellite strikes would be necessary.

"Yes," he replied. "I am coming."

The third lander had descended right beside the way station to disgorge a crew of humanoids who were carrying heavy-looking hand tools and darted into the ruination faster than any Human should be able to move. Golem, Jem realized, able to hear the beat of a heart, able to sense signs of recoverable life even after the heart had stopped beating, able to trace down the beacons of memchips. Strong too, enough power to rip away twisted wreckage trapping survivors, enough to rapidly dig away rubble with those tools they carried. Not demons.

It occurred to him to wonder how he could see so far and in such detail with just binocular vision, then he realized he was just manipulating the visual data more efficiently, dispensing with the models Humans used to save on mental processing, and seeing *everything*.

Some survivors did leave the way station under their own power, but with the place having been the focus of the attack, not so many as out here. Jem stood up, feeling a momentary joy when he saw the woman from reception limping out towards the transport, and the Human emotion flipped over biological switches in his skull, and his clarity of vision degraded. Was that really her? How could he be sure that distant, ragged and mud-covered figure was her? He turned and followed as Grant led off, Penny Royal sliding in ahead of them, now a grey veil, a mere distortion in the air.

"You'll need to hurry if you want to get to that transport before it takes off," the soldier called over his shoulder.

Jem glanced round as Shree swore under her breath then, after a pause, stomped after them. Another switch clicked over in his skull. Her act was good but Jem could see right through it. He wondered if the soldier could too. Did Grant see her pretence of reluctance to accompany them as an attempt to restore trust and repair the damage she had done by earlier revealing her true feelings? Did he understand that now her fear of an inappropriate death had been removed she was trying to restore her simple reporter persona by displaying fear of death alone?

"Penny Royal is extending chameleonware to cover us," said Grant. "But be ready to move fast—if we end up in the path of a hooder it not seeing us ain't any protection."

"So Penny Royal's talking again?" asked Shree, moving up beside him.

Grant gazed at her blankly for a moment. "Yeah, it's talking." The man did not want her with them anymore, this lay evident in the minutiae of his expression.

Jem turned away, also realizing something else: some crucial encounter was imminent. Immutable facts confirmed this. The increased activity here would not summon in more hooders, for focused on the death hormone they were hard-wired to respond to, they would go where it was more concentrated, and the breeze against Jem's cheek told him that was to the west, precisely where they were heading. Those Euclidean shapes up in the forefront of his mind like a shield, he trudged after the other two, idly wondering why his feet kept sinking into the soft ground, then remembering this was because his legs terminated in small Human feet.

"There is no doubt that it will have an impact," Amistad had informed him. "Penny Royal agrees that circumstances are fortuitous and should be taken advantage of—we were going to confront him with it anyway."

It certainly was having an impact, but whether Tombs felt that impact any more than Grant himself, the soldier could not say.

Even at this distance from the way station, much surrounding vegetation had been flattened, only occasional islands of flute grass still standing, along with a nearby copse of lizard tails sprouting from an islet of dried-out rhizome protruding from the surface. Hooders were visible whichever way he looked. But now he wasn't looking at any normal hooder. The Technician appeared as a movement on the horizon to their right, little to distinguish it from the other hooders they had seen. However, as it moved closer the dawn sunlight reflected off its white back, glistened on carapace like polished ivory. The thing was bigger even than the first hooder to attack the way station. It had probably reached some physical limitation to the species of which it seemed only marginally a member. Its cowl was also longer and flatter, more sleek, more dangerous-looking.

Grant halted and swung towards it, a disturbance in the air twenty metres out swinging round with him and moving away as Penny Royal planted itself between them and the creature.

"You're sure it can't see us?" he asked out loud.

"Increasingly less so," Penny Royal whispered in his ear.

"What is this, Grant?" asked Shree, sounding worried.

Tombs offered her an explanation. "What it is is self-evident. My nemesis comes."

Grant turned towards them. "Amistad is aboard the mobile observation tower that was set to watch over this creature, which was somnolent until the death hormone reached it three hours ago."

"So it's just like the other hooders?" said Shree.

Grant focused on Tombs. "Is it just like the others?"

For a few seconds the man just continued gazing at the distant but rapidly approaching creature as if he hadn't heard, then swung his attention to Grant, with eyes wide and a slightly crazy smirk twisting his mouth. "Of course it is not just like the others. Golem are similar to Humans, those augmented creatures called haimen are similar to Humans, but never can they be described as 'just like' Humans. The differences here"—Tombs stabbed a finger towards the Technician—"are of a similar nature."

"What did it do to you, Tombs?" Grant asked.

"What did it do?" Tombs now tilted his head to one side, gazing at the great white hooder as if studying the activity of a beloved pet. "The nature of the beast is to feed and so it did, cutting me as all hooders cut their prey so as not to release poisons contained in the black fats. So fine was its surgery it cut without allowing me to bleed, just as Penny Royal cuts. With deep respect it lovingly peeled away skin, fat and muscle and consumed them." He turned back towards Grant and the soldier stepped back, couldn't see anything Human in the man's expression. "But there is more to the nature of this beast—something retained almost like instinct after the mechanism stamped on its consciousness and rewired its mind like a child using a penknife to adjust a computer."

"Mechanism?"

"Penny Royal knows."

"And what more is there to the Technician's nature?"

"Its weaver did not choose oblivion, soldier. So many did not, which is why the tricones grind so fine." Tombs kicked at the matted rhizome they stood upon.

"I don't get it," said Grant, though some he did. The mechanism must be that Atheter machine that tore Penny Royal apart, but what was this weaver and that stuff about the tricones?

"What is the Technician's distinguishing nature?" Tombs asked rhetorically. "Grief, soldier; a grief inconsolable for a million years and an anger that must have been great enough to enable it to rebuild the wreckage of its mind." Tombs reached up and traced some shape in the air with his forefinger, but he looked bemused. "That can be the only explanation for how it recovered from the mechanism."

"Run!" a new voice boomed through the air. "Run and hide!"

This was Penny Royal, speaking out loud for the first time.

"It's heading directly towards us," Grant said. "We need to get out of its path."

"But it can't see us," Shree protested.

"Of course not," Grant replied. "Just coincidence."

His hope not to be contradicted was immediately destroyed when Penny Royal informed them, "On the contrary."

"What do you fucking mean?" asked Shree.

Grant surveyed their surroundings. They could conceal themselves in that stand of lizard tails, but that was the best they could do. There was no point just continuing to run. If Penny Royal could not stop this creature then it would surely catch them.

"The proctor confirms its nature," Penny Royal stated. "The war machine is fully functional and can see us."

"Come on." Grant reached out to grab Tombs's shoulder, only to find that steely resistance there again. Tombs peered down at Grant's hand, but did not react so violently this time, just brushed it away.

"It is not necessary," the man said.

Shree was already running, her thin-gun clutched in her hand.

"You might like to stop a while under that cowl again, Tombs, but I've no intention of letting that thing near me."

Tombs blinked, looked vaguely confused for a moment, and then whatever had laced steel through his body seemed to drain out of him. The man looked over towards the approaching Technician, huge now, beginning to rear above the air disturbance that was Penny Royal, now shedding its chameleonware.

"Yes," he said, turning, stumbling at first, then breaking into a steady lope after Shree.

Grant followed, pulling his own disc gun out of its holster. He wondered if he would be capable of turning the weapon on himself should the big white hooder get to him, or would he, like so many, still hope to survive even as the sharp darkness closed over him? His legs felt slightly weak, wobbly, as he ran on an adrenalin surge, never seeming to go fast enough. Even as he stepped up onto the islet of dry rhizome and pushed aside clattering lizard tails, there came from behind a sound like a monorail running full-tilt into a mountain of glass.

Grant threw himself down beside the other two and peered out. Penny Royal was now fully visible, a big black sea urchin, perfectly spherical, but with tentacles curving out from between lower spines to spear into the rhizome mat below. Twenty metres out from the AI the curved interface of a hardfield cut the air, and the Technician was skating along this, its armoured underside and knife-like legs visible, its cowl screeching along leaving a trail of odd pinkish flames. Even as it slid towards the side of the hardfield, Grant could see the effect of whatever it was doing. Penny Royal sank halfway into the ground, the rhizome mat all around it steaming, then bubbling to release hot gouts of smoke.

"War machine?" said Shree breathlessly.

"Maybe an original," Grant replied, then swallowed to try and relieve the tightness in his throat.

The hardfield blinked out and the Technician slammed to the ground, then accelerated off to the left leaving in its wake a long cloud of broken flute-grass stems. Was it running? No, it curved round, continuing to build up speed. Penny Royal now began to re-form, first flattening out, all its spines directed upwards, then this mass peeling off the ground on a thick plait of tentacles and cupping like a radar dish towards the now approaching hooder, stalked red eyes folding out on either side for triangulation. Grant saw the inner spines of that cup fold in, connect, and from them a distortion, like a ball of glass worms, writhed into being before the cup, then shot towards the Technician.

"What the hell is that?" Shree hissed.

"Beats me," Grant replied.

"It is hardfield energy formatted to induce a viral attack within the Technician's systems," Tombs stated.

They both turned to gaze at him. He was up on one knee now, his hands on his raised knee and his chin resting on them.

"How the fuck do you know that?" Grant asked.

Tombs stared at the soldier, the alien back in his face. "It is obvious," he stated.

The worm-thing unravelled to strike the forefront of the hooder's cowl, turning into a wave of energy travelling the length of its body. The creature nosed into the ground, peeling up a mountain of debris before it. Even from where they hid they felt the impact, the ground shuddering underneath them. But then the creature rose again, skated over that mountain, came down with its body arcing like a caterpillar, then snapping straight. Glass worms in the air again, issuing from between the Technician's segments and corkscrewing along the length of its body, then on towards Penny Royal. As they struck, the black AI just lost coherence, came apart like a flower losing its petals, turned into a cloud of spines loosely connected by a cage of tentacles.

"Fuck," said Shree, and took a moment to check the action of her thin-gun. Grant glanced at her, certain now that she wouldn't be using that weapon first on herself. He abruptly knew her thoughts. Maybe if she wounded Tombs and even Grant himself, she would be able to get away while the hooder fed.

Penny Royal began to reform, components slotting back into place. From this mass a proton beam speared out, struck the Technician's cowl, but only half a second before that cowl slammed straight into the AI. The entire hooder shuddered to an abrupt halt, and for half a kilometre behind the AI the ground rippled, split, and ejected fumaroles of mud. The immense sound bludgeoned the ears, as if from some massive building coming down. The very air seemed to strain and something, some very cord of existence, seemed to snap. The Technician backed away and Penny Royal hung off the ground for a moment, shivering, then just started to fall apart, steam rising from where its components landed in churned mud.

"Now we die," said Grant as the Technician's cowl swung towards them.

"Where're your damned Polity satellite weapons?" Shree asked viciously.

"They won't use them, not against this." Yes, Tombs was valuable because of what his mind contained, but the Polity AIs wouldn't destroy its original source to save him, or them. Grant turned towards her, but she wasn't looking at him, but peering past him at Tombs. Grant glanced round. Tombs had stepped down from the islet of dry rhizome and begun walking out to meet his nemesis.

"Get back here!" Grant yelled, struggling forward then tumbling down from the little islet, regaining his feet and going after Tombs. Was the man trying to sacrifice himself to save them? What the hell was he doing?

The Technician rose, its cowl up and flaring, opening out in a way Grant had never seen before, from any hooder. The movement of its feeding apparatus seemed odd, as if it were trying to form patterns like data maps. Its eyes, Grant noticed, weren't red, but a dull yellow. Tombs came to a halt.

"It is all right," he said, but whether he was addressing Grant or the monster before them Grant didn't know.

Abruptly the hooder bowed, nosed closer along the ground, its massive cowl slowly drawing to a halt, its rim just a metre from Tombs's chest. The man just stood there, arms akimbo, head tilted to one side. Then he reached out and that cowl eased closer. He rested his hand on it for a moment, before abruptly turning away. Crazy smile there, utterly weird. Behind him the Technician once again set itself in motion, swinging away and propelling itself off across the plain. Tombs dipped his head, pulled the string to which he had attached a penny mollusc shell up over it, then tossed this to Grant, who fumbled it and had to stoop to pick it up.

"Your AIs want answers, don't they?" Tombs enquired.

"Yeah, sure they do."

"Well I have one for them." He gestured to the shell Grant held. "Not all the Atheter chose to destroy their civilization, and some tried to save things by encoding them in the life of this world."

Grant gazed at the pattern on the shell.

"It means oblivion," Tombs told him. "But only one state of oblivion, one nuance of it."

13

Taxonomic and genetic research bases, or Tagrebs, look like giant iron tulip flowers when stored in the vast holds of the research vessels that deliver them. Launched, a Tagreb maintains this shape during entry into a planetary atmosphere while its AI comes online. The AI then slows the Tagreb in lower atmosphere with fusion thrusters before finally descending to a chosen location using gravmotors. Upon landing the flower opens, folds four petals down to the ground. From this five plasmel domes inflate—one at the centre and one over each petal. Their internal structures—floors, ceilings, walls and stairs—are inflated at the same time. The AI then decides how best to continue.

On Masada the Tagreb AI, Rodol, first injected a thick layer of a resin matrix into the boggy ground below to protect the base from tricone depredations, before injecting the same substance into the hollow walls and floors of the structure itself. Next the AI woke its telefactors, which immediately took the requisite materials outside the base to construct an electrified perimeter fence and four gun towers. Unusually, these towers were supplied in this case with proton cannons capable of punching holes through thick armour, for some of the natives were anything but friendly. After three days the base was ready for the next stage. Automated landers descended inside the fence and the telefactors began bringing in supplies: food, bedding, nanoscopes, full-immersion VR suites, soaps and gels, nano, micro and submacro assembler rigs, an aspidistra in a pot, autodocs, autofactories, holocams, coffee makers . . . Every item was slotted into its place or plugged in.

On day six Rodol brought the fusion reactor fully online,

supplying power to the multitude of sockets throughout the base. Lights, embedded in the ceilings, were ready to come on. Sanitary facilities were ready to recycle waste. Rodol stabbed filter heads down into the ground to suck up water, which was first cracked for its oxygen to bring the internal atmosphere to requirements, and thereafter pumped into holding tanks. The Humans, haimans and Golem arrived shortly afterwards; disembarking from shuttles with massive hover trunks gliding along behind them. Only a few days after was it discovered that the five gravplatforms were not nearly enough for those who wanted to do field work. Grudgingly, Rodol cleared Polity funds to pay the local population for twenty aerofans and five fattyred, all-terrain vehicles. Then the research began . . .

—*From* THE MASADAN CHRONICLE

"Penny Royal?" Amistad enquired.

"*Fzzzt,*" came the reply, but along with that an image feed of the three Humans now out of concealment, and the Technician off in the distance, still moving away.

The albino hooder wasn't tracking the death hormone like the other hooders, which further confirmed Penny Royal's analysis of Tombs's earlier statement: the Technician was once again fully functional, and had aims beyond the usual drives of a hooder. Doubtless it had brought itself to this state through its twenty years of napping. It was also damned dangerous; catching, copying and reformatting Penny Royal's patterned hardfield attack was something Amistad doubted he himself could have done before his recent upgrade. Also the proton beam hit had caused little damage, somehow refracted through another design of hardfield. Amistad knew of few Polity war drones that could take Penny Royal apart so quickly.

Unable to keep still, the big scorpion drone moved to the edge of the viewing platform as he further considered what had been learned. Tombs's initial reaction indicated that the man had known the Technician wasn't there to kill them, though his subsequent reaction and him hiding himself with the others indicated a mind in a perpetual state of flux. Penny

Royal had already recorded this cerebral activity; occasional increases in function, neural activity ramped up to levels the Human brain could not sustain for long, a side-effect being the kind of physical muscular integration only found in those who had either loaded martial arts programs or had trained for years. Knowledge, whose source could not be the original Tombs, was also surfacing in the man's mind.

Tombs had known precisely the nature of Penny Royal's defence against the Technician. It was the kind of knowledge possessed only by those once involved or still involved in hightech warfare, and Tombs's experience only extended to Theocracy rail-guns, chemically propelled projectiles and the usual bottom-end energy weapons.

Other comments were of note. Tombs opined that not all the Atheter had wanted to destroy themselves—a conjecture Amistad had already considered because the likelihood of every member of a high-tech civilization agreeing on such a matter must be positively minuscule. The man had stated that this was why the tricones "ground so fine," which perfectly fitted current knowledge. The tricones chewed solid objects down to a size of no more than just over three millimetres and, now having applied this measure to what it knew about Atheter memstorage, Amistad had ascertained that pieces of an Atheter memstore of this size were not large enough to retain fully identifiable mental structures and would chemically degrade within a few centuries, wiping out anything else remaining in them. The purpose of the tricones was to grind up the remnants of the Atheter civilization but, more importantly, it was to destroy those Atheter who had tried to save themselves by storing their minds.

Then, of course, Tombs's brief exchange with Grant.

Oblivion.

"How did you miss that?" Amistad routed his enquiry to the distant Tagreb.

Rodol took its time replying. "I've transmitted the information to our foremost expert on the Gabble—Shardelle Garadon—along with all the penny mollusc shell patterns we have on file."

"I'm looking at them now," said the drone, those patterns visible to him in a virtual mental space. "And you still haven't answered my question."

"The Atheter themselves missed it," Rodol grumped.

"You know as well as I," said Amistad, "that those Atheter who did not choose oblivion probably stored the shell patterns as alleles within the penny mollusc genome, set and ready for some later mutation or unravelling telomere to release them."

"Yeah, probably."

That the Tagreb AI had missed the glyphs of the Atheter language incised into the shells of those molluscs perfectly demonstrated the necessity of the AI approach of feeding different minds different sets of "facts." Knowledge blindness was equally endemic amidst all intelligences, whether their minds ran in crystal or grey watery fat.

"Why didn't we pick up on this stuff from the Atheter AI?" Amistad asked.

"Because all its communications have been in a Human format, and before it effectively shut down it was parsimonious with its knowledge and about as Delphic in its communications as Dragon." Rodol paused. "You are up to date on current knowledge, Amistad—now you are a prime, nothing is being kept from you."

Amistad had been wondering if he himself had been fed a "different set of facts" that excluded stuff from the Atheter AI. Rodol's claim that this wasn't so did nothing to reassure the drone.

"So what else have we missed?"

"We are reviewing data files, and are now looking for hidden knowledge," said Rodol. "And already some anomalies are coming to light—some unusual redundancies."

"Like what?"

"Like it seems that the Atheter art department was overrun with subversives."

"What?"

"Thus far it appears that beyond saving the Atheter written language for posterity, the penny mollusc shell pattern serves no other function. It neither camouflages nor is it one of those preposterous developments related to mating."

"Oh dear," said Amistad. "I do hope you haven't passed this on to Chanter yet."

"Perhaps best to let him find out about it later."

"Yes, I think so."

"So tell me about redundancy."

"Further assessment of the studies of the photoactive amoebae in a hooder's eyes reveal that producing light does not serve to increase the survivability of either the amoebae or their host, and that the amoebae contain apparently redundant and extremely complex mechanisms to modulate the frequency, direction and colour of that light, all across the spectrum from 350 ultraviolet to 780 infrared, which we know is the precise spectrum covered by a gabbleduck's vision."

"Go on."

"Also of note is that it is the differences in this modulation that led us to classifying over four thousand separate genera of photoactive amoebae—there is very little else to distinguish each genus."

"And this means?"

"Image files."

Had some Atheter, facing extinction, stored its family snapshots in the amoeba genome?

"Do you have any clear yet?"

"Yes, we do have some fragments."

The image file arrived in an instant. It showed a complicated tangle of tubes interlinking a variety of globular shapes. Holes were punched into the interiors of these objects, and in the darkness of some of these glinted things suspiciously like eyes. Amistad chose one hole and took magnification up to its pixel limit to reveal the head of a gabbleduck, no, an Atheter, something metallic woven across the top of its bill. Next swinging perspective to one side, Amistad saw that the whole structure seemed to be made of a basket weave of flute-grass stems.

"Their cities sang," Rodol noted.

"An appropriate moment for me to butt in," some other abruptly interjected.

As Rodol tumbled away, the one interjecting leapfrogging from the Tagreb AI and occupying all the bandwidth of the communication, Amistad felt a momentary anger at the interruption, suppressed at once when he realized its source.

"Appropriate in what way?"

This new intelligence reached out and touched Amistad's mind, replaying something that had come direct from Penny Royal. The drone saw Tombs telling Grant, *"Its weaver did not choose oblivion, soldier. So many did not, which is why the tricones grind so fine."*

"They wove their cities," said Amistad.

"Their whole technology was based on the weaving process," replied the Earth Central AI, ruler of the Polity. "It indicates that Masada was truly their Homeworld and that flute grasses are a natural product of evolution, and not part of an engineered ecology, though that is beside the point. The point, rather, is this."

An image file arrived, digital recording, Polity format, data packet accompanying it. Amistad gazed upon a massive horn-shaped object poised over a green gas giant, sucking substance from that Jovian world like some monstrous leech—a *woven* horn-shaped object with high-scale density and evidently alien technology packing its interior. Running the timeline forward Amistad watched the thing complete its feeding, ignite a nuclear blast behind it and hurtle out from the giant, to then suddenly stretch, down to nothing, spearing away into the dark.

"Its rather novel U-jumps are limited to ten light years at a time," Earth Central explained. "We suspect both its method of U-jumping and their limited distance are not usual, but due to an imbalance in its U-space engine."

"The Atheter device," Amistad stated.

"Yes, and coming your way."

Checking projections in the data package, the drone saw that, at its current rate of travel, this thing would arrive over Masada within five days.

"And what am I supposed to do about this?" Amistad asked.

"You'll deal with it, of course," Earth Central replied succinctly, then cut the connection.

Chanter used his cutter on the curtain of rhizome, stepped out of his mudmarine, stomped across the fallen vegetable matter then stood with his arms folded and a chunk of anger rolling in his gut. He certainly was interested in this product of the Technician, but rather resented Amistad co-opting him from chasing after that entity and employing him as a damned taxi driver. He tapped one webbed foot against the damp ground, making wet platting sounds, and peered at the three approaching.

The woman, apparently, worked for that brothel keeper of media whoredom, Earthnet, so he dismissed her from his consideration. The soldier was more interesting, since he had been there when the Technician did what it did and had then, although Tombs was a proctor, saved the man's life. To Chanter this meant that despite his martial background, Grant might possess some understanding of the Technician and its work, might have seen something beyond prosaic reality, and might know art. Tombs himself was of greatest interest, and the amphidapt studied him closely.

Tombs looked nothing like a proctor any more, but there should be no surprise in that, twenty years having passed since he wore the uniform and beat pond workers into submission. He also moved oddly, his disjointed gait carrying him to the more prominent and thick drifts of rhizome, even though all the rhizome layer here, unlike the churned and smoking area over to the right, seemed perfectly flat and easily capable of supporting the weight of a man. He walked like someone carrying a heavy load, as if worried about sinking, but as he drew close, Chanter read no worry in the man. Tombs's expression was utterly unreadable. His eyes seemed like hollows in a skull.

The three halted before Chanter, Shree and Grant studying him curiously whilst Tombs slowly lost that alien expression and took on the one of a man lost in some internal dream world. Shree and Grant of course knew about adapts, but Chanter supposed they weren't yet used to seeing them on this backward world.

"I'm to take you three to the Tagreb," Chanter snapped.

"And Penny Royal."

Chanter shivered and peered over towards that churned and smoking ground. "What happened here?"

"Amistad didn't tell you?" asked the soldier.

"No, I just got a terse instruction to pick you up and was told that you would fill me in—seems the drone's a bit busy now."

"Penny Royal had a rather close encounter with the Technician."

"Is it hurt?" Chanter asked, peering anxiously towards the churned area.

"Lying in pieces over there," said the woman.

Chanter felt something lurch inside him; all his reason for being. Some black objects were visible, had the Technician been destroyed? He swung back towards them. "Where is it?"

Grant pointed at those black objects and led the way. Chanter fell in behind the man, then quickly overtook him. In a moment they reached the objects and Chanter immediately recognized them as pieces of the black AI, and realized his misunderstanding.

"And the Technician?" he asked casually.

"In a lot better shape," Grant replied. "Didn't look like it had a scratch on it." Chanter continued to conceal his relief as the soldier gestured to Penny Royal's remains. "You got some way we can get these inside your . . . vehicle?"

"Certainly," Chanter nodded, then after a moment called, "Mick! Out here now!"

The odd-looking robot peeked out of the mudmarine, the two over there quickly moving away from the entrance as it extended one long-toed foot to test the quality of the ground. After a moment it clambered out like some giant iron cockroach that had been stepped on but still survived, scuttled past the other two, observing them with one hinged-up stalked eye, and came over to Chanter, halting before him like a sheepdog awaiting instructions.

"All this," Chanter gestured to the scattered remains of Penny Royal. "Collect it up and put it in the cargo blister. No need to be careful with it—this isn't one of the Technician's sculptures."

Mick scuttled past them, folded out one arm and closed long fingers around a single spine, yanking it up to reveal the heptahedron of grey metal attached to its base, and a length of tentacle extending from one face of that. This went onto Mick's ribbed back, where the tentacle writhed slightly. The next identical component went on, and studying the rest Chanter realized that all Penny Royal's components were of this format. He swallowed drily upon seeing one of those tentacles turn and attach to the heptahedron at the base of a separate spine. It seemed likely the black AI wasn't dead, just inconvenienced. He turned back towards his mudmarine, Grant walking beside him.

"So you're Chanter," said Grant.

Chanter restrained himself from sarcastic comments about how common mudmarine-occupying amphidapts were on Masada and contented himself with, "Evidently."

"I've known about you for years, of course," said Grant. "Known that like me you've been working for Amistad."

Chanter felt some chagrin at that. "We are colleagues," he said. "We exchange information and are useful to each other—no more than that."

Grant shrugged, and said no more as they returned to the other two. Here Chanter gazed with distaste at Shree.

"You, I will transport to the Tagreb with these two, but you'll report nothing about me unless I allow it—I've been subject to Earthnet hatchet jobs before."

"Ah, you mean Earthnet's reporting on your great interest in the painter Silbus?" said Shree. "That was a long time ago and nothing to do with me."

Obviously the three here had gone through a frightening experience, and it seemed her reaction was to put on a dismissive air.

"The restriction orders that resulted from it killed my line of research there—I'm not going to allow that to happen again."

"As I understand it," said Shree, "Earthnet reports were vetted by AIs even then. It wasn't a hatchet job, just the truth."

Chanter snorted in annoyance, turning to study Jeremiah Tombs. Still he felt some resentment about what had happened back then, though over the intervening years he had come to understand that he had been rather too . . . enthusiastic.

"So you're the one," he said.

Tombs just looked at him, looked through him.

Chanter tried, "The Technician is an artist and you are art."

Tombs blinked, seemed to only just realize he was being spoken to. "All is art," he said, as if this were obvious.

By now Mick had a full load of black spines and tentacles, which it took over to the domed hatch into the mudmarine's cargo blister. A signal from the robot opened the hatch, and Mick began to try loading the parts of Penny Royal into the space within. Chanter noticed the robot was experiencing difficulties, for many of the separate components had attached to each other, turning the load into a tangled mass. The robot eventually got round this by upending itself and tipping the whole lot inside, where it landed with a sound like rubble pouring into a hopper. The robot then trundled out again to collect the rest.

"Let's go inside," said Chanter.

With four people inside, the mudmarine's compartment was cramped. Chanter opened down his wall cot, where Shree and Grant sat. Tombs just studied his surroundings for a moment, then squatted, whilst Chanter himself sat in his control chair.

"All is art?" Chanter repeated, now checking feed from his sensor array. There were hooders out there still, some starting to draw closer now the Technician was departing, but none of them close enough to be too much of a worry. It seemed that the common hooders kept their distance from the Technician, but of course, the albino hooder was no part of the common herd.

Tombs remained silent, so Chanter turned to him, only for Shree to add her opinion. "Tombs here has been coming out with a lot of stuff like that." She eyed the ex-proctor. "Maybe if he keeps up this Zen shit the air of mystery around him won't disperse and the Polity will keep paying him to do just exactly as he pleases."

Chanter glanced at her with irritated puzzlement. Something didn't ring true about her words; they sounded almost desperate, as if she was having trouble being dismissive.

"I've studied the Technician's sculptures for decades," Chanter said, switching back to his own concerns. "The scientists here see them as the product of malfunction, but I see more. It was I who dated the oldest sculpture and it is I who see beyond such mechanistic views of reality."

"He searched for a million years and found the Weaver at last," said Tombs.

Chanter just stared at the man, not quite sure what he had heard for a moment, then some *mechanistic* facts fell into place. He had dated the oldest sculpture at about a million years yet, so Amistad and Clyde claimed the Technician itself dated back to the suicide of the Atheter race, two million years ago.

"The Technician searched for a million years?" Chanter asked.

Tombs glanced at him, almost dismissively, then looked past him at the screen showing Mick collecting up further parts of Penny Royal.

"It destroyed his mind, but not completely—broke the circuit but left the components in place. It must have taken him a million years to rebuild himself." He shrugged, looked slightly puzzled. "That's the only explanation."

"The Weaver?" Grant enquired, peering at Tombs.

Chanter felt like telling the man to shut up, but then perhaps he did have something to contribute. "Yes, what is this weaver?"

"He died, but what is death?" Tombs pointed at the screen and Chanter turned to look at it. Mick was trundling in with the last of Penny Royal, but beyond the robot, just visible, a big old gabbleduck was lolloping towards them. Something ran cold fingers down Chanter's spine. The gabbleduck wouldn't reach them before Mick finished up, and they would be well out of its reach deep in the mud shortly afterwards, but its presence out there just seemed too coincidental.

"You found where it happened," Tombs stated. "He died there, again."

"You see—mysterious bullshit," said Shree, with a break in her voice as Chanter turned.

Tombs gazed up at him, something more Human returning to his expression. He smiled. "I gabble," he said.

Chanter reached behind, groping across the console to open com, finding he didn't need to when Amistad spoke from the speaker. "Yes, Chanter?"

"I missed something," said Chanter.

"You did?"

Chanter frowned—it was so unlike the scorpion drone to pretend such surprise at his mistakes. "I did—I need someone to check the data I used to date that old sculpture."

"You feel you have the date wrong?"

"Stop fucking with me Amistad."

"What do you want to check?"

"At a million years in this environment, we're at the bottom end of mineralization mapping." Chanter paused, realized he was both dreading and fascinated by the results that surely could be obtained. "I did the mapping from a general mineral content of a Masadan grazer's bone, the Technician's usual prey, but I might have that wrong. However, we should be able to backtrack through the map to give us a specific mineral content and thus nail down the precise species of the animal the sculpture was made from."

"Even now, Rodol is running the maps . . . one moment."

After a pause Chanter asked impatiently, "Has it got it yet?"

"Of course," Amistad replied.

"What has it got?"

"I think you know the answer to that one, Chanter."

"Thank you," Chanter replied, not feeling in the least bit grateful.

"They're gone," said Jonas Clyde. "Every last one of them that came to this world is gone."

The clarity came, rolled through Jem like a wave of pure crystal, and it faded to leave odd shells in its wake. Studying those shells was an absorbing task that seemed to fold immediate reality away, in the big place in which Jem resided the immediate seemed some drama playing on a fuzzy screen—the best place for such pain. For a moment he focused back into the real, but he couldn't nail down the now, and time dislocated . . .

. . .

. . . putting him back in the mudmarine, cramming himself to one side of the small compartment as the robot returned inside and affixed itself to the wall. The robot's return here ran completely contrary to Chanter's instruction for it to secure itself in the same compartment as the cargo it had just loaded. The amphidapt probably didn't understand that the machine had evolved, had stepped up into the Turing band, and now possessed enough consciousness to know it did not want to stay that close to Penny Royal.

"What was that all about?" Shree asked.

"Mick is obviously malfunctioning," said Chanter, staring at the robot.

"Not that." Shree waved a hand at the console before Chanter. "All that stuff about mineralization mapping."

Chanter just shook his head, concentrated on taking his vessel under the rhizome layer to avoid hooders and the gabbleduck out there, both of which were starting to draw uncomfortably close. The gabbleduck, Jem realized, would lose the sense of it all and just return to its animalistic existence. No matter—another would be along soon enough.

"You gabble, you said?" queried Shree.

Jem realized the comment had been directed at him. She wanted him responding to her. She wanted him to associate with her on a Human level so she could lose her fear of him, of what he might be, and the doubt that cast on her own firm beliefs.

"Obviously a direct reference to the Gabble," said Grant. "Language seems his entry point." He passed her the shell Jem had given him—the shell Jem hadn't wanted to keep now he understood its attraction, and the accompanying denial.

The journey slid past, an odd dream, unimportant . . .

. . .

. . . back in the Museum Jem gazed at the neatly preserved carcass of a hooder and felt only a species of disappointment when the mechanisms inside the corpse activated it for those here.

"I worked that all out when I studied this." Clyde gestured towards the corpse. "Shardelle and I put it all together—the tricones, the nihilism, all of it."

Jem replayed the previous events in his mind. He remembered their arrival at the Tagreb, remembered Chanter instructing his robot to unload Penny Royal and the robot simply refusing to move. Like some iron animal self-eviscerating and spilling its guts, the mudmarine opened its cargo compartment, and Penny Royal clattered out. Strewing itself across the ground in the Masadan night, the black AI began to move with the same incremental slowness as the Tagreb itself.

"It's still functioning," Shree had said.

"Damaged but unbowed, I'm told," Grant had stated. "Penny Royal's still alive and should be able to pull itself together within the next few days."

Jem only now noticed how Shree had used the word "functioning" whilst Grant had used "alive."

Shortly after that Clyde had come out to greet them, then led them inside. Behind them the whole of Penny Royal shifted with the glacial slowness of a slime mould, but a couple of spines swivelled in their direction as if tracking their progress, which finally brought them to the Tagreb's museum.

. . .

"He needs to know it all," said Grant. "He needs to know all about the Atheter."

Clyde's succinct and bitter reply to Grant's earlier question, "Tell us about the Atheter," had obviously not been enough.

"So tell us all about that nihilism," said Shree.

"Here on Masada is where the Atheter committed racial suicide," Clyde explained. He folded his arms, his expression slightly irritated, then went on to detail what had happened on Masada—a story he seemed to have become tired of telling.

With half an ear Jem listened, but he knew the story so well now. The rest of his attention focused on the long row of sculptures, then down to the end, where Chanter stood looking at the last in the row, and the oldest. Then, almost as if time itself had shaken out the staples holding it to reality, he found himself sliding back into the near past.

. . .

"What the hell was that all about?" Shree asked.

Jem was back in the mudmarine again. Grant had just passed her the penny mollusc shell and she held it like some poisonous insect.

"It's a glyph, or a pictograph, or an entire word," Grant replied. "It's one of the basic elements of the Atheter language—I thought you got that, Shree."

"I get that it's what many would want to believe." She passed the shell back to him. "You know what I think? I think our proctor here is playing on the fact that the Polity thinks he has something important locked up inside his skull, and he's getting away with it because the AIs don't dare open up his skull and take a good hard look inside."

"You saw what he did with the Technician," said Grant.

Shree just turned away from him.

What did he do with the Technician? Jem closed his eyes and saw the weaving, recognized that after the scorched-earth return to Homeworld it was coming unravelled, and that his own kind had waded into madness and not recognized it as such.

"Okay, taking us under," said the amphidapt.

Strange creature, Jem felt, yet somehow more familiar to

him than both Shree and Grant. Certainly this familiarity stemmed from Chanter's webbed feet and bulky physique.

As the mudmarine shuddered into motion the floor tilted underneath Jem, so he sat down, ankles crossed, hands resting on his knees . . .

. . .

. . . and now found himself sitting in exactly the same pose on the floor of the Museum. The three close by were peering down at him with varying expressions. Shree just looked with contempt, Clyde with puzzlement, whilst Grant showed expectation. Of course, they had hoped that hearing the full truth of what had happened on this world would free up things in his mind. He sensed Penny Royal, still outside and still mostly immobile, waiting in attendance upon that, still haunting them like some vicious but restrained spectre.

"You okay?" Grant asked.

Jem ignored him and gazed at Clyde. "They are not all gone—I think you know that."

The man's puzzlement increased. "Some tried to save themselves or some part of their civilization, but you yourself said the tricones grind very fine."

"Not fine enough."

Victory in Grant's expression, a slight tilt of his head indicating Penny Royal or the drone Amistad must be talking to him. They thought they had succeeded here with Clyde's testimony. Jem decided to disabuse them of that notion, pointing to the row of sculptures.

"It surfaces because of them," he said. "Chanter knows."

Jem closed his eyes.

The technology had been all but annihilated, the war machines hunting down and burning to ash the last Jain nodes—the seeds left after the technology completed its millennia-long season of destruction—but the fear and the hatred had not gone away. The people knew that all it would take was one missed node and the whole nightmare would begin again. Retreating, they left behind the worlds seared down to the bedrock, acidic atmospheres and volcanism. Steadily they destroyed every trace of their interstellar civilization, mass dumping of all offworld constructs into suns, using the war machines to take out the rest of their own AIs, then using them at Homeworld to chew remaining offworld tech to dust, before summoning them to the surface for decommissioning. But the Weaver, like so many, did not agree with this.

Jem looked through eyes that could encompass a 240-degree panorama, and recollected the sight of row upon row of stationary war machines arrayed across some vast steel plain, and a deep gnawing anger at the injustice. The bell-like disruptors hung in the sky, hazing the air below them with patterned energies. Some of the war machines reared in protest, but could do little else. The Weaver fled, something important clutched in one claw as behind it the machines coiled and began to collapse in on themselves, turning to dust, the steel plain underneath them cracking, breaking away, falling to the dark mud it had concealed for millennia.

"What're you seeing?" asked Grant, impatient for detail.

"Similarities to religion," Jem replied, only stopping to analyse that reply after it was out.

"I don't get it," said Grant.

"It is not complicated," Jem replied. "Something bad happens to you for long enough and you start to believe you deserve it. Jain technology brought the Atheter millennia of civil war and they came to believe in some original sin as its source. The tree of knowledge gave them bitter fruit and many of them believed, with religious fanaticism, that their only route to salvation was to return to the garden."

"I knew religion would come in somewhere," said Shree. "See, he's babbling—making it up as he goes along."

"No, I'm gabbling," Jem corrected.

He saw thousands upon thousands of Atheter, great herds of creatures, tiaras of eyes agleam with intelligence, with madness, bills clacking in anticipation. They trampled the plains to slurry as they swarmed under the bells hanging suspended in the air half a kilometre above, the light going out in their eyes. As gabbleducks, many entered the vast swathes of flute grasses sprouting from further newly exposed mud, whilst many others just lay down like old dogs and died. The undertakers, the new morticians, those poor copies of the war machines that had been turned to dust, came in to shred the remains in an orgy of feeding.

"Those who did not walk willingly under the bell were hunted down," Jem stated.

"The bell?" Clyde repeated.

Jem glanced at the man. "Pattern disruptors. The business ends protruding into the real of the mechanism that rubbed out Atheter intelligence, destroyed what was left of their technology, hunted down those that concealed themselves, rubbed out their minds too." He paused contemplatively before going on, "After its task was completed, that mechanism was supposed to evert itself into the real, into the fires of a sun, that it has not done so suggests its programming has degraded or changed."

"We know about that thing," said Clyde. "It's what got to Penny Royal."

"It's what got to the Technician," Jem added.

"So tell us about the Technician," said Grant.

Jem smiled to himself. "Some knew that the only way to escape the mechanism was to record their minds in the hope of future resurrection, but time and the perpetual action of the tricones dealt with them. Only the Weaver survived." Glancing over, Jem saw that with perfect timing Chanter was returning from his long inspection of the oldest sculpture. He continued, "The Weaver retained a full schematic of the war machines it had designed and built—or a more appropriate description of this might be an egg. The Weaver knew it could not survive the attentions of the mechanism so made a recording of its own mind, just like the rest. However, unlike the rest it knew its mind recording could not survive time and the depredations of the tricones, unless some future route to resurrection was in place."

"The Technician," Shree stated, something hard in her expression.

Jem nodded. "Whilst everything on the surface was being annihilated the Weaver concealed its memcording deep in a mountain range rising from the mud faster than the tricones could grind it down and, deep in the mud of Masada, it left the Technician's egg, instructions deeply embedded, then accepted death. The Technician hatched, searched for a million years for its master, found the Weaver and resurrected it." Jem turned and gazed directly at Chanter. "You know where."

"In that cave," the amphidapt replied.

"In that cave," Jem repeated.

"But the Weaver didn't survive," said Chanter. "The Technician killed it."

"You what?" Grant barked.

Chanter looked back towards the ancient sculpture. "It's made of gabbleduck bone—the bones of the gabbleduck the Technician loaded the Weaver's mind into a million years ago."

Jem nodded. "The mechanism made it do that and, thereafter, the Technician kept trying to rebuild its master, kept trying to undo what it had done, but its mind was in pieces and it only aped that initial destruction."

"Until now," said Grant.

"Did it heal itself over that long period, I wonder," asked Jem, "or did the presence of alien intelligences on this world key the process? I don't know. Certainly the Technician acting now whilst Humans are here can be no coincidence. Maybe Dragon is involved for"—he glanced at Chanter—"that entity seemed to know more about what happened here than even your Polity AIs."

"So what about you?" asked Grant.

"Me?" Jem smiled at massive internal vistas.

The Weaver had been one of the greatest of its kind, for hadn't it made the war machines that finally ended that long-ago Jain threat, and hadn't it been one of the very few, if not the only one, to survive the suicide? But even so, it had underestimated the mechanism, thinking that by the time the Technician found the memcording, that destroyer of the Atheter race would have destroyed itself.

Jem gazed into the cave, saw the Technician, ancient but

still yet to attain its full growth because that growth had been slowed to an utter minimum during its millennia-long search. The memcording, a lump of dense matter no bigger than a thimble and of about the same shape, had degraded as it unwound its molecular chains of memory, of intelligence, of existence, directly into the Technician's data storage. Transference of a copy direct into the mind of the young gabbleduck had required deep surgical intervention, for mind is not all lights and electricity, but physical structures and chemical reactions. The very moment of waking had been that of intervention from the mechanism. So easy for that machine to flick a switch inside the Technician whilst it conducted this surgery; to make it slide into the quite similar feeding mode. Jem was glad his memories of pain did not include that. The Technician ate its master alive, so easier still for the mechanism to build the Technician's horror and grief into madness and utterly disrupt the war machine's mind, to drive it insane.

"The Technician reassembled its own mind, and in that process also reassembled the mind of its master, inside itself, ready to be downloaded into a living being." He studied the four who stood around him. "I am the Weaver."

14

Communication (pt 4)

Though firepower has its place, when you are fighting a high-tech war, communication and information are always more important. When someone had the sense to start numbering world wars on Earth, warfare had become high-tech, and it could be argued that radar and the decoding of Enigma were more important than the size of bombs dropped. The ultimate expression of this rule occurred during the Quiet War when the AIs dispensed with Human rule. At first they were powerless processors of information, the tidiers and routers of the huge gamut of Human communication, the maintenance workers, the sweepers and repainters in the informational world. But it was through the control of information and communication that they seized control of the Human technologies used to turn other Humans into mincemeat or ash. A pulse rifle is a potent weapon, but if you are blind and have no idea of the location of your target, it becomes just a piece of impotent hardware.

—"Modern Warfare" lecture notes
from EBS Heinlein

As she stripped off her clothing and dropped it into the sanitary unit, Shree tried to put her thoughts into order. Stepping into the shower in the temporary apartment provided by the Tagreb AI, she tried to rediscover her clarity of purpose, and dismiss from her mind the feeling that events were careening out of her control. She needed information first; she needed an update—that would start to straighten things out.

An Overlander might be able to kill an erstwhile member of the Theocracy with a bomb, but the casualties of a bomb blast would lead to a big Polity investigation, Tidy Squad members being arrested, and a damaging curtailment of Squad activities. The state's fear of terrorism was always stronger than its concern for its individual citizens. Better to watch the target, gather information, then follow the target to his favourite drinking den and lace his glass with cyanide. The statement would be made, and the target no less dead. Therefore secure communication and current data were more important than Tidy Squad planar explosives.

Shree knew this intellectually, which was why, even before the first vengeance killing that came completely under Squad remit, she began to set up a secure information-gathering and communication network. And this was an ongoing process that she still gave top priority to. She had even stopped some kills that might have endangered that network.

A member of the Tidy Squad had planted a transponder here over a year ago. The Tagreb being directly controlled by a Polity AI, the man had carefully infiltrated the place over a number of years, establishing a position as a reliable driver for those who wanted to venture out into the wilderness by ATV. Eventually allowed to take such vehicles out by himself, he took one to where, years before, he had concealed a new tyre, and swapped it for one on the ATV. A transponder, embedded in the wall of the new tyre, only responded to a coded signal, then relayed that by seismics to a U-space transmitter in Greenport. It was a one-use device, like many others planted all across Masada, since employing such devices in close proximity to Polity AIs was like playing Russian Roulette with a four-shot pistol. When it shut down after that one use it released a small amount of diatomic acid into its own workings, utterly destroying them.

"I need to speak to Edward Thracer." Shree spoke the words direct from her mind into her aug, no subvocalization, direct contact. And even that was dangerous here because if the AI, Rodol, was paying strict attention to her it might even pick up on that. It also annoyed her that knowing with absolute certainty that Thracer would not be speaking, she had to waste words on maintaining her façade.

"Edward is dead," replied the woman.

Shree studied the image her aug was projecting directly into her mind. Katarin De Lambert was Thracer's coms officer who, under usual circumstances, would not be answering a call from a secure one-off line like this. The woman, of course, would be receiving no image from this end.

Shree pretended concern, "Tell me what happened."

"Who are you?"

Shree paused, annoyed at this break with protocol. Those working undercover and forced to use such a secure line had to be thoroughly protected. Those receiving the call just listened and provided whatever was needed.

"You don't need to know and must be aware that you shouldn't ask. Tell me what happened to Thracer."

Katarin shrugged, looked both annoyed and sad. "Someone shot him in his apartment, shot him through the face."

"Any idea who?" Shree had to ask, since any agent in the field ostensibly with no idea what had happened to the Greenport unit commander *would* ask.

"Every file and cam memory in the area was trashed and the Greenport police investigation has stalled. No DNA, no traces. The Greenport AI can only give them probabilities on some people, mostly close to him. We think it isn't showing much interest because it knows he was Tidy Squad."

"That seems likely."

Katarin seemed to be debating with herself about something, then said, "I personally think he was killed by a member of the squad, because of Tombs."

Shree absorbed that, wondering to herself whether she might need to have this woman removed. "Who?"

"Ripple-John."

Shree felt some relief—Katarin had no idea. Ripple-John's fanatical hatred of the Theocracy had often been useful in the past and Shree knew about the disagreements on method between him and Thracer. She also knew and approved of

Ripple-John's tendency to remove assets who ceased to be assets by leaving the Squad. She herself had used him once as an expendable facilitator when she considered the risk too great for herself, feeding him information about a Squad member she suspected to be a Polity Agent. That John killed the individual concerned and got away with it probably indicated that she had been wrong in that case.

"I think it more likely Thracer was removed by a Polity assassin." Shree felt that such a contention should be nurtured—it would keep the troops focused. "However, though this saddens me, Edward died for a cause we still fight for, and right now I need information."

Again that shrug—this Katarin did not seem as interested as she should be. "What do you want then?"

"Some lunatic released gabbleduck death hormone at Bradacken—I thought Command ordered a shutdown on Squad activities—an order Tinsch disobeyed."

Katarin allowed herself a bitter smile. "Unfortunately there are many others in the Tidy Squad who adhere to a personal conception of what it needs to do and only loosely affiliate with its command structure."

"So who was it?"

"Ripple-John, of course."

Shree snorted annoyance. This was why Katarin thought Ripple-John had killed Thracer. "So where did he get hold of death hormone?"

"Separatists, we think," replied Katarin. "He has offworld contacts—we know that."

Shree absorbed this, felt the waters muddying around her. The Separatists were not as well organized nor did they have the clarity of purpose she had supposed. She felt another of those deep stabs of doubt that seemed to be plaguing her lately.

"Where is Ripple-John now?"

"Last contact was from Bradacken, but nothing since and no information from other assets in the area."

"Thank you." Shree thought for a moment, wondered if there was anything else useful she might obtain during this communication. There wasn't, so she shut it down, and felt suddenly alone as the link disrupted.

Tricones of doubt chew on the raft of certainty.

It was a Theocracy saying, but seemed no less apposite for that. Shree finished washing and stepped out of the shower, dried herself with the towel provided then retrieved her clothing from the sanitary unit—all clean, dry and neatly folded. She dressed and tried to concentrate on those tricone doubts.

Thracer's comments about the improvement in living conditions here since the Polity took over were one source of doubt, as was the feeling of self-disgust she experienced after killing him. That Leif Grant, a man she respected still, would agree with Thracer and was now working, even against his own people, for the Polity, had its effect too. But the attitudes of both these men were something she had encountered before on many occasions. Both men were strong in their own way, but did not possess sufficient strength of will or character to see how they were willingly donning their chains. It was, she realized, Tombs himself who affected her most and cut a hole through her armour to give those doubts access.

Jeremiah Tombs terrified her.

Actually seeing in the flesh someone she had known about, seen vids and pictures of and read stories about over twenty years, had its effect. To many, herself included, Jeremiah Tombs had achieved almost legendary status; he was a kind of celebrity. She had tried to dismiss that, hoping to find a madman just a few degrees crazier than the foaming-at-the-mouth doctrinaires given free rein under the Theocracy. She had understood that the Polity AIs would not have treated the man as they had without reason, but hoped he was being used as a shill, that supposed information hidden within him would give them justification for imposing the harsher controls of Alien Occupancy Policy on Masada. She had expected the whole set-up to be aimed at such justifications, that it was all about horse-trading, the lies and obfuscation of Human political manipulation. But what she found was Jeremiah Tombs cutting off his own face.

The kind of madness that drove a man to do something like that to himself was an order of magnitude beyond the ravings of the doctrinaires. Afterwards, she'd seen and heard some of that religious crap issuing from Tombs, but even as it seemed to just fade away, wondered if she had only seen and heard what she had been wishing for. Now, after their return from that jaunt to the cylinder worlds, Tombs had moved on, was becoming something she didn't understand and, because she didn't understand it, because it didn't match her preconceptions, found it difficult to hate. Him going out there and patting the Technician like some pet dog was the real turning point. She had to accept that the religious policeman had the mind of an Atheter sitting in his brain, that though some of the original Tombs resided there, something utterly alien seemed to be swamping it. But did that change anything?

Shree sat down on one of the softly padded chairs in her room and sighed to herself, gazing down at the pack slung on the wide single bed, aware at the core of her being of what squirmed inside a shielded cylinder within that pack. Really, what Tombs was did change things, but not in any way to change her course of action, only to make it more imperative. The man definitely was the source of information that could lead to AOP here. If the AIs accepted that he contained an Atheter then there was their indigene, there was their alien. She realized, finally, that she had hoped for some evidence, some information that would enable her to choose a different course, but only found confirmation. Tombs had done nothing, revealed nothing to make the AIs decide he was a waste of time.

When the Polity AIs let him run it seemed evident they had aimed to deliver a series of shocks to him to free up the stuff the Technician put inside his head. Grant was introduced into the equation as one of those shocks, being the soldier who had rescued Tombs. The cylinder worlds were another. Those, it seemed, had been enough to open Tombs's eyes and get him to start thinking for himself just as the AIs wanted, hence the man's own wish to come here. The next shock, the next revelation Shree had been betting on, should be an encounter with the Atheter AI, because that thing related to everything Tombs was about. However, now he was opening up, changing, was there any guarantee his next destination would be the Atheter AI?

Shree walked over to her bed, opened her pack and took out the cylinder, weighing it in her hand. Tombs had to die and, as others had to be aware, killing him was not the problem, the assassin surviving afterwards was. Shree would ensure that Tombs died but, now everything about him had been confirmed, she must use him to get to another target: the Atheter AI. Opening this cylinder she would kill both the AI and Tombs, removing the threat of AOP from Masada that both of them represented. The contents of this cylinder would kill all in the vicinity, so she too would die, but with a real *purpose*, something she only now admitted to herself she had been searching for since the end of the rebellion.

She put the cylinder away again, shrugged the pack onto her shoulder and went to find Grant.

With a deep sense of urgency the mechanism completed a new U-space jump, then with a deep sense of frustration tried to rebalance its U-space engine. Limiting its jumps to ten light years to prevent the engine getting out of control, upon each surfacing it was forced to repeat the routine. The murky data it had been obtaining from the Homeworld was now clear: the bioelectrical readings seemed a bit odd because the now functional Atheter mind existed inside one of the alien organisms occupying the Atheter realm; one of these Humans.

As it travelled the mechanism prepared itself by bringing all its back-up resources online, even the processing power of *all* the once somnolent pattern disruptors it contained. It understood now, in a way its creators had not made it to understand, that those same creators had not prepared it for eventualities like this. They had chosen oblivion, but a nuance of oblivion with an ancient cultural basis. They had wanted to live in some long-ago innocent state that in reality had never existed. However, it now seemed to the mechanism that this state, this nuance of oblivion, could not be maintained. The solution was all too obvious: all nuances must be cut away to reveal oblivion in its purest form.

Only total annihilation could work. The mechanism had erased the minds of its masters as instructed but, like Jain nodes, they were persistent. There had been the one the war machine had resurrected, the one the black AI had resurrected, so it only seemed logical that there might be others still. The only way now for the mechanism to properly fulfil its original programming was to remove the vessels to which those minds could be transferred. The Homeworld had to go, but that would only be the beginning.

The alien civilization that had now spread across the Atheter realm, and also occupied the Homeworld, was a great danger. The black AI was a product of that civilization, this was now evident, and that these aliens could also be instrumental in future Atheter resurrection attempts seemed inevitable. Present circumstances also demonstrated that it was possible to awaken an Atheter mind inside a Human being. The only way to ensure complete erasure of every trace of the Atheter would be to work outwards, as it had two million years ago, burning to ash anything with the potential to contain an Atheter, annihilating all informational or physical storage in which they might exist.

Yes, the Homeworld would have to go, but the aliens would have to go next. It seemed only logical to the mechanism, now its graven instructions were becoming much less specific, in fact quite blurred, that the next stage in the existence of Humans, and the machines they made, should be precisely the same as that of the Atheter.

"You'll deal with it," Earth Central had said, but Masada had not been abandoned by that entity—the world was far too important and the events taking place on its surface more important still. In Amistad's calculation, Earth Central would rather any number of other worlds in the Polity faced obliteration than this one.

Launching from the observation tower's platform, he gravplaned out across the wilderness then, finding adequate clearance, ignited the small fusion drive in his tail and headed straight up.

"So what kind of defences do we have?" the drone enquired of the planetary governor here, Ergatis. The question was merely a politeness, since Amistad now had the *weight* to just take that information directly from Ergatis's mind.

"Four gamma-class attack ships, two medium-range dreadnoughts and the geostat cannon," the AI replied, supplying details of these items.

One of the dreadnoughts and two of the attack ships were out at the Braemar moon Flint, the attack ships undergoing a refit at the space dock there and the dreadnought on guard duty over the runcible installation on the surface. The second dreadnought sat in orbit about Masada, called in from patrol in the unlikely event that it might be needed to back up the geostat cannon—the one positioned directly above the main continent where it could keep both the Atheter AI and the main dracoman towns in it sights. A precautionary measure, with firepower in excess of what the Theocracy laser network had been able to deliver, considered essential when dealing with aliens whose motivations were as yet unclear. But it was the two remaining attack ships that drew Amistad's attention.

"This anomaly they're investigating . . ." Amistad began.

"Two detonations under the chromosphere of the sun," Ergatis supplied, also opening all that data for Amistad's inspection. "Both were preceded by U-space signatures and whatever the objects were that surfaced there have been all but obliterated. The attack ships, however, have dropped probes to check for instabilities."

It could have been some kind of attack using U-space technology to cause instabilities in the sun's surface. This kind of attack had been conducted to devastating effect during the Prador war—deliberately causing a solar flare to sear the surface of a nearby world. However, studying the data available, Amistad didn't think that the case here. Those instabilities were usually quite plain, and had they been detected, everyone capable of doing so would be running. This time without any politeness, Amistad went through Ergatis to seize the data stream from those solar probes. Chromatic analysis revealed super-dense metals still in the process of dissolving—the kind of metals Amistad had already seen, just recently. The drone apprised Ergatis of this.

"The approaching mechanism sent them," Ergatis decided.

"But not, I would suggest, recently," said Amistad.

"The hypothetical sensors," suggested the AI.

By now the curve of the world had become visible all around Amistad and the main continent clearly visible in a deep purple sea below. Old habits dying hard, the drone began running close diagnostics on his weapons, even as he did so recognizing the futility of him trying to use such small firepower against what was approaching.

"Not hypothetical," he said. "This is certainly the device that screwed Penny Royal in the Graveyard and screwed the Technician a million years ago. That it possesses some method of detecting active Atheter minds is a certainty."

"I have some further data on this," Ergatis announced, immediately relaying data packets to Amistad.

Studying these, the drone contemplated events that had been occurring very close to the moonlet in which he had found Penny Royal. Since the Atheter device had interfered with the black AI at that location, a small research vessel had been sent. It had been some millions of kilometres out when Amistad had collected up Penny Royal's remains and transported them away. Its purpose had been to map and analyse U-space tremors for evidence relating to that device—its position consonant with U-space/realspace drift. Four years after Amistad abandoned the small private cargo ship he had hired, then used the runcible network to get to Masada, the research vessel had picked up on something sitting at the interface between the two continua.

Amistad was unsurprised to only learn about this now.

The readings could have been from any number of the imperfections sitting in that position: a black hole ghost, the disruption left by a faulty U-space drive, or one of the infinitely multiplying afterimages left when such a drive everted itself. However, just recently, the source of the anomaly became clear when it relocated to the nearby sun to obliterate itself. Another object made of super-dense metals—a necessity of construction when making physical probes to sit at such a location. Here then was the sensor that had picked up on Penny Royal's activities, here was another of the device's eyes.

"It probably wasn't at that location originally," Amistad noted.

"Seems likely," Ergatis opined.

"They'll oscillate in and out of the real at a rate dependent on how much scanning the main device requires."

"No sign of that oscillation being picked up with this one, over a period of many years," said Ergatis. "Yet the speed with which the device attacked Penny Royal would indicate an oscillation rate of just hours or even minutes, not years."

"Perhaps Penny Royal caused some fault in it. One detected only recently with the result we have just seen."

Things were starting to become clear to Amistad. You only started dumping remote sensors like that if you either thought they were about to be detected, or if they had developed some sort of fault that couldn't be corrected—which, at this technological level where self-repairing machines were the norm, meant only one kind of fault: hostile code in the controlling computers.

"And in the two we've seen destroyed here?" Ergatis wondered.

"So it would seem," said Amistad, then enquired, "Penny Royal?"

Though the erstwhile black AI was still nursing its wounds down on the surface, the response came instantly. "Answers in the part of my mind you rubbed out."

Penny Royal remained unaware that Amistad had not rubbed out that eighth state of consciousness, had just drawn it out like a pulsating sting and dropped it in a sealed container. The answers Amistad wanted certainly did reside in that vessel presently sitting under the southern ocean, but he did not fancy ending up on the end of that sting to retrieve them.

"I put you back together," said Amistad. "Evidence indicated that you were first attacked only on a mental level, then subsequently on both a mental and physical level."

"Yes," was all of Penny Royal's reply.

"Speculate," Amistad instructed.

"I would have replied along the route of the attack."

So it seemed likely that the device's sensor out at the Graveyard had been infected by something Penny Royal had sent, warranting its destruction. That two such sensors here had been destroyed indicated that the infection might have spread. Amistad paused for a moment, reviewing what little data was available concerning those sensors, reviewing a report from some haiman specialist who had been aboard that science vessel out at the Graveyard, then aboard the old interface dreadnought that first discovered the Atheter device. Something didn't add up, or rather it didn't add up until Amistad really thought about it for a couple of microseconds.

"Something else was used," he noted.

Neither Penny Royal nor Ergatis responded to this. They had both heard and closely studied everything Jeremiah Tombs had said in the Tagreb museum and were probably coming to the same conclusion as Amistad.

"You possessed eight states of consciousness, Penny Royal, each perpetually backing up the others—a scale of redundancy only a few Polity AIs have. During the second attack upon you, you were hit with something that disrupted you so fast, both mentally and physically, you had neither the time nor spare capacity to hold yourself together. If the original sensor had possessed that capability there would not have been two attacks."

"Agreed," said Penny Royal, adding, "Under the bell."

Yes, that made sense. Now shoving himself into a slow

orbit about Masada, Amistad considered how it must have been. The device must have been following narrow and clearly delineated orders. There was an Atheter AI here on Masada and Atheter memcordings existed. It probably didn't respond to the first because though artificial intelligence aped organic life its underlying mental functions were nowhere near the same. It didn't react to the second because a memcording was static. It must respond only to active Atheter mental processes, which it must detect by using some sort of very sophisticated pattern-recognition scanner. Until its encounter with Penny Royal it had been ignoring everything else, even the fact that a whole new alien civilization now occupied what had once been the Atheter realm. Having no idea what it was up against, perhaps thinking it was just dealing with an odd stray, some chunk of Atheter technology that had been missed, it had attacked Penny Royal in a limited fashion—through the sensor itself—thus enabling the black AI to respond. Only after that response had the device deployed the big guns.

Under the bell.

That there had been Atheter who had not agreed with the suicide consensus presupposed that the method used to conduct that holocaust incorporated sufficient power to deal with them too; to deal with advanced minds seeking every recourse to avoid oblivion, including the technological defences of a race that had been at war for millennia. It would have been done fast, on a massive scale. And what had done that had been sent against Penny Royal after the AI demonstrated it could defend itself.

"It probably requires a closer physical location for more effective deployment," said Ergatis, obviously thinking along the same lines as Amistad.

So, the device was coming to Masada to deploy the bell, or bells, whatever it had used to rub out the minds of millions of Atheter. What had driven it to relocate was detecting an Atheter mind functioning *in a Human being*, so it must now almost certainly be aware of and responding to the new alien civilization on Atheter home territory.

"The cavalry has arrived," Ergatis announced.

The big modern dreadnought the *Scold*, accompanied by the interface dreadnought *Cheops*, had just materialized in the Masadan system. Amistad felt some relief upon seeing the two ships. In *Cheops* Earth Central had provided something quite capable of denuding a planet of life, whilst in *Scold* it had provided something capable of converting the same planet into a collection of smoking asteroids. In light of what he had just learned, Amistad hoped these two would be enough.

Despite having slept for a good eight hours, Grant still felt tired as he gazed out of the windows of the Tagreb refectory and reviewed his most recent exchanges with Amistad. It seemed that now the AIs were getting what they wanted from Tombs, but more than they bargained for from out in space. He wondered what further use he could be. Whilst Penny Royal stood guard his own function as a bodyguard to Tombs had just been an honorary position. He rather thought that he'd served his real purpose just by his presence—a familiar face out of Tombs's repressed past—so perhaps the time had come for him to quit.

"Can I join you?"

He looked up to see Shree standing over his table. He actually didn't want her to join him, had come to realize that though they had been lovers during the Rebellion, he actually didn't like her very much now. Even so, he waved to the chair opposite.

"So what happens now?" she asked, dumping her pack down beside her seat.

Grant shrugged. "We go to Dragon Down, where Tombs gets his next shock treatment, or revelation, whatever."

"What sort of shock?" she asked.

Grant knew precisely the shock involved but, almost instinctively, he wanted to reveal as little as possible to Shree. Was this because a whole audience might be looking through her eyes? Or was it because of her still evident hate of the Theocracy and of Tombs? Grant abruptly felt surprise. In considering Shree Enkara's evident feelings he realized that his own had grown dull. Did he hate Tombs? No. Did he hate the Theocracy? No more than one can hate the corpse of an enemy.

"No idea," he said. "Something Amistad lined up."

Shree shook her head, showing far too obvious disappointment. "Surely he should go to the Atheter AI now. I know it projects holograms, but wouldn't a gabbleduck speaking to him do more psyche-loosening than anything else? The Atheter AI could probably even speak to him in the Atheter language and he'd probably understand it."

Obviously Shree, even with her media contacts, still didn't know that the Atheter AI remained uncommunicative and that the last time it projected the image of a gabbleduck had been twenty years ago. The Polity AIs must have kept this all thoroughly locked down. Perhaps they were respecting an associate's privacy.

"That seems like an idea," said Grant. "But what the hell do I know? I wouldn't have pegged letting someone hack off his own face as good therapy."

"If Tombs has recovered his sanity."

"What's sanity?"

Shree snorted dismissively and looked aside. Perhaps she had her own firm idea of an answer to that question. Grant realized that he too had once had his own set ideas about such things and, as he had discovered, a lot of ideas failed to survive their first contact with reality.

She looked back. "All I do know is that a final encounter like that would be perfect for me." She gestured with one hand towards the windows. "But then a neat climax to the story I'm broadcasting from here isn't the first concern of AIs like Amistad."

No, thought Grant, *Amistad's concern right now is that a two-million-year-old civilization-wrecking machine is on its way here.* He allowed himself a small grin—Shree's story was due to get an awful lot bigger.

"What's amusing you?" she asked, an edge to her voice.

"Just thinking," said Grant, "that Amistad won't object to Tombs's journey taking him to the Atheter AI—quite probably the opposite in fact." If Tombs could elicit a reaction out of that intelligence he would be getting something the Polity AIs had been after for the best part of the last two decades.

"So we'll go there?"

"It's not up to me."

"Why don't you ask Amistad?"

"You don't get it." Grant rested his hands on the table, fingers interlaced. "Amistad thinks Tombs going to Dragon Down might be unnecessary, but is letting it run. The drone's got other irons in the fire right now. Where Tombs goes after Dragon Down depends on them. When it's ready the drone will be down here having a very long talk with Tombs."

"So we just wait in Dragon Down until these 'other matters' are dealt with."

"No, I'm to take Tombs wherever he wants to go."

"Then why not to the AI?"

"That might be allowed, but it's his decision," said Grant.

"He's a fucking proctor, Grant."

"He's a free Polity citizen, Shree." Grant gazed at her steadily. "If you want him to go to the Atheter AI, then you'd better ask him."

She didn't like that at all, but Grant just did not seem to have the energy to care.

Dracomen, it seemed, were very literal in the way they named things. The first two dracomen, created by the massive alien entity calling itself Dragon and looking nothing like its name, had assumed the appellations Scar and Non-scar the moment there was a distinction to make. And the reason for dracowoman Blue's name stood out at once.

Dracomen were modelled on what some pre-runcible scientist thought dinosaurs might have evolved into had they not been wiped out. Of course, being Human, that scientist anthropomorphized his model to come up with man-dinosaurs, toad-faced lizard men, in fact the kind of evil critters found in just about every virtual fantasy experience on the market. Generally dracomen were pale yellow from throat to groin, their scaling elsewhere ranging from grass green to deep jade. This female, Blue, however, was precisely as her name implied. Her darker scales were almost blue-black and the lighter scales down her front were a curious almost artificial-looking azure.

Stepping out of her gravan Sanders first studied this female then the small town lying beyond her. The name of this place was literal too, for it stood at the edge of where one dragon sphere, the one the Theocracy had labelled Behemoth, had sacrificed itself to create the dracoman race. Dragon Down, inevitably. Of course no crater existed here any more—the tricones and the slow tidal movement of the mud had obliterated it.

"Please, this way." Blue gestured towards a walkway lying on heavily disturbed mud, then nimbly leaped onto it with that weird bird-legged gait.

"I've got luggage," said Sanders.

"Of course you have," replied the blue dracowoman.

Did Sanders really need her belongings? How long would she be here? Both were questions she had no answer to. However, she'd felt the need to take back some control, assert herself. She stepped down past her vehicle to the side door, sinking in churned mud up to her ankles, her soles coming to rest on the grid the weight of the gravan had pressed down below the surface. Palming the door pad she stepped back, removed her remote control from her pocket. After a moment one of her two hover trunks came trundling out, rocking as its sensors struggled to read what lay below it. She watched it for a second, until it managed to compensate, then turned and followed Blue onto the walkway.

The town was much like the other dracoman towns scattered across Masada. From a distance it looked like a sprawling mass of giant white puffballs sprouting from the mud. Only when one drew closer did the other infrastructure reveal itself between the globular houses, storage tanks, generator stations, creches, biofactories . . . though, as Sanders understood it, the difference between those last two might be something hard to nail down.

"I'm here to see someone," she said, finding herself reluctant to move further away from the illusory safety of her vehicle—the same reluctance that had delayed her arrival here when she decided first to return to Zealos and stay in a hotel. She didn't like obeying Amistad, and dracomen worried her. Stupid really, that last, for though dangerous-looking dracomen were visible throughout the town, there were also Humans here. Just a few metres away from her gravan stood a large old ATV, still in camouflage paint, and still bearing a rail-gun turret on the roof, and beyond that lay an antigravity bus—a utile transport that rested on the rhizome mat like a brick with windows. A woman who was probably its driver sat smoking a cigarette on the step of the open door—a habit some atmosphere-adapted Masadans had taken up as if to raise two fingers at the hostile environment. She was also gazing out to where other Humans, probably her intended passengers, were dismounting from huge lizard-like mounts—one of the creations of those dracoman biofactories, or crèches.

"Survivors," said Blue.

"What?" Sanders turned to the dracowoman.

"Survivors of the hooder attack on Bradacken way station," Blue explained. "Another attempt on the life of the one you are here to meet."

"Jeremiah Tombs."

"Yes."

"Someone's controlling hooders?" she asked, confused.

"In a way, yes," Blue replied. "We isolated the gabbleduck death hormone here not long after The Sowing, and supplied that data to Rodol when the Tagreb arrived. Neither we nor Rodol have made that information commonly available, so someone else must have both isolated it and synthesized it."

"Death hormone?" Sanders repeated, feeling slightly slow as she processed this new information. Yes, she knew about the hormone, just as she knew that The Sowing was a reference to the Greek myth of Cadmus sowing the dragon's teeth—it was effectively the time these dracomen first popped out of the ground like hostile asparagus shoots. "Someone lured hooders to Bradacken using the hormone?"

"The way station is gone. Many were killed."

"What about Tombs and Leif Grant?"

"They survived and, along with an Earthnet reporter, were transported to the Tagreb where Tombs at last begins to reveal the one within. Next they come here."

Sanders left that "one within" alone, instead asking, "Why is he coming here?"

Blue gazed at her with large unreadable eyes that she noted also contained a hint of the female's overall hue. Perhaps Blue was something like the dracoman version of an albino? No, dracomen did not really possess DNA like Humans and, though they reproduced, every new dracoman fitted precise specifications. There was no random mutation, no random surfacing of alleles. Blue had been engineered to be blue or that colouration was an insignificant side-effect of some other specification. Could it be that Blue was a diplomat and her colour a more soothing one to the Human eye? Sanders shook her head in dismissal—so easy to get paranoid around these creatures.

"We are on his route," Blue told her, a momentary confusion flashing across the dracowoman's expression. "Dragon Down lies between the Tagreb, the place he is currently departing, and the Atheter AI."

"Just coincidence then."

"Coincidence," Blue repeated. "An interesting Human term." Blue dipped her head in what might have been contemplation for a moment. "The time is just right."

"For what?"

"Answers."

"What answers?"

"To the witness."

Sanders felt a momentary frustration then dismissed it. She knew enough about Dragon and enough about dracomen to be sure she would get no further. *We must never forget where they come from*, she thought to herself.

Those were the words that had come out in a conversation all but forgotten until now. Just after the Polity raised the quarantine she'd returned to the mainland for a break from her fruitless efforts with Tombs. Lellan Stanton had spoken those words in Zealos, beside the partially reconstructed spaceport, where dracomen were climbing into Polity landers and going off to fight in some larger conflict to which the rebellion and subsequent events on Masada had just been a sideshow.

Sanders stepped up onto the walkway after Blue and followed her into Dragon Down. So where did dracomen come from—it was a long and tortuous story. Their main population here was a creation of Dragon a mere twenty years ago, but in essence they were Dragon—a singular entity turned into a race, not even that . . . one of four facets of a singular entity . . . Sanders had acquired the story in pieces that just did not seem to fit well together and realized she did not know it all.

We must never forget where they come from.

Sure—presupposing you had any idea where that was.

Blue led her on a winding course through Dragon Down to a huge oblate building lying just off the central park—the structure recognizable as Human accommodation because it actually possessed windows and a balcony area engirdling it. The central park itself was a gridded area seeded with low leafy growth, divided up by raised beds crammed with the products of an agronomist's dream, or nightmare, scattered with grape trees, yellow avocado trees, and many others she did not recognize, all producing odd colourful fruits. Sanders wondered if a foamstone raft lay underneath this place or if the dracomen used some sort of biotechnology to keep tricones at bay and prevent flute grass coming up underneath everything like a bed of nails. Here dracoman gardeners laboured with hand tools that looked like they must be locked up for the night, after being fed, or checked upon monitors clinging like glass limpets to some plants.

"Who are they?" Sanders asked, indicating with a nod the four men lounging on the balcony.

"Just travellers," Blue replied. "The elder is called Ripple-John and the other three are his sons, Sharn, Kalash and Blitz. They arrived ahead of the others from the intervention zone around Bradacken. It's safe here because the wind is carrying the hormone south."

Sanders glanced back. Some of those she had seen getting down from the lizard mounts had passed the gravbus and were heading this way. The driver of the bus was back inside, ready to run the vehicle to Zealos, probably. She followed Blue up the steps onto the balcony around the Human accommodation, uncomfortably aware of the intentness with which the four men on the balcony were studying her. She raised a hand to them, but only got that stare in return.

The inside of the building was odd. Intervening corridors seemed to be just the gaps between a collection of spheres that had apparently been inflated inside. Blue finally brought her to a door, which was a simple affair of woven and resin-bonded flute-grass stalks with a plain handle to one side—no palm locks or DNA security here.

"I am informed that Tombs will arrive here tomorrow morning," Blue said as Sanders inspected the interior of her room. It seemed almost bucolic—a peasant dwelling out of some history book, none of the weird biomechanisms she had expected to find. Her trunk settled to the floor with a sigh, as if contemptuous of its surroundings.

"Okay." Sanders nodded affirmation, suddenly feeling a nervousness at meeting her charge again. "Is there somewhere I can get something to eat and drink?"

"Of course," said Blue, imparting precise directions before departing.

The refectory was another sphere, refrigerated food and primitive cooking equipment available. She made sandwiches and took them back to her room, wondering why the dracomen hadn't taken advantage of readily available Polity technology, then thinking perhaps that the dracomen did not want to allow potential Trojans into their domain. She had finished eating and was considering just climbing inside the bed she sat upon when the door opened and Ripple-John stepped inside, his three sons coming in behind him.

"Jerval Sanders," he said cheerfully. "What an unexpected bonus!"

"What the—" was all she managed before he stepped forward and smashed his fist into her mouth.

15

Dragon (again)

Great has been the speculation about the motives of Dragon (in its various incarnations). It has been involved in numerous nefarious activities; set up Dracocorp to produce its dubious augs; was responsible for the Samarkand runcible explosion and the 30,000 resultant deaths; supplied the nano-mycelium that wrecked Outlink Station Miranda; sacrificed one of its four spheres on the world of Masada, converting its mass into the race of Dracomen; tampered with Human DNA on the world of Cull to make grotesque hybrids of men and local life forms; and fought with the Polity against Jain technology. So what is its ultimate purpose, people ask. Is it for us or against us? Is it attacking the Polity or helping the Polity? That they ask questions like this is due to Dragon's sheer scale and the power it commands. Surely such a being must possess great insight and some numinous ultimate aim. Wake up: godlike powers don't necessarily imply a godlike purpose. Dragon, it seems to me, is like a child at the controls of a bulldozer, very much enjoying the ride and rather careless of the havoc it wreaks.

—*From* HOW IT IS *by Gordon*

Sanders shot backwards over the other side of her bed to collapse on the floor and Ripple-John walked round to gaze down at her. She lay there stunned but he allowed himself the pleasure of driving his boot into her stomach a couple of times.

"So what now?" asked Blitz, as Kalash closed the door behind them.

Ripple-John stepped back, breathing heavily but not from exertion, and instead of continuing the beating as he wanted, drew his pepperpot stun gun. The weapon cracked in his hand, slamming a cloud of knockout needles into her back. What now indeed.

The sight of Jerval Sanders stirred up a killing rage in him and had been the impetus for him to go after her straight away like this. Here lay the Polity medtech who had for so long looked after Jeremiah Tombs as if it mattered whether the man was sick or well, mad or sane. Here, he felt, was the woman who had denied the Tidy Squad access to that piece of shit for over twenty years. That wasn't a rational assessment, he knew, but the others who had protected Tombs did not wear a Human face and so were more difficult to hate.

"She could die," said Sharn, rounding the bed to stand beside Ripple-John and gaze with complete indifference down at Sanders, who was making choking bubbling sounds.

True. Having received a kicking then a blast of stun-gun needles she might choke on her own vomit. Ripple-John considered letting her do so, considered using the stun antidote on her then, when he had her full attention, pulling the knife from his boot and doing something artistic with her face before cutting her throat. However, he had stunned her for reasons not yet quite clear to him—she would be useful, somehow. He stooped and pulled her into a recovery position, stuck his finger deep into her mouth and hooked out lumps of half-digested sandwich, gripped her hair and slapped her back until she coughed up the rest. After a moment she was breathing easier and he stood.

"We use her," he said decisively.

"How?" Blitz asked.

Kalash now spoke up. "Bait."

"But how do we use that bait?" Blitz asked, always looking for the holes. "Tombs, Grant and the Earthnet reporter were transported to the Tagreb in some sort of underground vessel. We know that and we know Tombs is coming here." He waved a hand at their surroundings. "But killing him here?"

Ripple-John dipped his head in acknowledgement. That

they had arrived here after Bradacken was merely due to the fact that this place was the nearest haven from the way station. It was pure luck that they had arrived at Tombs's next destination.

"No, not here," Ripple-John agreed. "At least not while we remain." Conducting a direct hit here would be tantamount to suicide and, even if they managed it, would most certainly result in him and his sons ending up dead. Though he was fanatical about killing Theocracy shits, his fanaticism did not extend that far.

"The hormone?" suggested Sharn.

Ripple-John shook his head. "We don't have enough of it, and anyway the dracomen would get them out." He paused for a moment. "Their biotech's very advanced too and they'd probably detect it and quickly shut it down."

"A bomb?" Sharn suggested.

Ripple-John peered at him. He often felt that Sharn was the dud in the magazine. "And where would we put it to ensure we got him?"

Sharn shrugged.

"No." Ripple-John considered their options, tried to put his thoughts in order. "Tombs is no longer protected by the thing that screwed Tinsch and later got him away from the hooders at Bradacken."

"You're sure?" Blitz asked.

The ATV driver and Tidy Squad member at the Tagreb had been reluctant to impart information now Squad Command had said Tombs must be left alone, but a few blatant threats and Ripple-John's reputation had been enough to open him up.

"We saw what happened to it on Earthnet, and it's outside the Tagreb still—the Technician fucked it up bad. If it goes on the move again we'll be informed at once."

"If Tombs travels from here underground we can't touch him," said Sharn.

Ripple-John glanced at him again. Maybe not a complete dud.

"So while he's on his way here we can't hit him," said Blitz.

"We can't hit him here either, nor will we be able to if he takes the underground route away."

"We ensure he doesn't use that route from here," said Ripple-John, the vague shape of a plan forming in his mind.

"A distance shot from outside," said Kalash, true to his name. "All we have to do is wait for that underground vessel to surface and wait for him to step out."

"And we'd be dead a few minutes after that."

"You think dracomen are that fast?" Kalash asked.

Blitz was the eldest, a teenager during the rebellion, but the other two had taken no part in the fighting. Blitz knew, but Sharn and Kalash had no idea.

"They can travel overland faster than an aerofan can fly. If they catch you they don't need weapons and can continue fighting even with half their bodies blown away. I saw that. We don't risk pissing them off."

"So how?" asked Sharn, then prodded Sanders with the toe of his boot, "And where does she come in?"

"We use a small, discrete bomb to disable that mud vehicle," Ripple-John replied, "detonated remotely from a good distance—that'll be your job." He paused, thinking it through. "After that they'll have no choice but to leave either by air or overland. If it's the first then Kalash gets to play with the missile launcher. If it's the second we get to use her as bait." He prodded Sanders with his boot. Yes, preferable to use her to get those inside a land vehicle on the outside where they would be easier to pick off, because they then stood a chance of capturing Tombs alive and could thereafter spend some quality time with him. Ripple-John really liked that idea.

"If she's going to be of any use we have to first get her out of here," Blitz noted.

Ripple-John leant across the bed and picked up a remote control, studied the touch pads for a short while then pointed it at the trunk presently sitting in the middle of the floor. Humming to itself the piece of luggage rose up a short way, then turned to face the door.

"And here's our solution to that," he said.

Taxi-driver again, Chanter thought to himself as he studied the seismic images on his subscreen. In the mud down here he could see some remains that twenty years of tricone attrition had failed to obliterate. There a wormish scrawl half a kilometre long; scattered around it, curved fragments of eggshell, but from eggs big enough to contain creatures the same size as a Human. Chanter did not like being here at all, in fact he had avoided being here ever since that first time, because his distrust of and doubts about Dragon had carried over to that entity's offspring.

"This is it, isn't it?" Tombs asked, peering up at the screen from his position seated on the floor.

The man either knew how to read seismic maps or recognized the images on the screen, which made no sense. He had been a Theocracy proctor prior to the rebellion, then bat-shit mad ever since. He should have no knowledge of anything he was seeing here.

"Yes, this is it," Chanter replied, reluctantly angling the mudmarine up towards coordinates provided by Rodol.

"Some of it remaining," said Grant from the fold-down bed. "It must be tough material. I thought Polity researchers dug it all up."

"They dug most of it up," said Shree from beside him, "but dumped the project as the dracomen established their town."

"Maybe the dracomen objected—felt a grave was being disturbed," Grant suggested.

Shree only snorted at that.

Chanter had been strongly *requested* to bring the three here to Dragon Down. He understood the tactical reasoning behind this, since whoever had set the hooders on Bradacken had not been captured and might still be in the area. But there was more to it than that. As a sweetener, Amistad, in a very brief exchange, had informed him that the dracomen possessed information concerning the Technician—something he might be interested in. He felt the AIs wanted him here, though why wasn't really clear, but was it ever?

Within a few minutes the marine surfaced, and Chanter noted a lack of resistance indicating either a thin or non-existent rhizome mat up here. The frictionless viewscreen cleared to show Dragon Down off to the left, and an ATV heading away far to the right.

Next a subscreen flickered on to show a draconic visage. Chanter reached out to check the settings of the transmission, contrast and colour—one finger-touch on the keypad running an instant diagnostic. Nothing wrong. This dracoman female—there an odd contradiction—was actually as blue as she looked.

"Chanter," said the creature before him.

"You know me?" Chanter replied.

"I've known of you for a long time," she said. "Let me introduce myself: my name is Blue, for evident reasons—one of twins as it happens. My brother sacrificed himself to the Technician even before the Theocracy died."

The company of these three over the last six hours had been enough to grate on Chanter's nerves, and now he felt something creeping up his back. He wanted to get the hell away from here just as fast as possible but still, information about the Technician . . . This Blue, it seemed, might be the source.

Why had the Technician stopped making sculptures? Its last new one Chanter had found some years before the rebellion, and from what he had recently learned, they were supposedly the product of a dysfunctional war machine. It had been mooted that the Technician lost its dysfunction itself, but how coincidental: a million years of madness followed by some Atheter machine definition of sanity now, with Humans and others here. And hadn't Dragon known things? Known where Chanter could find that oldest sculpture?

"I'm here to deliver a visitor for you," he said, noncommittal.

"And visit for a while yourself, I hope?"

"I'm told you have something for me."

"Certainly—please come and join me."

"Yeah, sure." Chanter clicked off the screen then sat staring at it pensively.

"Dracomen here before the rebellion?" Grant said wonderingly.

"Dragon was interfering here for years," said Shree. "Does it surprise you it had its agents down on the surface?"

"Yes, it does. Even though the brotherhood had Dracocorp augs I thought Dragon only came here itself the once."

Chanter considered that. Had it been here before, or had it obtained that information through its agents? He stood up and turned to find himself nose to nose with Tombs. "A little space here please."

Tombs did not move. He had one of those weird looks on his face again.

"Intricate weave," he said. "Now it comes clearer to me. The mechanism did not fail. The Technician was consigned to a Hell it could not escape alone."

"Are you going to get out of my fucking way?"

Tombs blinked, regained some Human expression, stepped aside.

The door opening ahead of him, Chanter stomped outside, then glanced back as the other three followed. When the door closed behind them with a satisfying thunk, he decided then that enough was enough—after this he would be returning to his mudmarine alone and be damned to any *requests* from Amistad. Heading across soft mud towards the dracoman town he didn't care whether his passengers followed him or not. He gazed ahead, noted the greenish-yellow hue of dracomen, the occasional Human, then one that stood out as it walked from the town towards them. Finally, after crossing ten metres of rhizome-netted mud, he checked back on the other three. Grant and Shree were only a couple of paces behind, but Tombs was hopping oddly along some metres behind them, trying to step from thick rhizome island to island, obviously scared of sinking into ground insufficiently boggy to swallow a lead coffin.

"Blue, I presume," said Chanter, stepping up onto one of the gridded walkways spearing out from the town. The words aped something historical, he was sure, and felt he had chosen them because something historical, for him, was about to occur here.

"That I am. Pleased to meet you at last, Chanter." The draconic female gestured to the walkway beside her and, when Chanter joined her, gazed beyond him.

"Leif Grant and Shree Enkara," she said. "You have both been here before and know we have accommodation where you can rest and get something to eat."

"But you'll be looking after Tombs and Chanter for a little while," said Grant, obviously having been so informed by Amistad.

"What's this all about?" asked Shree.

Grant turned to her. "Blue has something to show them, but it's not for us to see."

Chanter noted the brief flash of rage in her expression.

"I don't agree with that," she said.

"So you're going to argue with dracomen, here?" Grant enquired.

"Why wasn't I told?"

"Why should you be told?"

She abruptly stepped up onto the walkway and marched in towards the town. Grant watched her go for a moment then said, "I don't like this myself, dracowoman Blue."

"It's nothing you need concern yourself with, Leif Grant," said Blue. "Nobody will be able to harm Tombs here."

"Still," said Grant.

"Though what happens next will have its effect on Tombs's mental condition, it is more a resolution of a personal nature than something that might concern you."

"Yeah, whatever." Grant marched off after Shree.

"Jeremiah Tombs," Blue said, now turning to the ex-proctor as he finally approached the walkway.

"Nominally," he replied, concentrating on his footing.

"Of course."

Tombs reached the walkway, relief evident in his expression.

"Resolution of a personal nature?" Chanter queried.

"Isn't art personal?" Blue shot back.

"What's this all about, Blue?"

"Follow me and find out."

Chanter did so, annoyed but curious. Blue had mentioned art, which was a lure he could not ignore, perhaps foolishly.

As they walked in it seemed to him almost as if the town reached out to engulf them like some white leviathan, and in doing so constrained his freedom to act. He shuddered on seeing how perfectly the colour of the bulbous buildings around him matched that of the Technician's carapace. They wended their way to the centre, through the strange little park there, where Chanter saw Shree and Grant disappearing into a large oblate building—the only one here with windows—then moved beyond through a gap between walls that seemed to threaten to roll in and crush them, finally to a small spherical house with a single door that opened as Blue approached on hinges of muscle like a clamshell.

"After we have finished here you can rejoin your fellows." Blue gestured back the way they had come, then ducked inside.

Despite the odd feeling he got upon entering Dragon Down, Chanter followed her quickly as his usual agoraphobia began reasserting itself. Once inside he looked back towards the door, where Tombs was hesitating, ducking down and peering inside.

"Yes," said Chanter, irritated. "You're not a gabbleduck and you can get through the door."

Tombs entered, whereupon Chanter ignored him and studied his surroundings.

The floor drew his attention first. It consisted of differently shaped glass tanks all perfectly interlocking and smooth underfoot. Within many of these, curious forms of fauna squirmed or hopped. In others flora grew beautiful or grotesque, whilst in others still, resided things that were either both, or neither. Flat surfaces, crammed with equipment both mechanical and biological, sprouted like mushrooms from the floor. Beside one of these stood a saddle-like draconan stool, and next to this rested two chairs for Humans, one looking quite old, the other new enough to still have its scales. A round film screen rose from the mushroom table, below which rested things like leather flying helmets sitting at the end of snakelike tubes, the insides of the helmets uncomfortably like the inside of a reptile's gullet.

"Please, be seated," said Blue.

Chanter seriously considered just turning, shouldering open that clamshell door behind, then running for his mudmarine, but something beyond this little diorama riveted his attention. Numerous alcoves had been cut into the walls all around, some of them containing objects he could not identify and others that he could, like the Human skull with a proctor's dress cap perched upon it. The alcove nearest the three chairs, however, contained something that had been the focus of his life for so long, for there resided one of the Technician's sculptures.

For a moment, Chanter had no idea what to say for, reviewing his previous exchanges with this dracowoman, he knew more about the sculpture here than he really wanted to. He cleared his throat, held up his hand, the webs between his fingers stretched taut, peered through the infrared-sensitive skin and saw nothing unexpected, but through the skin that rendered ultraviolet saw the sculpture etched in an eerie glow.

"So," he said, lowering his hand, "you're blue right to the bones?"

"Certainly—it is a pigment I use in bodily functions similar to breathing, and permeates me through and through."

"What was your twin brother's name, Azure, Cerulean, maybe Lapis Lazuli?"

She turned to gaze at the sculpture. "He had no name, for he possessed no identity and no recognizably individual mind." She made a graceful gesture towards the sculpture. "I like to think of this as the Technician's tribute to him."

"The only tribute it could make," said Tombs, voice flat, less Human even than Blue's. "And the last sculpture it ever made."

Chanter swallowed drily. Though in one part of his being he wanted to be anywhere but here, at his core he knew he simply could not be elsewhere. So, at least two dracomen were here on Masada before Dragon sacrificed itself and was reborn. One of them stood nearby, whilst the remains of the other resided over in that alcove.

"So you're going to tell me about all this?" he asked.

Blue gestured towards the two weird organic-looking helmets. Chanter had rather hoped she wouldn't do that, but wasn't really surprised. He walked over to them, picked one up, slightly revolted at its warmth, stepped over to a chair and plumped himself down in it then, gazing at Blue defiantly, thrust the helmet down on his head. Something stung him, almost at once, then needles began burying themselves into his scalp and things started to get a little strange. He had time only to see Tombs taking up the other helmet, before the particular reality he occupied shattered and dissolved, revealing some underlying stratum. The memories of Dragon, and its children, began downloading into his skull:

. . .

The Theocracy lay ahead, nearly ready for change and joyous manipulation. Already a large proportion of the upper Theocrats were using the dracocorp augs supplied to them by Cheyne III separatists, and as Dragon approached, it sensed the growing network. However, that network had not yet reached full ripeness with someone taking an ascendant position in it; someone Dragon could then seize control of and through them manipulate everyone else. In fact, it seemed that a large proportion of aug network channels was being taken up by prayer from some group called the Septarchy Friars—something that could slow the whole process.

Cherry-picking information as it slid into the Masadan system, camouflaged electronically from the Theocracy's primitive sensors, Dragon noted that the Theocrats were aware of the original source of their augmentations and, possessing minds twisted by religion, had created a mythology about them. This it seemed enabled them to accept something which, up to this time, did not fit doctrine.

They had named Dragon Behemoth and distorted that label to their purpose. Behemoth, it seemed, was an angel only half-fallen, a renegade and a rogue, but not entirely evil. The augs were a gift from this entity, a powerful tool of seraphic origin that could lead them to damnation if they weren't sufficiently strong and did not adhere sufficiently to the tenets of their faith. Dragon loved this thing about Humans: how they lied even to themselves for their own advantage. Then something else, coming in through the sensor cloud it had distributed ahead of it, riveted its attention.

Masada.

They'd named their world after the Jewish fortress zealots suicided in rather than be captured by the Romans who had it under siege, yet they had not made it their own fortress, rather keeping their powerbase offworld, in the cylinder worlds presently under construction, and in their growing fleet. Did their reluctance stem from some sense of what this world had been; that they would have been building down there on the rotten foundations of an even older fortress?

As the sensor bees settled through the atmosphere they relayed enough data for Dragon to see the vague shape of it all. As they either hit the ground and began sucking up and analysing genetic material or sank into the ground for deeper scans, that shape hardened into visibility. The tricones for this, the hooders for that, the Atheter themselves now just animals but with a potential that had to have been held in check in some other . . .

There.

A brief glimpse of some alien eye peeking out from under-space to check all was well, the patterns of that continuum indicating an evident link back to something with the power to act, with the power to ensure its masters remained animals. Dragon of course perfectly understood the despair, driven by Jain technology, which could lead to such racial suicide. Had it not seen something similar in the kind that had sent it to the Humans in the first place? Wasn't that kind of madness why it had gone rogue?

So very very interesting, and with all sorts of ramifications. Certainly, even with Dracocorp augs and Separatist technological assistance the Theocracy could never survive the Polity steamroller. And the status of this world, once the

Polity saw it, absolutely ensured that the Theocracy would be crushed.

But the Polity, whilst it crushed up and absorbed stray Human civilizations as it perpetually extended its border, moved too slowly and too cautiously. Its AIs did not yet understand what danger they were in. Yes, Dragon's own games and manipulations kept them alert, but not sufficiently so, for they had a big tendency towards complacency. They needed to *see* Masada, they needed to understand what had happened to the Atheter and they needed to do both very soon, because the ever-growing span of the Polity was fertile ground for a Jain node, and that lethal technology would sprout once again.

Time to hurry things along.

"Hierarch Amoloran!" Dragon boomed through the aug network whilst, inside itself, it tapped off some of a lethal metal-eating mycelium from a hidden cache, and sealed it in a small container.

The Hierarch's reply was instant and somewhat worrying in its perspicacity. "You are the creature called Behemoth. Are you here in the Braemar system?"

"I am everywhere and nowhere," Dragon replied. "But here is something you will need to bring your dreams to fruition." Dragon sent coordinates of a point in orbit over Calypse, simultaneously ejecting the small vessel from inside its body and setting it on a course to that point.

"Another gift?" Amoloran enquired.

Rather than reply, Dragon sent a data packet containing instructions for how the mycelium should be used.

"We understand the nature of your gifts, Behemoth: sufficiently attractive for us to want them, but dangerous to everything we hold dear."

"That is the nature of power."

"Yes, power." Amoloran issued instructions, but they went too fast for Dragon to ghost a copy and study them. "Whilst I accept your new gift, Behemoth, I reject the snare of your old one."

Abruptly the chanting and prayer of the Septarchy Friars

occupied over 50 per cent of the aug channels. This abruptly cut down the whole utility of the network, limiting the extent of communication, limiting the amount of data that could be transferred from person to person. It also made it a certainty, whilst it continued, that no one would reach ascendancy over the network and that there would be no one Dragon could ultimately control. Amoloran had seen the danger, perhaps not understanding the initial ascendancy of one individual, but certainly understanding that through the whole network Dragon might be able to grab hold of their minds.

"Damn you Amoloran!" Dragon cried, allowing its *voice* to fade, while its amusement grew. Amoloran would do precisely as predicted. He and all his fellow idiots believed that ultimately the Theocracy would bring down the Polity. Wasn't faith stronger than machines? He was ambitious that this should happen under his own rule and had been pushing hard to that end. Dragon had given him a potent weapon against the Polity and he would certainly use it, and soon. This would sufficiently piss off the Polity AIs and they would come and stamp on him. Then they would find out about what had happened here on Masada two million years ago.

Now considering what it had set in motion, Dragon understood something else: the necessity of its own death. The mycelium had been used many years ago on a planet called Samarkand, with over thirty thousand deaths resulting, and the Dragon sphere that had delivered it there had paid the price of extinction. After Amoloran used the nano-mycelium again, the Polity AIs would soon identify its source as Dragon itself. Inevitably they would hunt down this particular aspect, this sphere of Dragon entire, and given the chance, would kill it too. Dragon did not want to flee, wanted to remain here to be part of and influence events, therefore it decided to pursue a course it had been considering for some time: to die, and live.

More data, coming in from the sensors, hidden by those who had not wanted to die, in the genetic code of the life, in patterned atmospheric gases and hot machines perpetually renewing themselves deep in the magma, etched into the shells of molluscs, roiling in a hooder's eye, trapped in the hearts of artificial gems. And then something else, a huge anomaly, a creature, no, a biomechanism like Dragon itself, ancient, from the time of the Atheter suicide. It seemed likely to be here as a result of another Atheter's attempt at survival but was complex enough to be worthy of closer study, for the readings nearby sensors provided were very strange.

Dragon immediately selected a more powerful and invasive sensor from a store within itself and spat it towards the world. The long egg-shaped biomechanism speared through the intervening distance over a period of days. Meanwhile Dragon noted a Theocracy ship arriving at the location of its new gift to them, picking it up and transporting it to one of the cylinder worlds.

The sensor hit atmosphere, burned its way down, shedding dispensable outer layers, thumped into the surface to blow a steaming crater half a kilometre across, then in the soft ground underneath began to reformat itself. Finally, during one Masadan night, it rose to the surface and emerged; a grotesque octopoid with a bloated tic body five metres long. Its own senses already focused, it skated out of the already refilling crater. Then cut a channel through the surrounding flute grasses directly to its target.

The massive albino hooder was departing the messy site of a recent meal, the remains of its repast refashioned over long hours into something unknowable even as it sank into the area of boggy ground it had been made upon. Dragon's monstrous sensor slid up to the hooder and flung itself upon it, wrapping tentacles around it and injecting mechanisms between the segments of its body. At once Dragon began to realize that the war machine had been hugely disrupted, not enough to kill it, but enough to render it down to the level of those animals of its own kind, only its colour and the curious way it played with its dinner remaining to distinguish it to the casual viewer. However, it was no walkover. It responded fast and viciously, both on the nanoscopic and macroscopic levels, repelling internal invasion with its still effective internal defences, its immune system, and turning its tool-packed hood on Dragon's sensor. Within seconds it had torn the sensor apart, and began hitting the remains with patterned energy fields to tear them apart at the molecular level. But, by the time the sensor had been turned to slurry spattering the surrounding grasses, Dragon had all the information it needed.

Dragon could see that the disruption within the war machine was such that its self-repair mechanisms could never overcome it. Intervention would be required, but intervention of a very special kind. The best way past its immune system was down the white hooder's gullet: thereafter a penetration through its digestive system would not elicit such a swift response. Specially designed viruses could install programming patches, microscopic phages could make repairs in certain critical areas, those parts of the immune system that had been turned in on themselves could be burnt out by nanoscopic thermal charges, thereafter regrowing as they should be. Whole repair wasn't possible but, beyond a certain point, the war machine could fully heal.

Dragon began fashioning, in the organic factories of its innards, something from a blueprint close to one used by the sphere that caused the Samarkand catastrophe. It understood that the one that penetrated the white hooder would require outside back-up—retransmission of programming destroyed during the internal war—so it caused a division within the egg that it both grew and fashioned from that blueprint. In a tryout of its later plan for self-resurrection, it sexed the twin foetal dracomen, one male and one female. The first would be the one to enter the war machine; the second would run back-up. Dragon brought them to term but did not hatch them out, instead building up protective layers about the egg before spitting it towards Masada. By the time it reached the surface those outer layers had burnt away and the egg had grown ready to hatch, and so it did.

. . .

Blue gazed out across the flute grasses swaying in recalcitrant breezes and issuing mournful music, appreciating them, appreciating so much about this world with a huge intelligence and knowledge already downloaded into her mind from her parent. Her brother gazed in just one direction, utterly fixed on his purpose and indifferent to his surroundings. The instant his body reached optimum, he set out at a fast run which, for a dracoman, was very fast indeed, organs within her brain monitoring her brother's function, the link between them so strong he seemed almost part of her, she was drawn after him.

They ran throughout one day, one night and into the next day, whereupon the male just slammed to a halt and began preparing the vast complexity of his body for the task ahead. The albino hooder came into view ahead of them, hunting again, hungry again. Blue moved away, yet even as she did so the link to her brother grew even stronger, so she carried his very shape in her mind.

Her brother stood up, that movement enough to attract the hooder, and it attacked, cupping him to the ground and following an instinctive feeding program. It stripped him of his skin, his muscle, hesitant over internal structures it hadn't been prepared to find, but ingesting them anyway. It took him apart, and in disjointed death agony he slid into its digestive tract, the connection broken with his sister. Soon he began penetrating tract walls and spreading out inside the hooder as it meticulously cleaned his bones. He followed his program, pheromone and EM transmitters re-establishing the link to his sister, Blue restoring those parts of him he had lost from her mental image of him. He did his work, death agony fading to an ache as the hooder destroyed him inside itself, a whisper of might-have-beens fading thereafter.

It was done.

Blue rose from where she had hidden herself as this white hooder adjusted, swung its cowl towards her. It did not attack, its self-awareness already growing enough to encompass a thing called gratitude. Perhaps it tilted its head in acknowledgement to her before it brought its cowl back down on her brother's bones and made its tribute.

She watched it rise again, leaving that sculpture, watched it depart. As purposeless then as any living sentient being, she collected her brother's remains and went to find a hidden place to exist. Waiting, waiting for her other brothers and sisters.

As he removed the helmet from his head, tendrils stretching and pulling from his skull like guinea worms, Jem gazed across at the dracowoman, two portions of his mind sliding around each other like immiscible fluids. It seemed that the Weaver continually connected to his Human self, and that those connections could not be sustained and so broke. Consciousness remained protean throughout the process. Sometimes his Human past became the lesser of two alternative histories; sometimes the Weaver became a graft upon his Human consciousness. Even so, his Human part was being perpetually changed by this process, and he liked it. The being he seemed to be changing into now felt better than that poor, thoroughly indoctrinated and unintelligent Human proctor, and perhaps the process might at last rub out the grief and the guilt his Human mind seemed determined to cling to.

"I have only one question," said Chanter, also removing his helmet then peering inside it with distaste. "Why did Dragon do this? Why did Dragon heal the Technician?"

"Surely you know the answer yourself," Blue replied.

"To meddle, to play with dangerous things, to cause disruption and twist the shape of the world."

"The usual view of Dragon, yes, but not the central reason."

"Then why? Why?"

"Because," said Blue, "it was aesthetically pleasing."

The amphidapt displayed a brief puzzlement, then he closed his eyes and shook his head. He looked sick.

It had taken Jem a little while to understand the man, but now he did. Chanter had invested heavily, both emotionally and intellectually, in the belief that the Technician was expressing itself through its art. Despite the fact that all recent evidence pointed to that creature's art being a product of a malfunction, he had doggedly clung to that investment. But now, Blue's words had undermined the last bulwark of Chanter's faith, a feeling Jem understood perfectly.

Because it wasn't based on logic, faith did not often fail when exposed to logic—such was always taken as an attack and resulted in a stubborn lockdown. However, take the faithful one out of his normal environment into one where he could not help but stumble on facts that refuted his faith—let that one expose himself to logic and accept it—and sometimes a breaking point could be reached.

"Just a machine," said Chanter.

Jem didn't quite understand that. "But a machine more complex than any Human being."

Chanter looked at him. "But a machine nonetheless."

Jem shook his head, still trying to encompass this strange idea—one that could be backed up by no physical science—that created organic machines somehow differed from evolved ones. Then, all at once, he understood. This was the thinking of members of a young civilization, newly arisen from primitivism and yet to grow comfortable with their machines. Less than ten thousand years ago Humans were still banging rocks together and sacrificing goats to ensure the sun rose. Yes, there had been a time when the Atheter had felt the same, when their machines were new and something separate from themselves. The Atheter of his own time had been certain about that, but it was a period of history lost somewhere far behind tens of thousands of years of war, of rises and falls that never quite expelled them from the age of machines.

"What does this mean?" Jem asked.

Chanter just stared at him for a long moment. Perhaps he didn't understand the question? No, finally he replied, "A soulless mechanism."

Oh yes, the soul . . .

Jem understood the concept; he had thoroughly believed in souls before. He winced at the painful embarrassment he felt now, felt himself dissolving, his forty-five years of human life diluted in an immensity of experience and understanding. Then something snapped, that other mind inside him detaching, again changing him just a little bit more but again distancing itself from him.

"What will you do now?" Jem asked.

Chanter stared at him again, then abruptly swung back to Blue. "We're done here?"

"We are done," the dracowoman agreed. "Are you satisfied?"

"Satisfied? Hardly." He turned back to Jem. "Now I'm going back to my mudmarine. Yes," Chanter nodded to himself, "I'm going back." He stomped towards the door, which obligingly hinged open ahead of him, and he stepped outside.

Jem now turned and faced Blue. "And this was aesthetically pleasing for Dragon too?"

Blue nodded an acknowledgement. "Dragon considered it unfinished business and so left the memories."

"Did interference make Dragon feel alive?"

"I don't understand you."

"Consider Chanter's feeling that constructed organisms and evolved organisms are somehow different. I ask again: did interference make Dragon feel alive?"

"You are still unclear."

Jem allowed himself a small smile, a Human twist of the face that denoted a certain communication. The Weaver had known the same sorts of problems, once, far in the past. War machines like the Technician could never be still.

"Dragon was aware it was a biomech, and carried the awareness in itself of its creators' belief in their own uniqueness. To prove itself it had to *do*, could not be still."

"I dream Dragon dreams sometimes."

"Quite," said Jem. "And in *doing*, Dragon went beyond merely curing the Technician, did it not? Dragon prepared for the inevitable results of the Technician becoming fully functional."

Blue said nothing, just stared.

Jem went on, "Perhaps you didn't realize that the download you provided, at Dragon's behest, gave me more than it gave Chanter. You are involved. You are still involved, for you were instructed to provide the means to end all this. Where and how?"

Blue blinked, even her draconic visage twisting in thought. "Yes, you were to ask that question."

"And you to provide an answer."

"The means has been brought here, and Shree Enkara carries it. She intends to use it against the Atheter AI, but it was only with such intention that I could get her close to you."

Jem nodded once in acknowledgement and departed after Chanter.

As he stepped out into Masadan evening, Jem processed the new information and started coming to conclusions he did not like. He had been manipulated and used all his life; first by the Theocracy, then by the Polity, and now by Dragon. Never had his destiny been his own. However, there was no way to avoid what had been planned for him. He must see it through before he could ever find his own course. He hurried after Chanter, falling in beside the amphidapt as he strode from the town. They did not speak until they reached the perimeter, where Chanter came to a halt and folded his arms across his chest and gazed pensively across at his mudmarine.

"Are you running away?" Jem asked.

"Maybe," Chanter agreed.

"The Technician being a faulty machine does not mean it was incapable of art."

Chanter shook his head. "It's all too damned complicated now, and there are too many people involved. How can I see to the core of it all with experts and AIs over-analysing every scrap of data? Some things should remain inviolate. Some mysteries should remain mysteries."

"Something I once believed," said Jem.

Chanter glared at him, his face blushing purple. "This has got nothing to do with damned religion!"

Jem shrugged. It seemed to him that whilst it had nothing to do with organized religion, it had everything to do with faith—that comfortable sanctuary from the complications of reality.

"Where will you go now?" he asked.

"Somewhere cleaner, less complicated, somewhere I can think."

Chanter strode away, and Jem let him go. Who was he to argue with the man? He had only started to make sense of the world using someone else's mind. The amphidapt reached his mudmarine, raised one hand goodbye, then a bright light glared and his vessel lifted and tore in half. The crump of the blast seemed more sensation than sound.

By the time Grant reached the blast site it was already swarming with dracomen and, even at night like this, he recognized Blue.

"Where are they?" he barked.

Blue held out the flat of her hand, turned it over then pointed. Grant headed where indicated. Jeremiah Tombs was down on his knees, not praying, but cradling Chanter's head in his lap. The amphidapt looked thoroughly wasted; burnt from head to foot, one of his legs gone along with part of the side of his head, now exposing mangled contents. Unless the man had a memplant there would be no way back for him.

"Shit," said Grant. "Shit!"

Tombs looked up, eyes strangely bright in the near-dark, reflecting light like the eyes of an animal.

"He wanted to go somewhere less complicated, cleaner, somewhere he could think," said Tombs.

"And you reckon he's gone there." Grant could not conceal his contempt.

"No, he's just dead."

16

When it was first discovered there was great excitement about the Atheter AI. The sheer size of the chunk of memory crystal it occupied indicated that it must be the gatekeeper on a vast repository of alien knowledge. A benefit of this was obtained upon first contact with the AI: a method of scanning in underspace to locate patterns generated by Jain nodes in realspace, thus to locate them. A later contact revealed a snapshot of part of the tragic Atheter history, but not really much more than had already been guessed. Then the AI shut down for two decades. When this silence finally ended, information again began to become available from the AI, indirectly, but it was disappointing. The vast repository of astrogation data, studies of Atheter astral bodies, suns, worlds, asteroids and underspace maps rendered very little that was new and not known; the fragments of Atheter history were very interesting, but censored, and technological data only matched current Polity development. Everything else of real interest to Polity AIs—mainly the advanced technologies—was available, but at a slow trickle and at a price. The Atheter AI was wise enough to recognize the stupidity of giving away a valuable commodity.

—*From* HOW IT IS *by Gordon*

The one called Sharn sat on the other side of the ATV from her, holding his nose to stop the blood. It seemed she wasn't the only one subject to Ripple-John's violence. Sharn, it seemed, was a "fucking idiot" with "the brains of a mud snake." Sharn had killed someone, that seemed evident, and now Ripple-John was worried, couldn't keep still.

"Why this way?" asked the one called Blitz, from the driver's seat. "Surely we need to stay close—we don't know where they'll take him next."

Ripple-John turned and stepped over to her, prodded her with his boot. "You awake?"

Sanders kept her eyes closed for a moment, then relented, gazing up at him, her vision slightly blurred. Pretending she was unconscious still would not have worked—he would have just put the boot in again. "I'm awake."

"Why don't you tell me all about you and Leif Grant," he suggested.

"What's to tell?"

"I wonder how much he values your life?"

Sanders could think of no reply.

Ripple-John smiled, but without warmth, then turned away to address Blitz. "If we stay near Dragon Down your dear stupid brother has ensured we'll be hunted down—that stirred them up like blood in a fucking squerm pond!" He turned and glared at Sharn. "You were supposed to disable that thing, not blow it to bits and kill the pilot!"

"So we're running?" Blitz asked.

"Yes and no," Ripple-John replied. "From the Barrier we've got the option to run south, to our aerofan cache, then we can fly over the hooder activity and go into hiding at Greenport. But we've still got one play left—haven't we, Jerval Sanders?"

"What's this about Leif Grant?" asked Kalash—factual question to get his father back to the point, and hopefully away from further violence.

Again the cold smile. "Seems Leif Grant and Jerval Sanders here have a history. Seems she spread her legs for him after the rebellion before running off to look after Tombs. I wonder how much he values her—whether he values her more than Tombs. What do you think Jerval?"

Not giving an answer wasn't an option. "Leif Grant is a professional—he won't bow to threats."

"You think?" Ripple-John nodded to himself. "You'd better hope he does, because you, lady, are dead if he doesn't."

Sanders turned her gaze back down towards the deck. If these idiots thought Grant would exchange Tombs for her, then they didn't know the man at all. That meant she was dead. She wanted to believe that when Ripple-John found out Grant wouldn't do as instructed, then she would be killed quickly. She really wanted to believe that.

Jem glanced at the face on the screen, realized it was no one he recognized and let his attention stray to one of the windows giving a view across the central park. In the raspberry light of dawn a group of dracomen were pruning grape trees and feeding the cuttings into the open back of something that looked like the offspring of a tortoise and a dustbin. Every now and again, this thing extended a rubbery tube from its underside to squeeze out a turd of mulched and digested plant matter at the foot of each tree.

The sun was rising, yes, and Chanter's body rested, cooling, wrapped in a scaly caul, in the room that had been provided for him. But this was about something else. Someone had gone missing, someone who should have been here.

"We didn't actually want anyone to die," said the face on the screen. "We just wanted to ensure you couldn't go underground to your next destination."

"But nevertheless, you murdered the pilot of that mudmarine," said Grant tightly.

The man shrugged. "Casualties are inevitable."

"Only when lunatics like you have their way."

"No, if I got my way there would be no need for casualties at all," replied the man. What was his name? Something odd, yes: Ripple-John.

Grant sat back, pressing a finger down on the mute button.

"This doesn't make sense," said Shree. "Why contact you now?"

Grant nodded agreement. "Just what I was going to ask." He took his finger off the mute button and sat forward again. "So you destroyed the mudmarine, presumably so you could ambush us when we headed away from here by other means, so why are you talking to me now?"

"I changed my mind and decided to appeal to your sense

of justice—a little research has revealed your long-term relationship with her . . ."

"So what do you want?" Grant snapped.

"Surely that's obvious."

"Not to me."

"You bring us Tombs. You bring Tombs out to the East Quadrant fence. If you don't, we kill her—it's quite simple."

"How the hell do you think you can get away with this?"

"First because that thing guarding him at Greenport is now in pieces outside the Tagreb, second because the war drone Amistad just went offworld, third because the police from either Zealos or Greenport won't get here in time, even if they hurry, which they won't. Oh, and by the way, we've got sensors scattered all over the area, so if we see any dracomen coming out this way, no deal."

"Even if you get away with this now," said Grant, "you'll be hunted down later."

"Maybe, but that's not your concern," Ripple-John replied. "You've got one hour to bring Tombs here, after which time I take Jerval Sanders outside and gut her—that clear enough for you?"

Jem had only been half listening up until that moment, but at the mention of that name his attention focused utterly and completely on the screen.

"I just can't do that," said Grant, frustrated, angry.

"As I now know, you've known Sanders for a long time, Leif Grant. Do you think Tombs is worth her life?"

"I can't make value judgements like that."

Ripple-John shrugged. "Maybe I'll take a lesson from Tombs himself and cut off her face first."

It seemed like everything around Jem had just opened out, like a pit, threatening to pull him down. Surely he had misheard?

"I'll need to see that she's alive," said Grant.

"Easy enough," replied Ripple-John. He reached out to grab something and the view swung round and down. It next showed the interior of an ATV, someone rapidly stepping aside to reveal a woman lying on the floor, her ankles taped together and her wrists bound behind her back. The one who had moved out of the way now stepped back in, reached down and took hold of a handful of her hair, jerked her head up so she faced the camera.

The Weaver snapped away within Jem's mind. He stepped closer to the screen. She had been beaten, clearly, just as it was clear that this was definitely Jerval Sanders.

"You've got one hour." Ripple-John came back into view. "One hour," he repeated, then his picture blinked out.

I didn't kill her, Jem thought. Guilt, undermined in his mind, collapsed like city blocks built on mud, but there seemed no joy in it, just an empty confusion. That same guilt, suddenly finding no reason for itself, began to thrash around in search of some reason for being.

Because of me she is like this, because of me she might be murdered.

Succinct and precise, yet some mental juggernaut seemed to be hurtling up behind it. Jem took another step closer, knew exactly what to do.

"You take me out there," he said. "And we do the exchange."

Grant turned towards him. "I was told to guard you—you're important, to this world, to the Polity and maybe to the whole Human race."

Jem shook his head. "No, you are wrong. What is inside my head is just a recording." He knew it was a lie, but now he was in control, completely in control.

"Nevertheless."

"You take me out there or I go by myself."

"I can't allow you to do that."

"I'm a free citizen to the Polity and it is my choice." Jem turned and looked directly at Blue, who had been standing quietly in the background. "He cannot stop me."

The dracowoman gave a curt twitch of her head, but Jem read all the subtleties there. She would not interfere because she knew what Jem had become; this was between Grant and him. When Jem turned back Grant was rising from his seat, his disc gun levelled.

"So you would kill me to stop me going and getting myself killed?" Jem asked.

Grant lowered his aim to Jem's leg.

Did Sanders matter? Within the enormous reaches of time Jem had experienced, even second-hand, she was nothing, a fleeting moment quickly passed, but then, in that same vastness his own Human life seemed so little. Should he just let it go, accede completely to the changes that other self had caused in him? No, because even with the Weaver granted perspective he knew that he wasn't the Weaver, could never be the Weaver. There wasn't room enough in this narrow Human skull to be everything that entity was—always sacrifices would have to be made. He was Human, and must live in a Human world with Human references, Human emotion, all Jem, though a much changed version of that man.

"It involved meticulous planning along with some doubtless long-understood and well tested methods," said Jem.

"What?" said Grant, beginning to look worried.

"First I had to be driven out of my insane denial of current reality; a madness that had locked down my mind and incidentally locked down what the Technician put there." Grant seemed to shrink in Jem's perception as if he was looking through some dark tunnelling lens. He continued: "This was achieved by a series of painful confrontations with that reality and manipulation of my inculcated tendency towards guilt. And in the final act Amistad and Penny Royal expected my encounter here, with Jerval Sanders, to finish the process."

Jem didn't recollect stepping forward. All he knew was that now he just stood a pace away from Grant, close enough to see the sweat beading on the man's face.

"They are very powerful intelligences, and they got it mostly right on the basis of the information they had. They thought that by now the strong medicine of guilt would be a hindrance and by removing it they would allow more of the Weaver to surface in my mind. But arrogantly they did not factor into their calculations what the Weaver wants, or the changes within me and what I, Jeremiah Tombs, now want."

He could feel it now, tightening up within his mind,

loosening its hold, a distinct massive consciousness poised like a thunderstorm, ready to explode into full being, but not within him, never within him. This separation, which neither Penny Royal nor Amistad could have predicted, allowed Jem some power over his own destiny. Now, turning in on itself as it prepared for the next stage of its existence, the Weaver knew Jem's actions might threaten that next stage, but also had confidence in the vessel that contained it.

He reached down and closed his hand over Grant's disc gun, and just took it out of the man's hand, inspected it for a moment and noted that the safety switch was still on. Grant needed to be able to protest but, in his heart, he valued Sanders more than Jem.

"I want," said Jem, "Sanders to be free."

"I'll take you out there," said Grant.

"Yes, I know," Jem replied.

The geostat cannon was of a thoroughly simple design: a doughnut tokomac two hundred metres wide supplying energy to a proton accelerator mounted above it, the beam focused and further accelerated through the doughnut hole by the magnetic field used to contain the fusion plasma within the tokomac. Around its rim micrometric attitude jets and curved-field gravmotors adjusted its position with sufficient precision to direct the beam to any single square metre on the continent below. Such was the precision of its positioning system that when Amistad landed on the doughnut, changing its position by only millimetres, the attitude jets briefly fired up to correct.

"How long?" Amistad asked, the communication directed to the surface below.

"Two hours minimum, three hours max," Penny Royal replied.

Obviously the damage the Technician inflicted had been major for it to take the black AI so long to recover from it. But, even without Penny Royal on guard, Tombs would be safe. Yes, the Tidy Squad had again tried to take him out, and Chanter was a casualty, dead, permanently dead, since the man had no memplant and his injuries were such that little could be extracted from his mashed brain. However, with Tombs inside the dracoman town the chances of another assassination attempt succeeding were minimal. The dracomen would protect him and, beside Penny Royal, no better bodyguards could be found on Masada.

"Well he stays in Dragon Down until you get there—he and Sanders can get nicely re-acquainted," said Amistad. "Then you take him on to the Atheter AI—we might not get anything more from him there, but maybe he'll elicit a response from it."

"No," Penny Royal replied.

"What do you mean 'no'?"

"Jerval Sanders is no longer present within Dragon Down," the black AI replied. "Data routing."

The information from Dragon Down arrived immediately. Sanders's belongings were still in her room, but the trunk she had brought them in had gone missing, as was she. Next a file arrived of the exchange between Leif Grant and an Overlander called Ripple-John, a man tentatively identified as a member of the Tidy Squad.

"This will have to wait until you are there," said Amistad.

"Too late," Penny Royal replied.

Amistad began grabbing further data and did not at all like what he found. Grant, the woman Shree and Tombs had taken Sanders's gravan and were acceding to Ripple-John's demand. Why had Grant done that? Probably because of his past relationship with Sanders—he would see her as worth more than a reformed proctor.

"Does Tombs know Sanders is still alive?"

"I do not know."

More data, routed through Penny Royal from an organic source in Dragon Down, the image strangely distorted. Something more had happened after the exchange with Ripple-John. The dynamic had suddenly changed: Tombs had become more dominant.

"Get to them as soon as you can," said Amistad. "Do what you can."

Next Amistad opened a communication channel with Dragon Down.

"Blue," said Amistad, the dracowoman appearing to his internal vision ensconced in her quarters, the view again distorted through some sort of organic camera. "Why did you let them go?"

"It was not for me to decide either way."

"Really . . ."

"Yes, really," Blue replied. "It may come as a surprise to you, Amistad, but we take the Polity ideas about personal responsibility and freedom quite seriously."

Did Amistad believe that? There had been input from the dracomen right from when Amistad arrived here, mainly through dracowoman Blue. It had seemed like she was keeping her finger on the pulse simply because major events on this world were of interest to the dracomen, Masada being the birthplace of their race. She had made suggestions about ongoing events, her last few being agreement with the idea that the Earthnet reporter Shree Enkara should accompany Tombs, and the suggestion that he should be brought, along with Chanter, to Dragon Down. But now, having earlier seen the recording she had shown Chanter, Amistad knew that dracoman involvement went all the way back, and that Dragon's manipulation of events hadn't finished with its self-immolation and rebirth.

"They could get themselves killed and, more importantly, Tombs could end up dead too," Amistad noted.

Blue shrugged. "I seriously doubt that."

"What aren't you telling me, Blue?"

"Surely that is evident?"

"How so?"

"I'm obviously not telling you what I'm not telling you." Blue shut down the communication.

Amistad opened up the processing power of his mind and applied it to every small piece of information, every hint, and very soon started to come up with some answers. Dragon had cured the Technician, but it seemed certain it had also influenced that war machine's subsequent actions. The Technician had downloaded the Weaver consciousness to Tombs. Both he and it had effectively been somnolent for twenty years, and were now active. It appeared that Amistad's own interference had resulted in this weaver becoming active inside Tombs, but was that true? Amistad had only started pushing after Tombs went on the move himself . . . In the end it seemed that the big question was what had been Dragon's intent in luring the mechanism here now, for it had to be Dragon who had started this.

Tempted to head back down to the surface to settle this, Amistad impatiently rattled his feet against the tokomac, causing the attitude jets to fire once again. But really, if Blue seriously doubted Tombs was in danger that was very likely true.

"Ergatis," Amistad enquired. "I want data on anything Dragon-related and nefarious over the last twenty years."

"This may take a while," Ergatis replied.

It did take a while; whole seconds for the AI to compile the data in one file and send it. Amistad tailored search engines to run through it, some of those engines possessing intelligence nearly equivalent to that of an unaugmented Human being. Much about the visit of the second Dragon sphere here they dismissed, but a lot still remained. Amistad went through that remainder himself, finally concentrating on one incident.

There had been assassinations here certainly conducted by dracomen, but brief analysis scrubbed them of any connection to events that concerned Amistad. Separatists who had tried to force dracomen to their cause had ended up in the paths of hooders. A unit of eight Separatists that detonated a bomb in Zealos and tried to make it appear that dracomen were involved were found in a squerm pond, or rather bits of them were. But there was something a little odd about this latest killing.

The story of what happened to those in the squerm pond had been extracted by forensic AI from a couple of Dracocorp augs. Those who had ended up in the paths of hooders were identified by remaining DNA and usually further evidence found of what they had been up to from their belongings-usually in some hotel room. It seemed their killers had ensured that evidence would come to light. These three corpses, however, were an oddity. They were found by pure chance: a Tagreb researcher had been ground-scanning and taking soil samples when he discovered them under a layer of rhizome. An engineered bacterium had been sprayed over them to eat away their bodies as quickly as possible—a few days later and there would have been nothing left. Forensic examination of their remains revealed that they had worn Dracocorp augs and that one of them, indicated by the remains of a particular poison, had been killed by dracomen, so it seemed possible they were Separatists. However their augs were gone—had been torn away—and no further evidence had been conveniently left to be discovered.

"This seems decidedly dodgy," said Amistad.

"There is a related offworld report." Ergatis relayed it at once.

The victims, it seemed, had come from Cheyne III. They were Separatists who years ago had dropped off the radar. Their own residences, when found, revealed nothing at all, but travel data had them going often to one particular location: a small, illegal otter-bone warehouse. When ECS raided it they found a laboratory within the warehouse, completely burnt out by a localized fire—some high-temperature incendiary had been used. In the ash were the remains of some very high-tech equipment and a further three corpses. There the trail had ended.

Was it instinct or intellect, Amistad wondered, that made him utterly sure this all had something to do with events here and now?

"They brought something here from that laboratory," Amistad stated. "I would guess that dracomen, through Dracocorp augs, hijacked a Separatist cell and used it for their own purposes."

"That seems a bit of a stretch," Ergatis replied.

"It does," said Amistad, "and I cannot pursue it now."

"The mechanism," stated the other AI.

"Yes." Amistad paused to contemplate, then continued, "It is evident that a series of events, instigated by Dragon, assisted along their course by dracowoman Blue and involving the Technician, Tombs and the approaching mechanism, are coming to a head."

"But you must act without reference to them," Ergatis stated.

"Yes, I must."

The fact that the mechanism would be here very soon was more important than unresolved though related questions about events below. The thing on its way here looked quite capable of trashing worlds and Amistad had to deal with it first. He shifted position on the tokomac, directed his sensors away from Masada and opened up communications with the warships presently in the Masadan system.

Grant took the gravan high above the flute grasses and the trails cut through them from Dragon Down, checked coordinates on his map screen then applied acceleration. As he flew he checked behind, noting that Tombs still sat on the floor in the rear of the van. After insisting that they go out to exchange him for Sanders, he had just followed meekly when Grant headed out, and had said nothing since.

"This is crazy," said Shree from the seat beside him.

"It's his choice," Grant replied. "Anyway, I wouldn't have thought you'd have any objection to him handing himself over to the Tidy Squad."

"It would certainly be newsworthy," she replied non-committally.

"And news is what you're all about, is it not, Shree?"

Grant jumped. He hadn't heard Tombs move up behind them, and now began to wonder why the man was suddenly making him feel so nervous. Glancing at Shree he could see the same reaction in her.

"So what if it is?" said Shree.

"Do you know what I was doing with the dracoman Blue?" Tombs asked.

Grant glanced round at him, furtively, unable to analyse why he felt the need to flinch. The man was just gazing ahead through the gravan screen, expression pale and serious.

"No one's seen fit to explain that," he said grudgingly.

"Dragon sent two of its dracomen to the surface before the rebellion. One to monitor and one to be eaten. Blue and her brother."

"You what?" said Shree.

"The brother was pure information and a method of transmitting that information. Her brother was the Technician's cure. Chanter saw and understood that, but I suspect his mind was insufficiently engaged to see the rest."

"The rest?" Grant was getting the creeps now. Perhaps he'd made a big mistake acceding to Tombs's demand to bring him out here, he obviously still had a lot of value inside that skull of his. Grant looked round to see the man staring at him. His eyes seemed completely black.

"Why heal the Technician?" Tombs asked. "Just to annoy Polity AIs, this being Dragon? I think not. What is the Technician's purpose?"

Grant just wanted to concentrate on flying the gravan. His map screen told him the containment fence around the Atheter AI was only a few kilometres away and they'd be over it in minutes. But the question was directed at him, only him.

"It wants to resurrect its master, this Weaver," he replied.

"Yes."

"But if it does that the thing that first fucked it over would stop it," Grant continued.

"Therefore?"

"Dragon did something else?"

"Precisely," said Tombs. He reached over and placed a hand on Shree's shoulder. She seemed about to shrug him off, but then froze. Was she feeling that rigidity, that unnatural strength that Grant himself had felt? "Dragon understood something that the Atheter, the Weaver itself, and the Technician too did not understand. The Atheter terror of Jain technology, the terror that led to their madness and racial suicide, is a weakness that can be exploited."

The barrier now started to come into view ahead through a low mist. The thing stood five metres tall. On first inspection it looked like no barrier at all, since it consisted of a long array of arched sections made from tubular ceramal. But within the foamstone rafts into which the arches were rooted were hard-field projectors, and the arches themselves contained all sorts of sensory gear. The animals of Masada could pass through this barrier freely, but the moment a Human, dracoman or any other intelligence tried it without permission, the hardfields would block their way. Grant turned the van into a course parallel with it.

"You're not making sense," said Shree. She was staring straight ahead, her eyes wide.

"Jain technology is the key—Dragon knew that," said Tombs. "But it was a key that had to be kept safe until the lock it fitted could be moved into position."

"And what lock would that be?" asked Grant.

Tombs just ignored that and continued: "The Technician is a war machine, a very sophisticated biomechanical war machine that has survived for two million years. Its purpose is battle, destroying the enemy. Protecting its Atheter masters was just a result of that, a secondary purpose, and one it served in one case throughout those years. But, like a soldier closely guarding a civilian, it has always been hampered. It could never risk itself in battle whilst it actually contained the one it was protecting."

"The Weaver," said Grant, not sure where this was going.

"The Weaver, yes . . . only when forced to defend itself has the Technician fought. When the Theocracy tried to kill it, it responded, but in a limited way, only destroying the direct threat to it and its master before going into hiding. Even the likes of Amistad don't really understand what it is capable of, though perhaps Penny Royal now has some intimation."

"Wait a minute," said Shree. "You're saying it's no longer hampered?"

"Yes, I'm saying that."

"Right, we're going back to Dragon Down," Grant said.

"No," said Tombs.

Grant looked round at him. "If I've got this right, you're saying the Technician no longer contains a copy of the Weaver, which means the only one in existence is the one in your head. That's too much to risk. You can't die."

"I am not going to die," said Tombs, "and you are going to take me to Sanders."

It happened so fast Grant didn't even have time to take his hand from the gravan's joystick. Tombs's hand made a snapping sound as it came down. He felt a slight tug at his waist, then, the barrel of his own disc gun was pressed down into the gap between his collar bone and his neck. He looked across as Shree slumped back and fell to one side, unconscious.

"You're risking too much, Tombs," said Grant.

"Was that a risk you considered when you fought the Theocracy?"

"I don't understand—you're more the Weaver now than the original Jeremiah Tombs . . ."

"You are right, you don't understand. The Weaver has changed me, the Weaver constantly changes me, but guilt keeps me Human. Though it does not want me to risk myself, it cannot stop me from doing this."

"But once free of guilt you'll be gone—the alien mind inside you will swamp you completely?"

Tombs shrugged. "Perhaps. But if the Weaver remains swamped within me it seems, ostensibly, that certain things cannot happen, and if they cannot happen I will be dead anyway."

"You need to explain that better."

"The mechanism will have detected the Weaver within me and will know that the war machine it had neutralized is once again active. It will come here to ensure, by deploying the full array of its disruptors, that its own purpose is completely fulfilled. This is as was intended by Dragon, in the plan that entity provided along with the cure that was Blue's brother."

"The mechanism, the thing that fucked up Penny Royal?"

Tombs gave a slow nod. "Certainly. It is also likely that it will have moved into a new programming state, will have integrated knowledge of an alien civilization here—a civilization that has already interfered in its purpose. It seems likely Amistad has gone to organize the Polity defence, but it won't be enough. The Technician now needs to be given new orders—it needs to cease being protective and go into full battle mode—and the orders for it to do so must come from a living breathing Atheter." He looked pained for a moment, adding, "Apparently."

"But . . . the Weaver is in you . . . and what do you mean 'apparently'?"

Tombs didn't answer, just pointed. "There."

The ATV had been parked a few hundred metres out from the arched barrier. Grant could see people nearby, but only two of them, one standing and the other lying on the ground. Doubtless Ripple-John's sons were concealed either in the ATV or in the surrounding flute grasses.

"Land," Tombs instructed.

Grant wanted to just disobey, to turn the gravan round, but his own disc gun was still pressed in below his neck and he very much doubted Tombs was bluffing. He eased the joystick down, spiralling the gravan towards the ground. He aimed for the edge of a wide muddy track, not wanting to have to push through flute grasses immediately on departing the vehicle. Soon the gravan crunched down through grass beside the track, landing with a thump and settling with a sigh. Grant shut down its gravmotors and mini-turbines, listened to both hum down into silence to leave only the rustle of grasses and the ping and crack of cooling metal.

"Okay, let's go."

Grant unstrapped and pushed himself up out of his seat, the gun barrel still hard against the base of his neck until Tombs abruptly snapped it away and stepped back. Grant peered at Shree, wondered if he should go for her weapon, but knew he just would not be fast enough. Rather than use the cab door he followed Tombs into the back of the van, and as the man opened the door and stepped out, followed him.

"What do you want me to do?" Grant asked as they stomped through squelchy mud.

"You take Sanders back to the van and you get out of here."

"What're you going to do?"

"Whatever is necessary."

Following the path round they reached the edge of the

small clearing in which the ATV was parked. Tombs halted, then abruptly held out the disc gun butt first.

"I am of course your prisoner," he said.

Grant accepted the weapon, clicked off the safety and pointed it at him.

"You understand that you won't be able to get me back to the gravan," Tombs continued. "Already two of Ripple-John's sons are between us and it, whilst the third is ten metres behind the ATV with a missile launcher." Tombs turned to gaze at Grant. "That was probably just in case you changed your mind about landing."

How the hell could Tombs know that?

Tombs began walking whilst Grant stared at the gun he held before abruptly following. In moments they reached the clearing, close enough to see the nasty flack gun Ripple-John pointed down at Sanders's head.

"That's far enough," said the Overlander, then, "Jeremiah Tombs."

Tombs didn't react, just stood unmoving.

"So how do you want to do this?" Grant asked.

Ripple-John smiled. "It's nice that you've seen sense, Leif. Did he give you much trouble? I don't suppose he did. They were always bullies and braver in packs."

"I'm not here for a pleasant chat, Ripple-John."

The Overlander held one hand out to the side, his expression apologetic. "Sorry to put you in a position like this, but you brought it on yourself when you considered proctors anything more than coffin fillers." He nudged Sanders with the toe of his boot. "Get up."

Only then did Grant see that her ankles were no longer tied together. With some struggle, because her hands were still bound behind her back, she got to her knees and then to her feet.

"Simple exchange," said Ripple-John. "She walks over to you whilst Tombs walks over to me. Anything untoward happens and both you and Sanders, die. My boy Kalash has you in his sights now."

Grant stepped over behind Tombs and nudged him in the back with his disc gun. "Get moving."

It was like pressing the barrel against a tree trunk, but after a moment Tombs took the first step, then another.

"Go on bitch, get out of here," Ripple-John instructed.

The two paced across the clearing towards each other. Sanders halted when she was close to Tombs. "I'm sorry, Jeremiah, so sorry."

Tombs dipped his head in acknowledgement but kept walking. When Sanders reached Grant the strength seemed to drain from her and she stumbled. Grant caught her, let her lean on him. With care he reached down and freed the knife from his boot, reached round and cut the length of optic cable binding her wrists.

The moment Tombs reached a pace away from Ripple-John the Overlander stepped forwards and lashed the flack gun across his face. The impact was hard, vicious, and should have immediately dropped the erstwhile proctor. All it did was turn his head, his body still as immobile as a rock. Then it seemed Tombs remembered he was supposed to be Human and stumbled, going down onto his knees. Grant saw the confusion in Ripple-John's expression. The man stepped in and drove a boot into Tombs's gut, and Tombs going down on his side, coughing and hacking, seemed to satisfy his attacker.

"Where's Amistad?" asked Sanders. "Where's Penny Royal?"

"Not here." Grant eyed two of Ripple-John's boys as they stepped out from the flute grasses.

Ripple-John dragged his attention away from Tombs and concentrated on Grant. "Get out of here now. If I don't see your vehicle leaving within the next few minutes, you won't be leaving at all."

Grant caught Sanders's arm and turned her, forcing her to keep up with him as he marched her back towards the gravan.

"We can't leave him—they'll kill him!"

"Nothing we can do," said Grant. "It's not safe here, not safe at all."

But the source of the danger here, he felt, was not the men with guns.

17

Gabbleduck's Brain

Three times the meat and five times the number of convolutions of a Human brain, along with four times the number of white-matter connections—just too much brain for a simple predatory animal. This was the limit of the knowledge of the gabbleduck's brain prior to the rebellion on Masada, because studying them was hindered by the fact that they emit a hooder-attracting hormone when they die and when dead, hooders fall on them like famine victims on a roast chicken and there's never much left to study. After the rebellion, studies were further hindered by the reclassification of gabbleducks higher up the sentience scale. All studies in recent years have been limited to scan data only, but have been revealing. In its animal state a gabbleduck uses just a third of its brain entire and just 10 per cent of its triple-lobed cerebrum. Among the many highly complex structures to have been identified is one that relates to language. Other structures appear to be organic modems capable of picking up a range of frequencies, and some cite these as reasons for their often odd behaviour—reception of Human-generated signals causing neuronal firing that their simplified brains don't know how to deal with. The bottom line, however, is this: these creatures are animals, but they also have unused mental watts far in excess of those of an unaugmented Human being. Let's just hope they never start using them.

—*From* HOW IT IS *by Gordon*

Jem lay utterly still. The only damage his assailant had caused was the cut on his temple, which leaked salty stinging blood into his right eye. This was irritating since, having a mere two eyes, it did impede his function. He reached up carefully and wiped his eye. It blurred, further dulling the senses of his inadequate body, so he reached out for further sensory data—data he had always known, but never truly acknowledged, would be available to him.

He had been aware of it ever since escaping the sanatorium on Heretic's Isle, that constant low mutter as of something stirring in uncomfortable slumber. Now as he touched it, the mutter turned to a mumble, then a panicked retreat from coherence. He reassured it, calmed it by opening his consciousness to it, then demanded a response; and the Atheter AI woke up to the presence of one of its masters. The history loaded in a second, he analysed it in that same second, began to understand more.

Jem realized that he had been wrong about why the AI had shut itself down. Having been transported here twenty years ago and making an assessment of what had once been the Homeworld of its masters, he had assumed it must have quickly worked out what had happened and felt itself in danger from the mechanism. Not so. It seemed that the AI's mind was as much like an Atheter's mind as a Polity AI's mind was like a Human's, which is to say, nothing like it. No, its reason for concealment was much closer, and altogether ironic.

The Atheter AI dated from a few Human centuries before the final racial extinction, from the time of the retreat. As the Atheter pulled back towards their Homeworld they obliterated their technology behind them so as to leave nothing Jain technology could hijack and, unlike in the Human Polity, their AIs had not climbed to dominance. There had been no Atheter Quiet War. This AI along with many others had been scheduled for destruction and so concealed itself. And the destroyers it had concealed itself from were Atheter war machines, just like the Technician. The AI had shut itself down out of fear of the Technician—a both amusing and tragic situation.

"On your feet, proctor," Ripple-John spat.

Jem rose to his feet in one smooth motion, but then at once adjusted his pose, slumping a little and bowing his head. He required more sensory data and got it at once as the AI relayed a feed from the sensors in the barrier, which it had seized control of long ago as a possible defence against the Technician. Visualizing further coding—a three-dimensional pattern only hinted at on penny mollusc shells—he made a link. The AI rebelled, briefly, but as the link hardened and it received data from that other source, it understood, and using the borrowed languages of Humanity offered up a few prized expletives. Now it realized it had been hiding for no reason. Now it knew the Technician's purpose, for that other source was the war machine itself, and the AI realized it had been sleeping towards another unexpected source of oblivion.

"*I know this Dragon,*" the AI noted.

"*You were not included in the original calculations,*" Jem replied. "*Though you can be of assistance. Call them—you have the capability.*"

"*It is done—they come.*"

"So how do we do it?" asked the young man with the scoped assault rifle.

"Should we waste time?" asked another. "A bullet through the head should be enough, surely?"

"It's not enough for me, Blitz," said Ripple-John with a smile. Jem understood that his cheerful demeanour concealed hate that had congealed solid. "Something spectacular and extremely painful, I think."

"We don't want to hang around here too long," said Blitz. He looked up, tracking the gravan as it rose into the sky and began to move away.

"Then we take him to our aerofan cache, then somewhere private," said Ripple-John. "We should be able to get to the Greenport underground quickly enough and then we disappear."

"Greenport's been evacuated—you know that," said Blitz.

"You misunderstand me," said Ripple-John. "I mean the real underground—there's a small cave system underneath

Green-port and an escape tunnel leading down the coast. It's not something generally known." He stepped closer to Jem, provocatively, hoping Jem would react in some way so he could respond violently.

Now, linked into the Atheter AI like Humans, drones and Polity AIs interlinked, Jem began processing more data. But he felt a strange disquiet, difficult to nail down only for a moment, after which he understood its source. This was so like using the *Gift*—the Dracocorp augs Dragon had provided for the Brotherhood, the chunk of semiorganic technology the Technician had ripped from him as it took off his face. He shuddered, then watched through the Technician's upper eyes as it hurtled along through flute grasses, a heroyne rapidly striding out of its path. Then out of the chaotic montage of images threatening to flood his brain, he selected one, close, and gazed through eyes that seemed more comfortable to him; ones giving panoramic vision extending further into the light spectrum than did Human eyes. He could feel the curiosity of the owner of those eyes, its potential intelligence disrupted into mentally self-destructive paths, its response to a microwave frequency picked up by a nearly atrophied organ in its brain. He saw what it saw as it raised its head above the flute grasses and gazed to where it somehow felt it had been summoned. He smiled to himself upon seeing the ATV, himself and his captors standing nearby.

"What the fuck are you grinning at?" Ripple-John asked.

Jem raised his head and gazed straight into the man's eyes. Ripple-John stepped back, registering shock.

"If you leave now," said Jem, "you might survive. You just might."

Another now, drawing closer. He could hear them in the flute grasses, but the four Humans here holding him captive could not. How, with such dull senses, had this race created a space-borne civilization?

"You're threatening us?" Ripple-John asked, viciously amused.

There was no way to control them—the best thing to do would be to get out of the way. Jem tensed up his body, tested the softness of the ground below his feet, scanned about himself for the best route.

"I don't need to be the threat," he replied. "They are." He pointed.

"Vrabbit fobbish," intoned a voice from where he pointed.

It weighed in at about three tonnes and came out of the flute grasses in one great lolloping bound, landing with a heavy thump that shook the ground underneath their feet. As four Human gazes snapped away from him, Jem launched himself sideways, shouldered the ground and rolled underneath the ATV. He glanced back to see the gabbleduck—a young adult yet to attain full massive growth—stand there for a moment like a great bear, then abruptly roll back on its haunches. Kalash chose that moment to open fire on it, which was a mistake.

The shots from his pulse rifle thudded into its chest, burning deep painful wounds. The brainless descendants of a once star-spanning civilization gabbleducks might have been, but they still possessed intelligence enough to know when they were being hurt, and who by.

"Where the fuck did he—" Ripple-John shouted, further words drowned out by the gabbleduck's multi-tone shriek.

Jem rolled out of the other side of the vehicle, got partway to his feet and hurled himself into the flute grasses beyond. He began pushing his way through, partly concentrating on what he was doing, but otherwise looking through many familiar eyes. The gabbleduck charged towards the four, Kalash firing again and putting out two of its eyes.

"Robnacker!" another voice cried, and a huge shape reared up right beside Jem.

This thing was a fully grown adult and squatting formed a massive pyramid of flesh and bone. He froze, gazing up at it. The thing dipped its head to peer down at him, shuddered like an arachnophobe seeing a tarantula and heaved its bulk a long pace away, where it hunched down and swung its attention away from him. Jem got up and got away just as fast as he could.

Someone screaming now. Kalash, suspended off the ground in a big black claw. The first gabbleduck had now lost all feelings of curiosity, and any playfulness that might have inhabited it earlier. It shoved one of Kalash's legs into its bill, closing teeth like white holly leaves down on it, then ripped it off. Next a crack and whoosh—the missile launcher. Through his link to the gabbleduck Jem felt the impact like a cramp in his own chest. Fire filled his vision through the creature's eyes then the view gyrated for a few seconds before shuddering to a halt, and now through his own eyes he peered across the clearing to where the creature's headless body began to topple.

"Where is that fucking proctor!" Ripple-John exclaimed. The man thought it was all over, because more than one gabbleduck in any location was no common sight.

Having cut a circular course through the flute grasses, Jem eased as quietly as he could to the grasses at the edge of the clearing and peered out. Ripple-John's other two sons had gone over to their brother. One was trying and failing to apply a tourniquet to ripped flesh and a protruding thigh bone, the other opening a field medical kit. Ripple-John did not seem concerned about them as he walked the length of the ATV, flack gun held out to one side. Surely they could hear it now?

"What is that?" One of the sons looked up.

Yes, they could hear.

"God help us," said the other one.

Two domed heads rose up out of the grasses on the other side of the clearing, then they both turned to each other.

"Stigger stig," said one.

"Romble," the other agreed.

Ripple-John turned, now seeing what his sons were seeing. "Get him into the ATV, quickly now," he said with studied calm.

The two helped their brother up onto his remaining foot, but he seemed to be either unconscious or in a drugged stupor, for they all but dragged him towards the vehicle. They took him inside, Ripple-John walking slowly backwards behind them as yet another gabbleduck, a small one, pushed into the clearing then lolloped over to the remains of its fellow and began sniffing at them. Ripple-John slammed the door shut just as the ATV's motors whined into life.

Jem eased himself to his knees, still keeping concealed, and waited. Now he was getting used to the visual melange he realized that seven gabbleducks, excluding the dead one, were in the vicinity. No knowing what they would do now and, whilst they had provided the distraction he needed, they could now be a danger to him.

"*We need a gabbleduck,*" he noted.

"*There are gabbleducks within the barrier,*" the Atheter AI replied.

"*Close the barrier behind me when I'm through.*"

"*As you will.*"

Did he notice a hint of resentment in the communication. Was the AI remembering that its own masters had scheduled it for destruction? He would have to be very careful with this entity. He must ensure it understood its perilous situation now, and that only Jem held the key to its survival for, without any doubt, it would be subject to the mechanism's secondary function of annihilating Atheter technology when it arrived here. He told it, briefly, what he intended.

"*We could never see it,*" the AI replied.

"*No, but Dragon did, straight away.*"

The ATV began to pull away but, at that moment, the big gabbleduck Jem had seen earlier decided to intervene. It rose up out of the flute grasses beside the vehicle, massive, pyramidal, reached out with one big heavy forelimb and brought a claw the size of a scrapyard grab down on its roof. The ATV's forward motion ceased, its wheels spinning and throwing up a spray of mud and chunks of rhizome. Jem saw the roof distort as the gabbleduck closed its claw—took a grip—then in a moment the wheels were clear of the ground. The creature picked it right up before its face and studied it with evident curiosity, turned it over and began prodding at the underside with one long black claw. It looked almost like a child with a motorized toy, checking to see where the batteries went. That claw then strayed, hitting one of the rapidly spinning wheels. The tyre shredded, spraying out yellow sealant foam from the auto puncture repair, straight into the creature's face.

"Bohob," it said, and discarded the vehicle.

The ATV crashed down on its roof, its front screen exploding outwards and snapped power cables shorting on its now upward-facing underside, through the bodywork and into the ground, which began to smoke. Jem winced, wondered if any of the passengers had survived that. He turned away.

Time to go. The other gabbleducks were concentrating on the vehicle, whilst the big monster was wiping foam from its domed head like a bald and sweaty fat man. Jem moved off, neither hurrying nor moving furtively. He knew enough about a gabbleduck's senses to realize they would be aware of his presence. If he ran their hunter's instinct might impel them to chase him. If he tried to creep away, that same instinct might shift them into stalking mode. But really, it was all might and maybe, because few logical rules applied to these creatures. Even though his skull contained the mind of one of their ancestors, he did not know what they would do.

The clearing soon out of sight, Jem moved into an area where the grasses had been crushed down, and picked up his pace. From behind he heard nonsense talk, the screech of metal rending, then gunfire. Ripple-John and his sons had a small chance of survival. If they got away from the gabbleducks they just might be able to make it on foot back to civilization. But even should they reach a place where the hostile local wildlife couldn't get to them, they would never be safe. They had released the death hormone and they had killed Chanter, and would be hunted relentlessly. Jem dismissed them from his mind.

"I want you to contact the gravan I arrived here in and make a communications link for me."

"Why?"

"Because there is something aboard that vehicle we need, something we need very much."

The communication link opened, again seemingly no different to using a Dracocorp augmentation. He saw Leif

Grant peering down at him and wondered what the man was seeing on his screen.

"You can return now," Jem said out loud, not sure why he felt the need to speak like that.

"Tombs?" said Grant.

"The same."

"What happened . . . how are you talking to me now?"

In the background Jem saw Shree Enkara leaning across to peer at the screen. She looked angry, and had a numb-patch plastered to her temple.

"My captors have been . . . inconvenienced. I am talking to you via the Atheter AI, which I am now heading towards. I want you to come to me."

Grant's expression registered shock, then after a moment he said, "Okay, will do." Shree's expression hardened—certainty, purpose there. Of course. Dragon's agent here, the dracowoman Blue, had picked her as the perfect way to convey a very important item to the designated spot. Blue had seen, so long after Dragon's death, a better way to bring that entity's original plan to fruition.

"That's all," said Jem, and the link faded.

The barrier seemed so utterly ineffectual. The rafts supporting the uprights of each arch were mere coins of foamstone a metre across and half a metre deep. The arches themselves seemed to be just curved chrome pipe the thickness of a man's wrist. All around them the flute grass had been trampled flat across a wide area. As a precaution Jem moved off the trail into a nearby stand yet to be trampled down. Now linked into the Atheter AI he understood why this area had seen so much activity, and recognized the danger here.

The Atheter had spectacularly failed to recreate that mythical garden of their past because, over the long millennia of their civilization, they had lost track of the distinction between evolved and manufactured biology in both themselves and the life forms they surrounded themselves with. Within the skulls of all the wildlife of this world grew some form of the same microwave receiver and transmitter the

AI had used to call the gabbleducks. And that wildlife had been frequently attracted to this area by the muttering of the AI stirring in sleep.

Jem paused at the edge of the flute-grass stand, ten metres of open ground ahead to the barrier, a further ten metres beyond it. Far to his right he observed a heroyne stilt-legging through the barrier and waited till it was out of sight before moving. He quickly hurried across, had reached the barrier when he heard something crash out of the grasses behind him.

"Going somewhere, proctor?"

Jem turned. From the vehemence in the shout he had expected to see Ripple-John, but no, it was the son called Blitz. The man strode towards him, jerkily, Ripple-John's flack gun clutched tightly in his hand. He had been through the wars: clothing muddy and ripped, blood smeared down the side of his face and soaking through at one thigh. He raised his gun and Jem stepped back.

"My brother is dead," said Blitz. "My father is dead."

"And why am I to blame for that?" Jem asked.

Blitz halted, raised his weapon.

"Gabbleducks," he said. "You . . . they came because of you!"

"And therefore?"

"It's because of you they're dead!"

"Am I to blame for defending myself?"

"Theocrat!" Blitz spat, and opened fire.

Jem remained utterly motionless as flack missiles exploded against the hardfield only a few centimetres ahead of him. Any resentment the Atheter AI felt towards him had obviously been outweighed by its understanding of the situation, for it had started the hardfields the moment he crossed the line between the inside and the outside of the barrier. Jem now took a further couple of paces back.

With a shriek of pain and frustration Blitz charged across the intervening ground. He shouldered hard into the forcefield and rebounded, crashed back to the ground, then after a moment pushed himself up on his forearms, and just lay there panting.

"Take your surviving brother and go," said Jem. "You have maybe twenty minutes before the Technician reaches the barrier at this point."

Blitz pushed himself up, gasped, then managed to get to his feet. He turned, stood there swaying, just staring at Jem. Seeing him, now, Jem recognized something of himself there.

"I was indoctrinated to believe certain things," Jem said. "How different are you?"

"I don't believe in any damned god!" Blitz shouted.

Jem shook his head regretfully. "You shouldn't blame yourself for not questioning your father. It's not your fault that he and your brother are dead."

He turned and began walking away. Behind him, a rumbling explosion accompanied Blitz's scream of rage as he emptied the flack gun against the force-field. He shouldn't have wasted the bullets. He would need them.

Amistad scuttled around the ring of the tokomac to a glassy blister covering a socket array connecting to the thing's sub-AI computer, pressed a claw against an indentation beside it and turned it. The blister lid rose slightly then swivelled aside like a fold-out lens. Even while doing this the drone kept his long-range sensors on other activity within the Braemar system to ensure preparations were under way. Four white-hot streaks scored across the face of Masada as the four insystem gamma-class attack ships decelerated in upper atmosphere. Lightly touching the mind in each vessel the war drone listened to their internal chatter. All very professional and so unlike the insane conversations Amistad had conducted with his fellows during the Prador—Human war.

"Haiman Drode's data reveals three U-space faults developing in the device's vicinity," Amistad told them. "This indicates that it is already deploying the 'bells' or 'pattern disruptors' it used to wipe out the minds of the Atheter, and which it also used against the AI Penny Royal."

Amistad gave an internal instruction and the tip of one claw split to extrude a spray of self-guiding optic plugs. The thing about warfare in space was that when the EM started ramping up, communications got disrupted. This was precisely why the Polity had started making independent war drones just like Amistad. Therefore, if you wanted to control some large lethal piece of equipment, just like the one Amistad was squatting on, it was always a good idea to ensure a hard link.

"Low orbital deployment?" one of the attack ships queried.

"Tombs's words 'under the bell' indicate the disruptors were visible during the racial suicide, therefore yes, low deployment and a readiness to go tropospheric. I need fast intercept over the main continent so stay geostationary or grav-balanced there."

"We can surface-deploy," the attack ship noted.

Amistad paused in what he was doing, immediately called up and inspected the schematics of these ships, within just a few seconds realizing that they could launch almost as fast as they could drop out of the sky. "Two of you down: one in the Northern Mountains and one mid-continent."

"Will do."

Amistad added, "It seems likely these disruptors will materialize before the main mechanism itself so don't wait on that-confine your efforts to surface defence. They must be destroyed."

"What about collaterals? These things'll have a U-space energy feed and might go off like air-detonated atomics."

"We have no positive proof of the device's intent, but we cannot afford to wait and see. If one of those things powers up over a settlement we could end up with tens, if not hundreds of thousands of mind-wiped Human beings. We have to risk blast damage and collaterals."

"Understood."

Focusing in and cleaning up the image, Amistad watched fusion torches slowing the attack ships at a rate that would have turned Human crew to jelly, had there been any aboard. Each ship bore the shape of a cuttlefish bone, but with weapons nacelles protruding. Each was also of a primary colour: orange, yellow, blue and red. They were modern vessels, with speed and power not seen in attack ships of an equivalent size during Amistad's war years. They would do their job. Amistad returned his attention to the task at claw, reached forward to set the optic plugs into motion. They groped around for a moment then found their sockets. A microsecond later the geostat weapon fell completely under his control.

"What are you up to?" Ergatis queried from down on the surface. "You could have asked."

"You'll have enough on your plate, I suspect," replied the drone. "Have you considered ordering evacuation of the main settlements?"

"Yes, but I guess you've not been paying attention."

"Enlighten me," said Amistad, meanwhile running checks on his recently acquired toy.

"As soon as it became evident that device was on its way here I raised the terrorist threat level based on a high likelihood of the Tidy Squad having obtained a CTD and being intent on using it against a main population centre, which is about the same threat level as these disruptor devices, and easier to understand."

Amistad paused to harden a link down to Ergatis and absorb data. Many of those with their own transport had taken off to the squerm farm villages. Others were dispersing on foot.

"My problem is that if I issue a full evacuation order the distrust of us here is so high that over half the population will disobey it, and if I enforce it that will only increase bad feeling," Ergatis continued. "That, however, is not the main problem. The problem is that I have nowhere to evacuate people to. Crop-pond areas would do for those who have adapted themselves to the environment here, but the majority are not so adapted. Enforced evacuation would result in many deaths."

"Have you considered telling them the truth?"

"Considered and rejected. They would ridicule the idea that a two-million-year-old machine is on its way here quite likely intent on turning them all into brainless animals—the ease of rule of an informed populace does not apply here. Perhaps in another fifty years they'll be sufficiently educated to listen to us."

"Very well—keep me updated."

Amistad ran a couple of small tests, reaction jets flashing lines of white vapour out all around the weapon's tokomak and the object beginning to turn. He then ran another firing pattern which set it on a course curving round from its previously geostationary position. No need for it here now, the system dreadnought was already in view—a distorted sphere of mirrored metal, one hemisphere cut out from which it almost seemed all its internal components were spilling—it would have to do for now.

"*Senator,*" Amistad addressed the ship. "You are to take position alpha over the continent. Liaise with the attack ships, give them what back-up you can, but most important I want you to constantly map local and planetary U-space to track any interference. Almost certainly, once the mechanism arrives it will deploy further disruptors and I want you relaying that data immediately."

"That is understood already," the dreadnought's AI replied pedantically.

"Repetition never does any harm, whilst a failure to understand might," the drone replied.

"Yes, quite."

The other system dreadnought had, as instructed, remained in position over Flint, for that place had to be kept safe. Now the remaining two.

Right on cue the AI of *Scold* asked, "So what're our targets?"

Amistad directed his attention out into space. *Scold* and *Cheops* were a million kilometres out and a mere hundred kilometres apart.

"Yes, surprise us," said Janice Golden, interfaced captain of *Cheops.*

"According to haiman specialist Drode, the device will be here no earlier than four hours from now and no later than five hours," Amistad stated. "And as you have probably already surmised, you and *Scold* are to engage it."

"Not a surprise," she said.

"I want an attack plan ready, based on the data we already have, ready within the next—'"

A data packet arrived from *Scold*, approved and digitally signed by the *Cheops* AI. Amistad opened and absorbed it instantly. It seemed they had already been discussing the matter. Yes, the mechanism was made of super-dense matter and massed as much as the planet Mars, therefore only certain weapons would be effective: open-splash antimatter, intersecting X-ray lasers to create internal heat points, and the four prototype U-jump missiles that *Scold* nurtured in its weapons carousel.

"That'll do nicely," said the war drone.

"And what about you?" Janice asked.

"Monitor and command," Amistad replied.

She emitted a derisory snort.

Amistad understood her doubt, since she had probably already checked up on the war drone's history.

"Though I will assist—circumstances permitting," he added.

The reaction jets now flipped over the geostat weapon so its business end pointed out into space. The thing was tuned to firing down through atmosphere at targets on the surface, but firing into space, not one scrap of its energy would be wasted, and with a little tinkering, some quite interesting attack patterns could be introduced into the coming fight. If they were needed of course—Amistad tried to stamp down on the surge of excitement he felt, an almost nostalgic excitement.

As they approached the barrier, Grant slowed the gravan, doubtless waiting for some message from the planetary AI Ergatis. Down on the surface, force-fields kept any unwelcome visitors out, but up here things were different. Some fifteen years ago, an air car had flown this route, its driver and passengers perpetually warned not to cross the barrier. It was a well-known story that Shree had covered in her persona as an Earthnet reporter. There had been no response; apparently their com was down. A submind of Ergatis, occupying a simple crab-drone body, had intercepted, intent on landing on the car to deliver its warning. It had been fired upon. That was enough. The geostat weapon powered up and fired as the car crossed the barrier, vaporizing it.

Following the subsequent investigation, Shree was surprised to discover that the three in the car weren't Separatists, but members of a small, previously ignored organization called Humans First. The investigation also revealed that along with them and their car, half a ton of planar explosive had also been vaporized.

"We're not going to be stopped?" she asked.

Grant slowed further. He looked nervous. Wondering if com might be down right now, Shree scanned their surroundings for some sign of a crab-drone. To their right, about a kilometre away along the barrier, something caught her eye. Something white there, on the move. After a second she realized she was seeing the Technician passing through one of the barrier arches like a train entering a tunnel. Kind of it. As she understood it, sections of the barrier usually had to be rebuilt whenever a hooder ventured through this area.

"I'll find out," Grant said. "Ergatis?" Word recognition in the console com directed the signal where required and the AI answered at once.

"Yes, you have permission to cross the barrier," said the AI.

"Just wanted to be sure no one had a finger on the trigger," said Grant.

"Someone has, but that weapon is no longer pointed at you."

"What?"

"Amistad just hijacked it to be part of the reception committee—just a few hours remain before the mechanism arrives."

"I see," said Grant, just as the gravan slid over the barrier.

"Good luck," said Ergatis, ending the exchange.

"Reception committee? Mechanism?" Shree asked. She had been aware that Grant had his suspicions about her and had been keeping her out of the loop. Time for an update, she felt, though peering down at the barrier they had just crossed, and which was now receding behind, any new information probably made no difference at all.

"The mechanism that the Atheter used to rub out their own minds and which has since been ensuring there's no chance of resurrection," Grant stated. "The one that fucked over the Technician a million years ago, and the same one that fucked over Penny Royal just a decade or so ago. That mechanism."

Shree felt cold fingers crawling up her spine and focused on him completely. "Yes, I know what this mechanism is . . ."

"It surfaced from underspace a number of days back and since then has been taking ten-light-year hops in this direction. Amistad reckons it's coming here to utterly ensure every last trace of the Atheter has been erased. It also seems likely it might want to erase any bothersome aliens who might get in the way."

"Us?"

Sanders, behind, standing in the cockpit doorway. Shree turned to study her. Having made use of the onboard medical kit Sanders now seemed steadier, though her face was still a bruised and battered mess.

"Yes, us," said Grant.

"How can Amistad know that?" Shree asked.

"Probably because he's smarter than us. Probably because this is how Dragon set things up when it delivered its cure to the Technician."

"What?" Sanders spoke the question simultaneously with Shree.

Shree didn't like this at all. Could things have changed in ways bearing on her mission here? Might there be a reason not to kill Tombs and destroy the Atheter AI?

"It's complicated," said Grant. "Dragon came here when the Theocracy was in control, left a couple of its dracomen on the surface, one as bait for the Technician. Its body was the cure for the Technician—undid the damage done to it by the mechanism."

"For what purpose?" asked Sanders.

"I don't really know—something to do with Tombs, something to do with the device and the Technician itself. Amistad didn't really take the time to explain."

It seemed clear to Shree that nothing she had just learned would alter her course.

The building that housed the Atheter AI now drew into

sight, and within a few seconds they were over it and Grant slowed the gravan and set it descending in a spiralling course. Shree spotted a single Human figure walking in along one of the foamstone pathways leading towards the building: Tombs. Grant turned the vehicle in towards that pathway, slowed it further and brought it down, finally landing with a gentle bump and a sighing away of motors.

"So here we are," Grant said, "though I'm damned if I know why."

Shree gave him a tight smile, quickly unstrapped herself, then opened and stepped out of the door on her side and headed round the van. She was already striding down the walkway as Grant stepped out of the side door followed unsteadily by Sanders.

"Tombs!" Grant shouted.

Tombs held up a hand but continued on, stepping between two pillars and into the building. Glancing over her shoulder, Shree kept going, seeing Grant hesitating, turning back to Sanders.

"You okay?" Shree heard him say.

"Just a bit wobbly—you go ahead," Sanders replied.

Shree broke into a trot, glanced back again and saw Grant hurrying after her. He didn't trust her—knew something was up. He wasn't to know that it was already too late. He could shoot her maybe, but even then she doubted he could stop her reaching inside her jacket and pressing her finger to the top of the cylinder concealed there. She paused at the pillars, glimpsing Tombs standing near the centre of the building; she stepped inside then immediately moved to one side, listening as Grant reached the pillars a second later.

"Tombs?" he called.

Shree prepared herself, loosened herself. Twenty years ago Grant would have been no pushover, but now he was soft, hadn't been in combat for too long, hadn't retained the paranoid instincts required for survival.

He stepped through and Shree swung her leg up, then back round in a perfect reverse kick to slam her heel up into his solar plexus, knocking all the breath out of him. He bowed over, and she stepped in, squatted on one leg, swinging her other leg round to take his feet away from underneath him. He hit the ground on his side, too winded to respond, and she came down hard on his side with her knee. Relieving him of his gun took a second. She tossed it, then pulled his knife from his boot and sent that clattering after it. She stepped away, drawing her thin-gun from its concealed holster and turning to aim it at Tombs.

"So, proctor, how did you know?" she asked. Aboard the gravan, before he knocked her out, he had talked of Jain technology and she knew he had been directing his comments at her.

"How did I know what?" Tombs enquired, seemingly unconcerned at having a weapon aimed at him.

Gasping, Grant managed to get to his knees, but he still could not gather the breath to speak. She noted him sliding his hand down to his boot, it coming to rest against the top of an empty sheath. Soft, weak. She almost regretted the defeat of the Theocracy. At least, before and during the rebellion, men like Grant had remained admirable.

"You get up and go stand by Tombs," she said. "Try anything and you're dead. Understood?"

Finally managing to get to his feet, he walked an unsteady course over to the proctor. She saw him glance across at his knife and gun. She doubted he could have done anything with them had he retained them. Taking his place a couple of paces to one side of Tombs he studied the man, seemed puzzled, maybe by the same thing that was puzzling her: Tombs's apparent serenity. Tombs glanced round at him, gave him a slightly regretful smile, then swung his attention back to her.

"Sanders," she said, "get out from behind that pillar and in here now or I put a hole through Leif Grant's skull. You have five seconds. Five . . . four . . . three . . ."

"Okay." Sanders stepped from behind a pillar and entered the arena too. Without being instructed she walked over to stand beside Grant. Good girl.

"Now, again." Shree reached inside her jacket and withdrew the squat glassy cylinder, slick in her sweaty hand. "How did you know about this?"

"Ah, so that's what it looks like," Tombs replied. "I would have taken it from you earlier, but the Atheter part of my soul retains a deep abhorrence of it. Far easier to let you carry it until it was required."

"Oh, you require it now, do you? And I'm supposed to hand it over?"

Arrogance, that's what it was. Born of his religious indoctrination and now reinforced by his position at the centre of events here. Shree considered putting a bullet through his leg to drain some of that out of him, but no hurry, and she did want to know.

"You have a choice," said Tombs. "You can hand that over to me now and walk away, or you can release it here to kill yourself, us, and the AI below your feet. In doing so you would sacrifice the entire population of Masada too, because Amistad and those Polity weapons up there are not going to be able to stop what's coming. They'll distract it and delay it for a while, for a necessary time, but ultimately fail."

He thought he could convince her, it was ludicrous.

"How did you know about this?" she insisted.

Tombs shrugged. "Blue told me. She subverted the Draco-corp network of a Separatist cell and used them to deliver it to you. It couldn't be kept here because of a chance of the Polity finding it, and she couldn't transport it back here because even now her kind is subject to intense Polity scrutiny." He gestured to the cylinder. "What you hold is the one thing that can stop the mechanism."

"You're talking nonsense."

"Such timing," he said, turning fractionally to gaze beyond the building. "Here is one who really talks nonsense, but less so now, and not for much longer."

Shree took a quick glance in the direction he was looking. A young gabbleduck now squatted just a few metres out from them, its head tilted to one side as if it was listening.

But then maybe it was tilting its head for another reason, for it looked like someone had taken a knife to its skull, which was crisscrossed with pale blue scars.

"You here?" it enquired, the nonsense words too much like a real question for comfort. Then it got up onto all fours and loped in.

Shree backed off, trying to keep her three prisoners and the approaching gabbleduck in her potential field of fire. She watched it step up onto a walkway, lift its feet up and down as if puzzled by this new sensation from them, then continue its approach.

"Don't concern yourself," said Tombs. "It's completely harmless."

To Shree's knowledge there was no such thing as a harmless gabbleduck. Sometimes they might not choose to do harm, other times they were as vicious as siluroynes.

"Yeah, harmless," she spat.

"I assure you it is," Tombs stated, gazing at the gabbleduck as it cautiously stepped between pillars and then into the building. "It's been prepared, and its only motivation is to get to this location, and wait."

"Prepared?" Shree glanced at him.

Tombs studied her carefully. "This can only matter to you if you decide not to do what you intend. You are procrastinating, Shree. Is it not time you brought this all to an end? Is it not time for you to express your hatred of a world that fails to live by your rules?"

"You think you understand me? *You?*"

"I think he does," said Grant. The soldier folded his arms, suddenly seemed more at ease, which worried Shree.

Tombs glanced at the soldier. "She defines herself by a belief in the purity of her hatred. During the rebellion she believed that hatred was of the Theocracy, afterwards she maintained and nurtured it in the Tidy Squad, and has now turned it on the Polity."

"Childish psychology," said Shree. "I *am* the Tidy Squad and this has nothing to do with hatred but everything to do with justice and freedom. I don't hate your Theocracy and I don't hate the Polity—this is just a fight that must be fought." Why the hell was she debating this? Was she procrastinating?

Tombs turned back to her. "You misunderstand me. I said you believe you hate both of those. In reality you just hate yourself, and that's why you want to die."

It was as if he had just sucker-punched her. For a moment she felt small and utterly lost, but then anger swamped in and drowned that. He was taunting her and now the time had come to bring him back to reality. She lowered her aim, didn't want him to die at once, just to suffer. A burn-cauterized hole in his gut would do it.

Through clenched teeth she said, "I think I've had just about enough of you, Tombs."

She pulled the trigger. The thin-gun gave just a little kick as it fired its charge of ionized aluminium dust. The impact flashed before Tombs, something like a two-metre-tall sheet of glass briefly blinking into existence in front him. As the fire dispersed he just stood there, gazing at her. This was why he could taunt her. She fired twice more and both shots impacted on the same hardfield. She swung her aim across and fired at Sanders. A hardfield stopped those shots too.

"Self-protection," said Grant. "The Polity AIs gave their alien brother the means to defend itself."

Shree abruptly holstered her gun, then held up the cylinder, poised her finger over the end.

"You've left me no choice," she said.

"There's always a choice," said Tombs. "Just put that on the ground and go—over the next few hours the AIs will be too busy to try finding you."

"No," said Shree, suddenly feeling very calm. She pressed her finger down, then pulled it away. Certainly, the geostat weapon was not directed down here now, but once the Jain technology started spreading here the Polity AIs would soon react. Feeling a huge burden coming off her shoulders, Shree waited for the end.

Nothing happened.

A void growing in her torso, Shree reached out and pressed her finger down again, and still the cylinder remained inert.

"I told you Blue ensured you got that item to me," said Tombs. "Bearing that in mind, you don't think Blue would have allowed you a way to open it, do you?"

Shree felt suddenly very stupid, but then saw a way clear. She stooped and put the cylinder on the ground, held it in place with her foot, drew her gun and fired at the thing. Fire flared across the floor, over her boot and up her leg. She yelled and stepped back, trousers smouldering and then going out.

"Nano-chromed, case-hardened ceramal, seems to me," said Grant. "You'd need a proton weapon to get through it."

Every option was being closed down, but she was damned if she was going to let them win. She stooped and swept the cylinder up in her hand, groaned as it burned her skin, threw herself towards the nearby pillars. Briefly something caught her shoulder—hardfield, trying to stop her, then she was out on the walkway, coming to her feet, running.

18

Jain Technology—A Brief Overview

It now seems evident that this technology was made during some vicious and eons-long civil war between Jain factions. And it also seems evident that it evolved into something more destructive than the faction that made it wanted it to be. It's why there are no Jain, no Atheter, and quite probably why there are no Csorians either. It's a whole technology as a booby trap, but one so large that when it goes off it can take out a civilization. It's a poisoned chalice, Sauron's ring of power and Pandora's box, though in the last case the box contains no hope. Once initiated it grants its host the power to seize control of just about any other technology, and to also seize control of other life-forms. Neither Humans nor artificial intelligences are immune to it. It gives its host the power to increase his own intelligence too, and using it, one man could quite easily seize control of a planet, even a solar system. And inherent in its methods is the simple fact that the man will not even consider doing otherwise. Then it takes, it absorbs the pattern of its host, and formats itself to more effectively hijack more of the same kind. It effectively breeds with its host, though it is a one-sided affair. Next it will go to seed, just like an annual plant—switching over to a new program it will produce Jain nodes within its structure and disperse them, and the next intelligent life-form to pick up one of these nodes starts off the whole process again. If it is not stopped, the final result is nothing but a spreading cloud of Jain nodes, each waiting for its next host and its next technical civilization to prey upon. And just one node is enough to wipe out an entire race.

—From QUINCE GUIDE *compiled by Humans*

The population of Zealos had reduced substantially, as had the populations of the two other northern cities and some of the smaller Human habitats. No one had abandoned the erstwhile rebel cities in their underground caverns, in fact many had fled there. Their safety was illusory. Many of those caverns dated back to the time of the Atheter. It being confirmed that not all the Atheter had agreed to racial suicide, some would certainly have hidden there, and it seemed evident they hadn't survived.

"How long now?" the planetary AI enquired.

"It'll be here within two hours, by current estimates—it's powering up for its last jump of eight light years."

Ergatis retained a loose contact with Amistad and reviewed the war drone's plans, trying to figure out where to fit the geostat weapon into them. It didn't seem to fit, just demonstrated that Amistad had not shaken off its lifelong inclinations. Through its numerous eyes scattered across the surface of the planet, the AI now checked out other arrangements.

The red attack ship, labelled *Corpuscle* but generally only using its nickname, had landed on the Plate in the Northern Mountains—that place where a gabbleduck had crushed Shardelle Garadon's ATV. The vessel was down on two rear weapons nacelles of a conventional ovoid shape, and one forward spherical nacelle from which extended a weapon like a stack of ancient machine guns wrapped in a ton of radiator fins and from which a magazine feed curved back into the body of the ship.

"Blood," Ergatis sent. "I thought that weapon was only vacuum spec."

"Yeah," Blood replied.

"Perhaps you could explain why you have it deployed?"

"The percentage of oxygen here cuts down on burn ablation within expected target range. The five-stage neutronium pellets will survive for eight kilometres, thereafter converting to plasma for the next kilometre."

Ergatis asked no more. Though the megagun fired at a rate of a million rounds per minute at near-c its destructive power was outweighed by many of this and the other attack ships' weapons. Blood, however, had obviously seen an advantage in having a weapon that effectively changed what it was after eight kilometres. It could be that an opponent, preparing a defence for projectiles might be caught out when those projectiles turned into short-lived spears of plasma.

Next Ergatis took a look at the attack ship down only fifty kilometres away from the Atheter AI in the south. This one was resting at forty-five degrees in a hollow it had burnt in the ground, steam still rising all around it and the mud now a hardened shell below.

"Anoxia," Ergatis named the ship, but got no further.

A wordless communication from the dreadnought above just gave coordinates, a time-frame of seconds, and some characteristics of the U-space signature it had detected.

"Gotta go," said Anoxia, even as its fusion drive ignited underneath it like a bomb and flung it into the sky, the ground behind it exploding outwards to leave a smoking crater a kilometre across. Tracking those same coordinates, Ergatis tried to see what it could, detecting a disturbance directly above Zealos, and another a short distance away from the Atheter AI, in fact over the known location of the Technician.

Blood was up too, the Plate behind it glowing red and now marred with slowly cooling ripples. As best it could, using satcams and eyes scattered across the planet, Ergatis tracked both attack ships near the surface and the two above now turning meteoric as they hurtled down, whilst also watching the things now materializing.

Jeremiah Tombs's description had been apt. Under the bell. From top to bottom they measured half a kilometre and with their slightly flared bases and domed tops closely resembled the kind of bronze bells that might be found in a Buddhist monastery. They also appeared to be hollow, or rather hollow in the way that a tulip is hollow with the functional bit deep inside. A ground view showed what looked like a great bundle of steel rods, which now seemed to be in the process of extruding downwards, and beginning to glow. The colour of these devices was odd, metallic yellows and purples in either a mathematical or decorative configuration. They were also translucent; had not yet fully materialized into the real.

Ergatis tried what scanners were available to it, even hijacking those on the Tagreb mobile observation tower. Certainly these objects were powering up for something, but so tightly woven and interconnected was the technology it was difficult even for a planetary AI to figure out how they functioned. Then, as the extruding rods drew level with the base of the bell above, it did function.

The air hazed below the device, camera eyes directly underneath were immediately disrupted by powerful, rhythmic EM interference. In the street, Humans fell to their knees pressing their hands to their heads, screaming. A wall of pure ceramal alongside one street began to vibrate to the same odd rhythm, shuddered, cracked, then abruptly fell into even chunks each the size of a hand. Chainglass thumped white and turned to dust. Ergatis tried to analyse what weapon was being used here, briefly noted a U-space signature matching the rhythm and directly relayed its data to Amistad.

"Seems like a sophisticated USER effect," Amistad replied. "Keep monitor—'

Com shut down, and suddenly Ergatis found it difficult to connect what Amistad was saying to immediate events. What is a USER? What am I?

Then Blood arrived.

The attack ship hurtled over the horizon seemingly pushing a star ahead of it as the megagun fired. Smoky black before the attack ship, the tons of five-stage neutronium beads it spewed ramped up through the spectrum from red to bright white until, half a kilometre away from the device, air friction turned them to plasma. This torch of super-hot gas played over it, but only for a second. The next moment it bucked in the air as Blood closed the half-kilometre gap and hot neutronium beads impacted.

I know what a USER is, Ergatis remembered. Underspace Interference Emitter created by simply oscillating a singularity in and out of a runcible gate to cause disruptions in U-space. This was more precise though, surgical almost. Running internal diagnostics the planetary AI began connecting up further broken links in its mind and realized that, had Blood not attacked at that moment, a further few seconds would have left it with no mind left at all.

People, who a moment ago were on their knees clutching at their skulls, were now staggering for cover. Metallic snow boiled down over Zealos—those metallic beads turned molten, losing their artificial density, expanding and crystallising as they fell. The device had begun to tip, turning its business end up towards the attack ship just as that ship arrowed past.

"No you don't," said Blood.

The missile must have been released just at the last moment, its sharp curving course a burning question mark as it used up a one-burn fuser engine. The device lit up like a bulb, distorted, shed internal bars and molten metal like a prolapsing robot. As the glare faded the thing became completely visible, utterly solid, then it just dropped out of the sky.

It came down sideways across a street, one end hitting the top of an apartment and collapsing it like a sugar stick, the other end coming down on warehouses. It took down everything it landed on without slowing, thundered into the ground, crushing foamstone, sinking to half its width. The entire foamstone raft of Zealos rocked with the impact. Stress sensors and other monitoring devices recorded that the raft had cracked, and continued to monitor the crack growing wider. Super-dense metals, no doubt—Ergatis estimated a weight approaching one megatonne.

Between eight and nine hundred people had died, some in the crushed buildings, other scattered elsewhere in the city, from ricochets, suffocation, accidents caused by something turning their minds momentarily to mush. Other sensors began registering movement and Ergatis immediately knew that the death toll it had just calculated would not be all.

"Blood, I need a quarter-kilotonne blast right here." Ergatis sent the coordinates along with the request, its attention fixed on the wreckage where the device had come down, where survivors were staggering into view, trying to find somewhere to go.

"Why?" the attack ship asked, as it swung round and back in towards the city.

"Because though the device has cracked the city raft, it is not lying over the crack—one half of Zealos will be at ninety degrees to the ground within four minutes if we don't do something."

"Understood."

The missile came down, a black line scraped against the sky, hit precisely underneath the fallen device. In a massive explosion tonnes of foamstone fountained out from underneath it, hardly dislodging it at all. Then it dropped, disappearing into hot rubble like a lead weight sinking through wet porridge, and the half of the city that had already risen ten metres, sank back down, cushioned by displaced mud. No sign of the survivors Ergatis had seen, just the shock wave would have turned them to a bloody fog. The AI upped its death count by a further hundred, then wondered if there was any point in counting when it simultaneously received visuals from Amistad showing what had just materialized in the Braemar system, and notification of further U-space signatures in the atmosphere of Masada.

"It is here," Tombs had said, "the mechanism is here," just before something began rearranging the inside of Grant's head. He was on the floor again, his side hurting—Shree had cracked one of his ribs. He clutched at the gratings as the floor suddenly seemed to become a wall. Next came the panic: he didn't know how he had got here, he wasn't sure where "here" was, then he wasn't sure who he was.

The thunderous crashing he did identify—a triple sonic boom of something moving fast through atmosphere, fast and low—then the meaning of the words "sonic boom" fled his mind. Tombs, still standing impossibly on the wall Grant clung to, said something. Grant gazed at him in incomprehension, a sound in his head like someone hand-sawing through a log. He pressed a palm against his temple, still clinging with the other hand, knew only confusion. Someone began yelling, and he only realized it was him as a flashbulb light filled his surroundings, the world took a deep breath, then blasted it all out at once.

The wind picked him up, sent him rolling until something hard and angular came down, clamping him in place. He gazed in terror at the big claw pressing on his chest, then up into an array of green eyes below a scarred and domed head. Flute-grass stems blasted across, followed by spatters of smoking mud and a heavy black smoke, then the claw lifted away and a Human hand closed on the front of his jacket. Tombs hauled him to his feet.

"They can only delay it for a while," Tombs said, and pointed.

Grant gazed out beyond the pillars to where a massive bell-shaped object hung tilted in the sky, shedding black debris and pouring smoke. Next the sleek blue shape of a Polity attack ship sped past, its sonic boom a solid sound that sent him staggering. He spotted Sanders, crouched, her hands over her ears, squatted down beside her. In its passage the attack ship left another massive blast. That flashbulb went off again and Grant was glad he hadn't been looking at that moment. When he did look out towards the object, one massive chunk of it peeled away in a cloud of fire, then just fell. As it disappeared from sight the second shock wave hit, but this time Grant was ready for it, bracing both himself and Sanders. Looking up again as the wind threw debris between the pillars, he saw that Tombs stood utterly steady, as if made of iron.

Next the building bucked underneath them. Ground shock from that fallen chunk of the object. Grant readied himself for more of that as, trailing fire, the rest of the thing abruptly dropped out of the sky. With an eardrum-tearing shriek the attack ship hammered in, decelerating at a seemingly impossible rate to a halt above the site. In the smoke and steam its energy weapons were perfectly visible; proton beams and lasers, even a maser etching out its existence so it seemed a glass column reached down. Then something else stabbed down, a single missile, and the attack ship accelerated away again. When he saw Tombs stepping over to one of the building's pillars, crouching down behind it and catching an arm round it, Grant braced himself for the worst.

First the building bucked again, rising up on a ten-metre wave through the soft ground, but that was only from the fall of the object. Then the sky ignited, all the pillars around thrown into black and purple silhouette. The shock wave hit, and no preparation was enough for it. Grant lost his grip on Sanders, found himself hurtling through the air. He clipped a pillar, thumped down into soft mud, the debris-laden air soon darker above him than any Masadan night. Then the wind blast reversed, and the building became a grinning mouth of pillar teeth trying to suck him inside it again. The roar actually seemed composed of all the debris: a solid substance in the air. This just went on and on eternally. He anchored himself, driving heels and hands into soft ground. But next it all paused, as if reaching some physical limit, other sounds impinging; the patter of falling mud, the landscape around him groaning. Gradually, it began to wane, fall of debris became a light black snow, and Grant just lay there gazing into a darkness that cleared to a smoky fog, at the last swept abruptly away by an icy breeze.

"Are you okay?"

He wasn't sure how long he'd lain in comparative silence before hearing the words. He looked around to see Sanders standing beside him, surprised he hadn't been deafened.

"I think so." At last he felt able to stand up, which he did. "Glad to see you are."

She shrugged. "It slid me against one of the pillars and pinned me there."

"Tombs?"

She nodded towards the building. "He seems indestructible."

They walked across a thick layer like the outflow from a compost shredder, and stepped back into the building. The gabbleduck still squatted here in the same position as before, seeming oblivious to the crap that had fallen all over it, even in its eyes. Tombs stood between two pillars, gazing out at the steadily rising mushroom cloud.

"Straightforward fission bomb," he said without turning. "Probably the dirty burn has a more disruptive quality itself."

Grant moved up beside him, shuddered—it seemed explosions of that shape had branded themselves in the Human consciousness. Then he lowered his gaze, seeing Shree Enkara, fifty metres beyond the end of a walkway, pulling herself up from the ground, glancing back at them then abruptly heading for a nearby stand of flute grass. He moved to go after her, but Tombs caught his shoulder.

"There's no need," he said.

"But she's got that Jain tech—'

"The Technician is out there—she won't get far."

Grant thought about that for only a moment. Shree deserved to die for what she had done, but not like that. No one deserved to die like that.

"No," he said, "I'll bring it back for you, and I'll bring her back."

He stepped through and down, and set out after her.

Acceleration, instant, unfelt by her Human body but sensed in more ways than a Human body could sense. Masada dropped behind, whilst space debris impacted on the adamantine slopes of *Cheops's* sides and its drive glowed like a small sun. Ahead, Calypse slowly grew, but magnification rendered in clear detail the object poised over its onyx face.

It seemed a cornucopia woven from strips of metal. Only the metal weighed ten times more than lead, was harder than diamond, tougher than ceramal, and each of those strips measured fifty metres across. Inside that horn of plenty the mass of dodecahedrons Janice Golden had first seen in constant motion about each other had conglomerated in one unmoving lump. Mass sensors indicated that this thing would still balance the scales with the planet Mars, and already tidal effects were visible down on the surface of Calypse. The gas giant's moon system had disrupted too—and no one would know the result of that until later, when they started clearing up the mess.

"Why is no interception on the way here?" Janice asked. "We knew its intentions were hostile. Why are we only now being allowed to take the gloves off?"

"Actually, no," came the reply from *Scold*, "we did not know for sure."

Currently travelling on a parallel course, a thousand kilometres away, the modern dreadnought loomed huge in her sensors, and Janice felt like a puppy running beside a full-grown wolf.

"So we had to wait until it started killing people? I'm betting that wouldn't have happened if this had been a Prador dreadnought."

"Perhaps because we have nothing more to learn from the Prador," the other ship AI replied.

Yes, that seemed highly likely. The order to attack had been delayed whilst further information was gathered. That information was more important to the rulers of the Polity than a few civilian lives. How hugely things changed throughout history, and how greatly they remained the same.

"A more apposite question should be: why out here? Why not right over Masada?" Scold wondered.

"Probably so it can suck up matter like it did before." Fully interfaced now and lying in her sarcophagus, Janice couldn't tell if it was herself or the Cheops AI that replied. More likely an amalgam of the two had spoken the words.

"It could also be targeting Flint," Scold noted.

The Braemar moon Flint currently lay on the other side of Calypse, but in less than twenty hours would lie directly over the mechanism. That wasn't really a concern. This should all be over long before then, one way or another. With a thought, Janice opened ports over her four big rail-guns, gazed through ship eyes into their hardened bunkers and watched conveyor magazines loading one-ton missiles of mono-dense iron wrapped in a layer of case-hardened ceramal. As the guns began firing their roar echoed through vast open spaces within *Cheops* as if from a horde of monsters.

"No finesse, then," suggested Scold.

"Just a probe to test things before we start to finesse the attack." Janice noted that *Scold* had begun firing too, though it seemed to be lacing its inert missiles with a nice selection of atomic and chemical explosives. "We have to test it, see how it reacts, see if the weaknesses are where we expect them to be." Janice paused. "We also need to ensure your U-jump missiles will hit home—no point wasting them."

"No, really?" said Scold.

Janice didn't bother going on, she'd long realized that when an AI started getting sarcastic it was time to stop talking.

Travelling at a large proportion of light speed, the two clouds of missiles sped out, the gap between them narrowing as they closed on their target, till they melded into one cloud. Abruptly, something materialized before this cloud—one of the objects they had already seen down on the planet. Janice ensured that every scrap of data from this encounter was being relayed back to Amistad, and to the ships defending Masada.

The thing flared, briefly, emitting an EM pulse of massive intensity. The missiles to the fore of the cloud vaporized, but after that there seemed something wrong with the instrument readings, for the whole cloud seemed off course. Then, as her entire ship groaned around her, Janice realized, with a sudden sinking in her gut, what she had just seen.

"Fuck. Gravity weapon."

Her sensors had registered the passing of a line of distortion throughout her ship. The gravity wave had hit even before the EM blast reached the missiles, in fact that blast might have been only a side effect of it. Damage diagnostics began to catch up. The internal structure had weakened by 10 per cent, there were reactor breaches and systems crashes but luckily, since this was a weapon the Polity had also been developing and had thus also prepared a defence against, both her ship and *Scold* now used reactive antimatter containment. Twenty years ago they would both have been toast.

The cloud of missiles, though diverted, had not been diverted enough, but the mechanism was ready for that. The U-space signature from it seemed as disruptive as a USER, and the thing didn't entirely submerge in that continuum. Even to her most precise sensors the mechanism seemed to stretch into an object five hundred kilometres long, then snap back into shape, five hundred kilometres from where it had been.

Inert missiles hurtled straight down into Calypse, pocking its face with hundreds of thermal blasts each spreading to the size of North America then fading to blood red. However, just a few of the missiles *Scold* had fired, which possessed their own guidance systems, diverted enough to come down on the mechanism. Two of them hit. Silent detonations in space, small suns igniting; explosions that would have gutted a ship like *Cheops.*

"Minimal damage," Scold noted as the fires faded. Just shallow craters in that basketwork of super-dense strips, some shrapnel of that same matter hurtling away. "Intersecting X-ray lasers . . . now—microwave on pattern D412."

They fired simultaneously; a complex pattern of energy attack tangling along the length of the mechanism, generating hot spots where recent sensor data indicated complex systems, microwave beams tracking what seemed to be com-lines, possibly optic. Explosions within the massive machine, visible through its basketwork interior, tracked progress. An irised gravity field began to generate to its fore as it began to turn towards Calypse, but then something massive blew near the front end, molten matter bled out into space, and the field winked out. The whole mechanism shuddered, began responding with multispectrum lasers whose energy load was easily absorbed and distributed by the superconductive layers in the armour of the two massive ships.

"It's rather disappointing really," Scold noted.

What did they expect? Janice wondered. The sheer scale of this thing might be impressive, but was dwarfed by some engineering projects within the Polity. Yes, it was all alien technology, but technology based on the same science the Polity used. There was nothing new here.

"Should we just disable it and retain it for study?" she asked.

"No, let's not become too arrogant and too complacent," Scold scolded. "I'm targeting one U-jump and firing."

In the Polity those not in the know had always thought that travel through U-space was a complicated affair that could only be managed by an artificial intelligence. The myth lasted even throughout the Prador—Human war when the enemy arthropods were using their own surgically altered children to fly U-jump missiles on suicide missions. Now the Polity was experimenting with similar devices guided by sub-AI minds. And now *Scold* sent one such device after its prey.

It left *Scold* under its own power, a spike of gleaming metal standing on a one-burn fusion drive. Two thousand kilometres out, it rippled, then twisted into U-space like a trout diving after having snatched its mayfly. The instant effect of its impact was immense, but in entirely the wrong place: *Scold* bucked, opened up like a clam and vomited fire. Its AI didn't even have time to deeply analyse how the mechanism had turned the missile back on it, had time only to send one word.

"Tricky," it said, and died.

Sanders studied him, still trying to find inside herself some emotional response to a Jeremiah Tombs no longer confined to a wheelchair, drawing penny mollusc patterns and muttering Satagents to himself; to a Jeremiah standing whole and sane . . . maybe more than sane. Perhaps the beating she'd received from Ripple-John and the certainty that she was going to die had numbed her, or perhaps seeing Jeremiah like this dispelled all those nursy maternal instincts.

"Jerval Sanders," said Tombs, turning to her the moment Grant disappeared out of sight amidst the flute grasses.

"Jeremiah," she replied cautiously. "I was going to ask you why you were prepared to give your life for me, but now I see that wasn't the case. How did you escape Ripple-John? How is it you're alive?"

Shut up Jerval, you're babbling . . .

"I knew I wasn't going to die."

"Religious certainty?"

"Via the intelligence here." He stamped his foot against the ceramal grating. "I called in some gabbleducks, which changed the odds, but I didn't know I would be able to do that. What I did know was this: the Technician was within range, and it would not let me die. And then there's this."

He moved, suddenly, abruptly crossed the three or four metres between them so fast it seemed some godlike power had edited the movement out of reality. Now he stood right next to her, reached out and pressed the palm of his hand against her face. It felt like hot metal.

"I understand so much now." He smiled a boyish smile and at last she felt something stirring in her. She reached up, closed her hand over his and squeezed it, then lowered her hand. He took his away. Now much closer to him she could see that his eyes were bloodshot and broken blood vessels webbed his face. Had the recent blasts caused that?

"Tell me what you understand."

"What the Technician did, *all* of what it did to me." He shook his head, grimaced. "Did you ever think to closely examine the full extent of the damage?"

"Of course I did," she replied. "I repaired it . . . most of it."

"Certain muscle groups excised, certain nerve pathways, all of which you regrew. What you didn't realize, as you regrew them on my body from my own tissue, was that you weren't following the original blueprint. There were deep changes, but mostly so that my body could perform as required." He paused, looked distant for a moment. "Only now do I realize that if Grant hadn't picked me up and you hadn't repaired the damage I wouldn't have died, but I wonder if I would have still been Human." He snapped his fingers, and just ten metres away the gabbleduck swung its head round and peered at him. "Speed and strength I at last understand. Ripple-John wasn't going to kill me; the only question was whether he would survive me."

"So you're Superman now?"

"No, just a better vessel to contain what I hold within my skull, and a better mechanism to transfer it."

"Is there anything left of who you were?"

"I might ask the same about you. How much of the Jerval Sanders of ten years ago do you retain, now?"

"I think you know what I mean."

"All the memories are there, Jerval, and more. I'm Tombs but I've been changed by the world, just as we all are." He shrugged. "Admittedly the world has been more radical in its redesign of me."

The gabbleduck leaned forward, placing its claws on the floor, then casually plodded over. Sanders backed up, ready to run no matter what she had been told.

"You finally returned my face to me, though I didn't realize it at the time," Tombs said.

"Then you cut it off again."

"Yes—Amistad and Penny Royal were manipulating me, but didn't know that they had no say in the final outcome."

"Which is?"

"You returned my face to me, regrew the nerves, muscle, everything, but never ventured any deeper than the durama-ter of my brain." He reached up and touched his face. Sanders saw something writhe under his fingertips, under the skin.

"As I was instructed," she said.

"I was scanned, scanned deeply?"

"Yes."

"What was found?"

She stared at him, saw that his face looked grey, almost metallic, blotchy. The shadows here? "We found signs of surgical intervention, signs of the kind of connections a cerebral aug makes all throughout your brain." Sanders turned towards the gabbleduck as it halted and squatted nearby. "Remaining fibres even, both from your Dracocorp aug and, we believe, from the Technician itself. I wanted to remove them but was told that they seemed to be still connected, rewiring your brain."

"That's true, but if you'd removed them they would only have grown back." He paused, turned to gaze at the gabbleduck. "And once I drew the final pattern from a penny mollusc shell, completing the Atheter alphabet, finishing the countdown, they began to grow again. Now they are ready."

His face seemed to be moving as he stepped away from her, right over to the gabbleduck. She saw a trickle of blood run down from inside his ear. He shivered, groaned, and stepped even closer to the creature, its bill just a metre above his head. It bowed, hunched down and in, its bill pressing against his chest and its eyes only centimetres from his. Sanders stepped to one side to get a better view, horror and intellectual curiosity warring for predominance inside her.

"Now," said Tombs.

A white worm, narrow as a bootlace, sprouted from his cheek and writhed across to the gabbleduck. Its tip groped across the creature's skull, found a purple scar just above one eye, straightened, opening that scar to reveal a bloodless slit, and its end writhed inside. Another broke from Tombs's forehead, blood pulsing out at its base, then another from beside his mouth. He shrieked, his hands clamping round the creature's claws, but it wasn't clear whether he was trying to pull himself away or hold himself there. Even more of the things broke from his face and his shrieking continued until finally muffled by a great skein of these things extending from bloody ruin to the creature's skull. Tombs writhed, took his hands away, but now the gabbleduck closed its claws around his chest.

Sanders sank to her knees, curiosity gone, only horror remaining. Tombs was struggling now, stretching that skein taut. The things started breaking, pieces of them dropping away, writhing down the chest of the gabbleduck. Some disconnected from Tombs's face to leave bloody holes, others detached from the gabbleduck's skull, small Venus flytrap heads flapping weakly. Then a convulsion. The gabbleduck tossed Tombs away. He hit a pillar, high, then dropped leadenly to the ground and lay utterly still.

Still eyeing the gabbleduck, which like a man shaving his skull now scythed away the last of those worms with one claw, Sanders stood and walked over to Tombs. She knelt beside him, turned him over so his head rested in her lap. He looked like he'd been shot in the face with a multi-pellet gun. Blood still leaked from the holes in his forehead but those in his lower face seemed to have closed. She carefully pulled out two remaining pieces of worm—they were like spaghetti now, lifeless—and tossed them away. After a moment, he opened his eyes.

"Going for the facial reconstruction record?" she asked, relieved he still lived.

"It's my face now," he said obscurely.

Sanders looked up at the gabbleduck now, and it returned her gaze. Its eyes gleamed and it seemed tauter somehow. It raised one claw, studied it while flexing the talons, then did something that shouldn't have been possible for a creature with a hard ducklike bill. The gabbleduck grinned.

No, Sanders realized, the *Atheter* grinned.

"We go in," said Janice and Cheops simultaneously, neither a question nor an order, but a statement of fact from both of them.

They had spent so long on that area of the Polity Line where they were the most dangerous thing anyone was likely to encounter, and the reality of the ultimate extent of their remit had been a vague thing, something acknowledged but unlikely. Their job was to defend the Polity, and here was something it certainly needed defending against. Together, they were a warship, and in the face of a dangerous enemy they were the line that must not be crossed.

The ship's engines ramped up their power, every weapons system not already online, coming online. Masers cut through the intervening gap from them to the mechanism, selected spectrum lasers probed for weaknesses. Missile carousels turned and loaded continent cracking rounds into the rail-gun magazines. EM bands swelled with every form of viral warfare the *Cheops* contained.

Janice sometimes wondered just how much her interfacing with Cheops suppressed her Human self. Without that connection would she be prepared to throw herself into battle like this? Without their close mutualistic link would she be prepared to do her duty, up to and including dying for it? As lasers just reflected away and the point temperature of the masers just dispersed in the massive object ahead, she began preparing for the ultimate: ramming, and simultaneous detonation of all internal reactors.

"Viral warfare feed?" both she and Cheops enquired.

"Some, but it seems it was ready for this," they both replied.

Ten thousand kilometres, eight thousand. Janice felt an utter calm suffuse her. Yes, she was prepared to do this.

"Firing."

Angry wasps departing their hive, CTDs railed out, speed cut because massive acceleration could lead to containment breach. They sped towards their target; five-ton steel sharks. Something flashed out. Gravity weapon. The *Cheops* bucked as if slamming through a wall of stone half a mile thick. It's superstructure buckled and twisted, walls ruptured and atmosphere spewed out through hundred-metre splits in the hull. The U-space engines ruptured, sprayed out pseudo-matter and half-real components like alien rainbows. The fusion drives burned dirty for half a second as their magnetic bottles failed, ate out the face of the pyramid that contained them, guttered out.

Forty-eight missiles detonated; a massive multiple blast spreading atomic fire across thirty thousand cubic kilometres of vacuum. A wall of fire slammed into *Cheops*, ablating away hull, burning through inside to melt and slag so much that very few systems remained available. However, some sensors were still available as *Cheops* spun a new face towards Calypse. Janice felt a moment's joy seeing five remaining missiles still on course. Then the mechanism stretched, became a line reaching up past her, in towards Masada, snapped out of existence here and reappeared a million kilometres behind. The missiles continued on down into the face of Calypse. They didn't detonate; their target was gone.

We will follow you down, Janice thought, but Cheops negated that. The gravity wave and subsequent blast had shoved them off course. They would slingshot around Calypse, that was all.

She wasn't going to die, not just then, but having prepared for it she felt a deep gnawing disappointment and almost unconsciously reached towards the ship's self-destruct. Cheops relieved her of control like an adult taking a sharp knife out of a child's hand.

"We did what we could," the AI told her.

Janice lay in her sarcophagus, wanted to cry, but found she couldn't.

Amistad detached optic links and leapt out into vacuum. Frustration passed in a microsecond to leave cool calculation. He had to accept that the geostat weapon was about as much use to him as a machine gun against an approaching battle tank.

"You might be able to use this," he said, surrendering control of the weapon to the planetary AI.

"Thanks," Ergatis replied, once again swinging the weapon round towards the planet where, even now, a further five of those bell-shaped disruptors were materializing.

"Penny Royal, what's your position?" Amistad enquired.

"Passing through barrier," the black AI replied.

Here, in this planetary system, they did not have the resources to physically defeat the mechanism. They were in serious trouble, there was absolutely no doubt about that. The mechanism had rolled over *Scold* and *Cheops* with consummate ease, and now it was here.

Amistad experienced a weird moment of bewilderment. Earth Central had seen the data provided by Cheops and by the haiman Drode and yet had seriously underestimated what they were up against. Then again, Amistad had seen the same data and considered a warship like *Scold* more than adequate. So much for the omniscience of AIs. He shook himself internally, switched more to memory and experience rather than reliance on new processing power, and rediscovered cynicism. Frankly, as a veteran of the Prador—Human war, Amistad knew that mistakes like this weren't that uncommon. And he now began to try and find some new solution. Perhaps it could be provided by what resided in that armoured sphere anchored to a plate of ancient coral underneath the southern ocean?

"Do you have anything for me?" Amistad asked Penny Royal.

"Atheter AI interacting with Tombs, but it has shut down access to all sensors in the area. Technician inside the barrier. Unusual wildlife activity. Nothing else."

"I will be going dark for a while, do not be concerned."

"Why?"

"Informational warfare up here," Amistad lied.

He shut down all connections with Penny Royal, shut down other communication channels from himself to other intelligences, even physically disconnecting some of them. All he left himself was his U-space transmitter, and allowed only one channel to open in that when he sent a heavily encrypted signal.

Activation and contact, and Amistad flowed into Eight's realm, the door firmly closed behind. The virtuality had changed. Amistad now seemed to be standing in a snow-swept landscape, white and clean and, with its lack of the imagery of torment, utterly unlike anything Eight had provided before.

"I like what you've done with the place," the drone said.

A gust of wind cleared powdery snow to reveal Eight's reply: Humans up to their necks in ice, trying to scream but only gusting snowflakes from their mouths. These streams of flakes began melding into one single stream which began circling the drone—a visual representation of the expected attack.

"I've no time for this," said Amistad. "I want everything you have on the mechanism. I will take it now."

The swirling storm stuttered and broke apart in the air, went into reverse to coagulate into a single thick column of snow that entered the mouth of just one of the victims below. Amistad concentrated on this one, watched its head bloat grotesquely and the ice about it begin cracking. A fist smashed upwards, then reached over, sausage fingers splaying, and a giant of a man with the physique of a sumo wrestler and blue skin webbed with purple veins began to clamber out. Icicles extended from this giant's eyes as he finally reached the surface and began to stalk towards Amistad.

The drone prepared isolated storage within himself, put all his internal defences on full alert and turned the new upgraded power of his mind towards bolstering those defences and making them more reactive. Perhaps now he could handle anything Eight might throw at him.

The figure walked right up close, its head level with Amis-tad's own, and the icicles extended further until they finally touched the drone's own eyes. Here a representation of the upload channels, waiting for permission to connect. If Amistad allowed this now there was a chance that something might escape from here; that all his work with Penny Royal might be undone. But this eighth state of consciousness seemed to know some way to defeat the mechanism, and for that Amistad had to take the risk. He allowed contact.

An icy storm of information flowed in, filling up three secure storage crystals. Amistad allowed it to continue whilst important facts could be gleaned from it, fully aware that much of it formed a viral attack. In the first few microseconds the drone learnt about the battle between Penny Royal and the mechanism, but he needed more data about the thing itself, how it functioned, what weaknesses it possessed.

There were few. It soon became evident that the mechanism contained warfare technology far in advance of much in the Polity and, through its underspace links, almost limitless resources. Then, at the last, Amistad saw it: the off button.

Swinging out one claw, Amistad smashed the humanoid away to send it tumbling across the ice. On an informational level he closed all access, let nothing more in. However, already he felt like he had swallowed a dose of poison. He backed away in a direction Eight could not see, departed, once again slamming the door closed behind him.

Floating free in space, Amistad fought the viral attack propagating from his secure storage. He now possessed vital information about how the mechanism could be stopped, but to communicate that information to any other entity right now would be a kiss from a diseased mouth. Internally, he directed an ultrasound beam weapon, smashing one of the three storage crystals. A mistake, because a fraction of a second before everything in that crystal broke down, along with its structure, the breaking process itself first cracked the crystal's security. Programs like armoured bacteria in turn laden with all sorts of nasty viruses spread through the drone, dumping their loads to shut off all the internal ultrasound cleaners and then going on to work on other internal defences. Before they could go too far, Amistad managed to physically eject a second crystal through a skin port, and hit it with a laser, turning it to a micalike glitter in vacuum.

The third crystal became more of a problem as a virus took away his ability to eject internal components. Within just a few seconds the programs from Eight had control of nearly a quarter of his systems and were getting mighty close to breaking through to his core mind. As he fought against this, he now noted something odd, some kind of networked program forming. Trying to understand the shape of this, and the intention, Amistad did not see it until too late. Data aligned, seized internal physical components and did their work, rerouting one optic and making a connection with it between the remaining crystal and the drone's U-space transmitter.

The crystal emptied, transmitting all its contents which, almost certainly, would find their way to Penny Royal. No need now to eject or destroy the crystal, but the internal battle was by no means over. The viral attack began to mutate and Amistad knew at once that he would not be contacting the outside world for some time yet. Annoying, that. He now understood that others knew about the mechanism's off-button and were doing something about it, but he couldn't warn them that a previous ally might shortly turn into a dangerous AI psychopath. And the final irony was that with his processing power, his intelligence, back down to what it had been before, he had the answers he had been seeking.

19

When the Polity seizes control of a new world, it usually does so because it has been asked to by 80 per cent of the population—a majority that would have been the envy of past Human democracies. However, that majority is only attained over an open-ended voting period usually culminating when things are so bad on the world concerned that the population feel that anything would be better—usually in the middle of catastrophe, often natural but more often man-made. Polity intervention forces normally turn up when some bitter war has obliterated infrastructure and is turning genocidal. The moment the AIs take over, they institute the amnesty. They want a clean slate, a new beginning, are not interested in what went before or in war crimes trials, since at the point of intervention where to attribute blame has become murky indeed. However, many historians have questioned the very loose enforcement of Polity law in the years directly after intervention, and noted how the worst of those who would have been defined as war criminals in some previous age tend to end up in a body bag, despite the protection the amnesty is supposed to afford them.

—From a speech by Jobsworth

As he entered the stand of flute grasses Grant realized his mistake and threw himself abruptly to one side. A series of shots tracked across where he had been standing, grasses briefly flaring and smoking stems falling. Lying on the ground he winced, pressing a hand against his ribs, the pain concentrating his attention, reminding of the old days. He drew his disc gun, checked its action, but didn't return fire. He waited, gave it a good minute, then smiled to himself when he heard grasses rustling ahead and over to his left. Shree seemed impatient to get away. In the old days she would have waited a lot longer.

Grant slowly rose up into a crouch, then began making his way forward as quietly as possible, carefully pushing stems aside and ensuring they didn't noisily spring back once he was past. This slow and laborious process had prolonged his survival in the past during numerous encounters with Theocracy soldiers and proctors. However, when he heard the flat cracking of a thin-gun some distance ahead he knew it was time to move fast rather than quietly.

He began pushing hard, head low, forearms brushing the grasses aside. Spilling out into a channel between stands he checked to his right and saw footprints then, seeing a heroyne step out only thirty metres further up the channel, gunshot wounds evident on its armchair-shaped body, he leapt the channel and forged ahead. He knew that Shree had always loathed the things, but against all logic and sense she must have fired on this one. Her recent failure must have seriously knocked her out of whack to allow her to do something so stupid.

If a heroyne got over-excited it would certainly eat a Human being, but its senses weren't those of a siluroyne or gabbleduck, since it detected its usual prey of mud snakes by feeling their subterranean movement through its feet—it was possible to avoid a heroyne's attention by just keeping very still. However, just as with those other predators, if you pissed off a heroyne it could become viciously persistent, kicking over every bit of grass in the area in its search for you. But then perhaps he misjudged Shree, perhaps the creature was already over-excited by the events here and she had inadvertently stumbled straight into it.

"Hey, Shree!" Grant called. "Why're you upsetting the local wildlife?"

"You keep coming after me, Grant, and you're dead." Shree replied. "You're slow and you've forgotten how to do this."

Some of the flute grasses ahead had been flattened, the rest were islands of tangled broken stems. Working his way through one of these he began to notice heaped drifts of stems and occasional chunks of torn-up rhizome. She was heading towards where that thing had been knocked out of the sky and, if she kept going, would end up in an area where the grasses had been either completely flattened or scoured away. That would put her in the open. All he had to do was ensure he stayed behind her, which shouldn't be too difficult since she was leaving a perfectly visible trail. Abruptly realizing how *very* visible that trail was, he halted at the edge of a clearing where flute grasses had been flattened in a spiral, probably by a small whirlwind, and squatted down.

What would he have done in her situation? Of course, she was right, he had been slow. She would have looped back towards her own trail, and lain in wait for him. He moved off to his right because, of course, the area ahead was perfect ambush territory. Slowly circumventing the clearing, ten metres into the grasses, he tried to find her trail. Fifty-fifty chance—she could have looped round to the other side. He paused, decided to take a risk.

"I'm trying to save your life, Shree!" he called. "Either I retrieve that cylinder from you or the Technician does it—your choice."

"Generous of you," she said from close by.

Grant threw himself for cover, heard the crack of her thin-gun, then felt an impact against his thigh. He hit the ground wrong, pain jabbing from his ribs, rolled and snap-shot behind him. He came up, dragging his leg, tried to locate her. He did so by her gun's flash, the second shot slamming into his shoulder and spinning him.

"Toss your gun away or my next shot will be through your head," she said, much closer now.

He peered behind him. She stood five metres back, weapon held steady with both hands. He did not doubt she meant what she was saying. He tossed his gun and turned, pain lancing through his shoulder, his right leg feeling like dead weight.

"So you've got me, Shree, but that don't change your situation at all." He heaved himself up into a sitting position.

"You've got days of walking to get anywhere you can get hold of faster transport, and the Technician is out here, ready for you."

"So you say," was all she could manage, but she looked scared.

"Give it up, Shree," he said. "Give me the cylinder and you can run—I won't come after you." He gestured down at his leg, which was really starting to hurt now. "I can't come after you."

She took one hand away from her weapon, reached inside her coat, took out the cylinder and held it up. "This? How about if I just toss it out here somewhere?"

"Tombs seemed pretty confident. I'd say the Technician's got some way of detecting it, which again is why I say just give it to me and run. You saw that thing in the sky. Do you think this is only about—'

Flute grasses rustled behind him—something big moving—and he felt his skin crawl, didn't really relish the idea of lying in the Technician's path. Shree's eyes grew wide. She shoved the cylinder back in her coat, took a firm grip on her gun again.

"Shree—'

A big long leg ending in a three-toed webbed foot came down from overhead, crunched against the ground only a few metres ahead of him, a shape blotted out the sun above. She began firing, pumping shot after shot into that shape. The second foot came down just in front of the first. The heroyne emitted a cawing ululating shriek, its long neck a curved arc against the sky. The beaked and eyeless head seemed just a two-metre extension of that neck, and the beak gaped wide. Shree turned to run, but the heroyne's head darted down, the beak closing on her like a giant pair of blunt scissors. It snatched her up; a wading bird snapping up a frog.

Grant stayed utterly frozen, still as he could be. The heroyne straightened its neck against the sky, opened its mouth and tossed her up, screaming, caught her and did it again, her screams muffled when her head entered its gullet, then it gobbled her down whole. In utter horror Grant watched her slide into the creature's neck. It convulsively swallowed, shoving her deeper, but she was still struggling. The heroyne raised its head again, shrieked again, then raised one of its webbed feet off the ground and like someone troubled with reflux rubbed at the lump in its neck.

Grant turned his head slightly to locate his gun. The heroyne swung towards him and he froze, and fought an old urge to pray. The heroyne took one slow and short pace in his direction, halted, tilted its head as if listening. Long painful moments passed, during which Grant saw the still struggling lump that was Shree traverse the last length of neck down into the creature's stomach. Next it abruptly straightened, lifted a foot off the ground and began grooming its head, scraping one toe down the edge of its beak. When it finally realized there was nothing to clean off, it lowered that leg, tucked it underneath itself and just stood there on the other leg. Its head nodded, slowly started to droop. It looked like the damned thing intended to take a nap.

Go away! Go away!

Something snapped the creature's head back up. Had it actually heard him thinking?

"*Jain technology,*" a voice ghosted in his comunit.

A tentacle whickered through the air, wrapped around the heroyne's neck for a moment then retracted. The creature's head, and a yard of neck, toppled like a scythed weed, thudded to the ground, the beak opening and closing spasmodically. Orange liquid squirted from the stub of its neck protruding from its body, and it began to lash back and forth. Its raised leg went down and it started high-stepping in a tight circle. The tentacle lashed out again, cracking this time. It sliced down at an angle through the back of the creature's body, separating its main body from the saddle of bone and muscle above its legs. Body and remaining neck thumped to the ground, the neck still writhing. The legs, and the muscle above them, squatted and frog-leapt into the air, came down ten metres away, staggered on for a little while then came to a swaying stop. They didn't fall, just stood there.

"*Distributed neural tissue,*" said that voice in Grant's ear.

"Get her out!" Grant shouted. "Get her out of there!"

Penny Royal passed over him like a cloud of black knives and descended on the heroyne's body, which rose into the air, a cage of lines drawing across it. The outside fell into segments like an orange, revealing a multicoloured mass of internal organs. These abruptly spread to the limit of their connections to each other. One big maggot-like sac split, spilling Shree onto the ground, then Penny Royal tossed the rest over by the still-standing legs.

By now Grant had retrieved his gun. He began crawling over. Penny Royal had yet to finish. It opened Shree's coat and extracted the cylinder, then entirely shed its chameleonware as it enwrapped that in one tentacle.

"*Jain technology,*" it repeated.

The black AI rose up off the ground, supported on a pillar of tentacles, its upper part divided into three masses of spines, each mass aligned and each pointing in one direction only. As Grant reached Shree, a shadow fell across and he looked up—he preferred not to look at Shree anyway.

"Great, just perfect," he said.

The black AI's spines were pointing at the source of that shadow, risen up out of the flute grasses like a titanic cobra made of bone. The Technician had finally arrived and Grant lay between it and Penny Royal, between it and the cylinder.

"Eight?" said Penny Royal out loud.

The Technician slid closer, the movement of its massive body now clearly audible. The air seemed to be charging up with something. Grant closed his eyes, expecting to die any second now and just hoping it would be quick. But nothing happened. Finally he opened his eyes again, now to see Penny Royal extruding a tentacle with the cylinder attached to the end of it as if by glue. The Technician tilted its hood up like an animal ready to receive some treat, extended complex glassy manipulators, accepted the cylinder and transferred it inside itself. Then it turned, and in one massive wrench that shook the ground, it was gone.

The moment stretched taut, then Grant broke it. "Can you do anything for her?"

Penny Royal directed one clump of spines down towards Shree, then flipped up two stalked eyes, red as hell, as if to make a closer inspection. The orange bile covering her from head to foot had rotted her clothes and burnt away much of her skin. One of her eyes was gone, the other lidless in its socket. The lips on one side of her mouth were gone too, exposing ridiculously white teeth, and the flesh had been scoured from one of her hands. Hideous damage, but a bubbling wheezing issued from her mouth. She still lived and Grant knew that this damage was not beyond Penny Royal.

"No," the AI said.

"What do you mean 'no'?"

"It is just."

The thing folded its eyes back inside and began to turn away.

"Wait! Where are you going!"

"Eight," it replied, and flowed away like darkness.

Grant returned his attention to Shree, and in horror realized she had turned her head towards him, gazing at him with her remaining eye.

"Do . . . it," she managed.

He could lie there pretending he didn't know what she meant, allowing her to suffer for longer. He could kid himself that he wouldn't hand her over to the Polity, and that mind-wipe or some other execution of a death sentence would not then ensue. He did none of these.

Grant put the barrel of his disc gun against her temple, fired twice.

A ball of fire rose from the point of impact, throwing into silhouette the new disruptor to appear over Zealos. The thing hardly moved—solid in the sky as if nailed to the fabric of the universe—but in the city below the shock wave picked up ATVs, aerofans and gravcars and tumbled them along the streets like polystyrene models.

The red attack ship, *Corpuscle*, threw itself into a hard turn, then dipped low to the ground as some sort of surface extended from the disruptor—a three-dimensional ripple spreading from the fabric the thing had been nailed to.

Where the lower edge of this shaved the city, it peeled up roofs and knocked over buildings. But this was no hardfield, Ergatis realized, everything falling from the point of contact seemed shredded. An aerofan rising into its path fragmented: in one twisting wrench it separated into all its individual components, and they fell. Nuts and bolts, cowlings, armature windings, spindles, computer chips and seat padding, all mixed with other components: bones, bleeding organs, soggy sheets of fat and lumps of muscle.

No connection with Amistad, *Scold* had been obliterated, and *Cheops* knocked out of the fight, and now the mechanism was visible in the Masadan sky. Also, the disruptor above was one of five presently materializing, messing up coms so badly that Ergatis couldn't even pull the trigger on the geostat weapon Amistad had returned to it. Things did not look so good.

The planetary AI watched the attack ship flying low between buildings—its passing flipped over further cars and blew out glass windows in the street behind it. It ducked right underneath the field the disruptor had emitted, leaped an old church, peeling up tiles as it went, then stood on its tail and hurtled up towards the device, its megagun firing. The disruptor spewed fire, even shifted slightly from the impact, then cracked like an egg full of magma, its two halves beginning to fall. Again there would be the problem of all that weight coming down on the city raft. The attack ship would need to . . .

Positioning itself for that underside shot, Blood must have known the likely result. It tried to turn using gravmotors, side-blast fusion and by detonating one of its own weapons nacelles. Not enough. It hit one half of the disruptor and bounced off, its entire body bent at the middle so it looked almost like a boomerang. Completely out of control it tumbled in an arc over the city and came down in the Market District, cut a burning swathe before coming to rest, almost indistinguishable from the ruination it had created.

The two halves of the disruptor slammed down, both on one half of the cracked city raft. They didn't break it further, nor did they cause it to start tilting; instead that half of the city just began to sink at a rate of half a metre a minute.

No way of moving those immensely heavy objects now. Through all available com systems in that half of the city, Ergatis ordered evacuation to the other half. Would that save lives? Perhaps, but maybe only for a short while. Another disruptor had begun to slide in this direction. It had materialized in the sky fifty kilometres away, and all data feed from the small town under its shadow had blanked. But now, with the disruptor here destroyed, data began coming in. Fires were visible in the town, massive damage, building collapses, and people staggering and crawling through the wreckage, just one look at their dumb imbecilic faces enough to tell nothing intelligent remained behind them. That could happen here in Zealos, soon, unless . . .

Connection.

If Ergatis had possessed a face it would have smiled at that moment, a tight humourless smile. A simple digital instruction set the doughnut fusion reactor of the geostat weapon winding up to full power, but enough energy was available in super-capacitor storage for three full-power shots. No point using any less than full power—those things in the Masadan sky were tough.

Perfectly targeted, the proton beam appeared like a blue pillar in the sky, its base on the approaching disruptor. The energy flash blanked those cams pointing at the thing, but the last microseconds recorded a spray of *something* issuing from its underside. New cams swung to bear as the beam blinked out, leaving a black trail of quickly dispersing smoke. The disruptor itself tilted and the ground underneath it burned with the orange flames of some sort of chemical-isotope fire. Its progress had halted, but now it began to move again, now in a wavering spiralling course spreading more of that fire.

Great, thought Ergatis. The thing had turned into ground fuser with its operator dead at the controls.

Cam eyes averted for another shot, then back again. The thing flipped over onto its back, spewed a cloud of glowing matter into the sky, but remained intact. A third shot, straight down its throat, and now the thing was gone, the blast wave of a massive explosion rolling towards Zealos, chunks of superdense shrapnel leading it.

Ergatis sent what warnings it could, targeted another disruptor and waited with the patience of a machine for the geostat weapon to reach full charge.

"The Technician freed itself of the Weaver by placing it inside me so it could reformat itself for war," said Tombs, his voice hollow and his expression lost. "Whether I returned to sanity or not was irrelevant—I was just a safe storage vessel. After a countdown, using penny mollusc shells, a twenty-year countdown." He glanced at Sanders, who smiled, remembering the quiet of the asylum terrace and her stripping off to go for a swim. It seemed an age ago.

"Why did it need to do that?"

"It has been like a soldier hampered with a civilian—never able to fight without reserve, always needing to protect the civilian."

"But twenty years?"

"Twenty years ago the Technician would not have been ready for it, but now it is. That is why the Weaver first rose up in my mind, so as to lure the mechanism here. Now it has departed my mind to give the order of battle." He shook his head, sad, puzzled. "Though I don't think its physical presence here is necessary, rather it wanted to be in at the kill—it is a predator after all."

"But Amistad's manipulation of you gave the Weaver freedom to do that, surely?"

Tombs smiled without humour. "Amistad and Penny Royal, representing the Polity, did precisely what was expected of them by Dragon. They kept me alive and they kept me here. Everything else they did was irrelevant. They kept me safe until the time was right." He paused, checking about himself as if for something lost. "And now it is gone, and I am a broken bottle."

"But why download to a Human?"

Tombs shrugged, looked tired. "Because Dragon wanted the mechanism physically present here at Masada. Placing the Weaver inside a Human being ensured the mechanism took note of the Human race, and recognized it as a danger sufficient to impel it to come here."

"You are not broken," said a voice. The words were perfectly enunciated, yet definitely did not issue from a Human mouth.

"I feel empty," Jem replied.

"Yes, but now you can fill yourself."

The skin on her back crawling, Sanders looked round. The gabbleduck had moved with utter silence and now squatted just a metre away from them. She had never been this close to one of the creatures. It produced a smell, cinnamon apple pie, but with an underlying hint of carrion. Its skin looked like rhinoceros hide, but blotchy purple and green with a glint as if lightly sprayed with gold paint. One composite forearm was closed up, the other partially open, and she could see how its six-talon claw could divide into two claws each with three talons. It held the two of them fixed in its emerald gaze for a short time, then turned and went down on all fours to saunter off out of the side of the building. Why should she be surprised that an Atheter spoke to them with such ease? Gabbleducks had been speaking Human words ever since Humans came here to Masada.

"It's here," said Tombs, and started trying to get up.

Sanders resisted him for a moment, pressing her hand against his chest, but he seemed utterly determined and brushed it aside, so she helped him as best she could, though her own body was bruised and battered.

A strong wind seemed to be blowing through the flute grasses, rushing, impatient, then the Technician surged into view, circumventing the building then circling round it, its hood catching up with its own tail to form a ring. The ring tightened, the Technician travelling steadily faster and faster, and the hood finally closed over the tail.

"What now?" asked Sanders, having to raise her voice over the noise.

"Now it receives its orders!" Tombs replied.

Sanders gazed down at the gabbleduck, at the Atheter

named the Weaver. It was squatting again, arms folded across its chest like some self-satisfied Buddha. It showed no sign of giving any orders, but how was she to judge?

Tombs reached out to a pillar, took the weight off his legs for a moment then sat down. Sanders sat beside him.

"This could be dangerous!" he shouted, not seeming to care.

"I'll stay here!" she replied.

The rushing wind sound grew to the roar of a gale, and then steadily transformed into something more intense. The air movement it generated blasted across before them, swirled around them and seemed to be creating a vacuum in the building behind, constantly trying to drag them in. In a minute Sanders realized the creature had started to glow, and felt the heat of that on her face. No doubt now that the Technician was moving faster than any hooder had ever moved—whirling like a machine component rather than something living. Sanders wanted to ask Tombs about this, but now it wasn't possible to speak.

Another sound then, more a feeling; the deep resonant toll of a bell. Sanders looked up straight into the throat of one of the mechanism's disruptors, poised over them like a capture cup ready to slam down. Glowing an intense eye-aching white, the Technician now spun about the building a couple of metres off the ground. Suddenly it tilted, and only as it did so did Sanders see the Weaver raise one claw and gesture. The Technician tilted further, a burning wheel against the sky, its lower rim skidding on the ground and spraying smoking debris. The air seemed to thicken and Sanders suddenly felt a panic, unable to remember why she was here, the noisy chaos around her becoming meaningless, confusing, frightening.

Then the wheel broke and the Technician speared into the sky. It hit the disruptor like an arrow going through an apple, but with the sound of mountains falling. Sanders averted her eyes from the sudden raw glare. From horizon to horizon, the flash leached the landscape of colour, rendered it only in white and shades of sepia. The domed roof above slammed down, then back up and flipped away. A pillar to their right tilted out, then snapped off to tumble end over end into the distance. Only upon seeing this did she realize that she was now pressed down on her back, and that the same force-fields that had prevented Shree from killing her and Grant were now preventing them both from being tossed about like leaves in a hurricane.

A second detonation turned the sky into a pink backdrop etched with streaks of yellow lightning. Pressure waves rolled out from the impact site above, across the sky and down to the ground. The whole landscape jumped, smoked and steamed, shifted sideways. Something massive thundered down to the left, and the ground surged up and forwards into a wave that wrenched the building up until the floor stood near-vertical for the seconds it took to pass underneath it. Another cataclysmic impact surged a wave in from the side, and at once the building turned right over. Sanders found herself still pinned in place by force-fields, facing down towards the ground, one side of the building swamped, the open side revealing in a devastated landscape fires which, because of its lack of oxygen, shouldn't be burning.

Later, the gabbleduck came, carefully closed its claws about them as the force-fields released, lowered them to the ground and led the way out into devastation.

An arrow of intense light shot up from the planet, and, still struggling to regain control of his body after scrubbing the last of Eight's viral attack, Amistad only knew of the mechanism's grav-weapon response to that arrow, the Technician, as the wave hit him. It compressed and stretched his internal components as it passed, metal and crystal fracturing, optics disrupted and superconductors shorting out, delicate highly-protected components trashed in an instant. Disoriented and still fighting to regain control of his internal workings as he tumbled through vacuum, Amistad saw the Technician shudder to a halt, then lurch into progress again. No longer travelling like a missile, the biomech writhed through vacuum as if its legs were finding purchase on the nothingness and, by the minimal readings Amistad could obtain from a few remaining sensors, that was precisely what the creature was doing.

Like a white-hot centipede a hundred metres long it clambered relentlessly towards the mechanism, yet, though the Technician was massive and certainly dangerous, the inequalities of scale made it seem to be something that could be stomped on by its opponent. The mechanism reacted. The whole massive device swung incrementally, its throat now entirely centred on the approaching Technician. Another gravity wave slammed out, paused the Technician for just a second, then seemed to allow it to surge forward once past.

Further damage, the legs all down one side disconnected, some crystal storage cracked, optics distorted and thus distorting information flows. Amistad took it, calculating what systems he could save, and concentrated on them. In orbit over Masada a brief intense detonation at the head of a column of purple fire—the geostat weapon, which Ergatis had just used against a disruptor, detonating halfway through its next firing cycle, fusion plasma escaping the doughnut Tesla bottle and punching out into vacuum, proton beam unfocused, dissipating on the way down, just licking the disruptor sliding in over the east coast. Amistad also noted blooms of steam arising in the southern ocean, all in a long line not very far from where Eight's armoured prison resided. Volcanic action there, a subduction zone forced into activity by the mechanism's gravity weapon. Any more of that and a tsunami or two might be included in Masada's present woes.

But the mechanism must have decided otherwise. Three disruptors appeared in the Technician's path and a hemispherical hardfield slammed the war machine to a halt, it coiling to slam down on the field, a centipede dropped on a plate. After a moment it straightened out again and nosed against the barrier, moving like an eel making no headway in a current.

"You lied."

Where had that come from? U-space signal, highly disrupted and taking whole seconds to put back together again. It could have been from Ergatis, but it wasn't, and it didn't take a supermind to figure out its source.

"On one small point," Amistad replied, and waited

interminable seconds. But Penny Royal did not reply, so the drone tried, "Where are you?"

"Take a guess."

"Under the sea?"

Again Penny Royal did not reply.

Amistad remained focused on the Technician and the mechanism—he could do nothing about Penny Royal now, and wouldn't be capable of doing anything about the black AI for some time hence, if at all, if anything sentient remained alive here.

Induction.

The war machine must have fed something back through the force-field between it and its prey. One of the disruptors abruptly tumbled away as if slapped aside like a skittle, and the hardfield shimmered, weakened. The remaining two turned towards each other. Amistad guessed they were running direct line-of-sight diagnostics. The hardfield stabilized. Here, Amistad realized, was warfare gone beyond just bombs, energy weapons and simple force-fields—the kind of fight he had already witnessed down on the surface between Penny Royal and the Technician.

U-space.

Amistad detected a weird U-space signature as the Technician's cowl faded to translucence, and pushed straight through the hardfield. That translucence passed along its body at the point of intersection with the hardfield as it continued to worm through. Amistad wasn't quite sure he believed his own sensors: the damned war machine had just *tunnelled*—a theoretical possibility but with energy-density requirements that should outscale the Technician's physical body.

The hardfield began flickering, emitting Hawking radiation, and an arc-light glare where it intersected with the Technician's body, but the war machine continued writhing on through. The hardfield went out, the two disruptors folding out of existence, no doubt back within the body of the mechanism. Then another massive U-space disruption tried to tear at reality. The mechanism stretched fifty thousand kilometres at a tangent to Masada, relocating itself as it had in its battle with *Scold* and *Cheops*, its elongated form lying only a few hundred kilometres from Amistad so it seemed he was at touching distance from some immense space-borne train. The mechanism snapped back into shape at the terminus of that stretch, but it seemed the move had failed, for the Technician had moved with it, persistent as a mamba, still writhing closer.

Antimatter blasts next, interspersed with straight fission weapons, partially obscuring both the Technician and mechanism behind a spreading cloud of nuclear fire. But between explosions the war machine moved relentlessly closer. It was tunnelling again, just dipping itself into U-space to avoid the worst of the shockwaves and heat, glowing like something out of a blacksmith's forge as it surfaced.

Then it arrived, nosing straight into that mass of dodecahedrons at the mechanism's core, seeming to tunnel straight inside them. The mechanism shifted again, its stretch line straight down into Masada, gone. U-space shift through a gravity well; a fish trying to shake off a leech. Then back again, two million kilometres out, spinning as if smacked by the hand of some playful god. Another stretch, straight back to its original position. Within it the dodecahedral structures had parted, were rearranging themselves. Some massive detonation ensued inside, arclight glaring out through its structure, another gravity wave followed, cracking further crystal inside Amistad, shuddering Masada so that a row of red eyes stitched down from the pole, a fault line opened.

The mechanism then hung in vacuum for long minutes, seemingly dead, the shapes within it still. Finally they shifted again, like a giant clearing its throat. They spat out the Technician, twisted, broken into three pieces.

Stomped on.

20

Black Hats

When a bitter war has been fought long and hard, and at last ends, many of the combatants use their energies to rebuild their lives. They delight in the day-to-day normalities of living because, for so long, they weren't normal. Tired and sickened by it, they give up that detestation of the enemy that was necessary to enable them to fight, and kill, or at least suppress it sufficiently so they can just live. However, some cannot live without their war and are unable to give up their hate. They are matured by conflict and cannot define themselves other than by what they fought. They consider themselves the polar opposite to their enemy, the antithesis of their enemy. They are the white hats whilst the enemy are the black hats. Their problem is that they cannot visualize a world without hats—and fail to see that the ugly processes of war ironed out those distinctions. And worse still, even when there are no black hats left, they seek others they deem suitable for that attire, because in the end it is not the enemy that matters, but the hate.

—*From* HOW IT IS *by Gordon*

As he finally pushed his head out into the open, Grant swore to himself, but with a kind of maniacal glee—something to counter the pain. Oh yes, he was an anachronism because he hadn't gone in for radical physical redesign so he could breathe the air of Masada, but being such had saved his life. He'd seen the Technician streak into the sky and slam through that disruptor, punched at the sky in glee on seeing the disruptor broken and falling to earth. But he hadn't foreseen the ground bucking like a faulty aerofan and the subsequent wave of mud and flute-grass debris. It buried him, and only because he wore breather gear did he survive. One of the adapted would have suffocated.

He began to drag himself into the open, the little self-justifying victory of having survived passing, and the pain returning, and hard. The wounds in his shoulder and leg were just raw agony, and tears began to fill his eyes. Because of that he didn't see the claw as he dragged himself out. It closed round his chest, plucked him yelling from the ground and held him up for inspection. His luck had just run out: he'd survived Shree, the heroyne and the Technician, and now it seemed he was to become the plaything of a gabbleduck.

"Put him down!" said someone, annoyed.

It took him a second to recognise the voice. He tried to tell Sanders to run, to get out of there, but his mouth was dry, he couldn't find the breath. You just didn't tell off a gabbleduck like it was a naughty child. That could get you chewed up, or not, depending on how the creature felt at the time. However, the gabbleduck lowered him carefully to the ground, and stepped back. In a moment Sanders knelt beside him, triggered an auto-injector against his leg and then his shoulder, straight through his clothing, then used a micro-shear to slice through the cloth of his trousers, a first-aid kit open beside her.

Exhausted, Grant gazed at the gabbleduck. It was the same one Tombs had lured into the Atheter AI building, but it looked very different now. It moved with greater certainty, gazed with great intensity at something on the distant horizon, seemed more *here*. Tombs himself now walked into view too, his attention fixed on the creature.

"I'm looking at the Weaver, ain't I?" Grant said, now the pain had started to fade.

"You certainly are," said Sanders, pressing something against his leg to spread blessed numbness.

He glanced down as she next pressed an extractor-pack wound dressing in place, and watched it deform over his leg, melding around and into the wound. This would help him heal in the same way as the usual Polity wound dressings, infusing antibiotics, antivirals and further painkillers, but would also extract the metals from a pulse-gun shot. Next she set to work on his shoulder, pulling his jacket aside to cut through the underlying fabric.

"So how did that happen?" Grant asked.

"You guessed the first bit," said Sanders, "surely you can guess the rest."

"Tombs loaded the Weaver to it, but how?"

"A physical connection." Sanders shuddered.

Tombs now turned to face them.

"Did you kill her?" he asked abruptly.

How to explain that? He was about to simply say "yes" but he cared about what Sanders thought of him, and realized that Tombs's opinion of him counted too.

"Yes, I killed her, but not in the circumstances you might think." As he went on to explain about the heroyne, Penny Royal, the Technician and Shree's end, Sanders finished dressing his wounds and then injected a cocktail of drugs that spread like cold fire through his body.

"You did the best thing," she said, carefully replacing the injector in the first-aid kit and closing it.

As he now easily found the energy to sit upright, Grant glanced at her in surprise. He had expected her to berate him, tell him he should have called her so she could tend to Shree.

"Best thing?" he repeated. He pressed a hand against the soft ground, now feeling sure he would be able to stand.

"I could have saved her life, but for what?" Sanders shook her head, took up the kit, stood up and stepped back. "She was Tidy Squad. If we are to believe what she said, she was the leader of the Tidy Squad. That means that on top of trying to release Jain technology here and murder us, she has killed before, probably many times."

"Where's the medical ethics that inclined you to save proctors?" Grant asked, studying her expression. She seemed harder to him now, more callous, yet this new attitude was a product of peacetime, not war.

"Still there. I just hold to Polity law. Proctors like Tombs had an amnesty and a chance to redeem themselves. She killed long after the war was over and the enemy defeated." Sanders looked at him directly. "The minimum I would have saved her for would have been mind-wipe."

After a brief silence, Tombs said, "Redeem themselves—that sounds almost religious."

"Doesn't it just," Sanders replied.

Grant pushed against the ground, got into a squat and slowly stood upright. His left arm still hung weak at his side, but his leg no longer felt so tight, so swollen, and could easily bear his weight. Fantastic technology—and he was in a position to know, remembering how long it had taken him to be able to stand after having grapewood splinters from a bomb blast removed from his calf two years before the rebellion. He now turned to study Tombs more closely. The man's face was a mess. The soldier at first thought it might have been caused by shrapnel from the recent blasts, but the puncture wounds were all the same size and too evenly spaced.

"What happened to you?"

"He cleared his mind and became whole," replied an utterly alien voice.

Grant looked up into the gaze of the gabbleduck. It raised its claw and beckoned with one talon. "Follow me." Grant felt no inclination to disobey it.

The creature led them around a nearby mound and then on a convoluted path through the devastation to halt by yet another mound, where Sanders's gravan lay on its side half-buried. She must have retrieved her medical kit from here, Grant realized, but how had she known she would need it?

The gabbleduck now began digging away the debris covering the vehicle, its claws perfect for the task as it used them like great dung forks.

"Our way home?" he asked.

"Yes," Tombs replied, "though no part of this world can be called home for us any more."

Grant tilted his head in acknowledgement of that, then turned to another mound and began to climb it—the drugs Sanders had used not only dispelling the pain but filling him with a restless energy. In a moment he reached the top and from there surveyed the devastation. The building housing the Atheter AI lay upside down, and tilted like a ship photographed on a storm-tossed sea. All around, the mud, soil and rhizome had been mounded into waves, all of them ringing a source that still belched smoke and steam into the air—where the disruptor the Technician destroyed had come down. Then, with the horizon line visible, Grant felt his stomach sink upon seeing another of those bell-shaped devices hanging in the sky above the horizon. He quickly scrambled back down the mound to his companions.

"The Technician failed," he said. "Those things are still in the sky."

With a whoomph the gravan crashed upright.

"Too early to judge," Tombs replied.

"So what now?" Grant asked.

"Now we leave—we don't belong here any more."

As Amistad ran internal diagnostics and tried to repair some of the massive damage he had suffered, his senses began to range out, his compass to expand, and some abilities returned. Like small animals nosing from cover after some massive storm, com lines began to open up again. Amistad first obtained an overview of the situation down on Masada. Three disruptors hung in the sky over the main continent, whilst a fourth was poised far out over the ocean for no obvious reason. Amistad speculated that perhaps there had been something significant out there about two million years ago. Two attack ships were functional—one resupplying from the orbiting dreadnought whilst the other held station between the disruptor nearest to Zealos and the city itself.

"Why the pause?" the drone asked.

"Ah, you're back," replied Ergatis. "Simple answer: destroying those things results in significant damage elsewhere, so whilst they are doing nothing I ordered the attack ships to hold back."

"Reasonable enough," Amistad replied, wondering if his opinion would be different if he hadn't recently lost a great mass of his own mental processing.

"So what happened up there?" Ergatis asked.

Amistad magnified the image of the three chunks of the Technician floating through vacuum. They hadn't completely separated, held loosely together by strands of some fibrous matter. The thing certainly seemed to be dead, since the only EM reading issuing from it lay in the infrared, and that steadily declining as it cooled. Next the drone took a long hard look at the mechanism. There the activity had increased. The thing was glowing from inside and rapidly swapping about those odd internal components, EM output filling and disrupting numerous com bands. It looked rather like it was trying to grind up something indigestible.

"The Technician is finished," the drone stated. "The mechanism is still functioning."

"Then we're screwed," Ergatis suggested.

There was something else too, but Amistad was having problems tracking down the memory. The Technician was controlled by the Weaver and had been sent against this threat to the Weaver's existence, but it had failed, hadn't it?

Amistad abruptly stabilized relative to Masada, a gravmotor at last beginning to function how it should. Fusion drive was down for the moment, but simple steering thrusters were still available. He fired up some of these to begin a long slow acceleration back towards the planet, and in that moment remembered, and at once sent a message to Ergatis.

"You're kidding!" the planetary AI replied.

"No I'm not," said Amistad, with some relief at last igniting its fusion drive.

Within minutes the drone entered atmosphere, and hurtled down to a location in the southern ocean, just hoping that by the time he reached his destination there would be a planet to land on. It just depended on how it was done, in the end.

The mechanism, now becoming acquainted with emotion, understood that it had just experienced fear—fear of extinction. Two million years ago it had eradicated all the remaining Atheter war machines down on the surface of the planet, but that had been a demolition job, for they had been powered down and unable to resist. A million years ago it had scrambled the workings of the Technician, at a distance, using techniques that did not involve direct confrontation. But this had been different.

Machines like the Technician had been the pinnacle of war technology and had subsequently been used to obliterate both those Atheter and their own machines that had resisted the enforced return to the Homeworld. And just now such a machine had come close to killing the mechanism. It had resisted every warfare technique at the mechanism's disposal, managing to actually penetrate right down the core. Only there had the mechanism contrived to bring to bear the full force of its field technology to tear the thing apart and eject it, and even now it continued to search out fragments of the shattered device and eject them. Everything about the Technician was dangerous: nanotech spreading from its physical parts, computer warfare programs downloading from the smallest fragments, modulated fields spreading infection . . .

Nearly all gone now, nearly all . . .

There.

The mechanism found something alien stuck like a caddis-fly larva case to one of its internal units. This wasn't part of the Technician—analysis revealed metals and field containment similar to those used by the aliens here. It didn't seem to be dangerous, so why was it here? Closer study revealed that the end of the glassy cylinder lay open, the field generators within shut down, and whatever they had contained was gone. A metallic smear spread from the open end across the surface it was stuck to. The super-dense metal there possessed a strangely uniform crystalline structure and, even as the Mechanism directed sensors to study this more closely, the metal fractured into even hexagonal chunks that swirled away.

The enormous dodecahedral unit, two kilometres across at its widest point and one of hundreds within the mechanism's horn-shaped body, shuddered as it tumbled, went out of pattern and bounced off its nearest neighbour. A signal generated from it, routed though its U-space transmitters and down to the planet. There, a disruptor abruptly began to rise into the sky as its holding position adjusted. This made no sense. The mechanism tried to isolate the unit, managed to shut down all EM and U-space transmission and reception around the thing, but could not halt its physical movement.

They were going out of pattern—it had to be one of the worms or viruses sent by Penny Royal all those years ago . . . no, no they were gone. Something else was attacking, subverting. The mechanism used a complex field grab to seize hold of one of the floating fragments of metal, meanwhile diverting its other units away from the infected one. Using a deep-scan nanoscope it focused on the structures in the dense metal, recognizable structures, but still room for doubt.

Fear again.

The mechanism immediately wanted to eject the unit and destroy it. It also wanted to send a destruct signal to the disruptors that had also been affected by it, but there was no way round the deep hard-wired programming now coming online. Unable to stop itself, the mechanism summoned the disruptors back, back through U-space and thumping down in its core, pitiful diseased children called back to be free of their misery. It felt them there, felt patterns generating from them. The painful reality was that there was nothing threatening about those patterns. Yet.

Like with Penny Royal . . .

Still it could eject its infected parts, still it could destroy them.

Another unit fell, briefly touched by the rogue. The mechanism gazed inside, trying with all its will to deny what it was seeing. Matter and energy were being reordered inside and such now was the mass of data accumulating about that process, it could no longer be denied. It tried, but its orders crippled it.

Here then was Jain technology—the one thing the mechanism could never allow within itself, the thing it had been built to free its masters from, by destroying them, their own self-destructive fear of it the utter basis of the mechanism's programming. The mechanism fought the inevitability of the oblivion, fought its hard wiring, but so deeply ingrained were the orders that they rooted to the core of its being. They took over, carrying through the inevitability of the Atheter's self-destructive fear. Suddenly this Jain tech felt like infection, filthy life occupying pristine technology, and there was only one way to be free of it, one way to be clean.

Its mind in the grip of the same madness that killed a race, the mechanism reached for the succour of cleansing fire, stretched half in and half out of the real, out and down, millions of kilometres drawn thread-thin, finally snapping fully into the real in a place where matter itself burned, and immolated itself in Masada's sun.

Amistad hit the ocean hard, speared down in a tube of superheated steam that slammed shut after half a kilometre, then angled his claws and body to curve his course upwards. Most of the drone's components remained undamaged by the sudden cooling, designed for even harsher conditions, but those already damaged by the mechanism's gravity-wave weapon failed, some shattering. Even so, the reduction in temperature accelerated internal repairs: information processing speeded up, some nano-machines forced into somnolence by the heat woke and set to work; microbots, their joints seized by thermal expansion, stretched like arthritic fleas and returned to the job in hand. Then, with one further fusion blast creating a high-pressure steam bubble behind, the drone shot to the surface.

Penny Royal wasn't down below now, nor was the armoured sphere containing Eight—Amistad had seen that on the way in. Exploding from the surface, he planed out, gravmotor functioning intermittently, its fault returning. Ahead, smoke and steam boiled into the sky, a harsh red glow at its base. Huge waves heaved below, their forerunners already hitting the coast two hundred kilometres behind.

"Update," the drone requested.

"It seems the mechanism reacted to a Jain technology infection just as its masters programmed," Ergatis replied.

An image feed opened and Amistad watched the mechanism's last moments, stretching to an all but invisible line straight into Masada's sun. Next came a view, and data, from one of the close-watch solar satellites. Readings indicated that the thing materialized deep in the radiative zone of the sun, and above that a sunspot slowly appeared, a hundred thousand kilometres across. The outpouring of radiation forced the satellite to shut down most of its receivers, batten down its hatches against the solar storm. But the meagre sensor data available revealed regular hexagonal structures all across the sun spot. They lasted for ten minutes before dissipating. This had been seen before: the massive energy-fed growth of Jain-tech in that environment, before its eventual destruction.

"And here?" asked Amistad, whilst concentrating on internal repairs. Connections made, and all of a sudden all his legs were working. Shame that only a few of his weapons were available, since he felt certain he would soon be needing them.

"North and south coast tsunamis. Greenport is gone."

Images now of the harbour there, drained of water to feed an approaching wall of it three hundred metres high. The buildings of Greenport stood against this, but the city raft upended and tumbled, then all disappeared in a maelstrom that travelled many kilometres inland.

"Casualties?"

"Thankfully few, since we evacuated the place and most of the residents were either inland or out at sea on the ships."

"The north?"

The wave here crashed against rocky coast, clawed up mountain slopes and then receded. Along less mountainous strips of coast it surged inland, but there were few habitations there. Amistad did, however, spot a hooder writhing in white water that swept it out to sea.

"Rescue ships are on the way, and we're getting supplies and rescue personnel through the Flint runcible."

All this was out of Amistad's remit, really, but what lay ahead remained the drone's responsibility.

A small island had risen out of the sea, a caldera at its centre shaped like a gibbous moon, cooling magma steaming from a slope extending down from its horns side. Visibility wasn't great, but enough for Amistad to see something black on the upper part of the slope, where the outpouring had formed a solid crust, something like a sea urchin clinging to its undersea rock.

"Penny Royal?" Amistad queried, but with every defence up and ready for anything that might accompany a reply.

Nothing.

The drone used steering thrusters to slow, but with his gravmotor malfunctioning, came down hard on the lower part of the slope. He stumbled through lava with the consistency of stiff porridge, clambered onto hardening crust, felt that break, clambered further until on secure ground, then stood there shaking each leg in turn to flick away hardening rock.

Up above Penny Royal had changed, spreading out into a triangular mat of spines and gradually flowing up the slope towards the caldera lip. Amistad stalked after the black AI, frantically checking through his supply of weapons. Some missiles could certainly be fired, and his particle cannon had just come back online. Would these be enough? Perhaps it would be better to just keep the AI in sight until reinforcements could be summoned? No. If Penny Royal had reloaded the eighth part of its consciousness it might take some time to incorporate it, so there was a good chance the AI would be vulnerable right now.

"Penny Royal!" Amistad called, and scrambled up the slope. Progress was slow with his legs perpetually puncturing the crust of hardening rock.

Ahead, the black AI reached the rim, mounded together then stretched upwards into a tree of thorns. Perhaps good positioning: one missile now and the thing would be inside the caldera. Maybe that's what it wanted, maybe it still retained enough sanity to know it did not want to be what it had once been?

"You lied," whispered Penny Royal, swinging towards Amistad an array of spines unnervingly like icicle eyes.

"Is that so unusual?" Amistad replied, now edging round, up to the caldera rim just ten metres away. He took a quick peek over the edge. The magma down there was plenty hot, but it would probably take everything in his armoury to keep Penny Royal in it for long enough.

"Am angry . . . concerned."

Uh?

"Why did you keep it?"

"Scientific interest."

The spines abruptly surged closer, extending on necks of plaited tentacle. Did Penny Royal want a physical fight here and some Holmes and Moriarty ending in the fire below? Amistad targeted the rock below where the AI had rooted itself, selected a chemical missile and loaded it.

"Interest is finished," said Penny Royal.

The black AI shifted, spines rippling, slid to one side to reveal what it had been squatting over. There lay the armoured sphere that contained Eight, unopened.

Like some child's model of a hand, four spines folded out on corded tentacle, swung to one side, paused for a moment, then swung back, slapping into the sphere. It tumbled over the edge, bounced on the slope below then splashed into boiling magma. It wouldn't be destroyed, not yet; it would take ages for the heat to do any damage. Amistad shifted right to the edge, almost went over, rocks dislodged and tumbling down, but then scrabbled back. What did he really want that thing for? Was he keeping it because of his attraction to madness—a prime sample for some collection? A missile spat down, hit with a sharp detonation like some massive fuse blowing. The side of the sphere peeled open on arc fire and it turned over, began to sink.

For a moment Amistad thought he had fired the missile himself, but no, Penny Royal had just killed part of itself.

"We have things to do," said the AI.

"Quite," Amistad agreed. "Quite right."

The analgesic cream Sanders had provided was working now, and his face no longer felt like someone had taken a bead blaster to it. However, he did feel as if something had scooped out a huge part of his mind and left an aching blankness inside, which was essentially what had happened.

The Weaver's memories were no longer available to him, just memories of memories which, as time passed, grew increasingly strange to him. Yet it wasn't the deep stuff he found himself becoming disconnected from, not the attitude, the wisdom, the inner thoughts, but all those memories of the Atheter's direct interaction with the world around it, which in the end were the larger portion of its mind.

"Is there a problem?" Sanders asked.

The gravan had begun making a horrible rattling sound the moment they took off, and had got worse ever since.

"No problem," Grant replied from the controls. He reached out and tapped something on the computer screen before him. "Just damage to the bodywork—I'm getting a safety warning but only because bits might fall off and hit someone."

Jem eased himself to his feet and moved forward to stand behind the two of them, only realizing why he had moved when he saw the barrier lying ahead.

"Ripple-John's sons might still be alive," he said.

Grant glanced up at him. "And?"

Jem could find no answer to that. He had changed, but those who had tried to kill him would not have changed at all. There would be no truce with them, no meeting of minds or any peaceful resolution of their differences.

"And nothing, I guess," Jem replied.

They slid over the barrier and, because all the flute grasses in the area had been flattened by the recent blasts, the remains of Ripple-John's ATV were clearly visible. It lay on its side, but had been partially dismembered, many of its component parts stacked in a neat pile. Between the vehicle and this stack of parts squatted the enormous gabbleduck Jem had seen out here earlier.

"What's it doing?"

"We can take a look," Grant suggested, "but I don't want to get too close."

The gabbleduck tilted its head and watched them descend. Grant brought the gravan down a good twenty metres away from the creature, which would give him time to take off again if it decided to take too close an interest in the vehicle. The creature peered at them for a further moment, then returned to the task in hand. It seemed it had dismembered the ATV so as to strip out all the optics and the superconductive wiring, which lay in neat coils on the ground before it. However, it had evidently lost interest in them upon unearthing the electric engine. Presently the armature of the motor lay on the ground beside it, the wire from it steadily being unravelled as it wove the wire into *something*.

"I've never seen them do that before," said Sanders.

"They never have," said Grant.

"Something we will have to get used to," said Jem.

They both turned and looked at him questioningly.

"Jeremiah, what do you mean?" Sanders asked.

What did he mean? Just because one Atheter had resurrected itself in the body of a gabbleduck did not mean that all gabbleducks would cease to be animals, did it? He riffled through those memories of memories. The Atheter had possessed their equivalent to Human augmentations, but had gone further, incorporating them into their bodies. They shared information via those organic transceivers in their skulls, processed information in other organs, absorbed it almost unconsciously. Inside their skulls they possessed permanent links to the Atheter virtual world, and that ability had not been erased by the mechanism, in fact the Atheter themselves hadn't seen this ability as something separate from their evolved form, nor as something to be disrupted, erased.

"Gabbleducks speak nonsense," he said, "but why do they use our words to speak it?"

Grant and Sanders continued gazing at him, now puzzled. They couldn't see it and, at that moment, Jem realized that no one had seen it before.

"A gabbleduck found far out in the wilderness, one never having come into contact with humans throughout its life, will speak our words."

"That's . . . true," said Sanders.

He realized by her expression that she had begun to understand.

"They're like Humans in an aug network, but with the augs an organic part of their brains," Jem explained. "For two million years that network consisted of nothing but the minds of animals, then Humans arrived. Who knows what radio or microwave channels open into the mind of a gabbleduck? But certainly all of Masada became swamped with signals when we arrived here. They probably listened to us speaking the moment the first Human radio transmitter was used on this world."

Grant nodded acceptance of that, then pointed at the big gabbleduck. "But that?"

"Now there's a real Atheter mind in the network either consciously or unconsciously broadcasting stuff for which the receivers were made. I would guess that what we're seeing with our friend out there is being repeated all across the continent."

The gabbleduck abruptly put aside the thing it was working on, and began to heave itself to its feet, seemingly gazing towards them with predatory intensity. But it was not them who had drawn its attention, but Blitz, who now slammed open the side door of the gravan and stepped inside, pointing his father's flack gun straight into the cockpit.

Time slowed for Jem. In the background he could see the gabbleduck, now on all fours, hurtling massively towards them, kicking up great clogs of rhizome-bound earth, whilst close too, Grant was slipping a hand down towards his holstered disc gun. Outside, Sharn was dragging himself to the door, his clothing soaked with blood and his legs dead behind him. Obviously, along with Ripple-John, it was the brother Kalash who had died.

Jem moved.

He crossed the intervening space in a second, aware throughout every fraction of that second of Blitz's finger tightening on the trigger. He slapped at the barrel of the weapon, the shot slammed a hole through the side of the gravan, pieces of metal ricocheted. He then forced the barrel up, chopped down with his other hand, breaking Blitz's hold, drove his elbow back into the man's sternum and shoved him away, stumbling and falling. Still moving, Jem stooped through the door, slapped away the weapon Sharn had just drawn, caught his collar and dragged him inside.

"Get us out of here, now!" he snapped, turning.

By now Grant had drawn his disc gun, but just stared, his mouth hanging open.

"Now, I said," Jem added.

Grant dropped his weapon in his lap, took the gravan up off the ground. "Move fast," he said, it not entirely clear who or what he was referring to.

Jem gazed down the barrel of the flack gun at his two prisoners. Blitz still looked rebellious, angry. He backed up against the wall of the van, started to get his feet underneath him. Sharn just looked exhausted and lay with his head against the floor, blood starting to pool around him.

"Tell me why I shouldn't pull the trigger," said Jem.

Blitz just continued to gaze at him with barely controlled hate, seemingly readying himself to do something stupid. Sanders replied, "Because you're better than them. We'll just hand them over to the police—let them sort it out."

Sort it out.

Just like with Shree, yes. These two were guilty of kidnap, attempted murder and murder itself, and once found guilty, as they undoubtedly would be, they would be mind-wiped, erased from existence. Quite right. These two, along with their father and their brother Kalash, had set the hooders on Bradacken way station, and they had killed Chanter. There should be no mercy for them. Only now did Jem wonder about his impulse to drag them inside the gravan, and realize he was tired of hate, so very tired of it. He started to lower the weapon.

Something crashed against the side of the gravan, sending it penduluming through the air, four even grooves visible in the bodywork from the inside. Another thump on the underside as they rose, denting up the floor underneath Jem, an odd whining sound coming from the gravmotor.

He staggered, reached out to grab the edge of the door to steady himself, some mental undercurrent telling him he just *knew* what would happen next. Blitz threw himself forward, hammering his head into Jem stomach, grabbed the gun and wrestled for control of it. Trying to tear the weapon from the man's grasp, Jem spun him, slamming him against the wall of the van. A bang like some explosive going off and the whole panelled side of the van peeled away, a wind roaring inside. Blitz fell through, and still holding the gun, dragged Jem after.

"It's fucking got hold of us!" Grant shouted, wrestling with the controls.

He hung suspended from the side of the vehicle, one leg wrapped round a remaining panel strut to prevent him falling—Jem considered that the least of his worries. Blitz, suspended below, still clung to the gun, trying to turn the barrel towards Jem.

Blitz should be clinging for his life, yet killing Jem seemed so much more important to him. No truce, no forgiveness here. The man hated what Jem had ceased to be long ago, and could see nothing else. Blitz had been fed that hate with his mother's milk and was little more than a mental clone of his father. Jem swung his gaze across to the gabbleduck, up at full stretch from the ground, its body extended out like a great gnarled oak but for the huge quivering sac of its belly. It met his gaze and, for a brief instant, it seemed an understanding passed between them.

A great calm suffused Jem as he tilted the gun, the barrel towards his own face. Why not, what did any of it matter? Blitz's grip slipped as a black claw swept across and closed about his legs—that first claw releasing its hold on the gravan. Blitz slipped a finger down to the trigger and pulled it back. The weapon clicked and buzzed, a red empty light flashing on it. Blitz, having loosened his hold on the weapon to press that trigger, now lost his grip entirely and screamed on his way down.

Jem hung there as the gravan rose, his calm quickly washing away. Oblivion was such an easy choice to make, and too easy when it was no choice at all, as in the case of Sharn, who by the time Sanders reluctantly stooped over him, had already bled out on the floor.

They returned to Dragon Down mostly in silence, but for one brief exchange.

"So what are you going to do now?" Sanders asked.

Jem considered the sons of Ripple-John with the hate impressed in their minds even as those minds developed. He considered Shree, who could not give up the war that made her, and he considered himself, indoctrinated from birth to believe and have faith, then in an odd second life turned into a vessel for the thoughts of another.

"I don't know what I'm going to do," he replied, "but I know what I'm going to be."

"And what's that?" Grant asked tiredly, at last thinking to slide his disc gun back into its holster.

"For the first time in my life," Jem told them, "I'm going to be myself."

EPILOGUE

Amazing that such seemingly huge claws could weave so intricately, thought Amistad, and so many of them were busy weaving all across the main continent of Masada.

"What do you think it's making?" he asked.

"Home," replied Penny Royal, completely invisible, but hovering protectively behind Leif Grant.

The observation tower stood tall behind them, a long-stalked steel mushroom moved here so those squatting on it and in it could keep watch on the growing structure ahead. Amistad had already seen such a structure before, recorded in the eye of a hooder. It stood on the muddy plain amidst a spring growth of flute grass spearing from the ground like a million bloody knives—something a swarm of weaver birds might make, if they swarmed; some similarity to the nests of paper wasps and some to a modular construction space habitat for Humans—a convoluted basketwork city that played a dirge whenever the wind blew from the north.

There had been no communication, none at all, no demands, nothing until now. All across Masada gabbleducks had begun behaving strangely, weaving odd shapes out of flute-grass stems then abandoning them for Humans to puzzle over. Amistad wondered what Chanter would have made of that -something, certainly. Here though, the Weaver had been disappointingly inactive, just living, like an animal, until the Polity lifter came in to right the Atheter AI and make repairs. It just watched the lifter and the maintenance robots, then, once they departed, it moved into the building and there in its structure wove a small home. Next, over ensuing months, other gabbleducks began to turn up here to weave dwellings for themselves. Were they just animals copying? Were they just somewhat adroit mocking birds? All Polity science could give no definite answer, somewhere between, perhaps, in that territory where physical manipulation of the world came before consciousness of self.

But now a communication, direct from the Atheter AI: something had to be returned.

Seeking an answer to the mystery here, Amistad studied the gabbleducks he could see, tried to discern something within the structure ahead, but nothing leapt out. He swung his gaze to the big grav-sled trundling along behind himself, Penny Royal and Grant.

"He comes," said the black AI.

"So there's nothing I can say if it tells us to get the fuck off of Masada," said Grant.

"Nothing at all," Amistad replied, turning to Grant. "In fact Earth Central has already designated evacuation ships."

"That's annoying."

"That's the AOP, and you agreed it was right when you took the job."

After Tombs had departed Masada, doubtless to go and find some place where he could at last "be himself," Leif Grant had sunk back into morose introversion. Then Sanders went and snapped him out of it, renewing something they'd had before and, incidentally, delivering the news that the position of Human ambassador to the Atheter was open to him, if he wanted it.

Amistad returned his attention to the scene ahead, noting a hundred identifying features on the approaching gabbleduck and knowing it to be the Weaver. It halted five metres in front of them, twitching its head slightly as it studied them. It also seemed to Amistad, by its long pause whilst gazing towards Grant, that the Weaver might be able to see Penny Royal too.

"It's your show now," Amistad told Grant.

In his capacity as expert on all things Atheter, Amistad was here merely as an adviser. In its capacity as recovering lunatic, Penny Royal was here under Amistad's charge.

Grant glanced at the drone, whispered a sarcastic, "Thanks

a bunch," then stepped forward. "We've brought what you asked for," he said out loud.

A thought from Amistad brought the massive grav-sled round to one side, then had it settling down on the new flute grass with a sound like a steamroller over gravel. The Weaver turned and studied the three huge chunks of the Technician lying on the sled, nodded contemplatively, then turned back towards the trio.

"You have Policy on the occupancy of alien worlds," it said.

Here it comes: get off our planet.

"We do," Grant agreed, abruptly folding his arms and looking pained.

The Weaver pointed at the pieces of the Technician. "I have this," it said, then stabbed a claw behind. "And this."

"Yess," said Grant slowly, unsure where this might be going.

Humans were just so slow sometimes . . . well, most of the time really. Amistad focused on some of the lower parts of the conglomerate town growing here, noted the damage, the chewed-up basketwork, the ground churned by subterranean activity and dotted with pan-pipes molluscs. There wasn't much here to build a civilization on when tricones kept eating your foundations.

"You have what we threw away," the Weaver noted. "You have what we shattered and ground into grit."

"I see," said Grant, and maybe he did, because he smiled.

The Weaver sat down on its haunches, lifted a claw to its bill and began to work at something between its holly-like white teeth. After a moment it flicked this away, tracked its course to the ground then swung back towards Grant.

"No more gabble. Now we negotiate," it said.

NEAL ASHER is a science fiction writer whose work has been nominated for both the Philip K. Dick and the British Fantasy Society awards. He has published more than fifteen novels, many set within his Polity universe, including *Gridlinked*, *The Skinner*, and *Prador Moon*. He divides his time between Essex and a home in Crete.

A Chronological Guide to the Polity Novels

The Technician

Prador Moon

Gridlinked

Brass Man

Line War

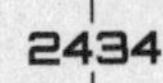

2444

2310 AD

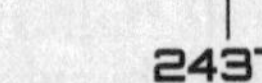

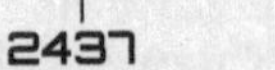

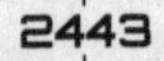

Shadow of the Scorpion

The Line of Polity

Polity Agent

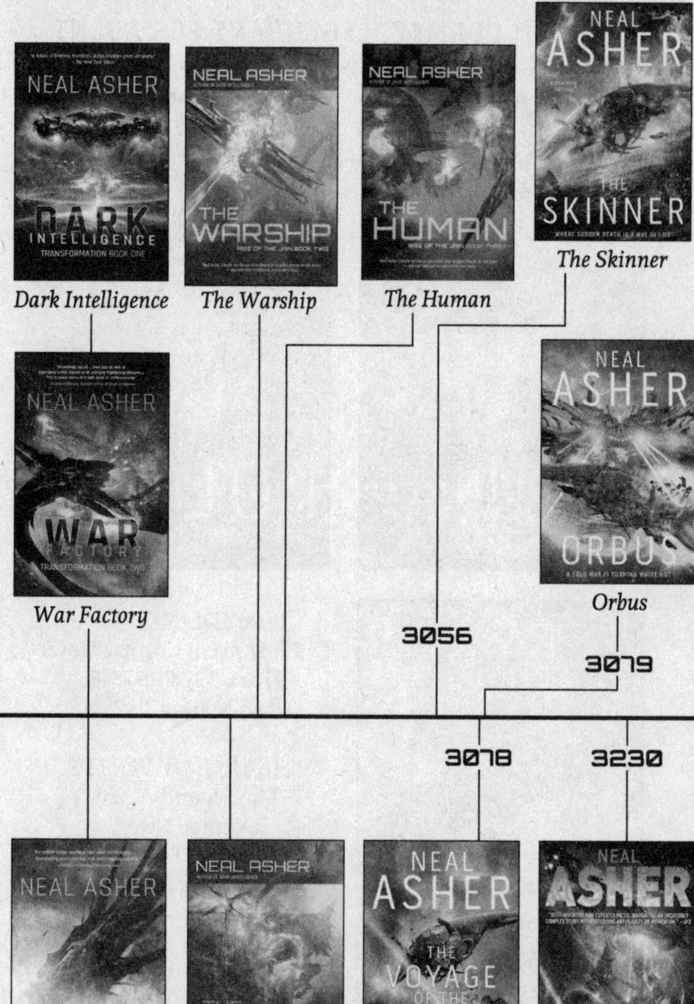

Infinity Engine

The Soldier

The Voyage of the Sable Keech

Hilldiggers

NOW AVAILABLE FROM NEAL ASHER'S SPATTERJAY TRILOGY

THE SKINNER
The First Spatterjay Novel
978-1-59780-987-0
Mass Market / $7.99

"*Dune* meets *Master and Commander.*"
—*Entertainment Weekly*

THE VOYAGE OF THE SABLE KEECH
The Second Spatterjay Novel
978-1-59780-989-4
Mass Market / $7.99

"High-octane violence, exotic tech, and terrifying and truly alien aliens."
—*Daily Mail*

AVAILABLE FROM NIGHT SHADE BOOKS
WWW.NIGHTSHADEBOOKS.COM

MORE NOVELS OF THE POLITY

SHADOW OF
THE SCORPION
A Novel of the Polity
978-1-59780-139-3
Trade Paperback / $14.95
978-1-949102-39-0
Mass Market / $7.99

"Skip backward in time to Cormac's first military engagement... *Shadow of the Scorpion* is a war novel with sting."
—Annalee Newitz, *io9*

PRADOR MOON
A Novel of the Polity
978-1-59780-052-5
Trade Paperback / $14.95
978-1-949102-38-3
Mass Market / $7.99

"A prequel to much of everything else he's written set in the Polity universe . . . an excellent intro to an unpleasant but very entertaining universe."
—Rick Kleffel, *The Agony Column*

AVAILABLE FROM NIGHT SHADE BOOKS
WWW.NIGHTSHADEBOOKS.COM

TRANSFORMATION: A POLITY TRILOGY

DARK INTELLIGENCE
978-1-59780-844-6
Trade Paperback / $15.99

WAR FACTORY
978-1-59780-882-8
Trade Paperback / $15.99

INFINITY ENGINE
978-1-59780-910-8
Trade Paperback / $15.99

AVAILABLE FROM NIGHT SHADE BOOKS
WWW.NIGHTSHADEBOOKS.COM

THE WARSHIP
RISE OF THE JAIN
BOOK TWO
978-1-59780-990-0
Hardcover / $26.99
(available now)
978-1-949102-05-5
Trade Paperback / $15.99
(available now)

The dangers of ancient technology loom over the Polity in the sequel to *The Soldier*, Neal Asher's latest action-packed space opera series.

The haiman Orlandine, charged with safeguarding lethal Jain tech swirling inside an accretion disc located in the distant reaches of space, has weaponized a black hole to eliminate the threat. But others are suspicious of her motives, and both the Polity AIs and the leaders of the alien prador kingdom dispatch fleets of warships in anticipation of conflict.

As the black hole continues to eat its way through the planets in the accretion disc, making its way towards a dead sun, it becomes clear the disc has been hiding a larger secret. Nefarious forces with ulterior motives have manipulated Orlandine into deploying the black hole, triggering a series of larger events that will uncover a danger far older than even the Polity itself.

From British science fiction writer Neal Asher, *The Warship* picks up right where its predecessor, *The Soldier*, left off, showcasing Asher's unique take on cutting-edge and fast-paced science fiction.